NNEWTS

BOOK ONE
ESCAPE FROM THE LIZZARKS

DOUG TENNAPEL
WITH COLOR BY KATHERINE GARNER

graphix

An Imprint of

SCHOLASTIC

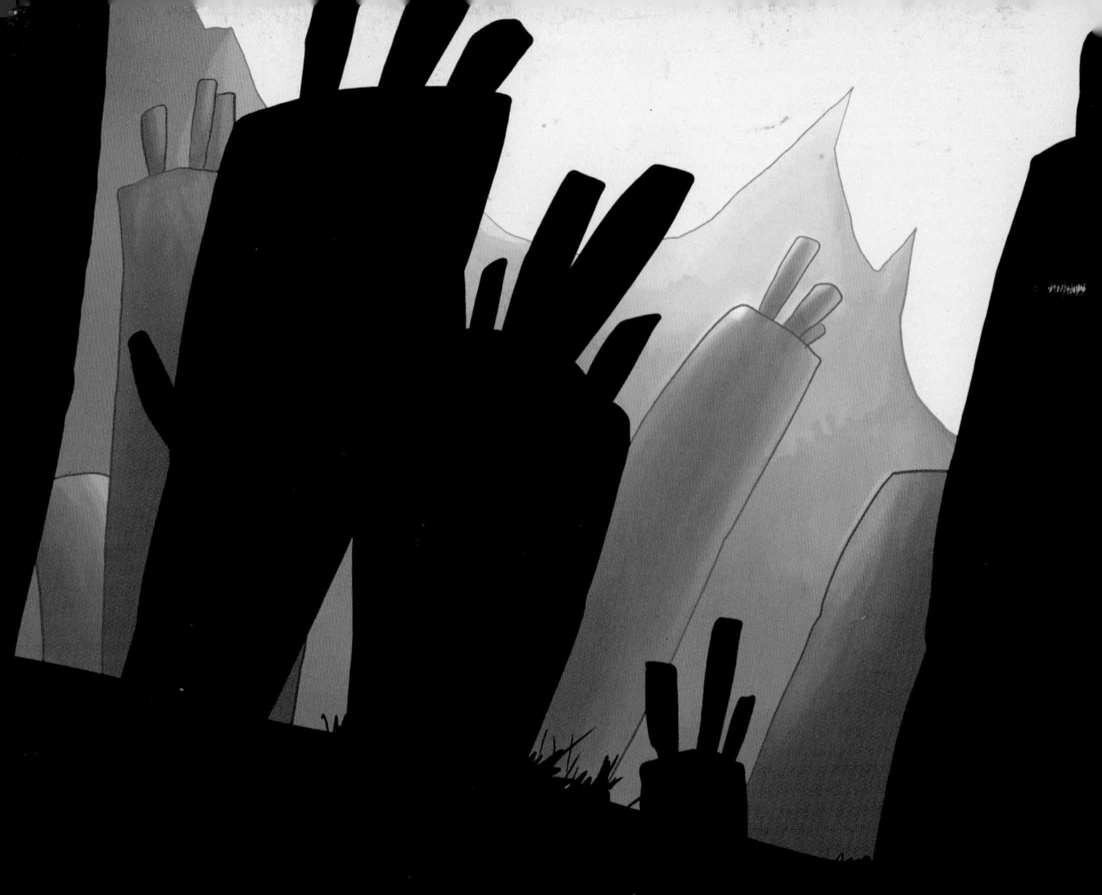

Library of Congress Control Number: 2014939372

ISBN 978-0-545-67647-2 (Hardcover)
ISBN 978-0-545-67646-5 (Paperback)

12 11 10 9 8 7 6 17 18 19 20 21

Printed in China 38

First edition, January 2015
Edited by Adam Rau
Book design by Phil Falco
Creative director: David Saylor

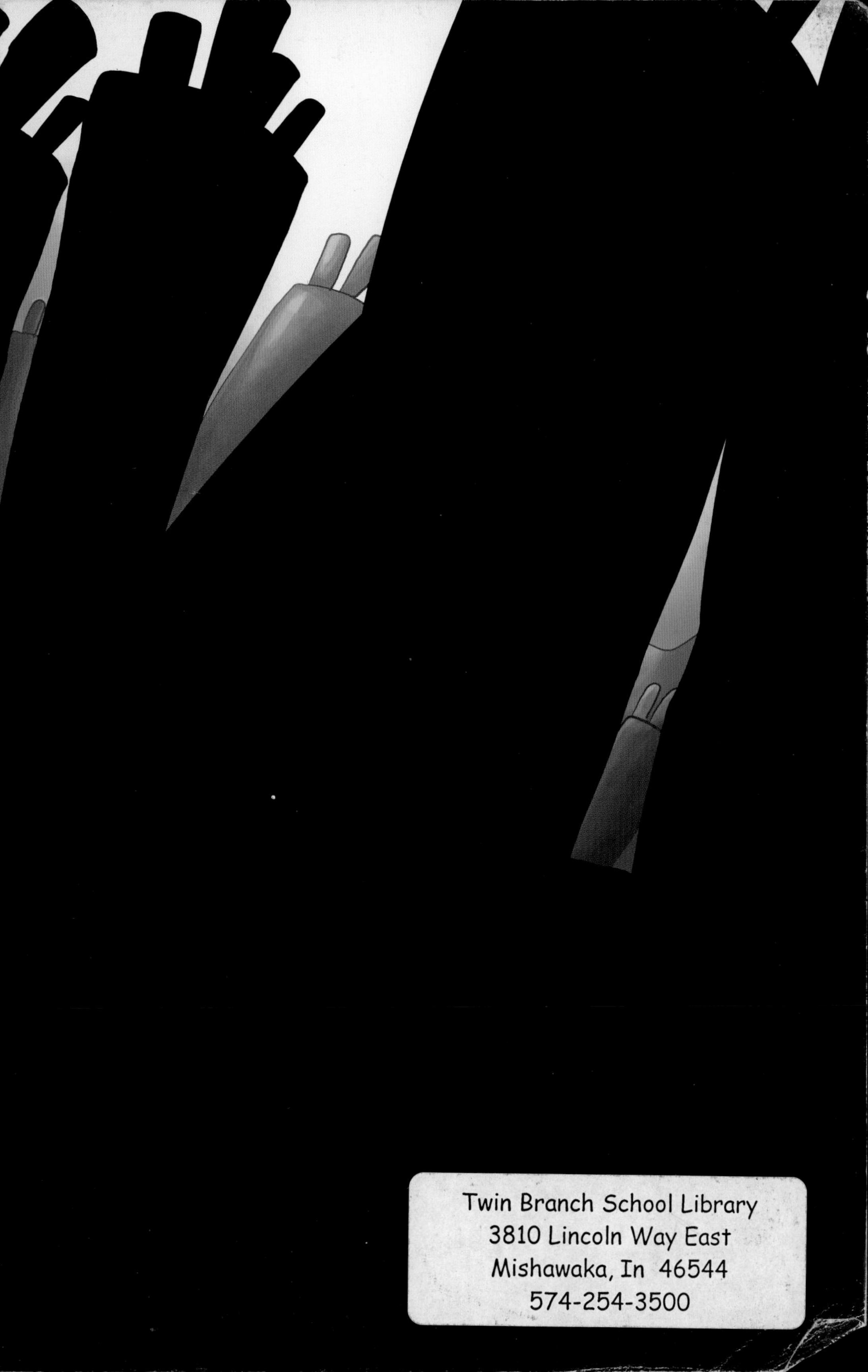

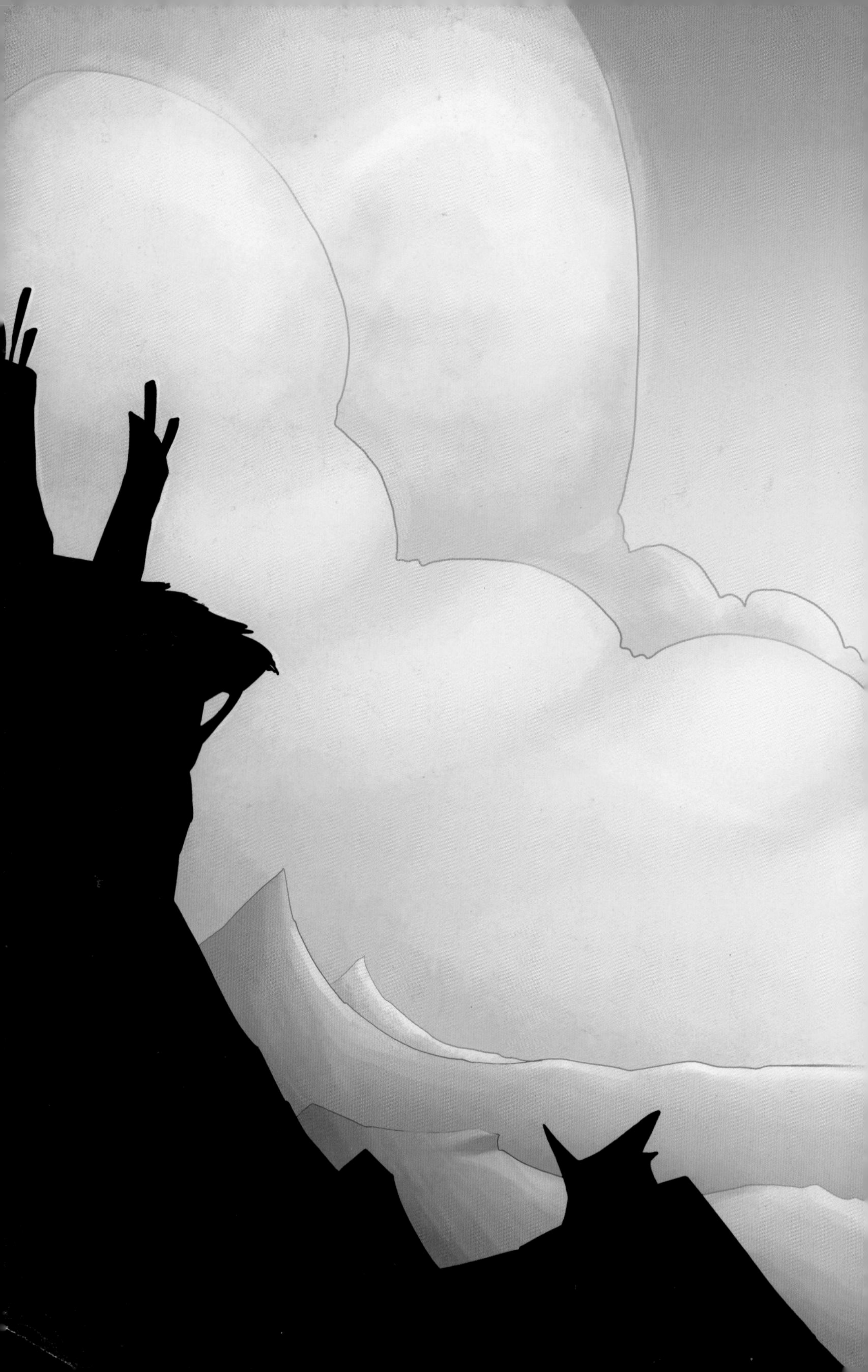

For Mr. Watanabe

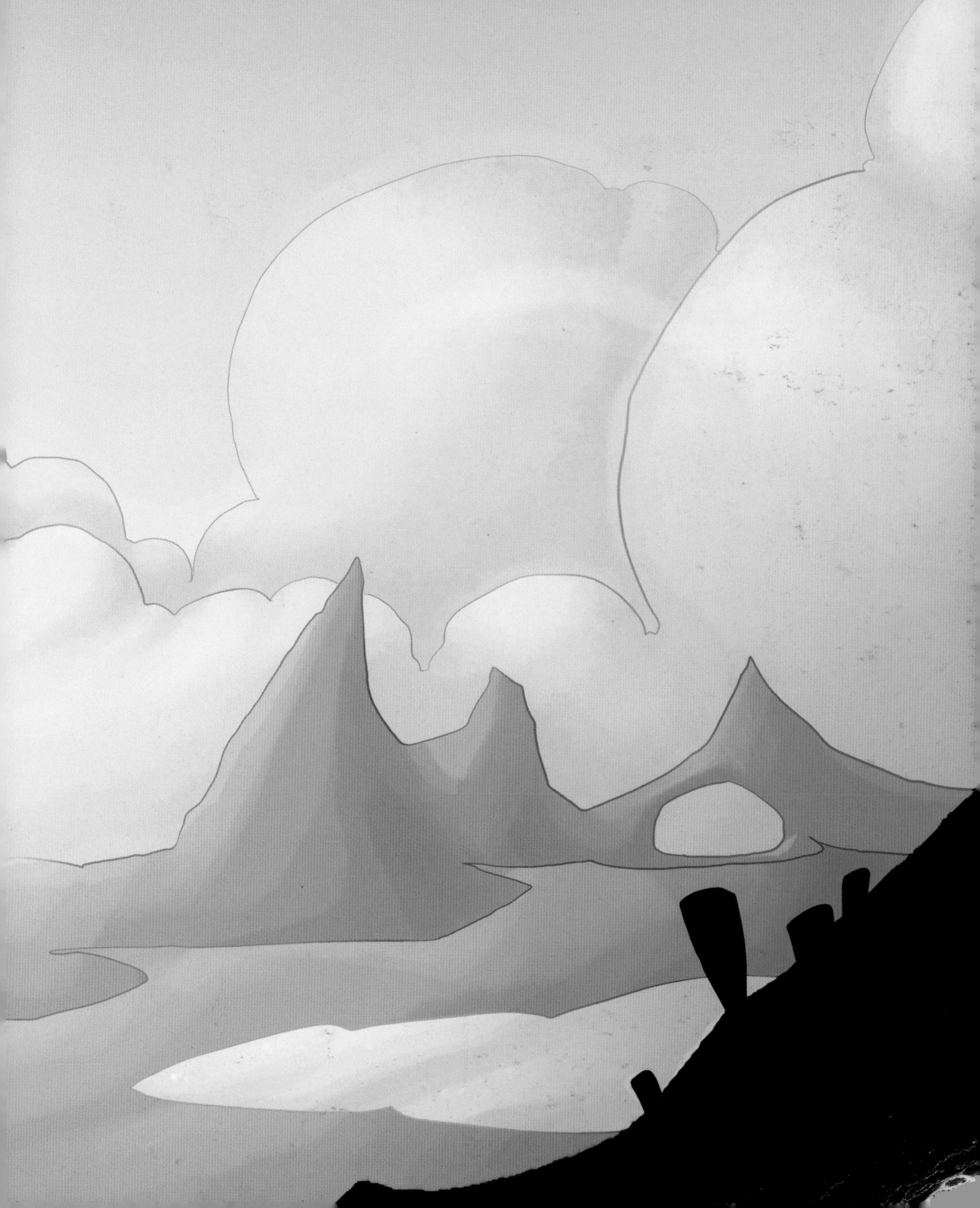

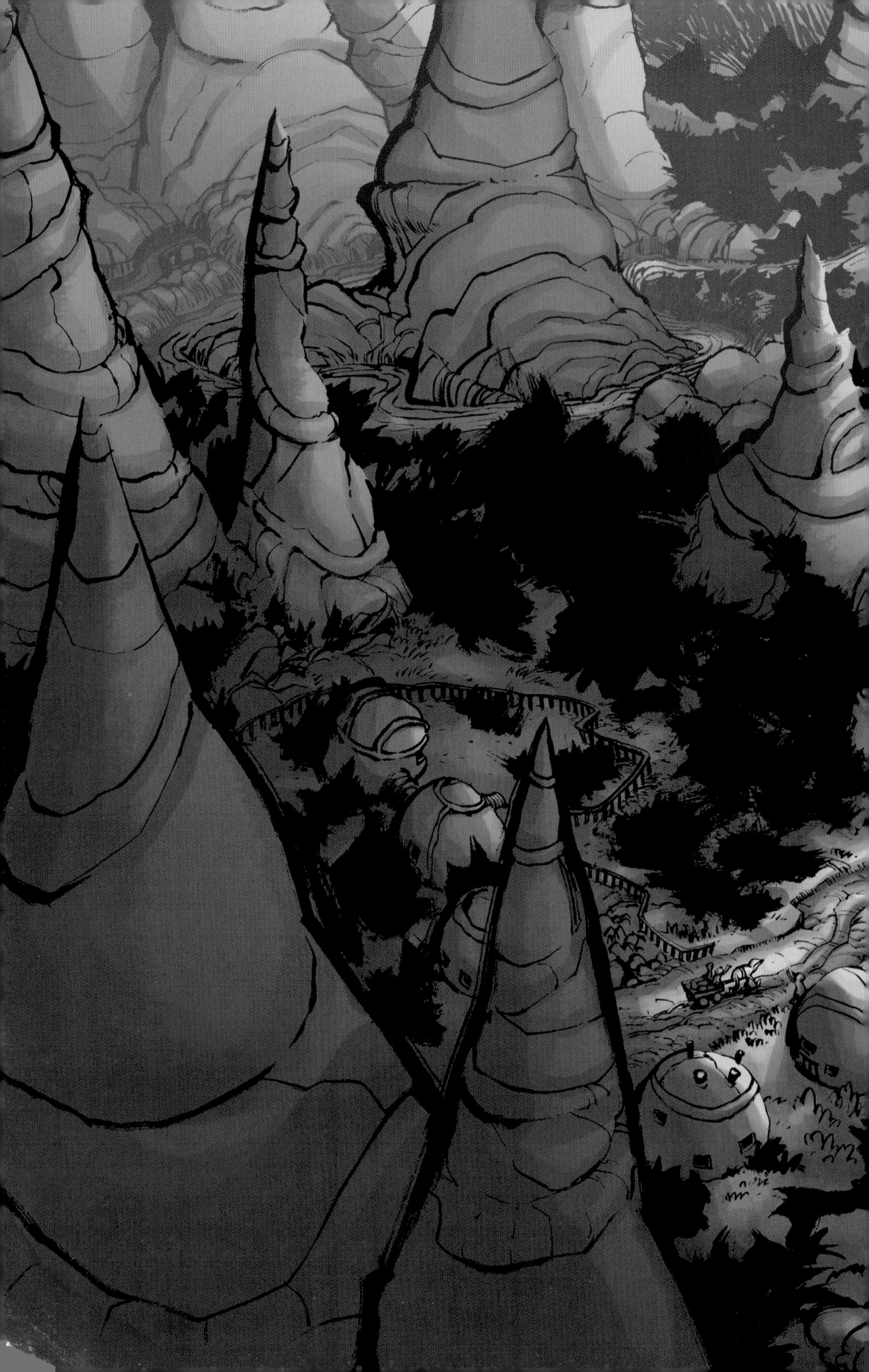

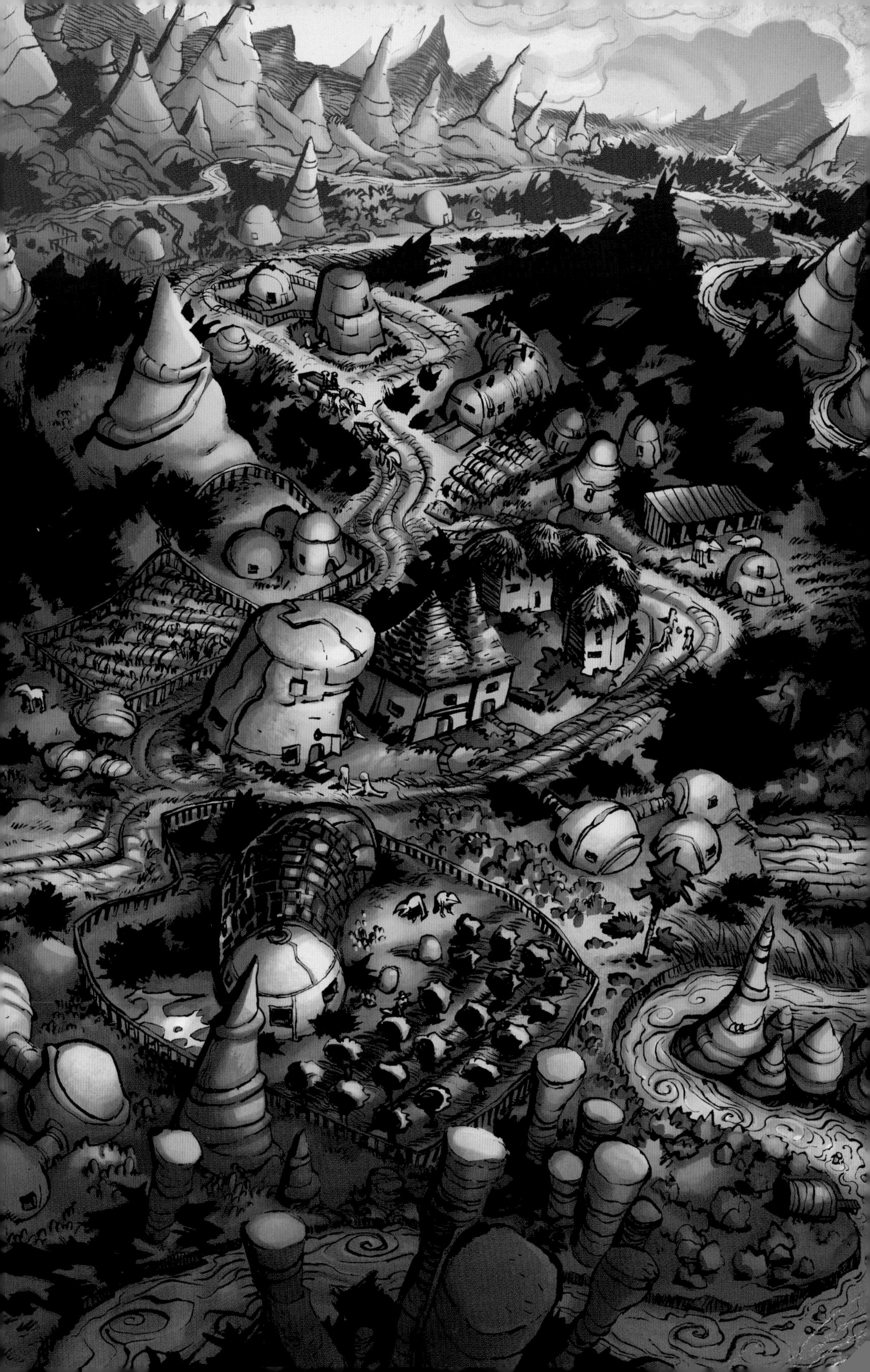

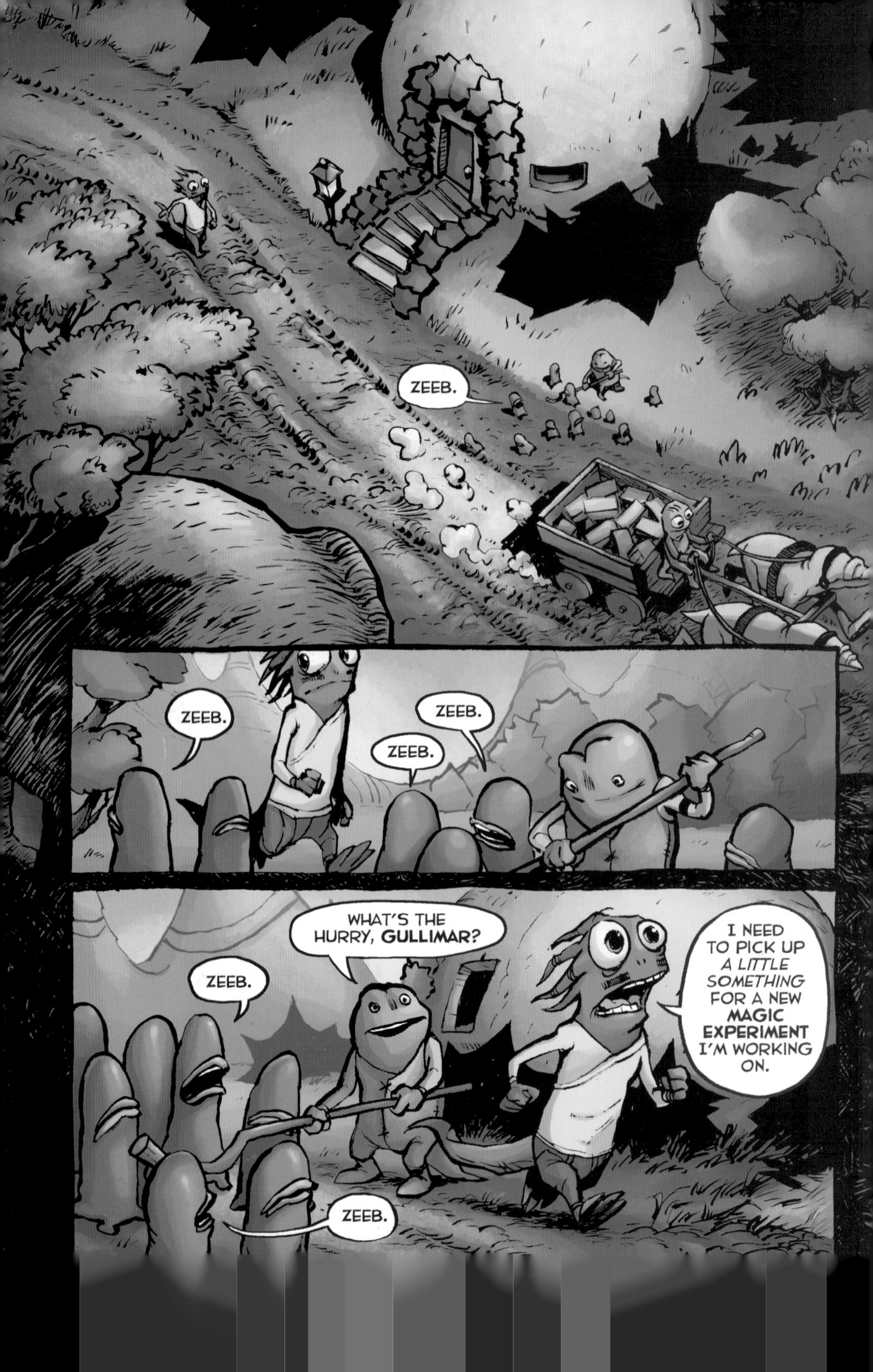
ZEEB.
ZEEB.
ZEEB.
ZEEB.
WHAT'S THE HURRY, GULLIMAR?
ZEEB.
I NEED TO PICK UP A LITTLE SOMETHING FOR A NEW MAGIC EXPERIMENT I'M WORKING ON.
ZEEB.

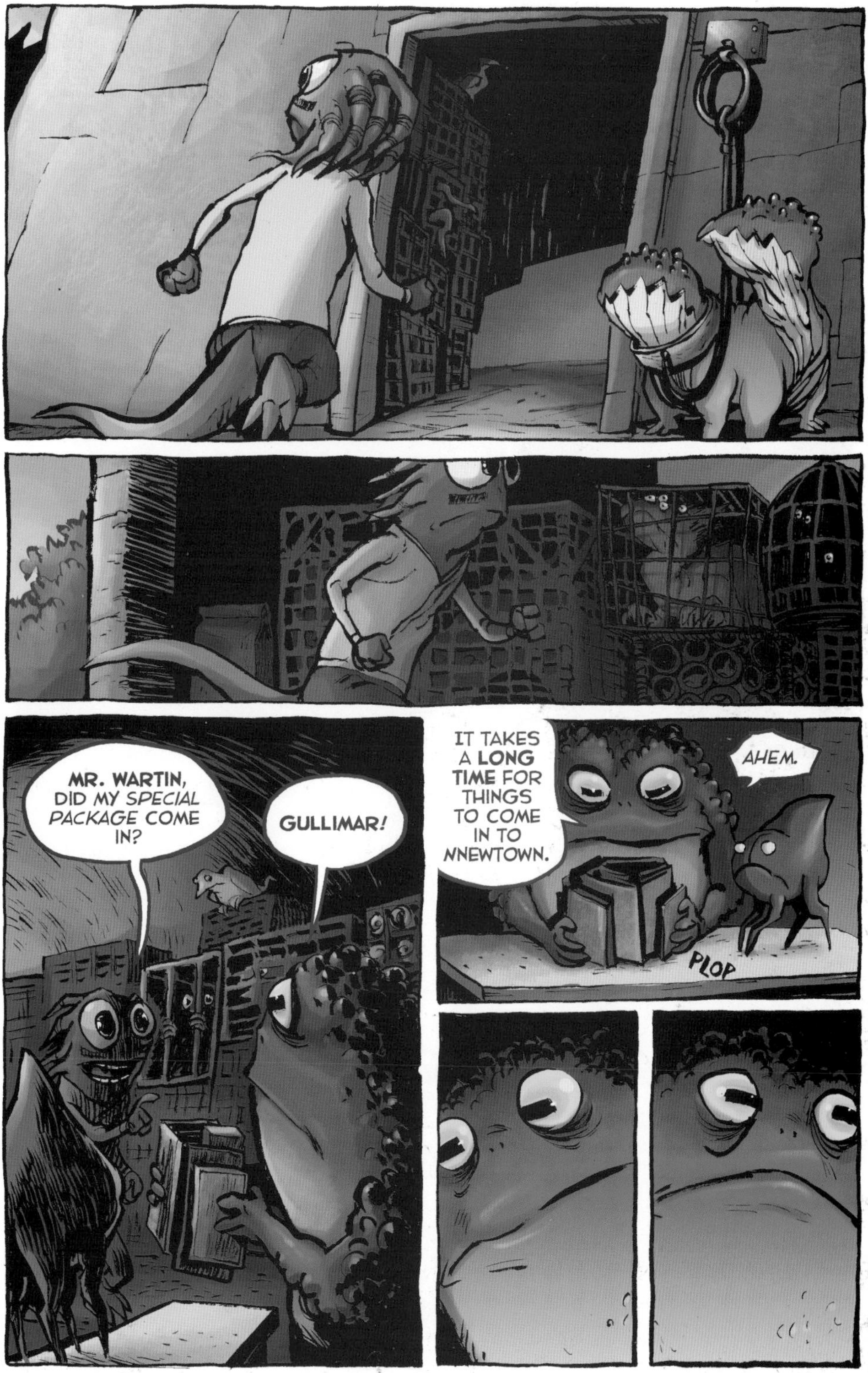
MR. WARTIN, DID MY SPECIAL PACKAGE COME IN?
GULLIMAR!
IT TAKES A LONG TIME FOR THINGS TO COME IN TO NNEWTOWN.
AHEM.
PLOP

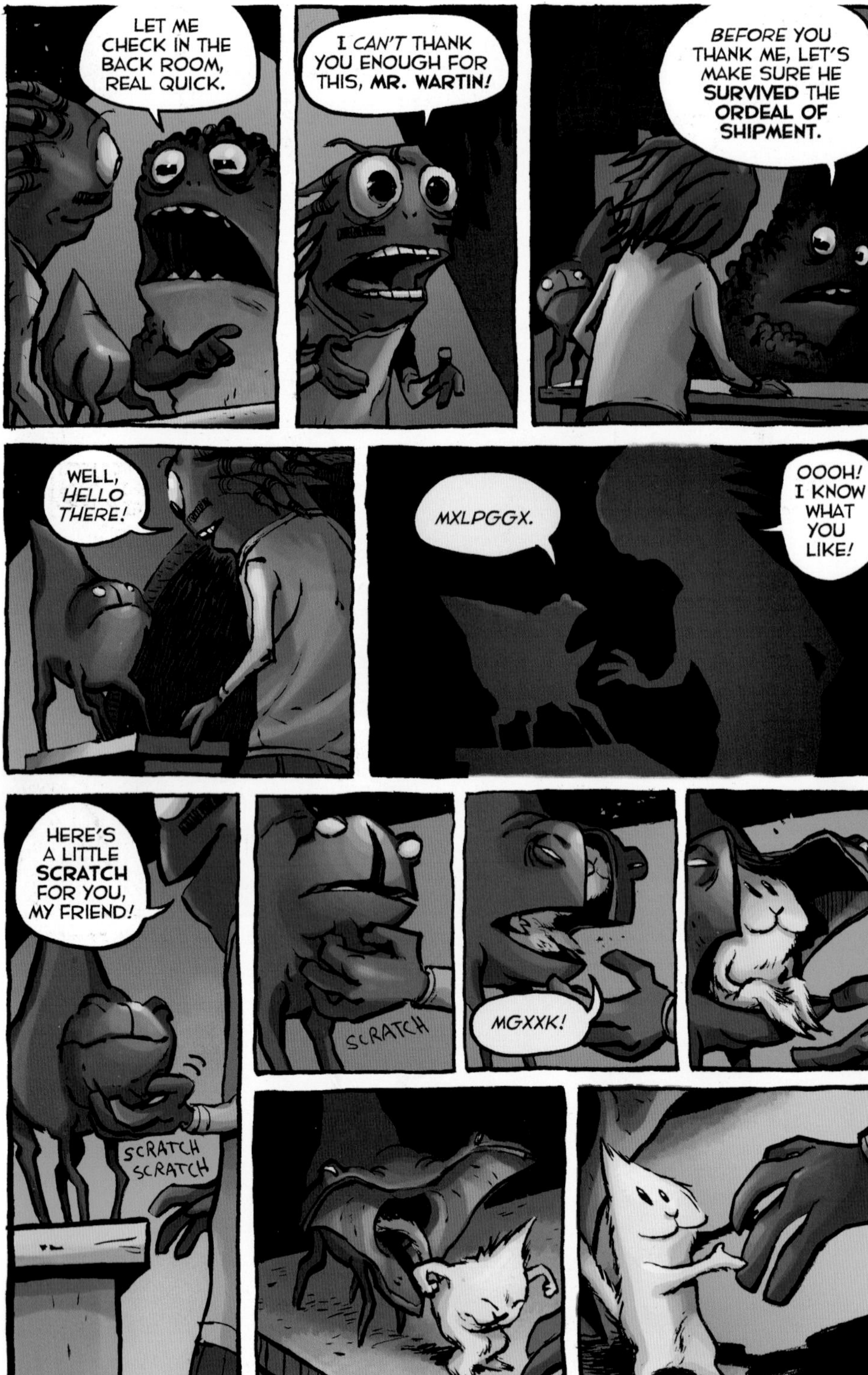
LET ME CHECK IN THE BACK ROOM, REAL QUICK.
I *CAN'T* THANK YOU ENOUGH FOR THIS, **MR. WARTIN!**
BEFORE YOU THANK ME, LET'S MAKE SURE HE **SURVIVED** THE **ORDEAL OF SHIPMENT.**
WELL, *HELLO THERE!*
MXLPGGX.
OOOH! I KNOW WHAT YOU LIKE!
HERE'S A LITTLE **SCRATCH** FOR YOU, MY FRIEND!
SCRATCH SCRATCH
SCRATCH
MGXXK!

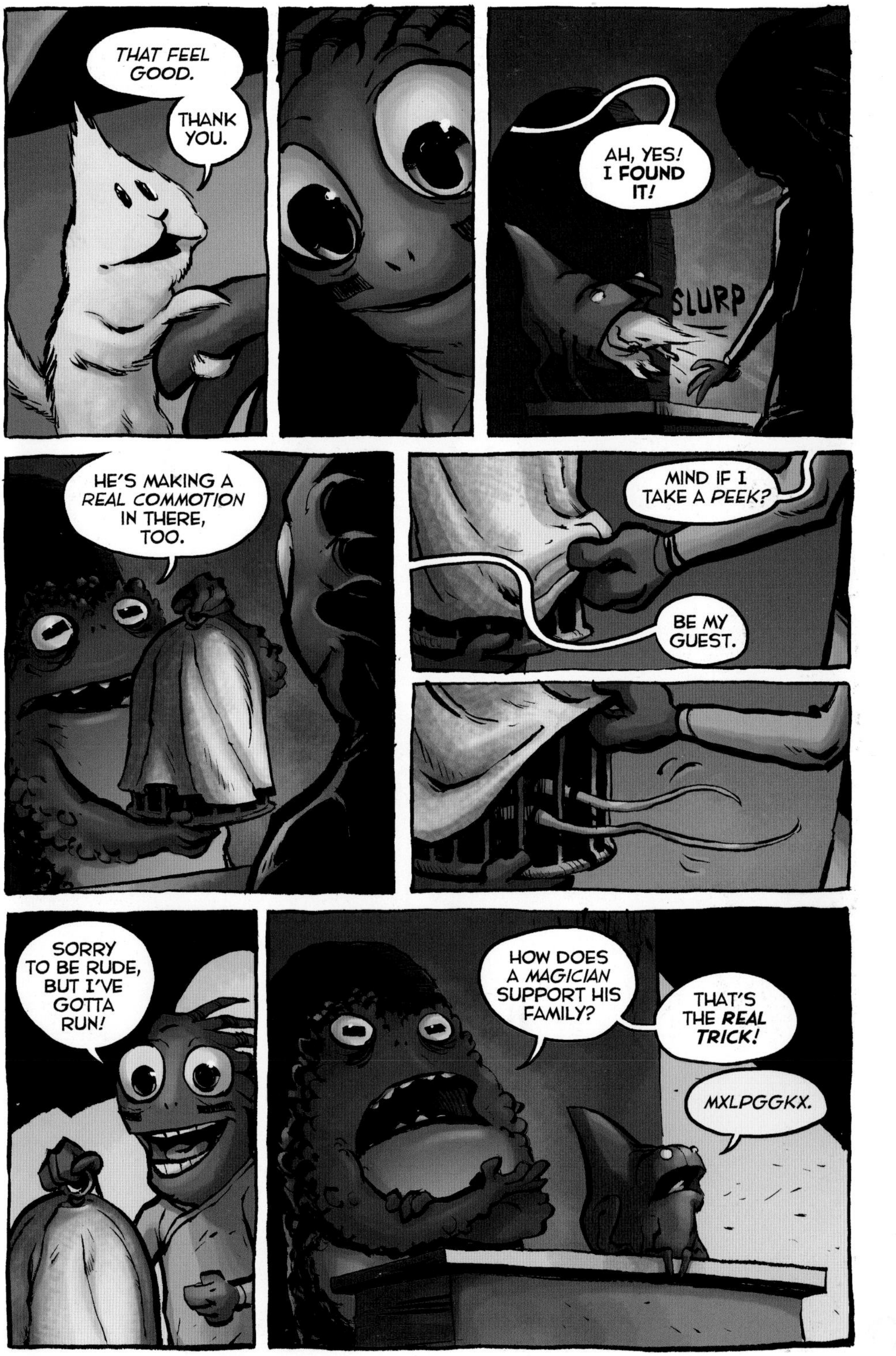
THAT FEEL GOOD.
THANK YOU.
AH, YES! I FOUND IT!
SLURP
HE'S MAKING A *REAL COMMOTION* IN THERE, TOO.
MIND IF I TAKE A *PEEK*?
BE MY GUEST.
SORRY TO BE RUDE, BUT I'VE GOTTA RUN!
HOW DOES A *MAGICIAN* SUPPORT HIS FAMILY?
THAT'S THE ***REAL TRICK!***
MXLPGGKX.

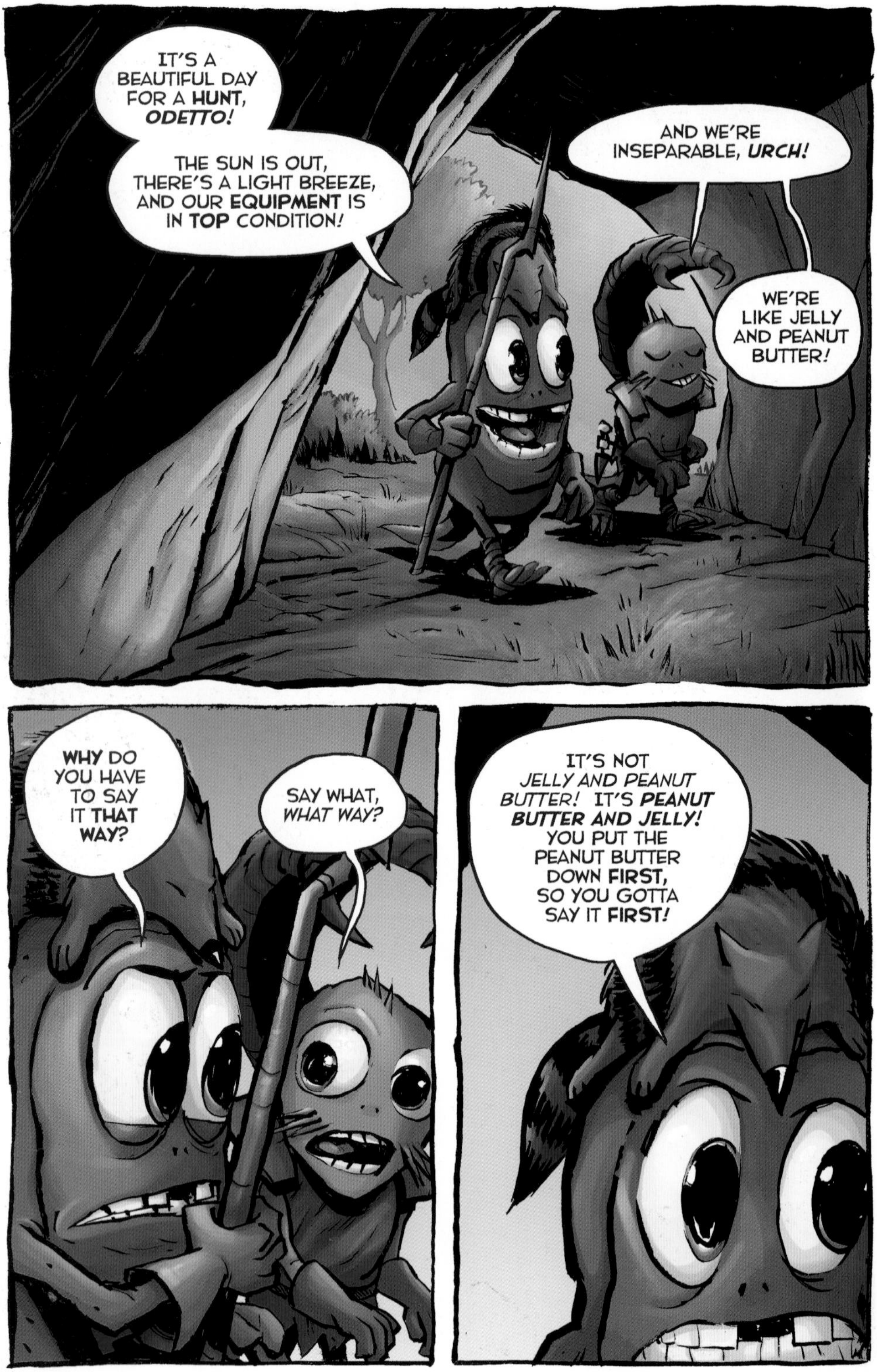
IT'S A BEAUTIFUL DAY FOR A **HUNT**, ***ODETTO!***
THE SUN IS OUT, THERE'S A LIGHT BREEZE, AND OUR **EQUIPMENT** IS IN **TOP** CONDITION!
AND WE'RE INSEPARABLE, ***URCH!***
WE'RE LIKE JELLY AND PEANUT BUTTER!
WHY DO YOU HAVE TO SAY IT **THAT WAY?**
SAY WHAT, *WHAT WAY?*
IT'S NOT *JELLY AND PEANUT BUTTER!* IT'S ***PEANUT BUTTER AND JELLY!*** YOU PUT THE PEANUT BUTTER DOWN **FIRST,** SO YOU GOTTA SAY IT **FIRST!**

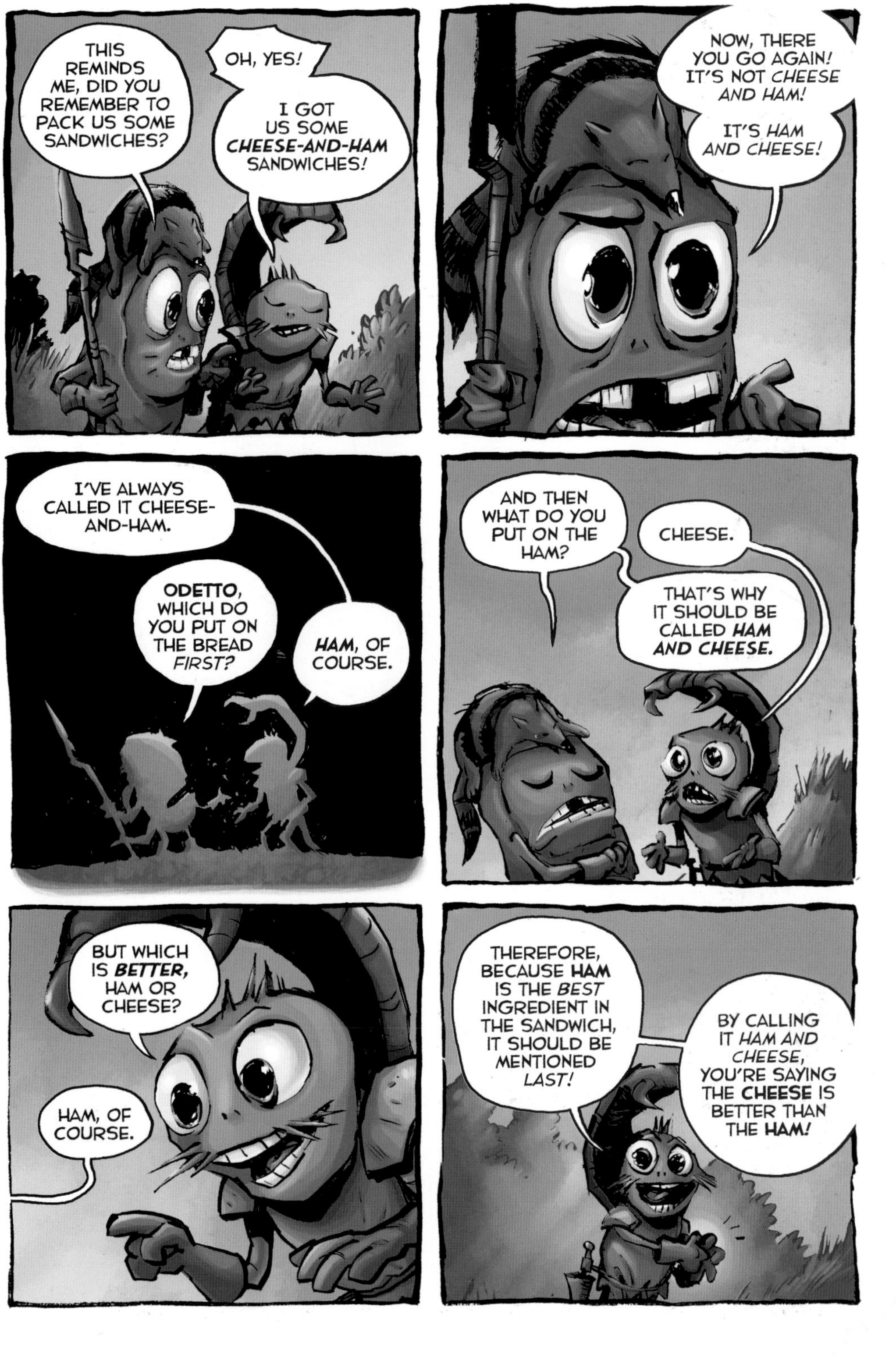
THIS REMINDS ME, DID YOU REMEMBER TO PACK US SOME SANDWICHES?
OH, YES!
I GOT US SOME *CHEESE-AND-HAM* SANDWICHES!
NOW, THERE YOU GO AGAIN! IT'S NOT *CHEESE AND HAM!*
IT'S *HAM AND CHEESE!*
I'VE ALWAYS CALLED IT CHEESE-AND-HAM.
ODETTO, WHICH DO YOU PUT ON THE BREAD *FIRST?*
HAM, OF COURSE.
AND THEN WHAT DO *YOU* PUT ON THE HAM?
CHEESE.
THAT'S WHY IT SHOULD BE CALLED ***HAM AND CHEESE.***
BUT WHICH IS ***BETTER,*** HAM OR CHEESE?
HAM, OF COURSE.
THEREFORE, BECAUSE **HAM** IS THE *BEST* INGREDIENT IN THE SANDWICH, IT SHOULD BE MENTIONED *LAST!*
BY CALLING IT *HAM AND CHEESE*, YOU'RE SAYING THE **CHEESE** IS BETTER THAN THE **HAM!**

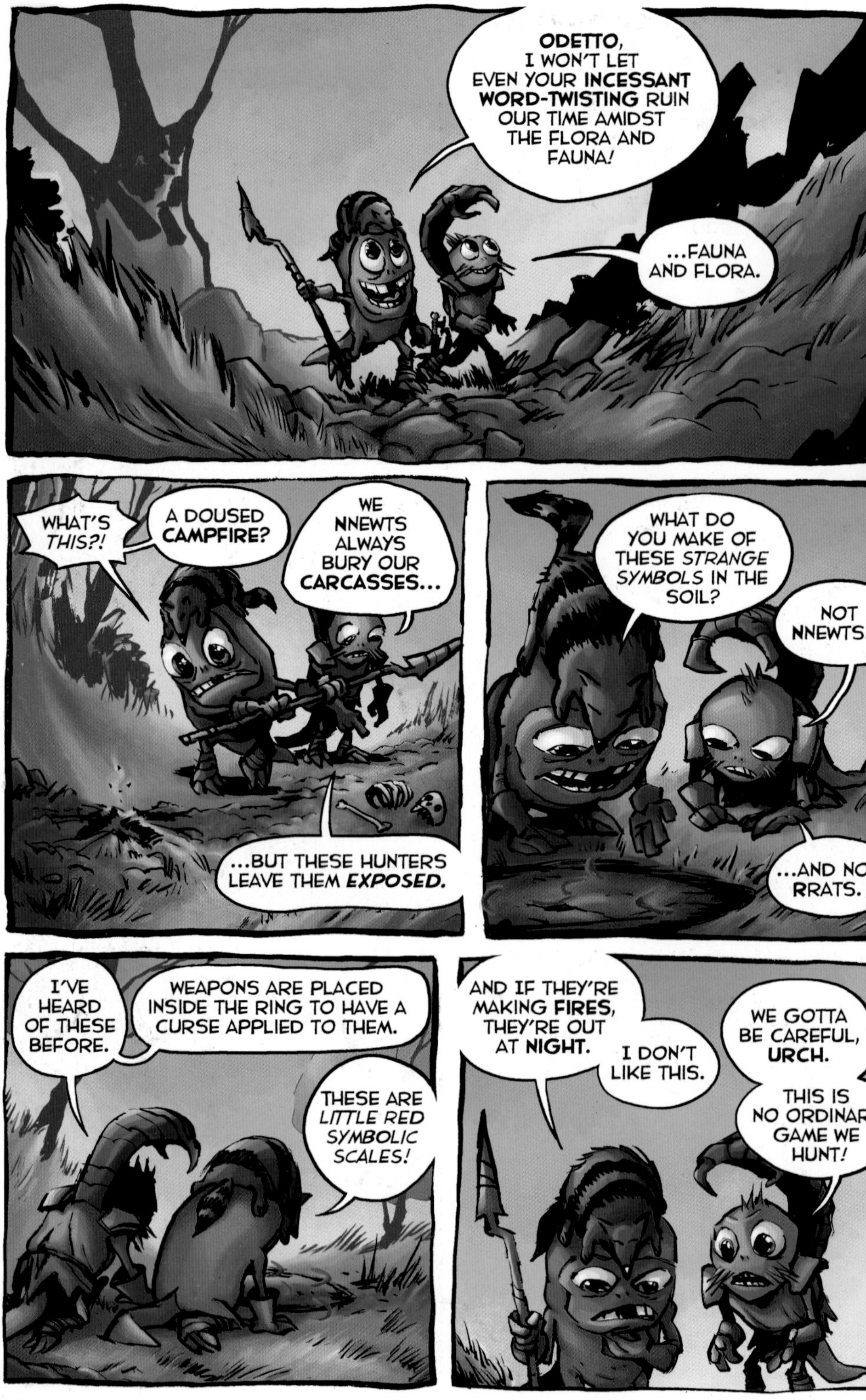
ODETTO, I WON'T LET EVEN YOUR INCESSANT WORD-TWISTING RUIN OUR TIME AMIDST THE FLORA AND FAUNA!
...FAUNA AND FLORA.
WHAT'S THIS?!
A DOUSED CAMPFIRE?
WE NNEWTS ALWAYS BURY OUR CARCASSES...
...BUT THESE HUNTERS LEAVE THEM EXPOSED.
WHAT DO YOU MAKE OF THESE STRANGE SYMBOLS IN THE SOIL?
NOT NNEWTS...
...AND NOT RRATS.
I'VE HEARD OF THESE BEFORE.
WEAPONS ARE PLACED INSIDE THE RING TO HAVE A CURSE APPLIED TO THEM.
THESE ARE LITTLE RED SYMBOLIC SCALES!
AND IF THEY'RE MAKING FIRES, THEY'RE OUT AT NIGHT.
I DON'T LIKE THIS.
WE GOTTA BE CAREFUL, URCH.
THIS IS NO ORDINARY GAME WE HUNT!

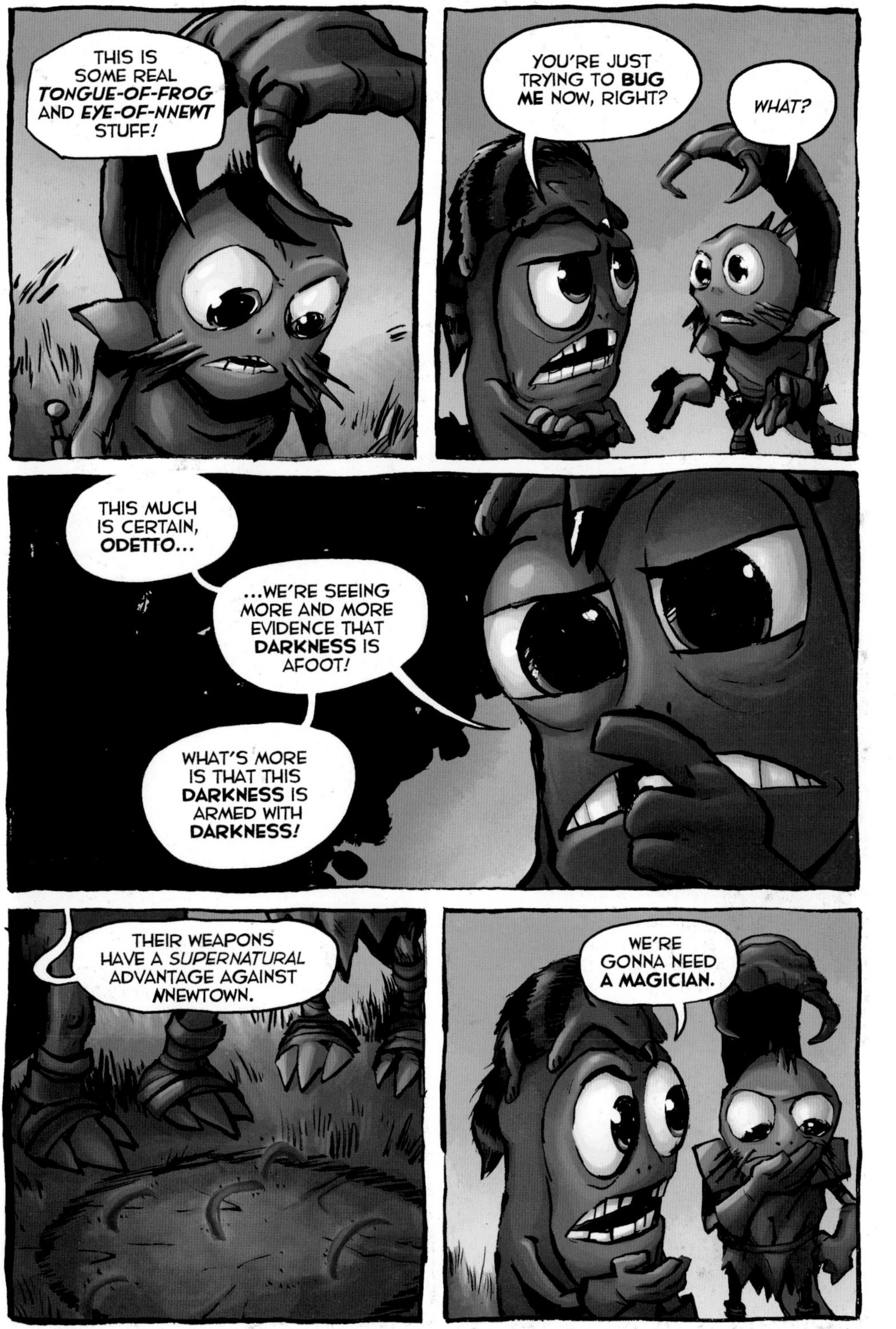
THIS IS SOME REAL *TONGUE-OF-FROG* AND *EYE-OF-NNEWT* STUFF!
YOU'RE JUST TRYING TO **BUG ME** NOW, RIGHT?
WHAT?
THIS MUCH IS CERTAIN, **ODETTO...**
...WE'RE SEEING MORE AND MORE EVIDENCE THAT **DARKNESS** IS AFOOT!
WHAT'S MORE IS THAT THIS **DARKNESS** IS ARMED WITH **DARKNESS!**
THEIR WEAPONS HAVE A *SUPERNATURAL* ADVANTAGE AGAINST NNEWTOWN.
WE'RE GONNA NEED **A MAGICIAN.**

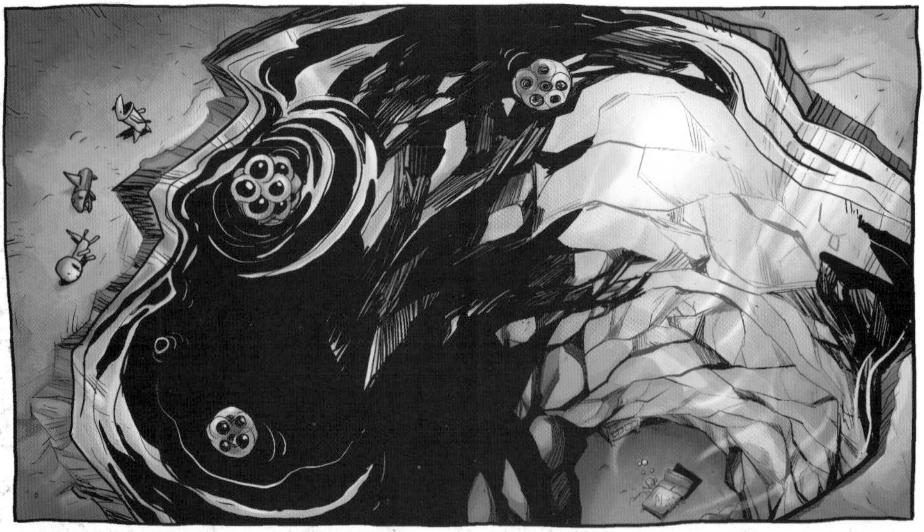

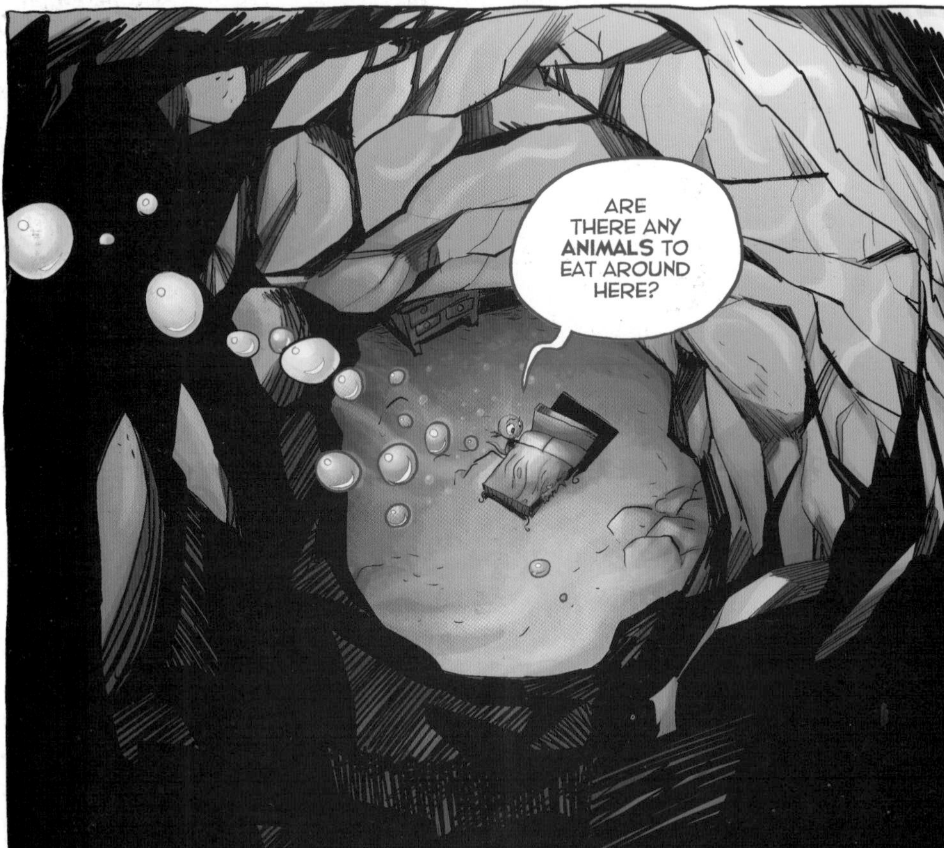
ARE THERE ANY ANIMALS TO EAT AROUND HERE?

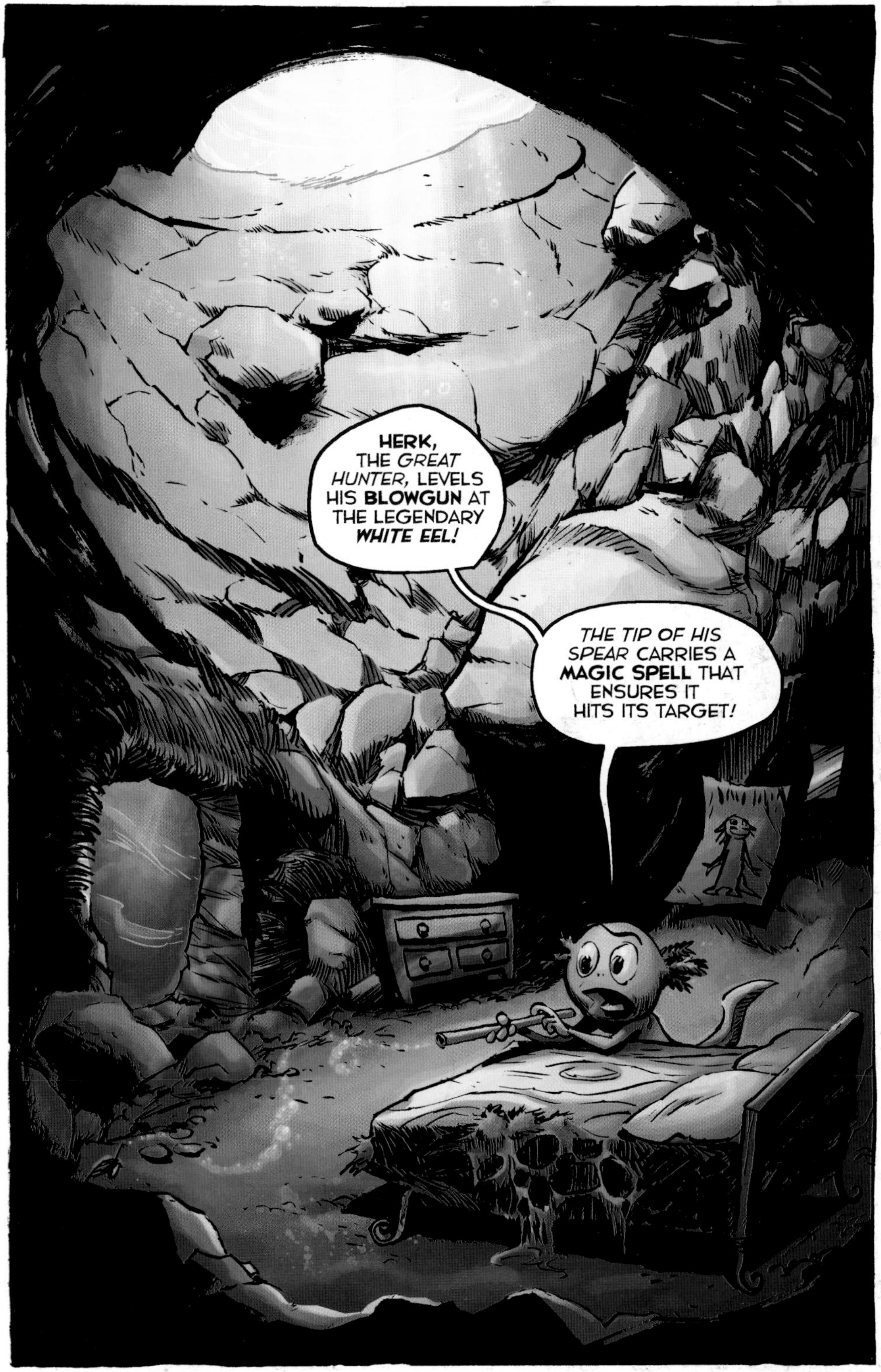
HERK, THE GREAT HUNTER, LEVELS HIS BLOWGUN AT THE LEGENDARY WHITE EEL!
THE TIP OF HIS SPEAR CARRIES A MAGIC SPELL THAT ENSURES IT HITS ITS TARGET!

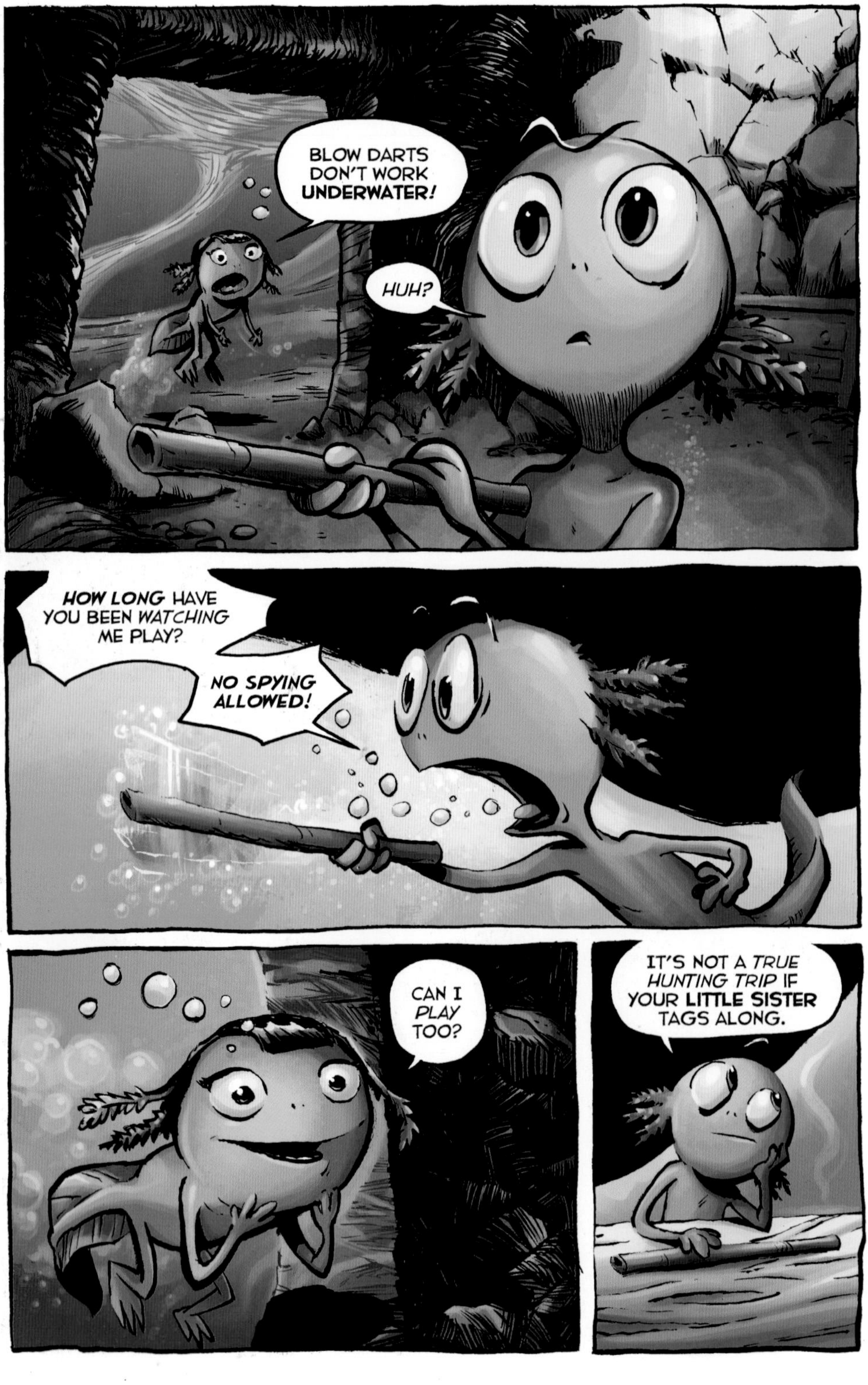
BLOW DARTS DON'T WORK **UNDERWATER!**
HUH?
HOW LONG HAVE YOU BEEN *WATCHING* ME PLAY?
NO SPYING ALLOWED!
CAN I *PLAY* TOO?
IT'S NOT A *TRUE HUNTING TRIP* IF YOUR **LITTLE SISTER** TAGS ALONG.

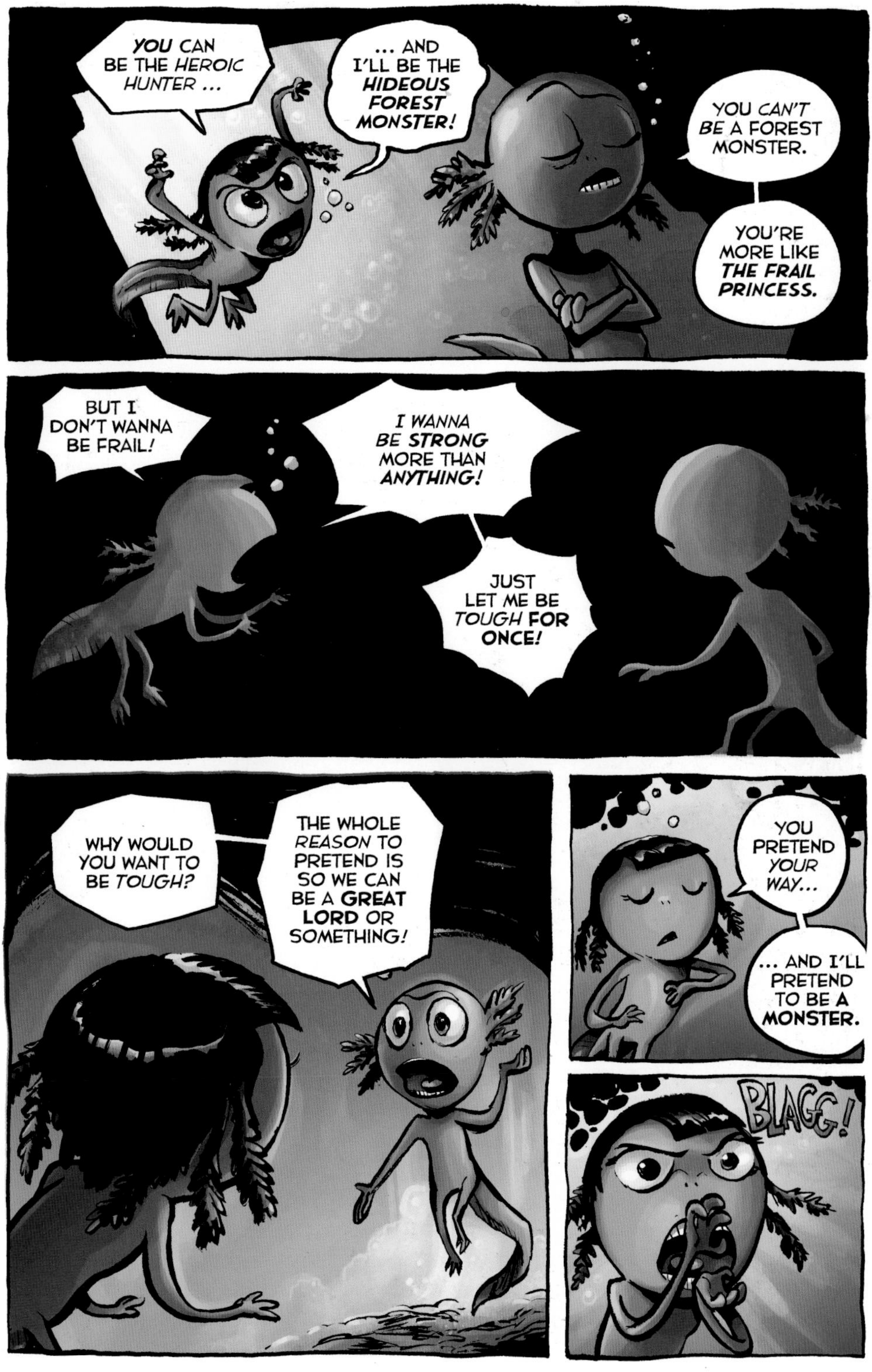
YOU CAN BE THE HEROIC HUNTER ...
... AND I'LL BE THE HIDEOUS FOREST MONSTER!
YOU CAN'T BE A FOREST MONSTER.
YOU'RE MORE LIKE THE FRAIL PRINCESS.
BUT I DON'T WANNA BE FRAIL!
I WANNA BE STRONG MORE THAN ANYTHING!
JUST LET ME BE TOUGH FOR ONCE!
WHY WOULD YOU WANT TO BE TOUGH?
THE WHOLE REASON TO PRETEND IS SO WE CAN BE A GREAT LORD OR SOMETHING!
YOU PRETEND YOUR WAY...
... AND I'LL PRETEND TO BE A MONSTER.
BLAGG!

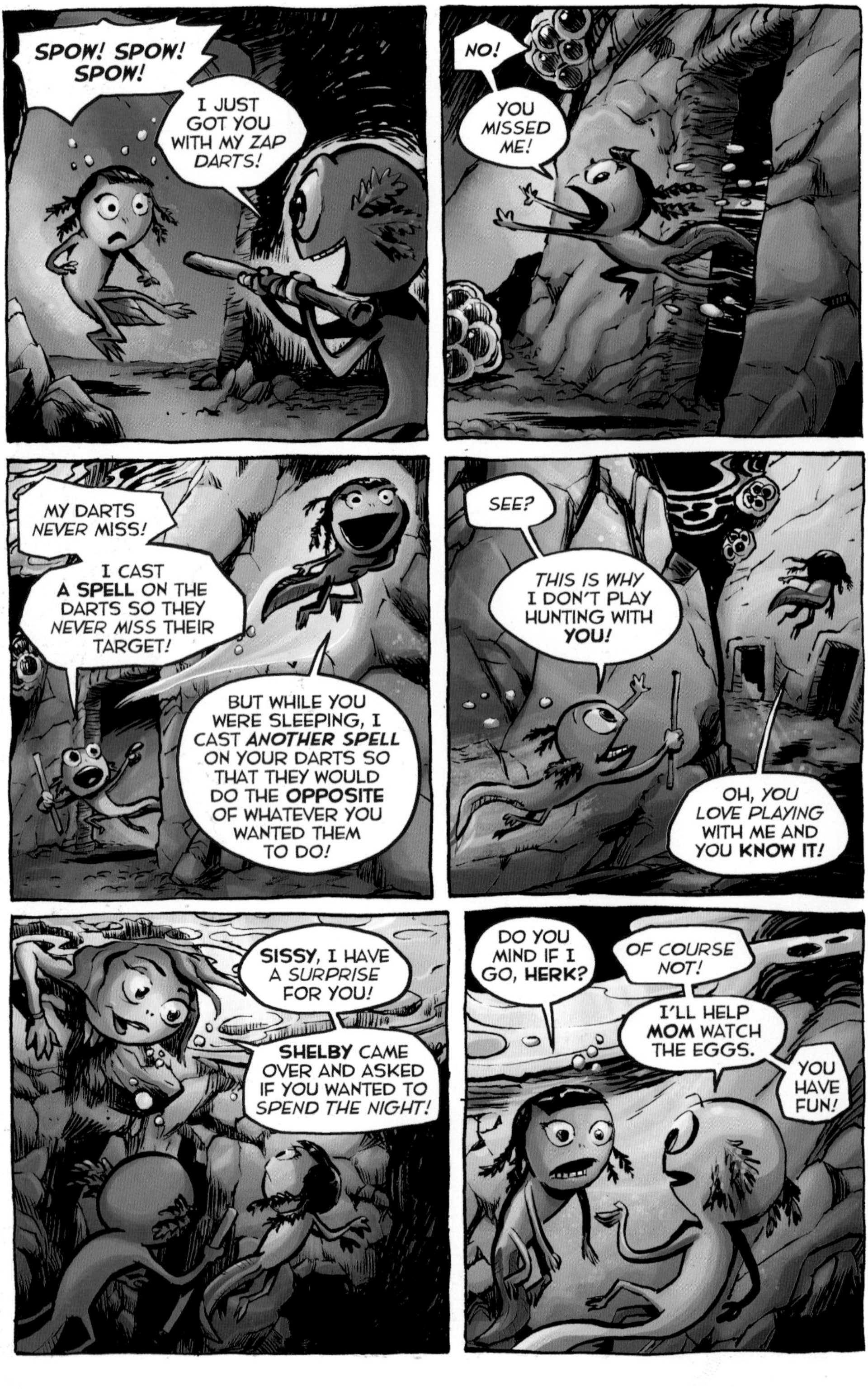
SPOW! SPOW! SPOW!
I JUST GOT YOU WITH MY ZAP DARTS!
NO!
YOU MISSED ME!
MY DARTS NEVER MISS!
I CAST A SPELL ON THE DARTS SO THEY NEVER MISS THEIR TARGET!
BUT WHILE YOU WERE SLEEPING, I CAST ANOTHER SPELL ON YOUR DARTS SO THAT THEY WOULD DO THE OPPOSITE OF WHATEVER YOU WANTED THEM TO DO!
SEE?
THIS IS WHY I DON'T PLAY HUNTING WITH YOU!
OH, YOU LOVE PLAYING WITH ME AND YOU KNOW IT!
SISSY, I HAVE A SURPRISE FOR YOU!
SHELBY CAME OVER AND ASKED IF YOU WANTED TO SPEND THE NIGHT!
DO YOU MIND IF I GO, HERK?
OF COURSE NOT!
I'LL HELP MOM WATCH THE EGGS.
YOU HAVE FUN!

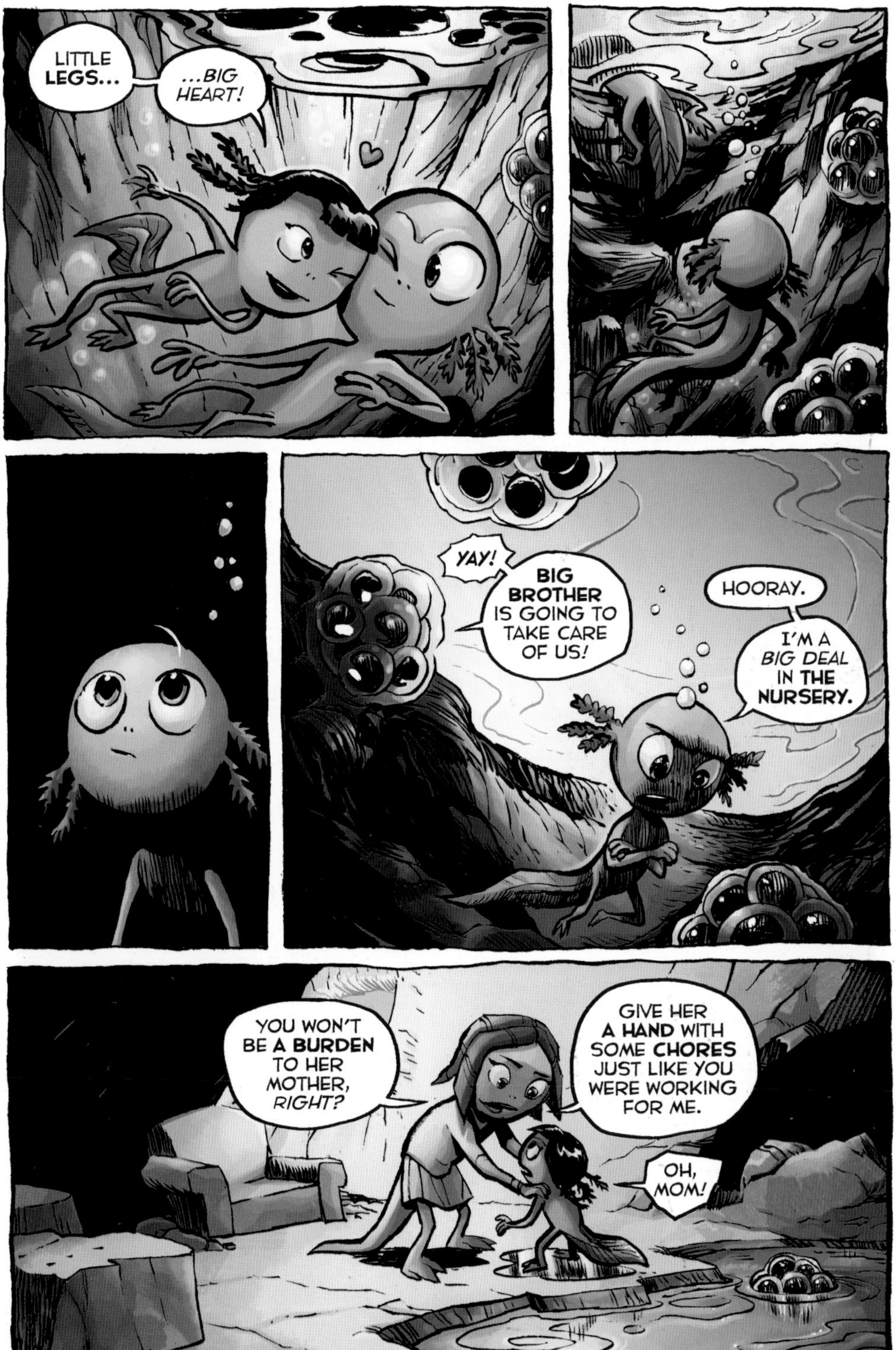
LITTLE LEGS...
...BIG HEART!
YAY!
BIG BROTHER IS GOING TO TAKE CARE OF US!
HOORAY.
I'M A BIG DEAL IN THE NURSERY.
YOU WON'T BE A BURDEN TO HER MOTHER, RIGHT?
GIVE HER A HAND WITH SOME CHORES JUST LIKE YOU WERE WORKING FOR ME.
OH, MOM!

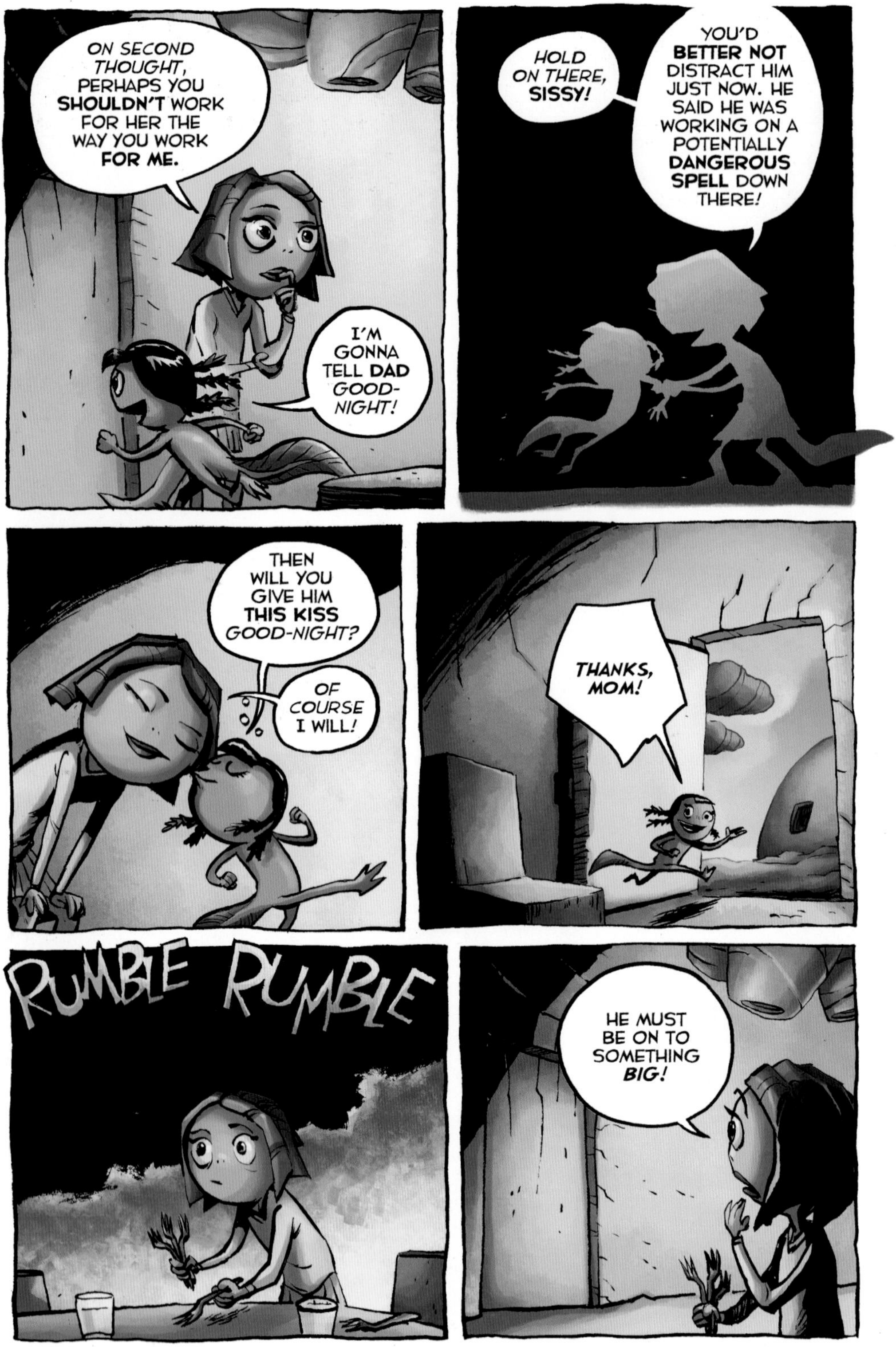
ON SECOND THOUGHT, PERHAPS YOU SHOULDN'T WORK FOR HER THE WAY YOU WORK FOR ME.
I'M GONNA TELL DAD GOOD-NIGHT!
HOLD ON THERE, SISSY!
YOU'D BETTER NOT DISTRACT HIM JUST NOW. HE SAID HE WAS WORKING ON A POTENTIALLY DANGEROUS SPELL DOWN THERE!
THEN WILL YOU GIVE HIM THIS KISS GOOD-NIGHT?
OF COURSE I WILL!
THANKS, MOM!
RUMBLE RUMBLE
HE MUST BE ON TO SOMETHING BIG!

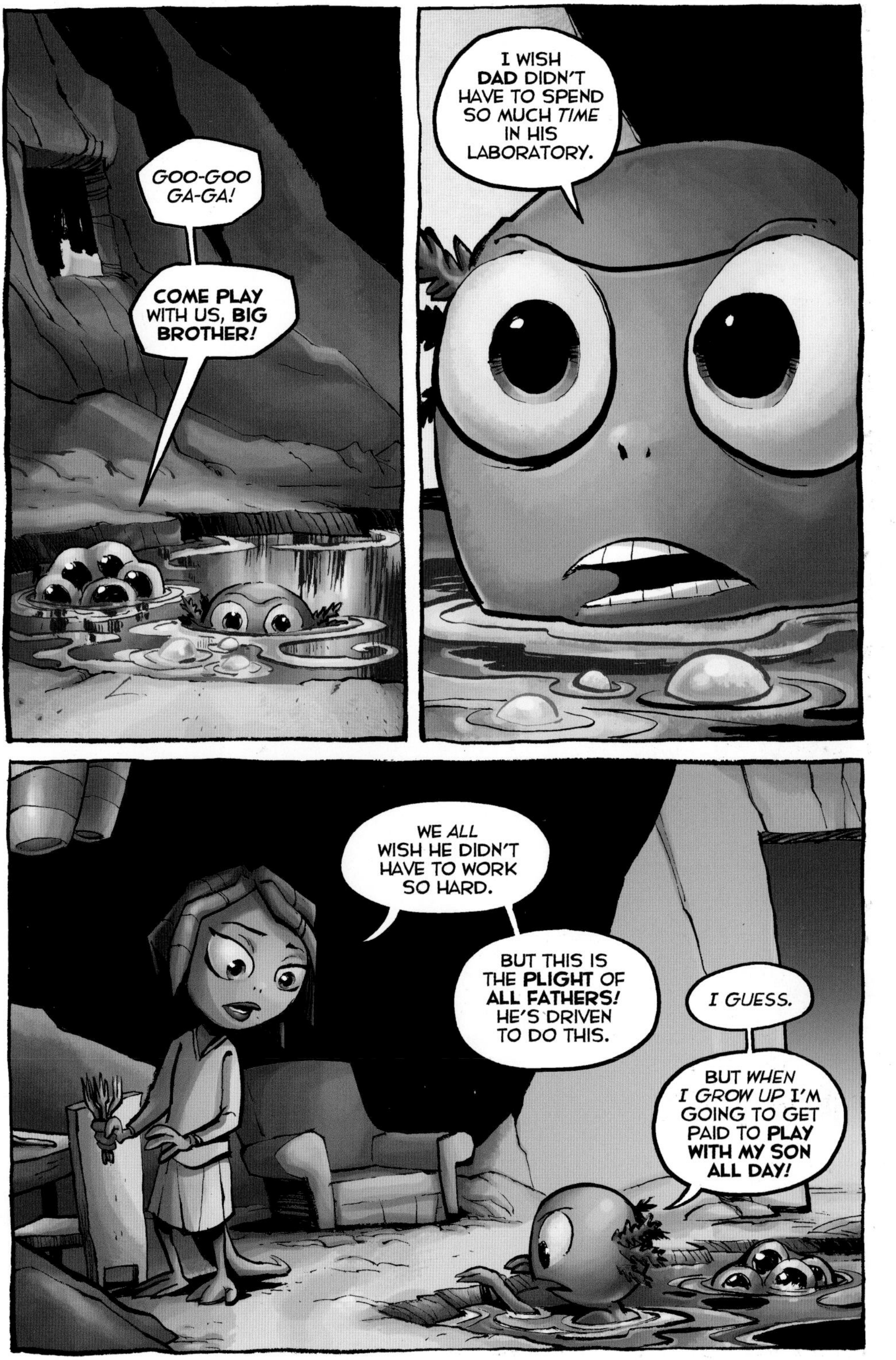
GOO-GOO GA-GA!
COME PLAY WITH US, BIG BROTHER!
I WISH DAD DIDN'T HAVE TO SPEND SO MUCH TIME IN HIS LABORATORY.
WE ALL WISH HE DIDN'T HAVE TO WORK SO HARD.
BUT THIS IS THE PLIGHT OF ALL FATHERS! HE'S DRIVEN TO DO THIS.
I GUESS.
BUT WHEN I GROW UP I'M GOING TO GET PAID TO PLAY WITH MY SON ALL DAY!

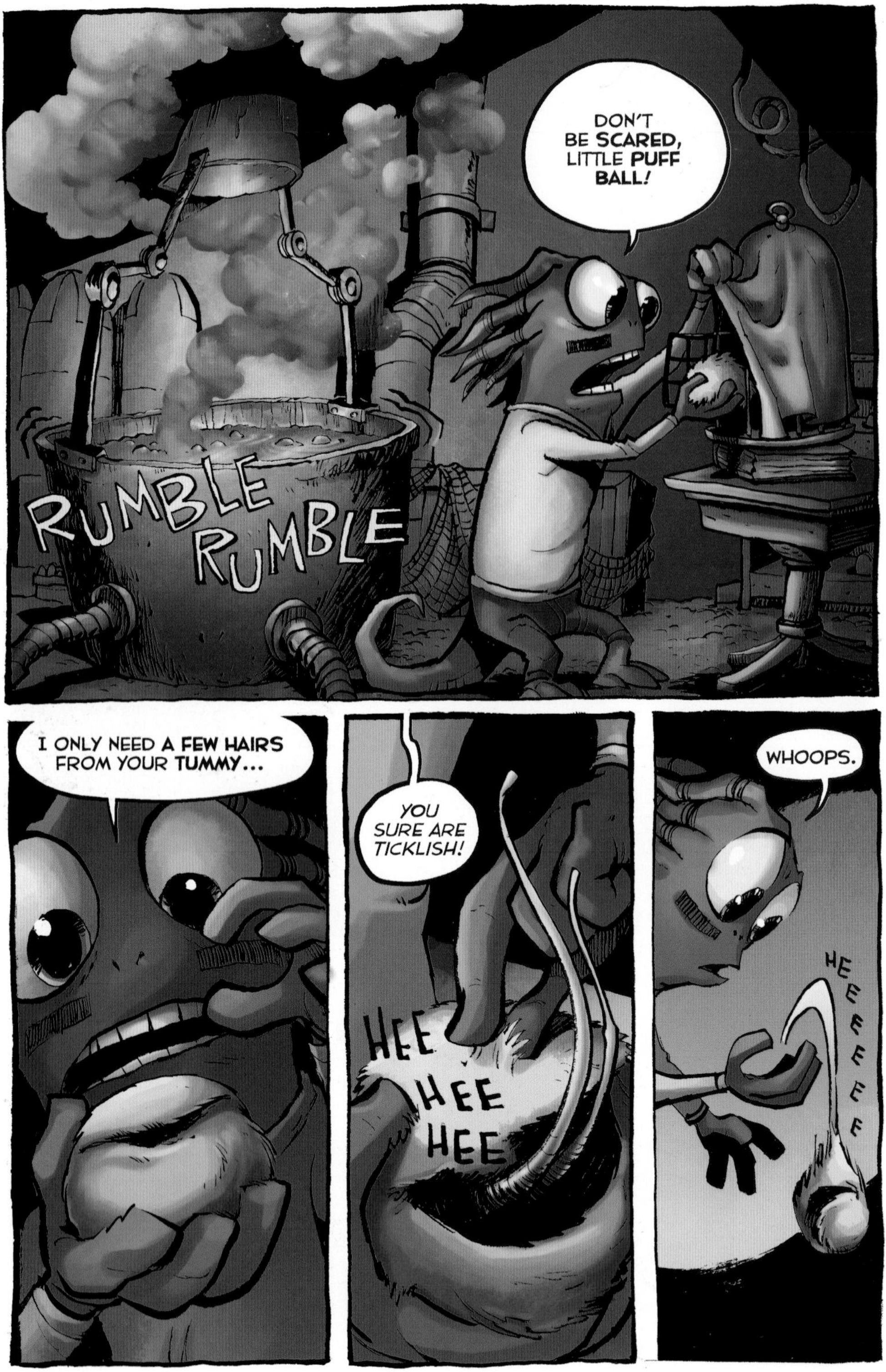
DON'T BE SCARED, LITTLE PUFF BALL!
RUMBLE RUMBLE
I ONLY NEED A FEW HAIRS FROM YOUR TUMMY...
YOU SURE ARE TICKLISH!
HEE HEE HEE
WHOOPS.
HEEEEEE

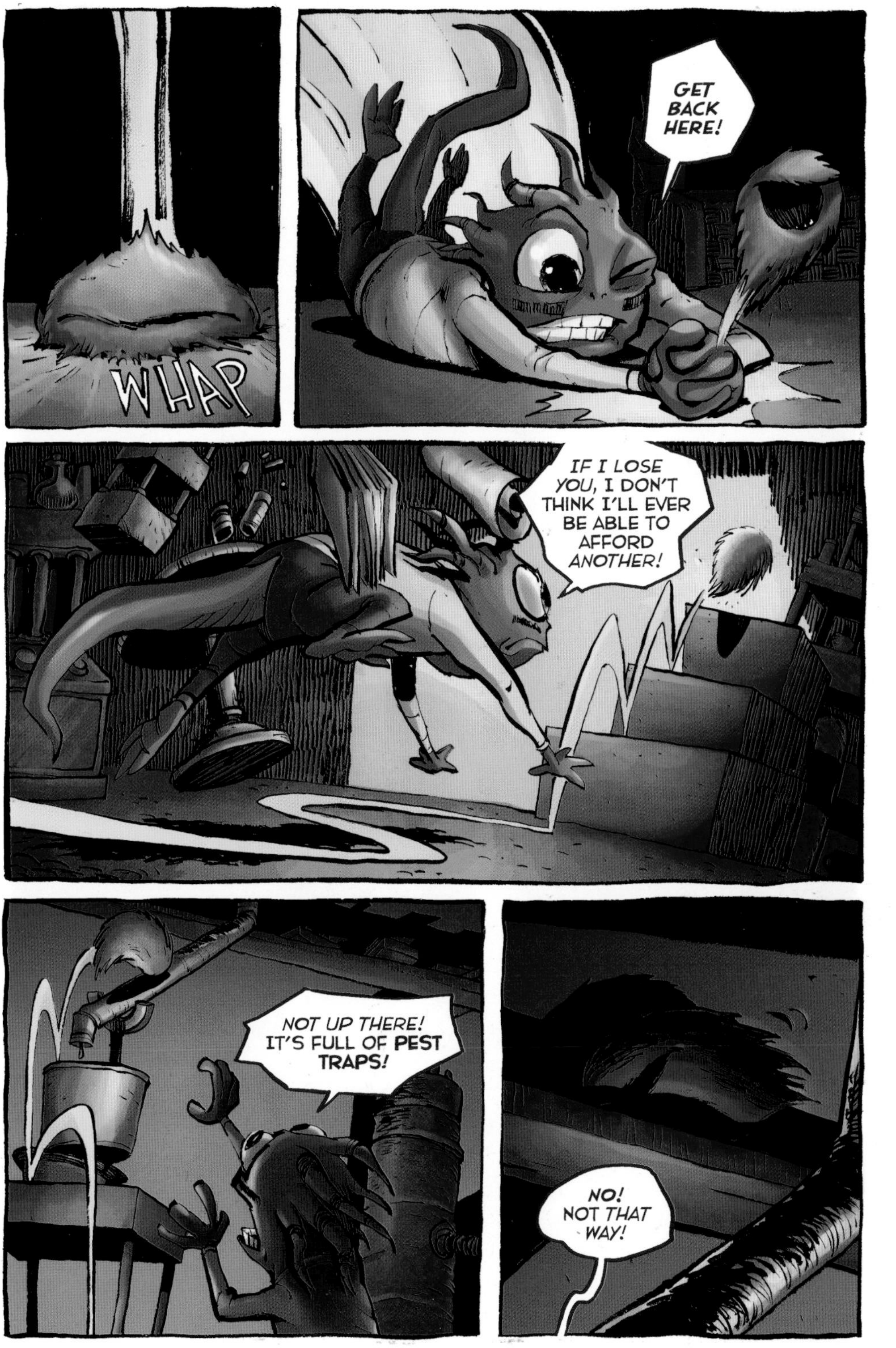
WHAP
GET BACK HERE!
IF I LOSE YOU, I DON'T THINK I'LL EVER BE ABLE TO AFFORD ANOTHER!
NOT UP THERE! IT'S FULL OF PEST TRAPS!
NO! NOT THAT WAY!

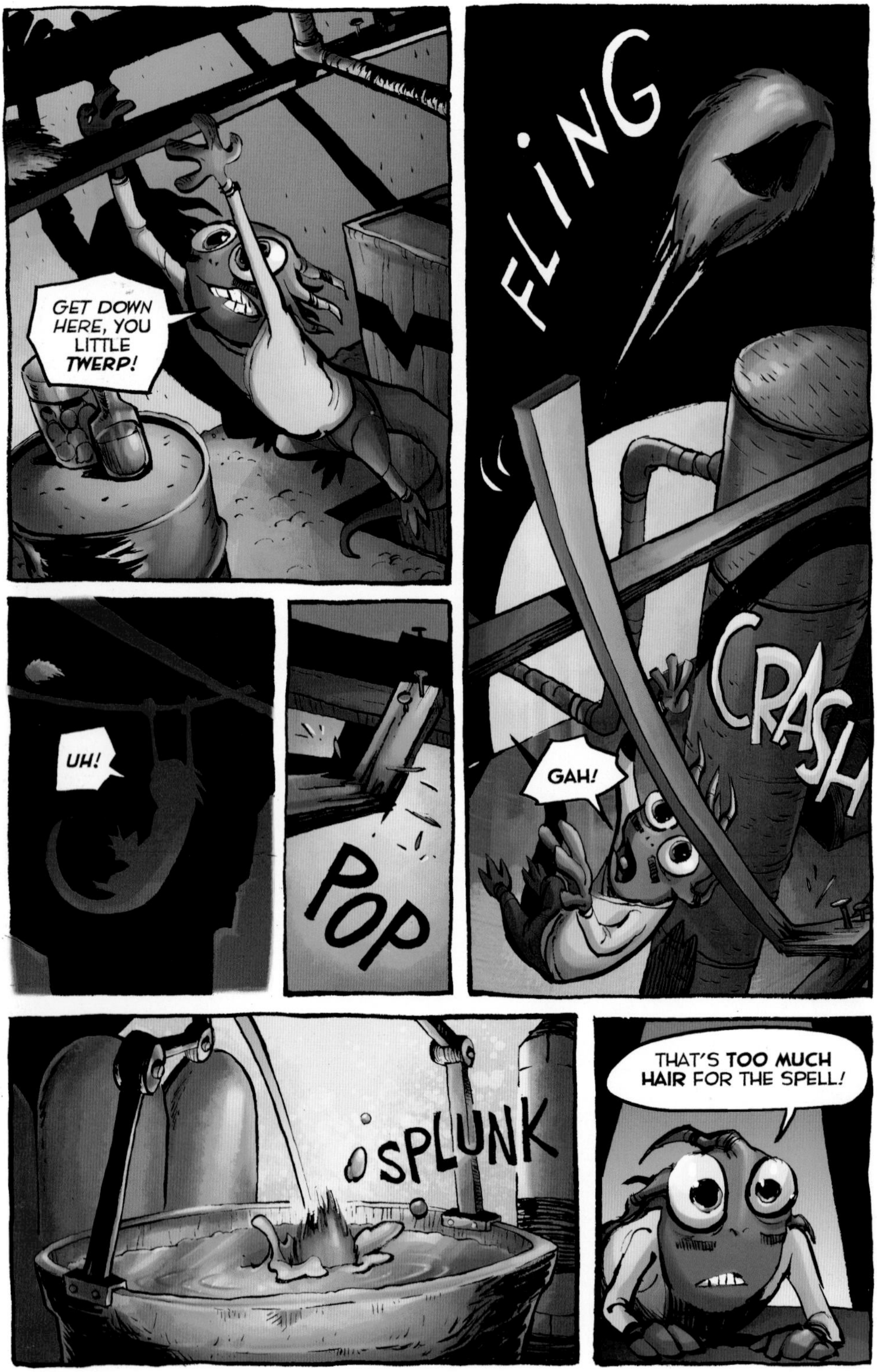
GET DOWN HERE, YOU LITTLE TWERP!
FLING
UH!
POP
GAH!
CRASH
SPLUNK
THAT'S TOO MUCH HAIR FOR THE SPELL!

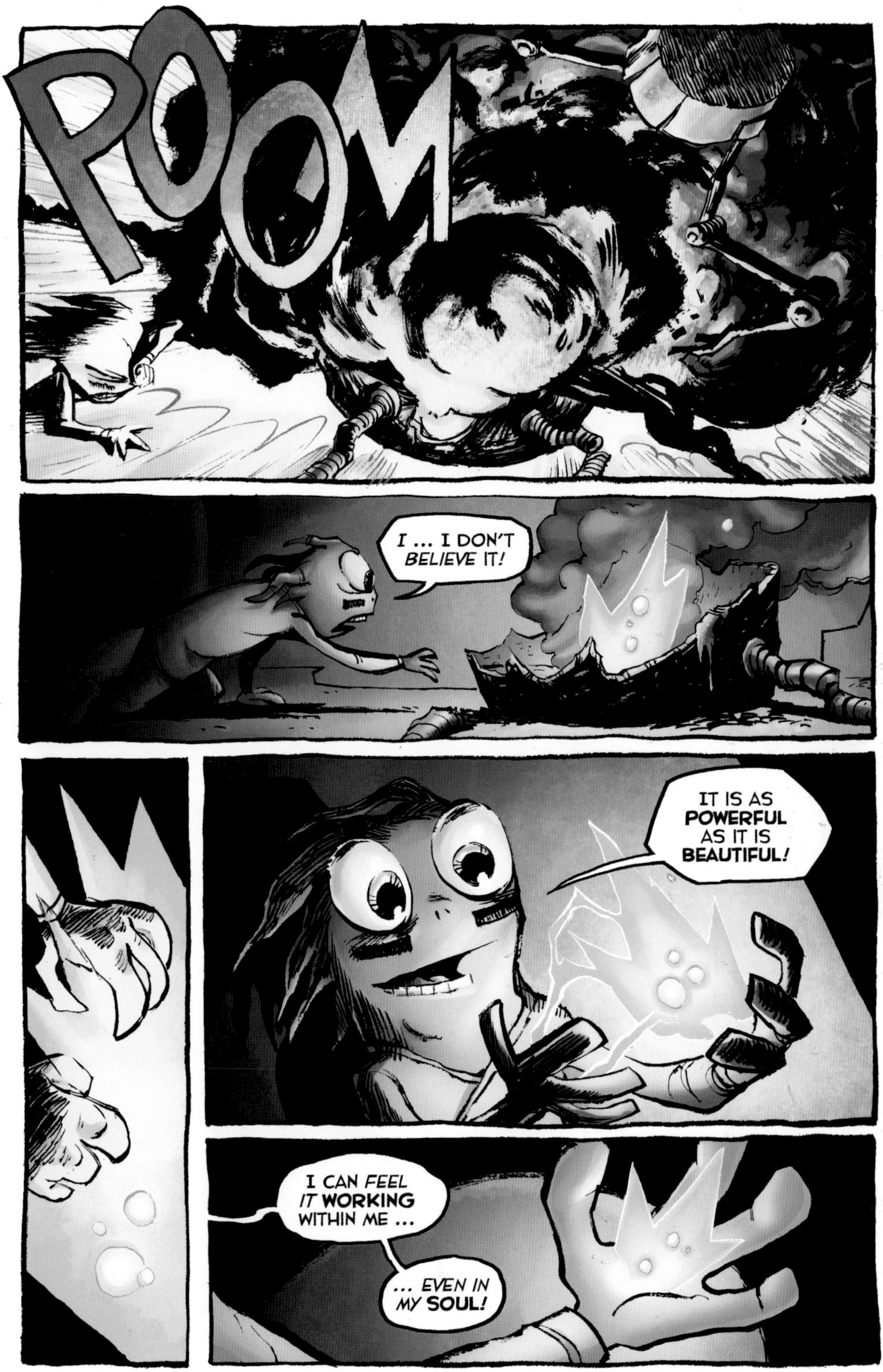
POOM
I ... I DON'T *BELIEVE* IT!
IT IS AS **POWERFUL** AS IT IS **BEAUTIFUL!**
I CAN *FEEL IT* **WORKING** WITHIN ME ...
... *EVEN IN MY* **SOUL!**

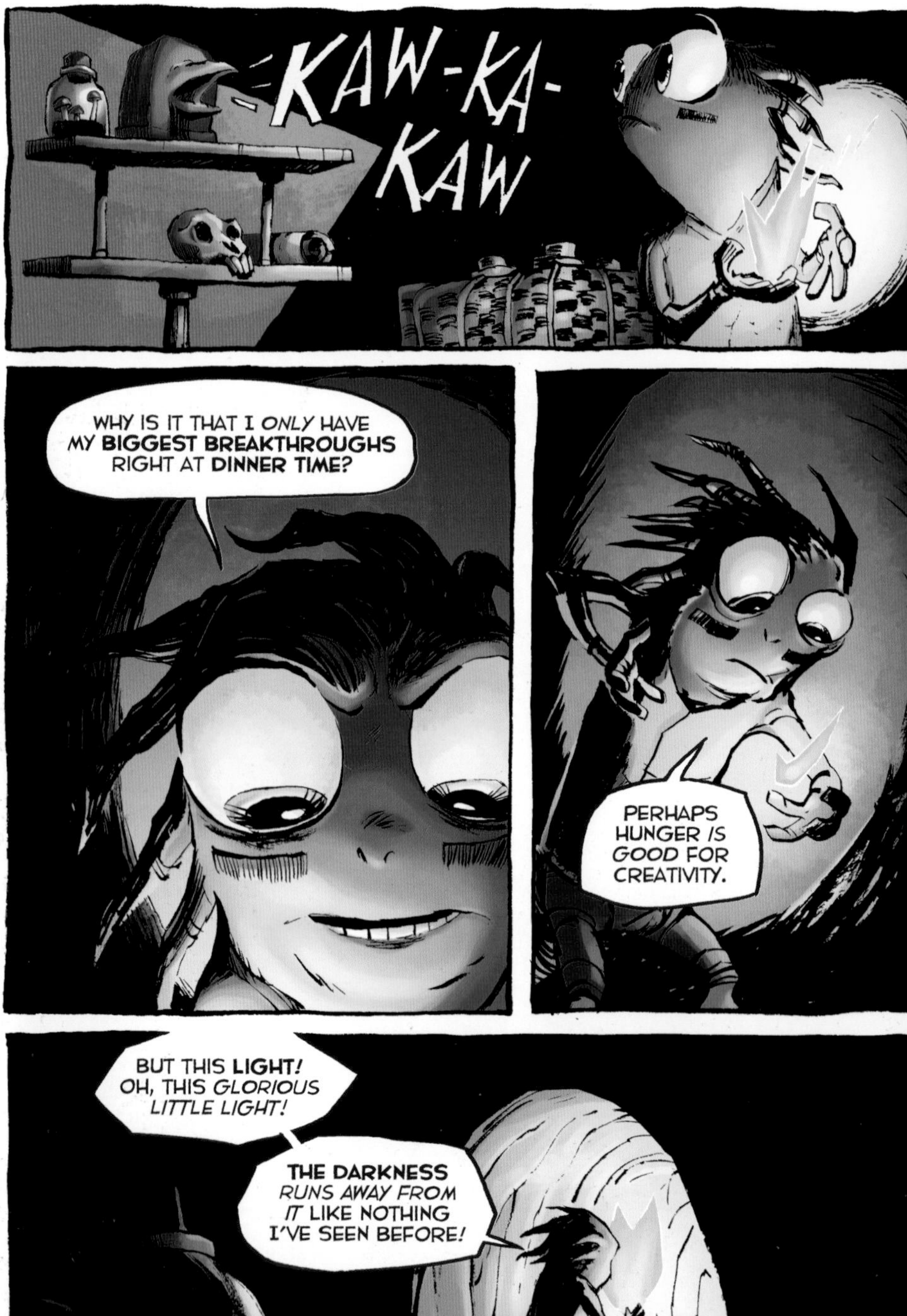
KAW-KA-KAW
WHY IS IT THAT I *ONLY* HAVE MY **BIGGEST BREAKTHROUGHS** RIGHT AT **DINNER TIME?**
PERHAPS HUNGER *IS* *GOOD* FOR CREATIVITY.
BUT THIS **LIGHT!** OH, THIS *GLORIOUS LITTLE LIGHT!*
THE DARKNESS *RUNS AWAY FROM IT* LIKE NOTHING I'VE SEEN BEFORE!

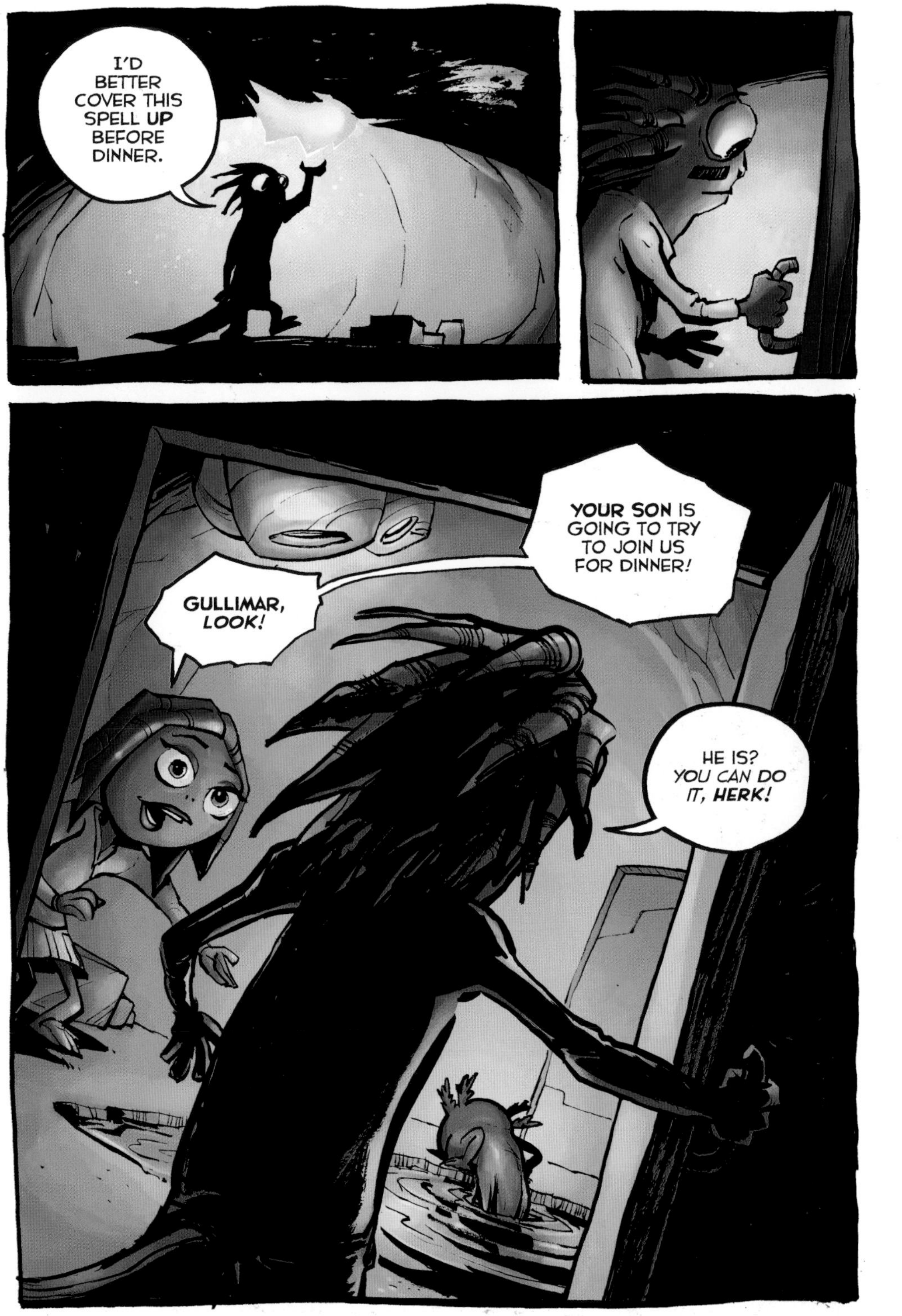
I'D BETTER COVER THIS SPELL UP BEFORE DINNER.
GULLIMAR, LOOK!
YOUR SON IS GOING TO TRY TO JOIN US FOR DINNER!
HE IS? YOU CAN DO IT, HERK!

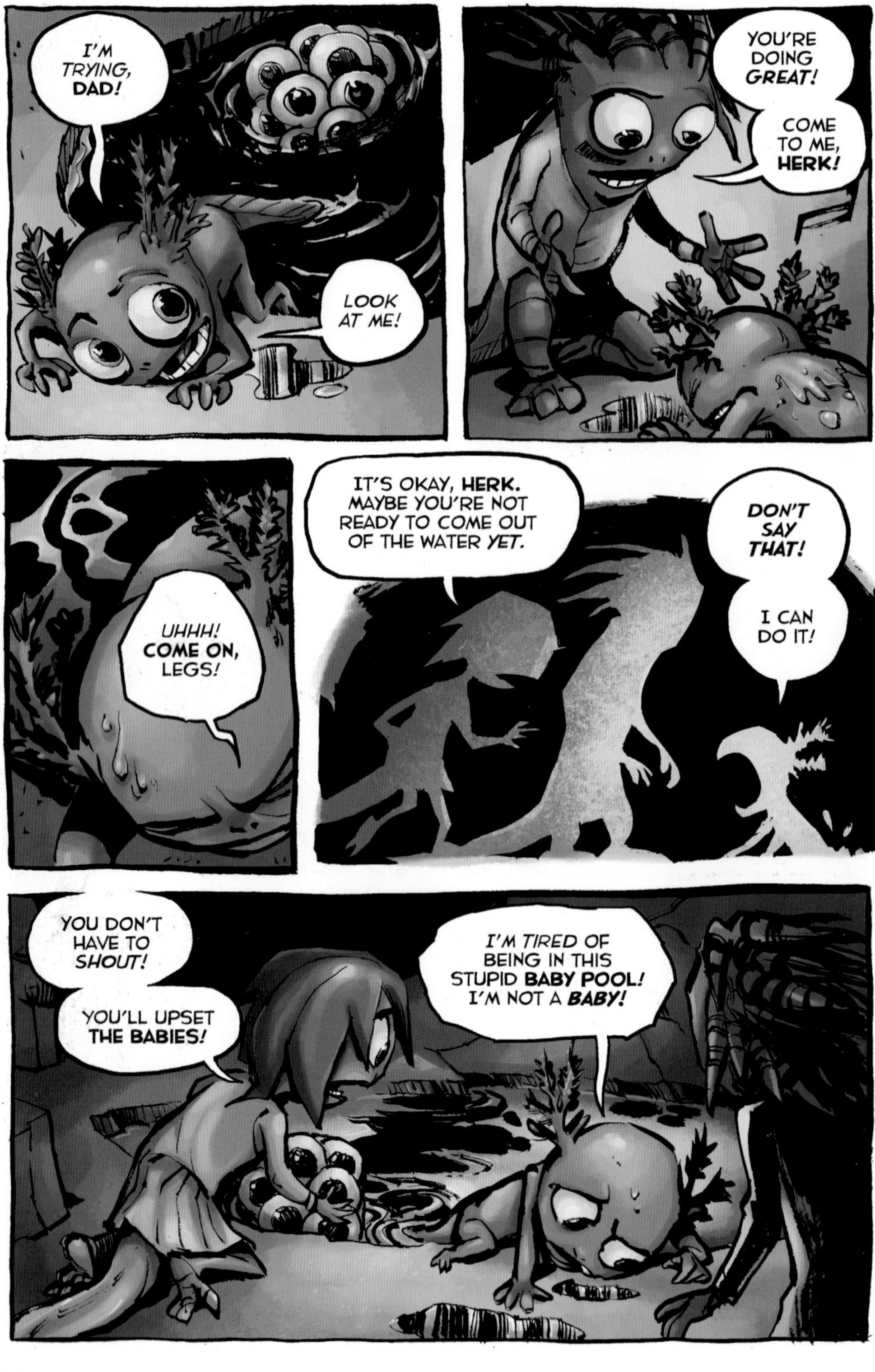
I'M TRYING, DAD!
LOOK AT ME!
YOU'RE DOING GREAT!
COME TO ME, HERK!
UHHH! COME ON, LEGS!
IT'S OKAY, HERK. MAYBE YOU'RE NOT READY TO COME OUT OF THE WATER YET.
DON'T SAY THAT!
I CAN DO IT!
YOU DON'T HAVE TO SHOUT!
YOU'LL UPSET THE BABIES!
I'M TIRED OF BEING IN THIS STUPID BABY POOL! I'M NOT A BABY!

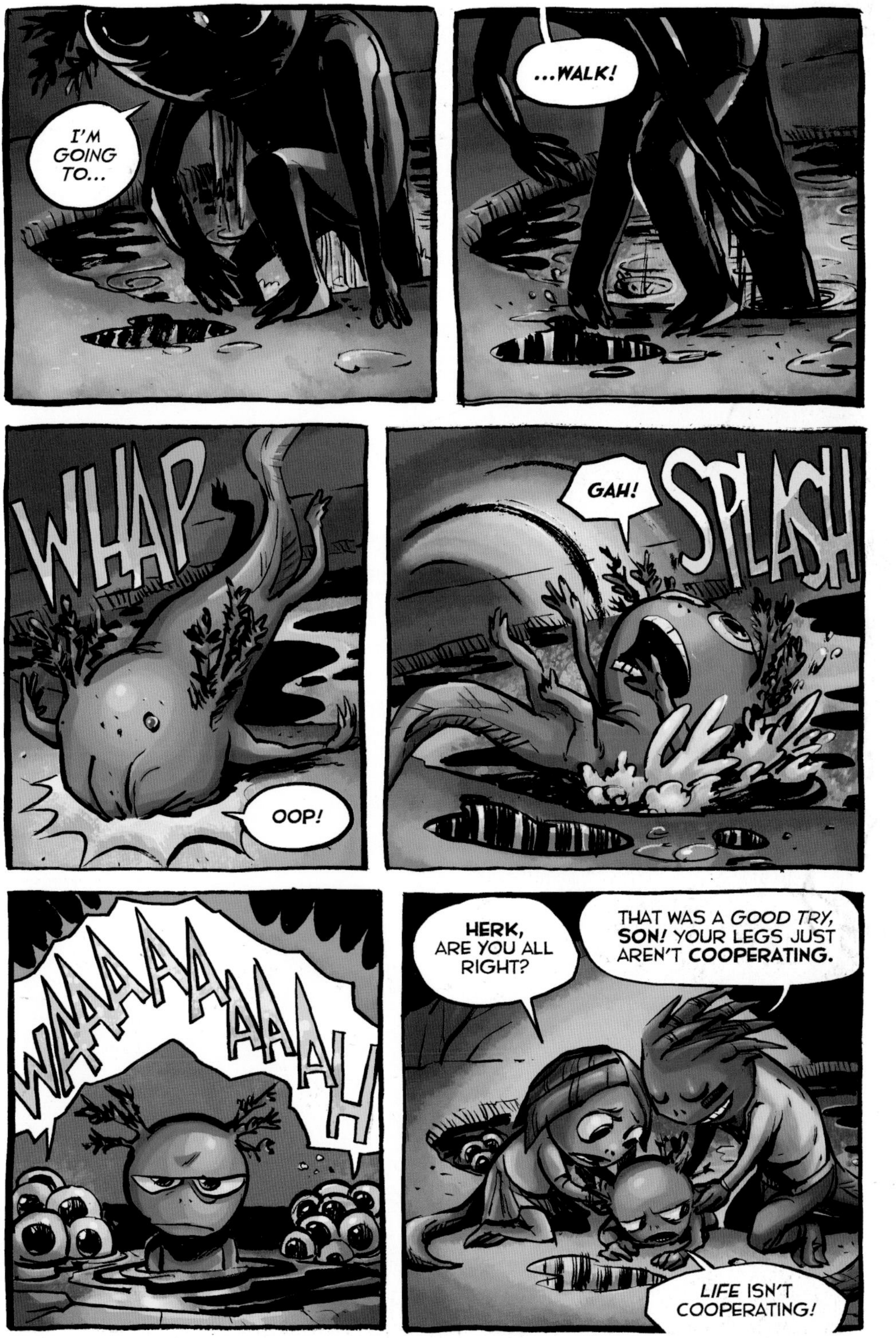
I'M GOING TO...
...WALK!
WHAP
OOP!
GAH!
SPLASH
WAAAAAAAAAH
HERK, ARE YOU ALL RIGHT?
THAT WAS A *GOOD TRY*, **SON!** YOUR LEGS JUST AREN'T **COOPERATING.**
LIFE ISN'T COOPERATING!

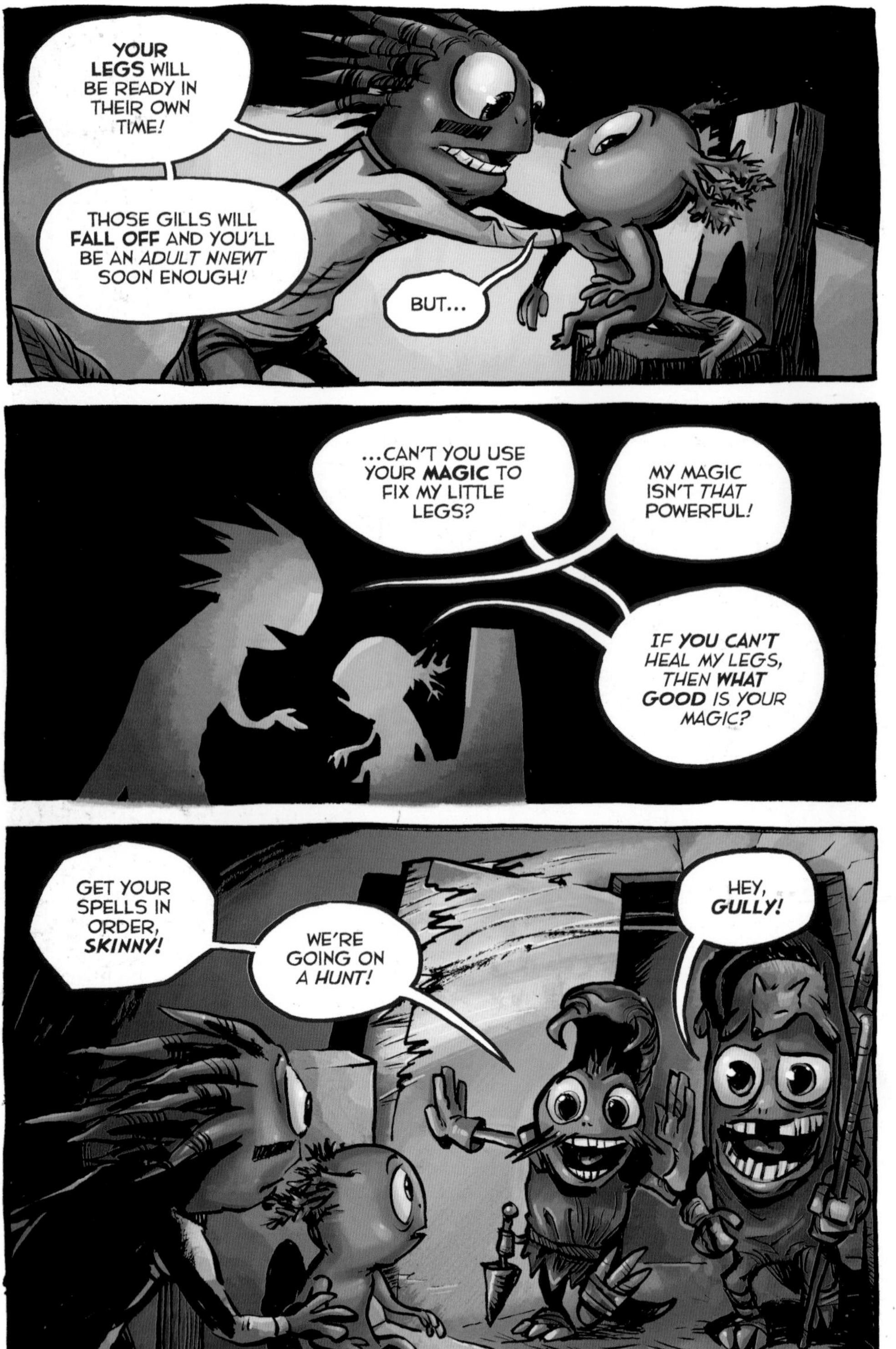
YOUR LEGS WILL BE READY IN THEIR OWN TIME!
THOSE GILLS WILL FALL OFF AND YOU'LL BE AN ADULT NNEWT SOON ENOUGH!
BUT...
...CAN'T YOU USE YOUR MAGIC TO FIX MY LITTLE LEGS?
MY MAGIC ISN'T THAT POWERFUL!
IF YOU CAN'T HEAL MY LEGS, THEN WHAT GOOD IS YOUR MAGIC?
GET YOUR SPELLS IN ORDER, SKINNY!
WE'RE GOING ON A HUNT!
HEY, GULLY!

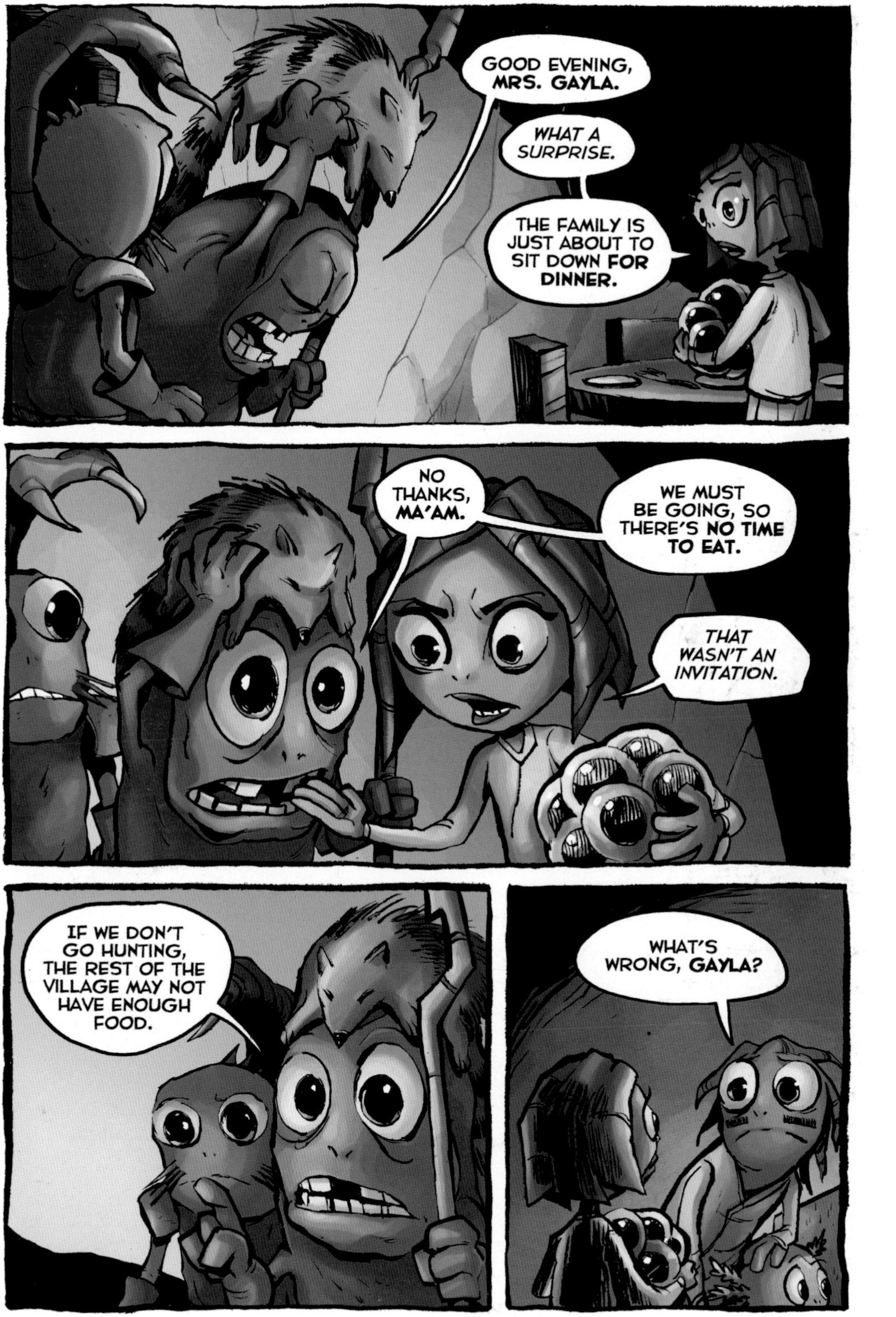
GOOD EVENING, MRS. GAYLA.
WHAT A SURPRISE.
THE FAMILY IS JUST ABOUT TO SIT DOWN FOR DINNER.
NO THANKS, MA'AM.
WE MUST BE GOING, SO THERE'S NO TIME TO EAT.
THAT WASN'T AN INVITATION.
IF WE DON'T GO HUNTING, THE REST OF THE VILLAGE MAY NOT HAVE ENOUGH FOOD.
WHAT'S WRONG, GAYLA?

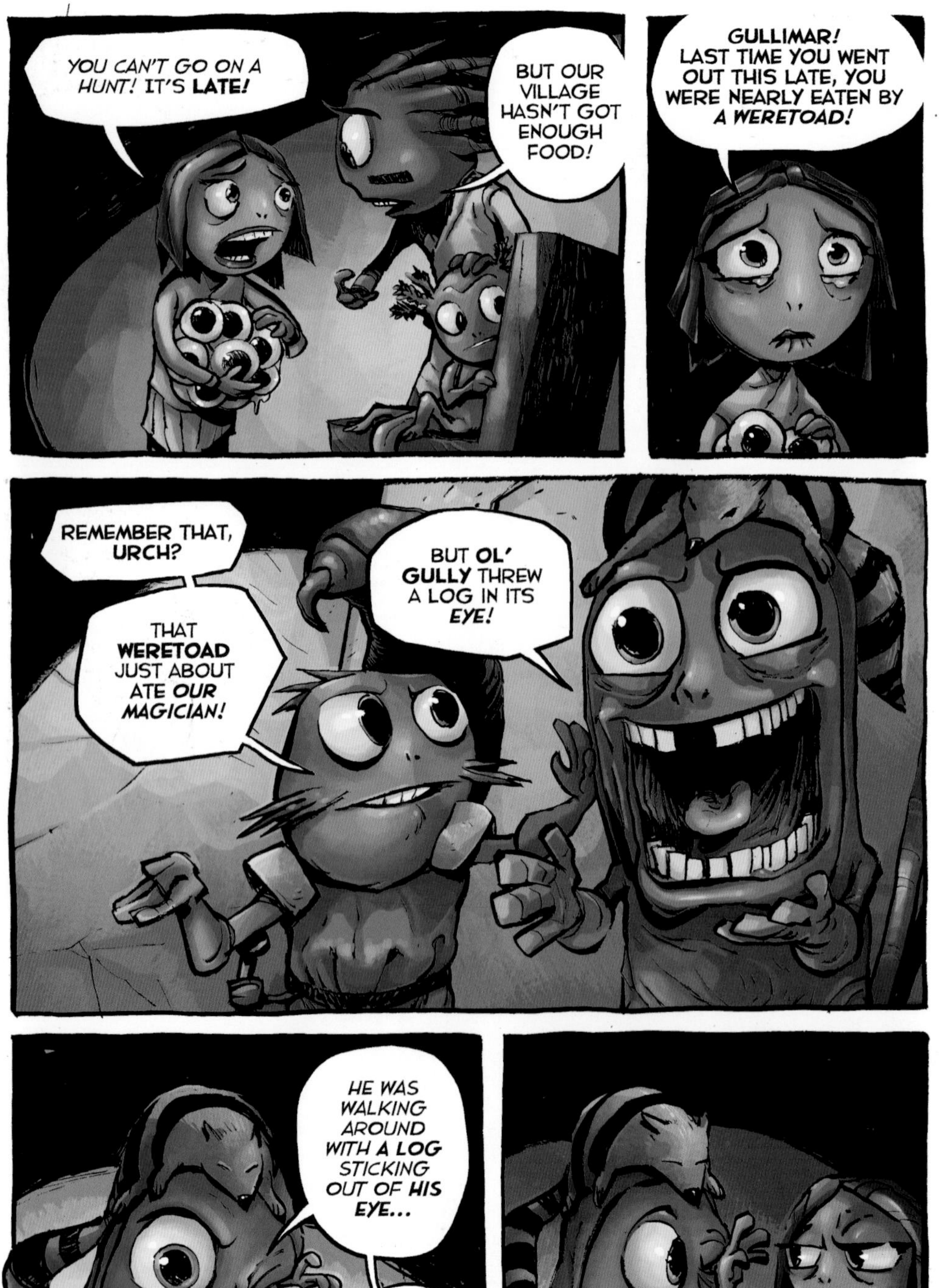
YOU CAN'T GO ON A HUNT! IT'S LATE!
BUT OUR VILLAGE HASN'T GOT ENOUGH FOOD!
GULLIMAR! LAST TIME YOU WENT OUT THIS LATE, YOU WERE NEARLY EATEN BY A WERETOAD!
REMEMBER THAT, URCH?
THAT WERETOAD JUST ABOUT ATE OUR MAGICIAN!
BUT OL' GULLY THREW A LOG IN ITS EYE!
HE WAS WALKING AROUND WITH A LOG STICKING OUT OF HIS EYE...
...LIKE THIS!

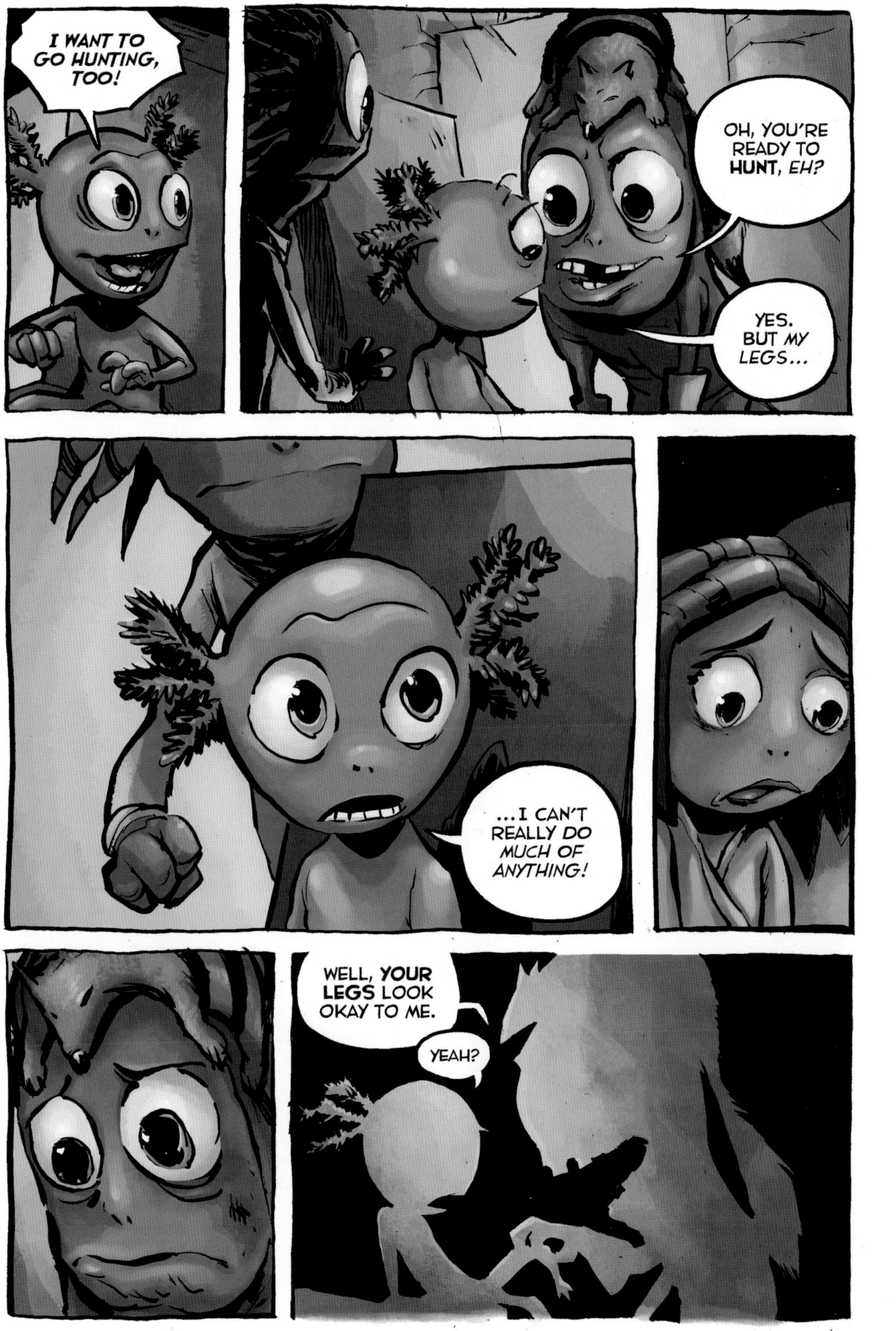
I WANT TO GO HUNTING, TOO!
OH, YOU'RE READY TO HUNT, EH?
YES. BUT MY LEGS...
...I CAN'T REALLY DO MUCH OF ANYTHING!
WELL, YOUR LEGS LOOK OKAY TO ME.
YEAH?

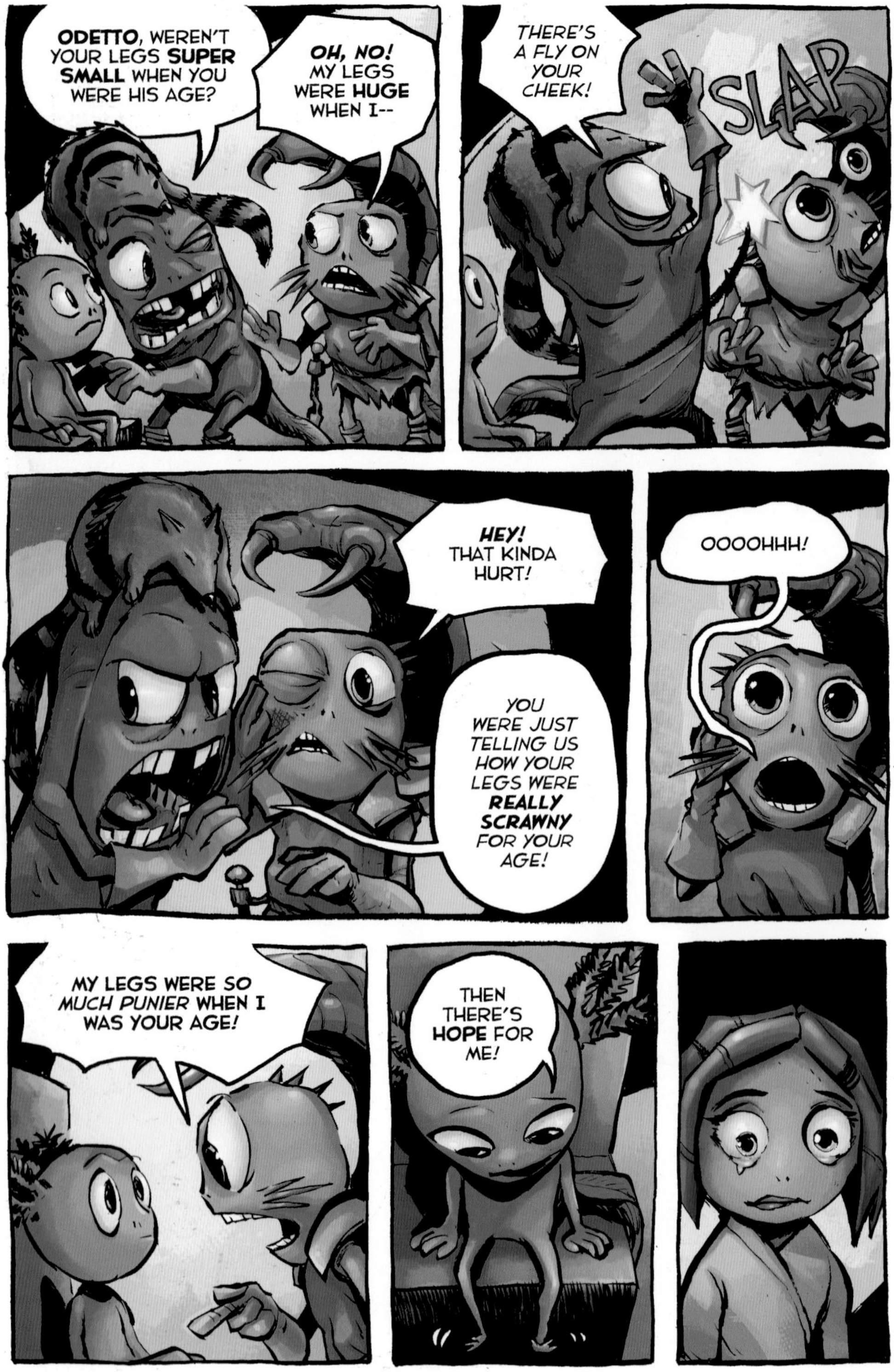
ODETTO, WEREN'T YOUR LEGS SUPER SMALL WHEN YOU WERE HIS AGE?
OH, NO! MY LEGS WERE HUGE WHEN I--
THERE'S A FLY ON YOUR CHEEK!
SLAP
HEY! THAT KINDA HURT!
YOU WERE JUST TELLING US HOW YOUR LEGS WERE REALLY SCRAWNY FOR YOUR AGE!
OOOOHHH!
MY LEGS WERE SO MUCH PUNIER WHEN I WAS YOUR AGE!
THEN THERE'S HOPE FOR ME!

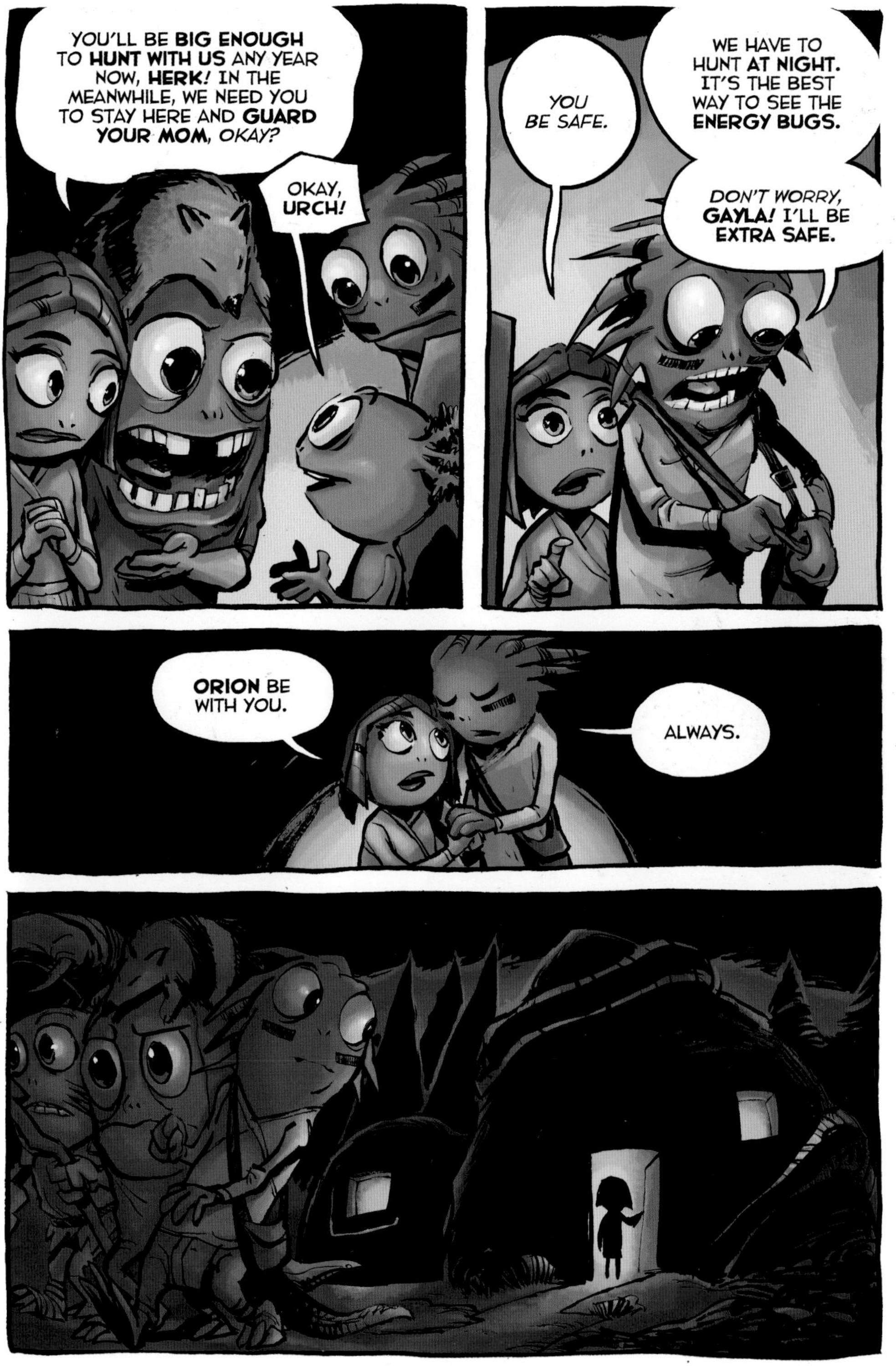
YOU'LL BE **BIG ENOUGH** TO **HUNT WITH US** ANY YEAR NOW, **HERK!** IN THE MEANWHILE, WE NEED YOU TO STAY HERE AND **GUARD YOUR MOM**, *OKAY?*
OKAY, **URCH!**
YOU BE SAFE.
WE HAVE TO HUNT **AT NIGHT.** IT'S THE BEST WAY TO SEE THE **ENERGY BUGS.**
DON'T WORRY, **GAYLA!** I'LL BE **EXTRA SAFE.**
ORION BE WITH YOU.
ALWAYS.

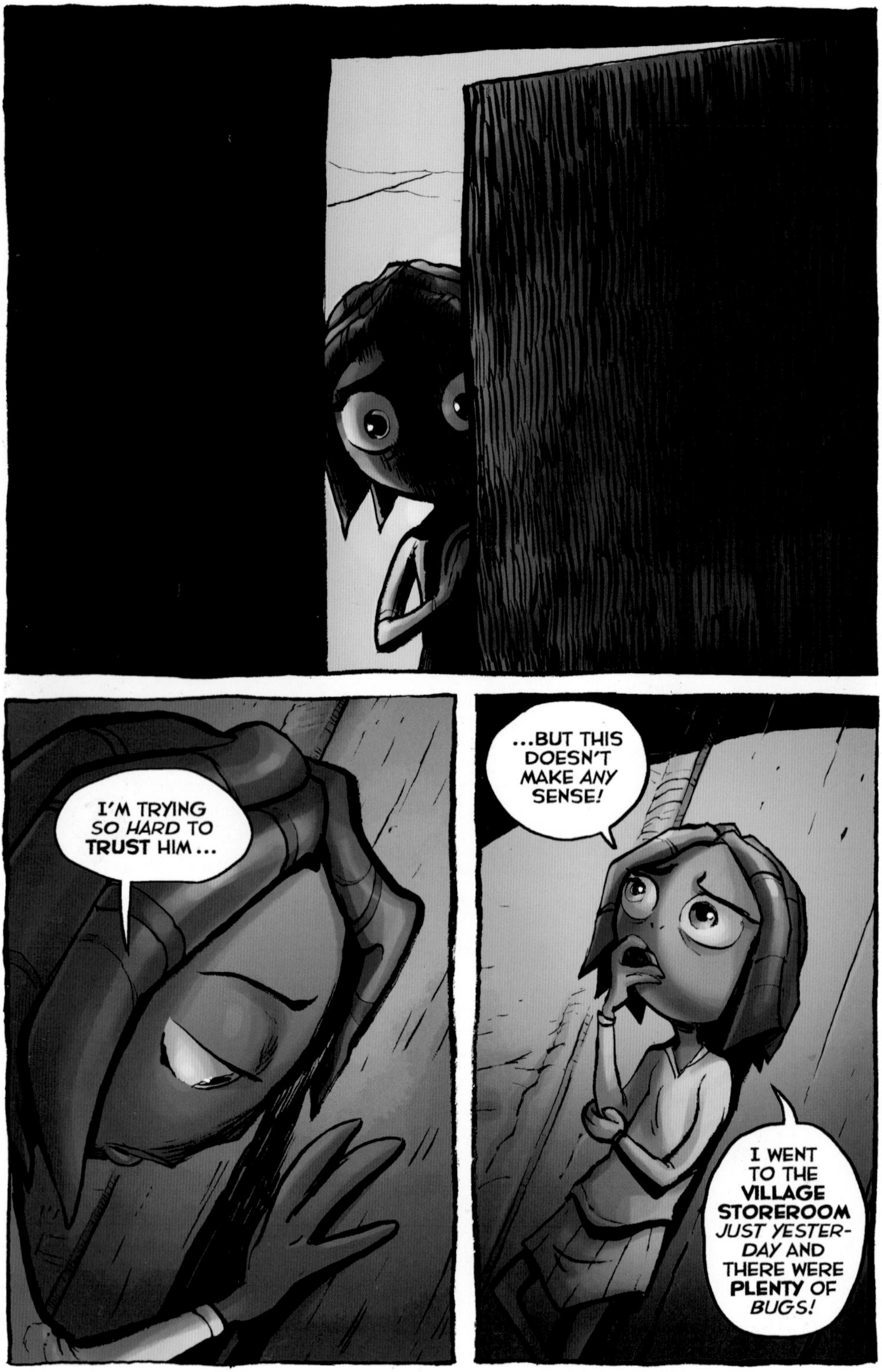
I'M TRYING SO HARD TO TRUST HIM...
...BUT THIS DOESN'T MAKE ANY SENSE!
I WENT TO THE VILLAGE STOREROOM JUST YESTERDAY AND THERE WERE PLENTY OF BUGS!

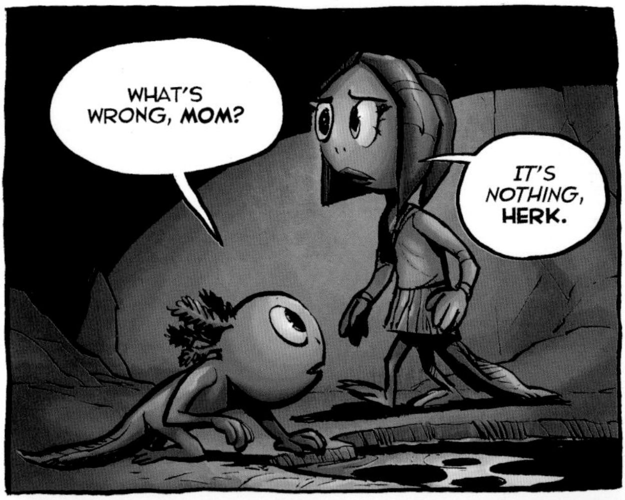
WHAT'S WRONG, **MOM?**
IT'S NOTHING, **HERK.**

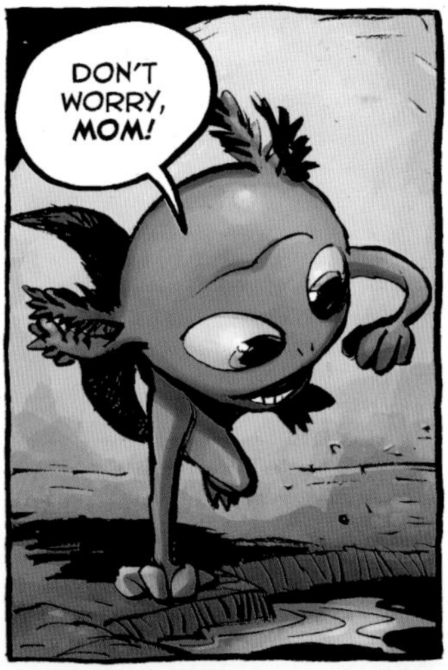
DON'T WORRY, **MOM!**

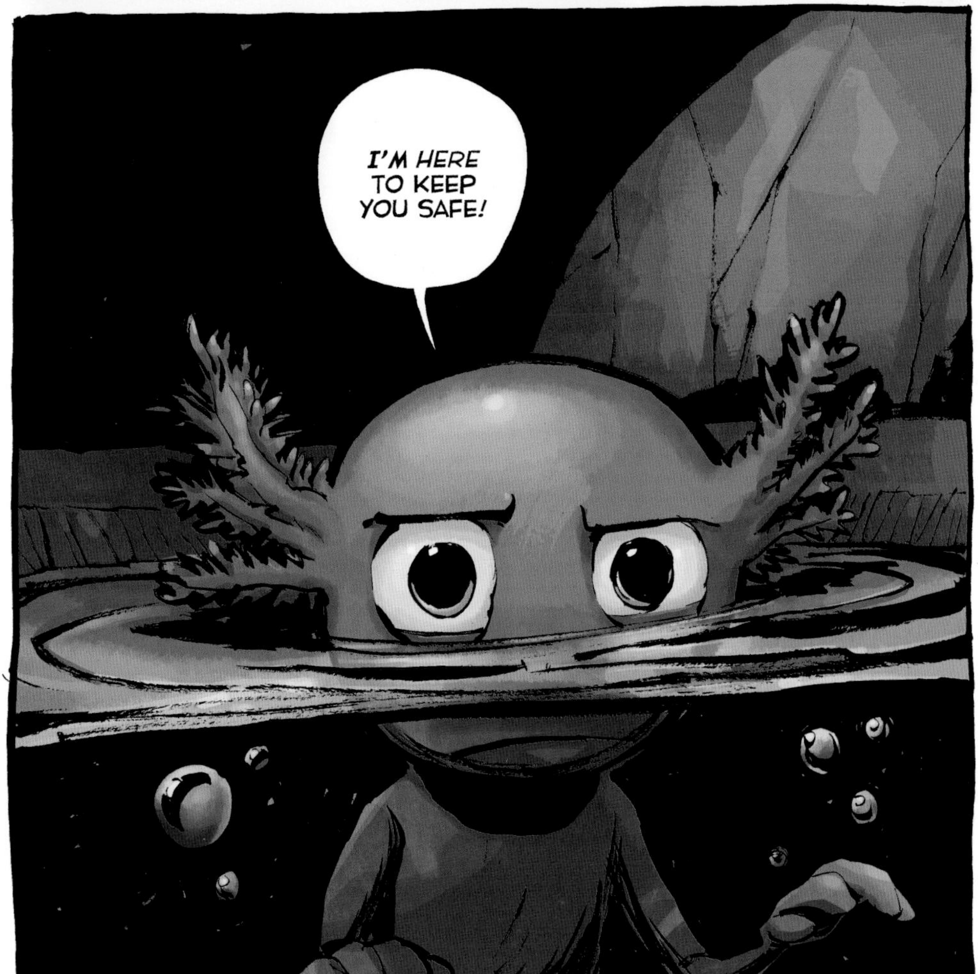
I'M *HERE* TO KEEP YOU SAFE!

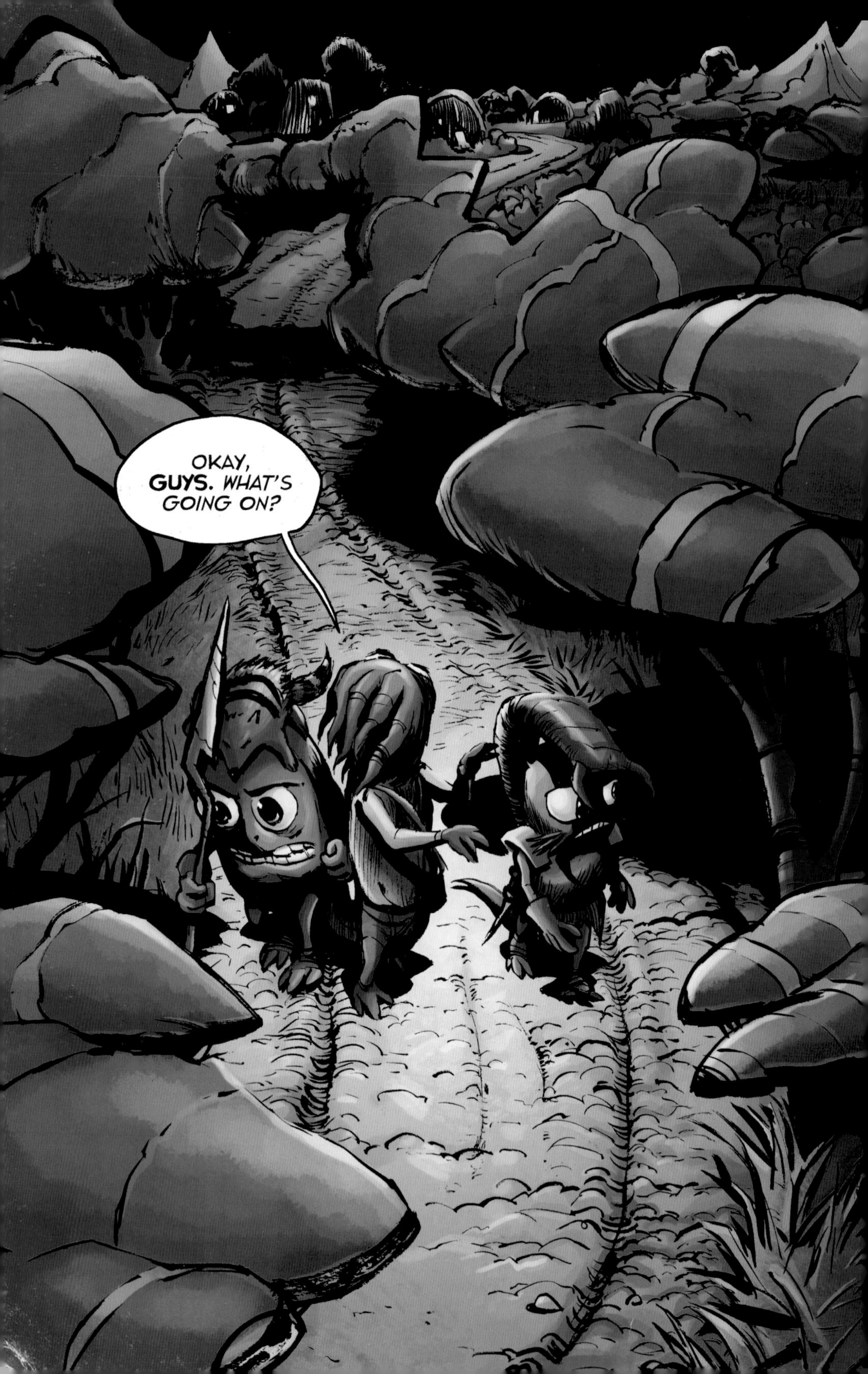
OKAY, GUYS. WHAT'S GOING ON?

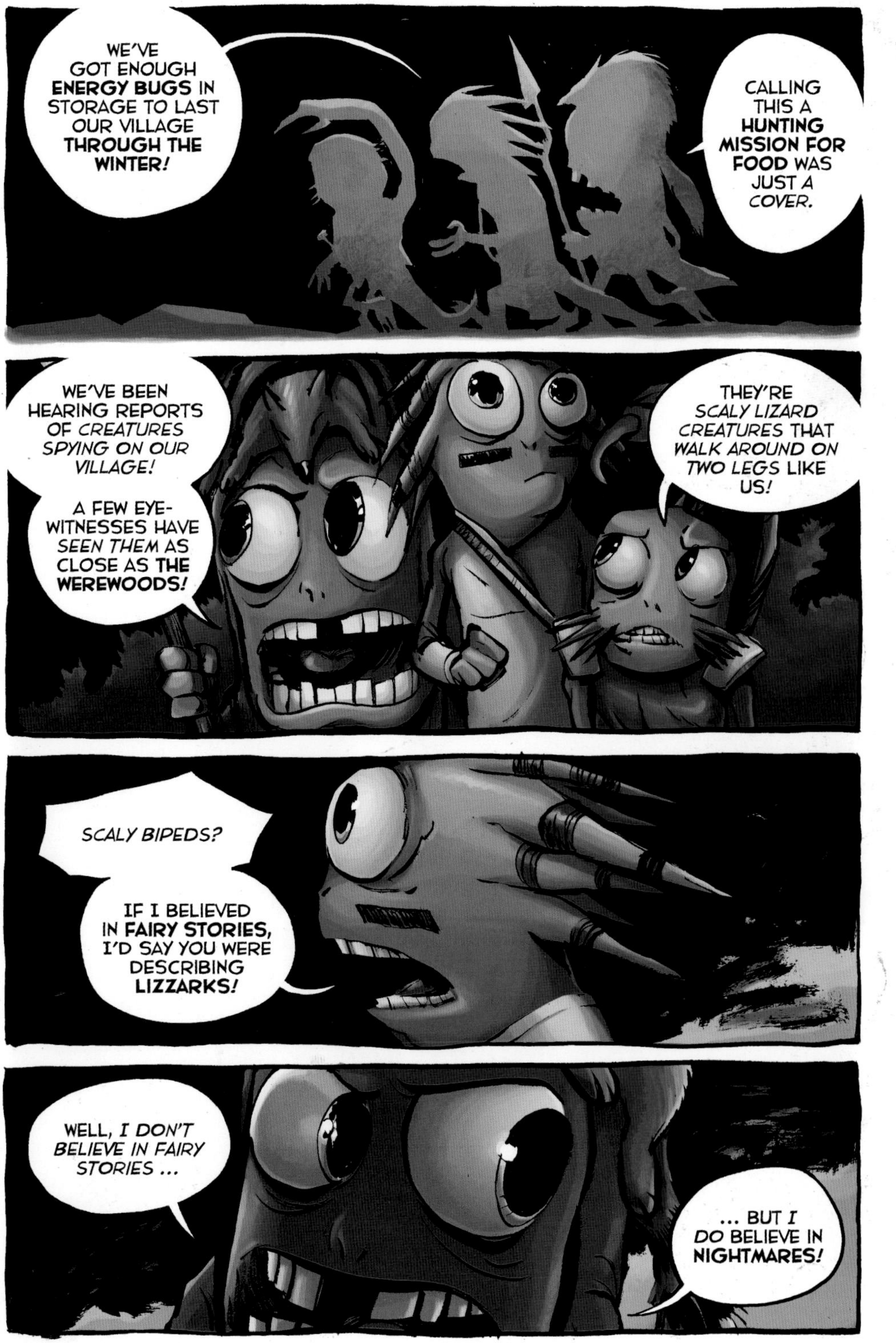
WE'VE GOT ENOUGH **ENERGY BUGS** IN STORAGE TO LAST OUR VILLAGE **THROUGH THE WINTER!**
CALLING THIS A **HUNTING MISSION FOR FOOD** WAS JUST A *COVER.*
WE'VE BEEN HEARING REPORTS OF *CREATURES SPYING ON OUR VILLAGE!*
A FEW EYE-WITNESSES HAVE *SEEN THEM* AS CLOSE AS **THE WEREWOODS!**
THEY'RE *SCALY LIZARD CREATURES* THAT *WALK AROUND ON TWO LEGS* LIKE US!
SCALY BIPEDS?
IF I BELIEVED IN **FAIRY STORIES,** I'D SAY YOU WERE DESCRIBING **LIZZARKS!**
WELL, I DON'T BELIEVE IN FAIRY STORIES ...
... BUT *I DO* BELIEVE IN **NIGHTMARES!**

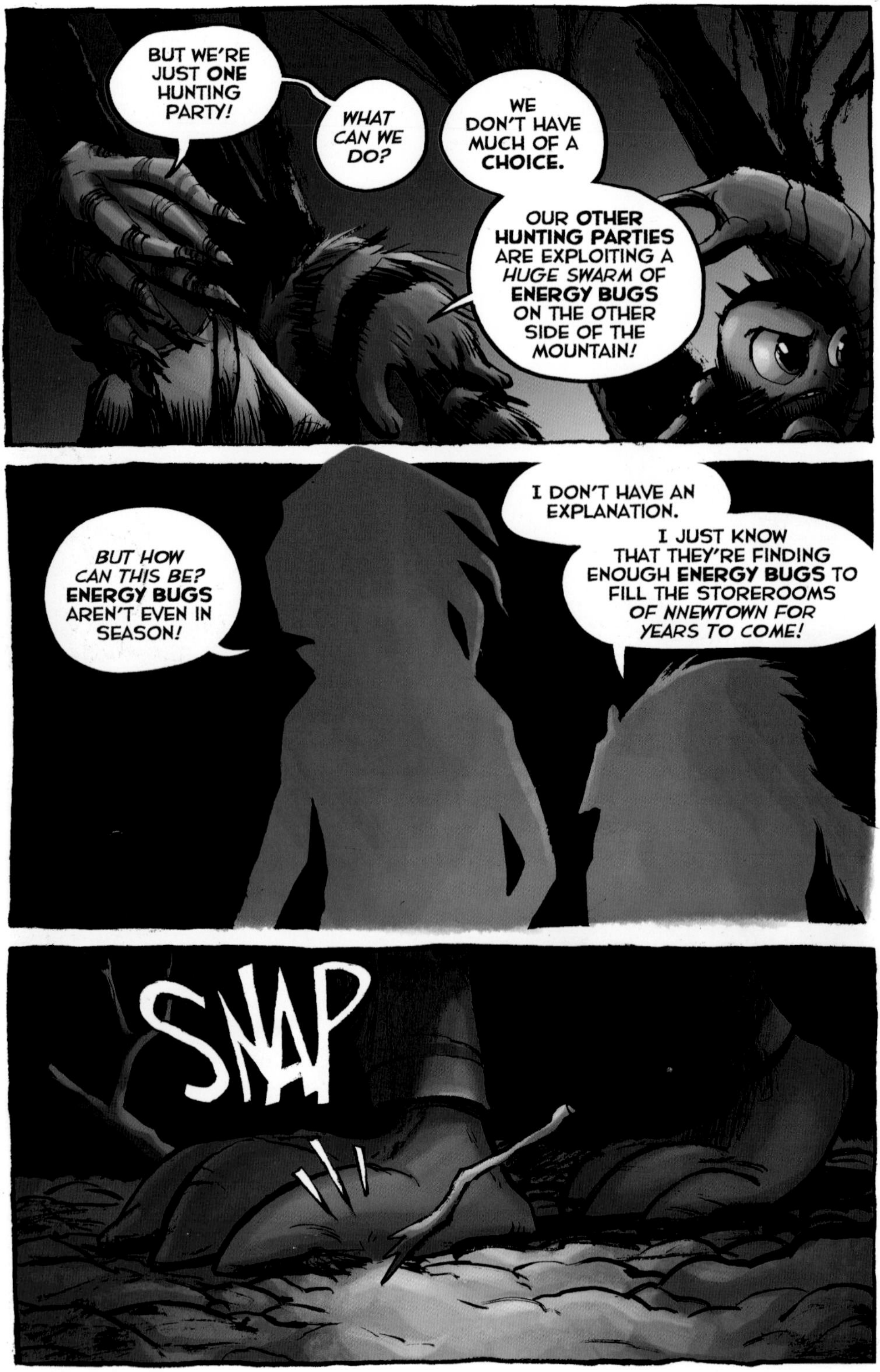
BUT WE'RE JUST **ONE** HUNTING PARTY!
WHAT CAN WE DO?
WE DON'T HAVE MUCH OF A **CHOICE.**
OUR **OTHER HUNTING PARTIES** ARE EXPLOITING A *HUGE SWARM* OF **ENERGY BUGS** ON THE OTHER SIDE OF THE MOUNTAIN!
BUT HOW CAN THIS BE? **ENERGY BUGS** AREN'T EVEN IN SEASON!
I DON'T HAVE AN EXPLANATION.
I JUST KNOW THAT THEY'RE FINDING ENOUGH **ENERGY BUGS** TO FILL THE STOREROOMS *OF NNEWTOWN FOR YEARS TO COME!*
SNAP

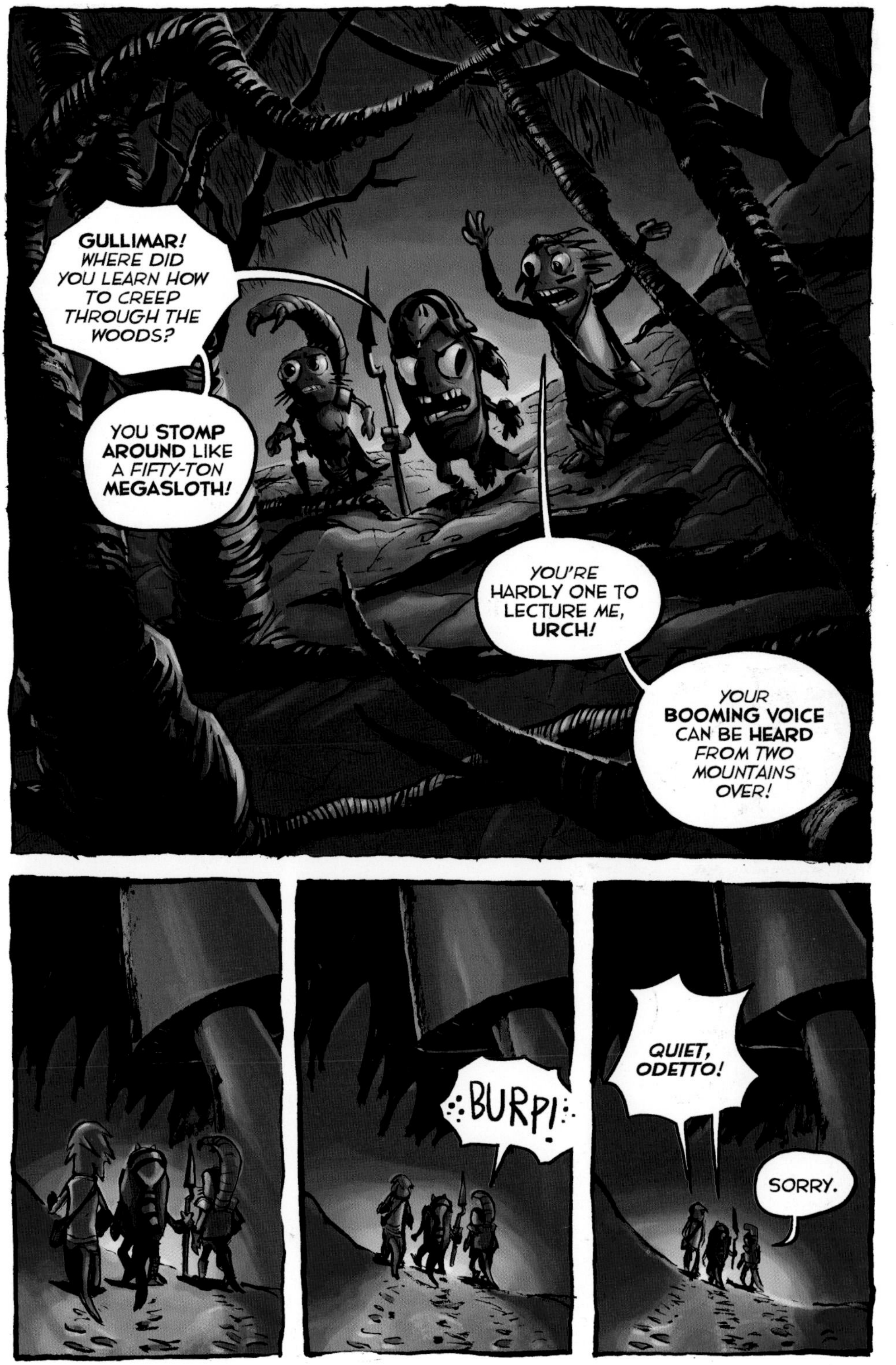
GULLIMAR! WHERE DID YOU LEARN HOW TO CREEP THROUGH THE WOODS?
YOU STOMP AROUND LIKE A FIFTY-TON MEGASLOTH!
YOU'RE HARDLY ONE TO LECTURE ME, URCH!
YOUR BOOMING VOICE CAN BE HEARD FROM TWO MOUNTAINS OVER!
BURP!
QUIET, ODETTO!
SORRY.

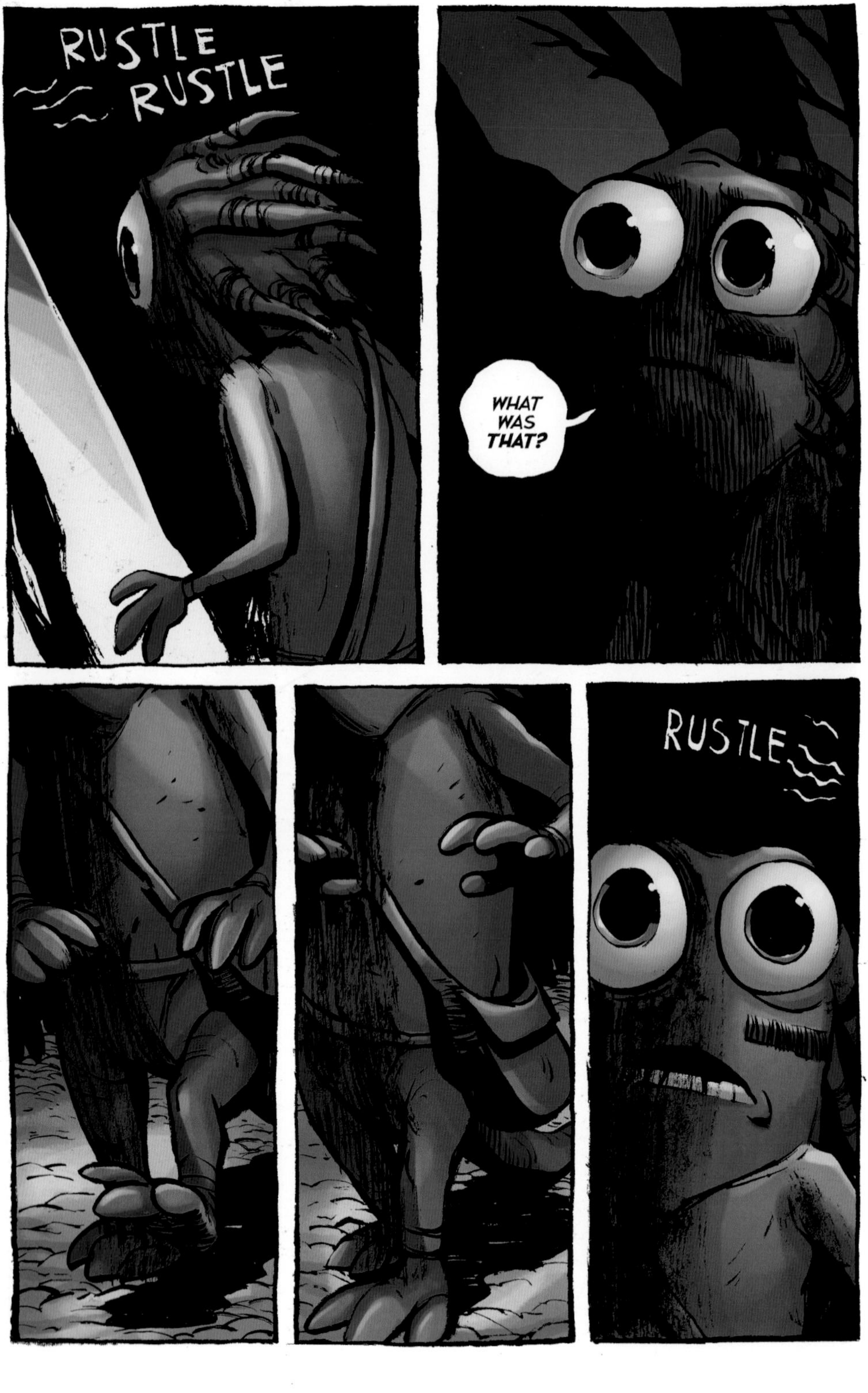
RUSTLE
RUSTLE
WHAT WAS THAT?
RUSTLE

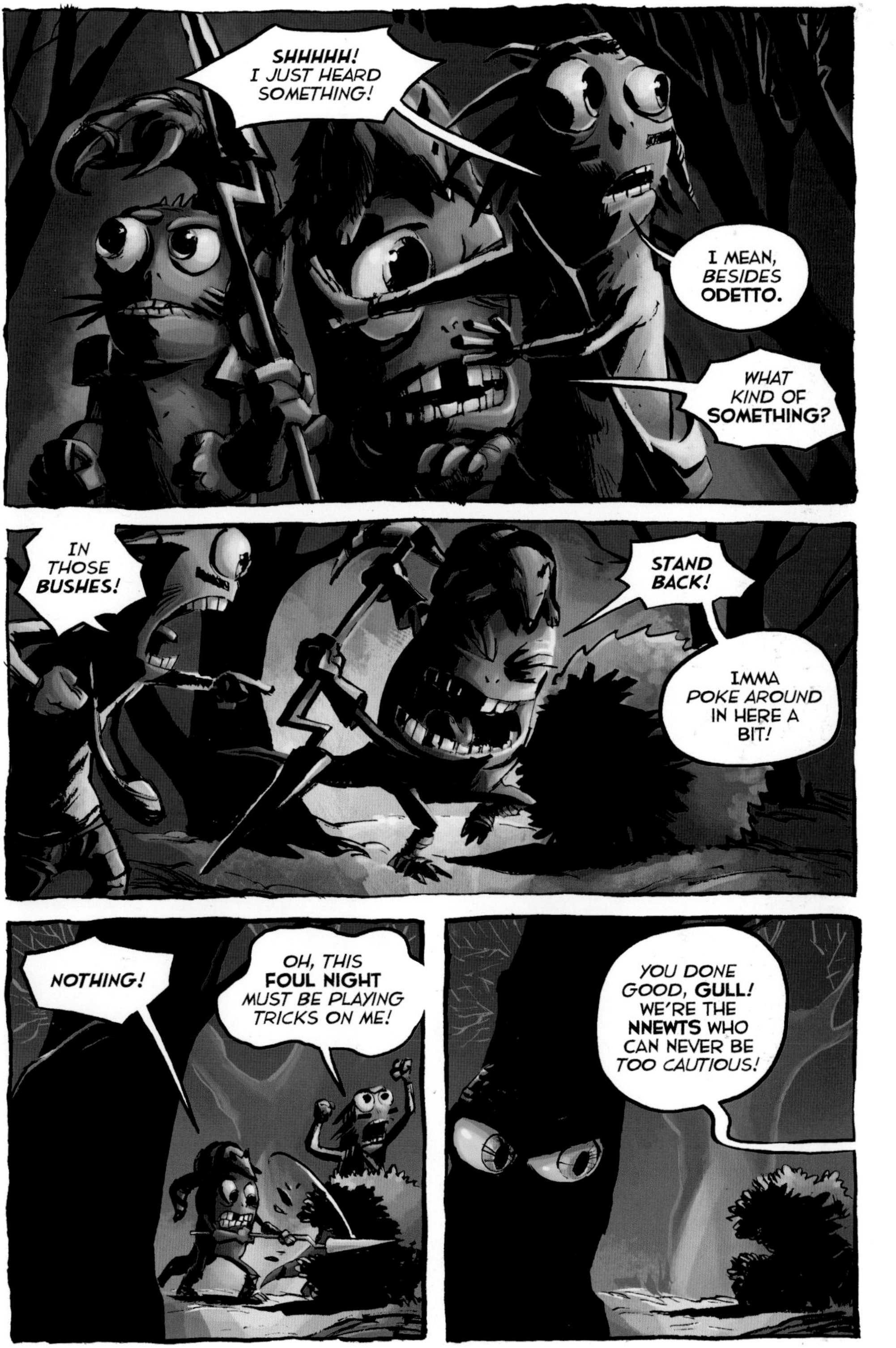
SHHHHH! I JUST HEARD SOMETHING!
I MEAN, BESIDES ODETTO.
WHAT KIND OF SOMETHING?
IN THOSE BUSHES!
STAND BACK!
IMMA POKE AROUND IN HERE A BIT!
NOTHING!
OH, THIS FOUL NIGHT MUST BE PLAYING TRICKS ON ME!
YOU DONE GOOD, GULL! WE'RE THE NNEWTS WHO CAN NEVER BE TOO CAUTIOUS!

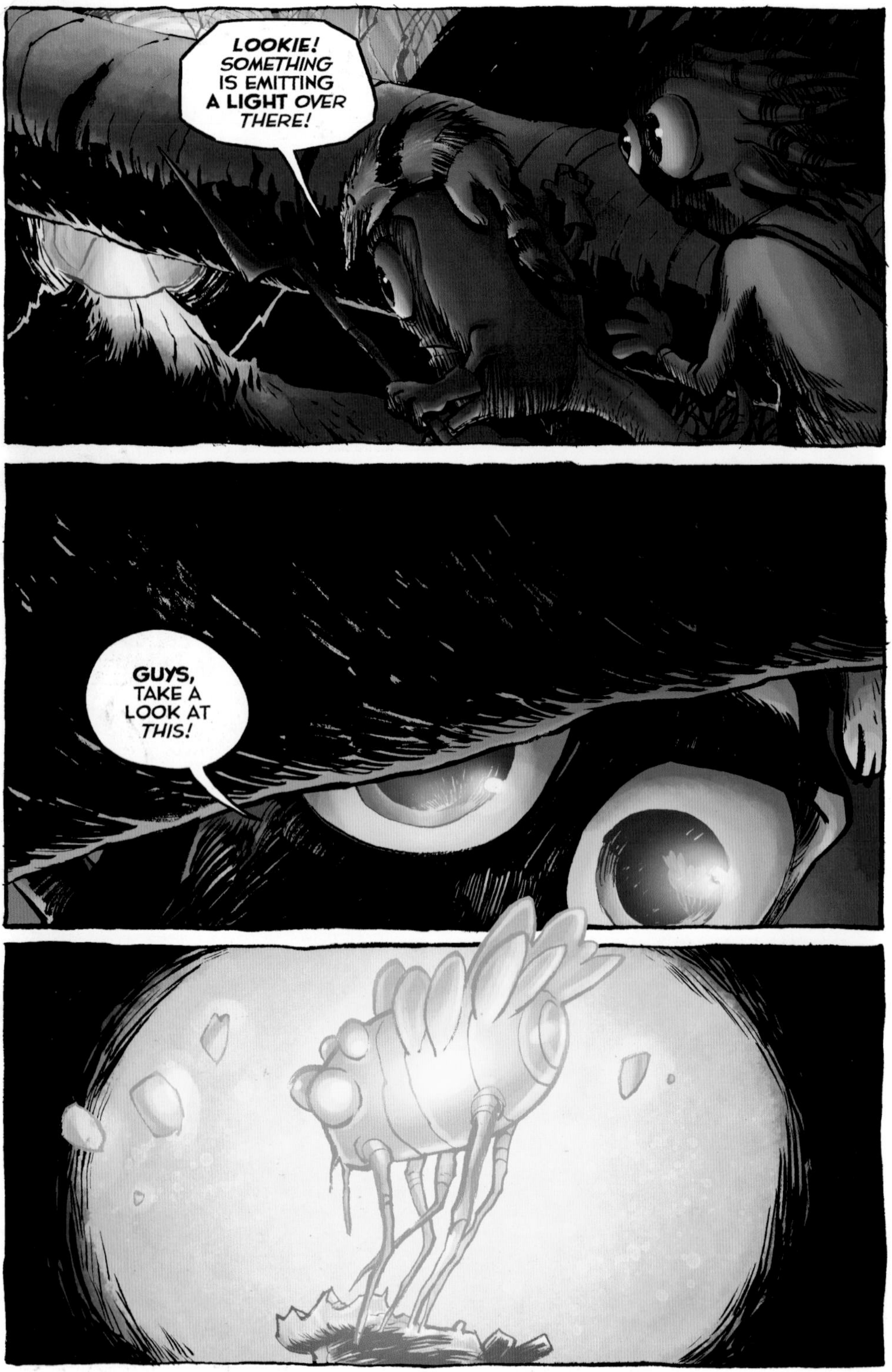
LOOKIE! SOMETHING IS EMITTING A LIGHT OVER THERE!
GUYS, TAKE A LOOK AT THIS!

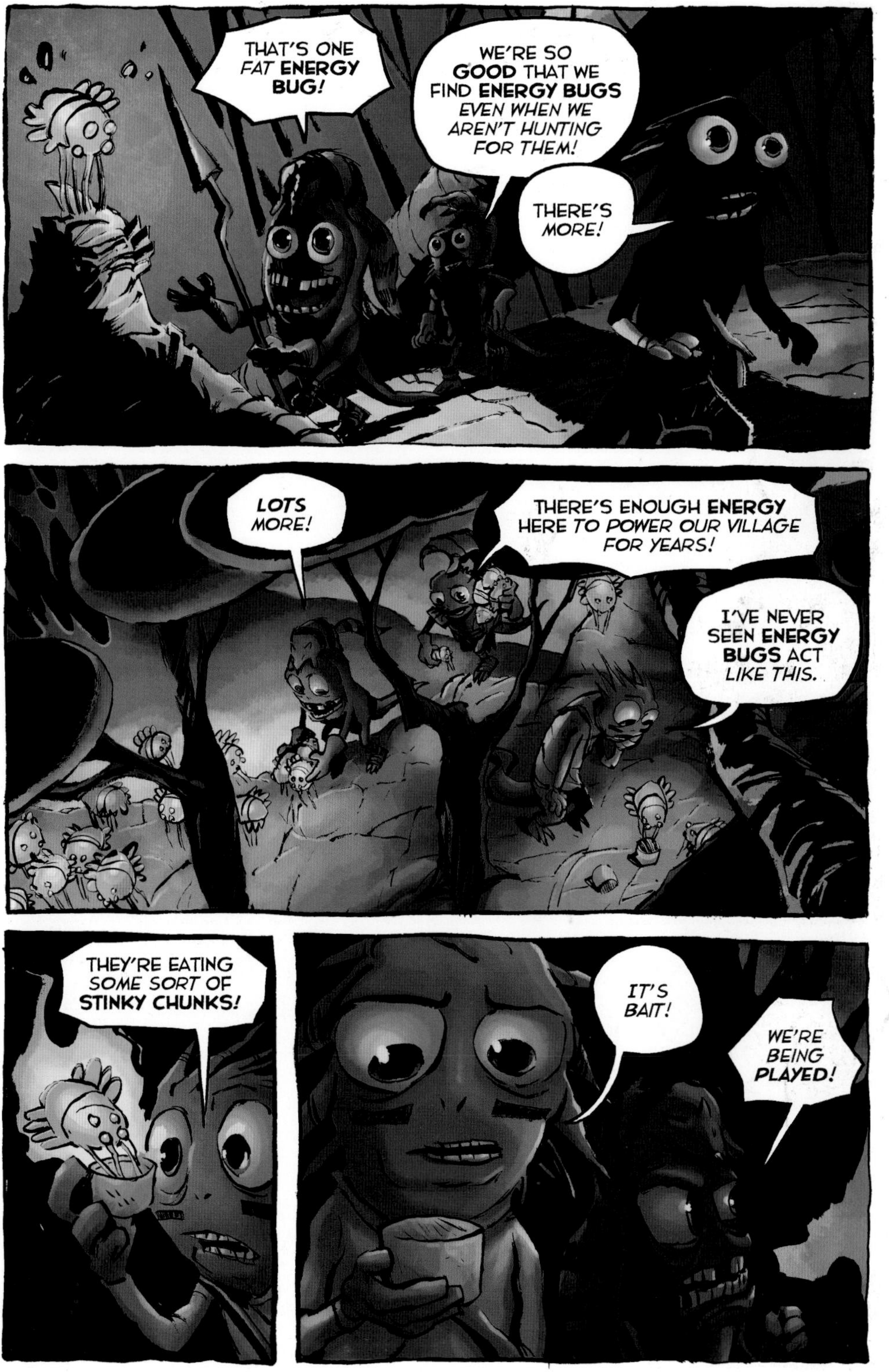
THAT'S ONE FAT ENERGY BUG!
WE'RE SO GOOD THAT WE FIND ENERGY BUGS EVEN WHEN WE AREN'T HUNTING FOR THEM!
THERE'S MORE!
LOTS MORE!
THERE'S ENOUGH ENERGY HERE TO POWER OUR VILLAGE FOR YEARS!
I'VE NEVER SEEN ENERGY BUGS ACT LIKE THIS.
THEY'RE EATING SOME SORT OF STINKY CHUNKS!
IT'S BAIT!
WE'RE BEING PLAYED!

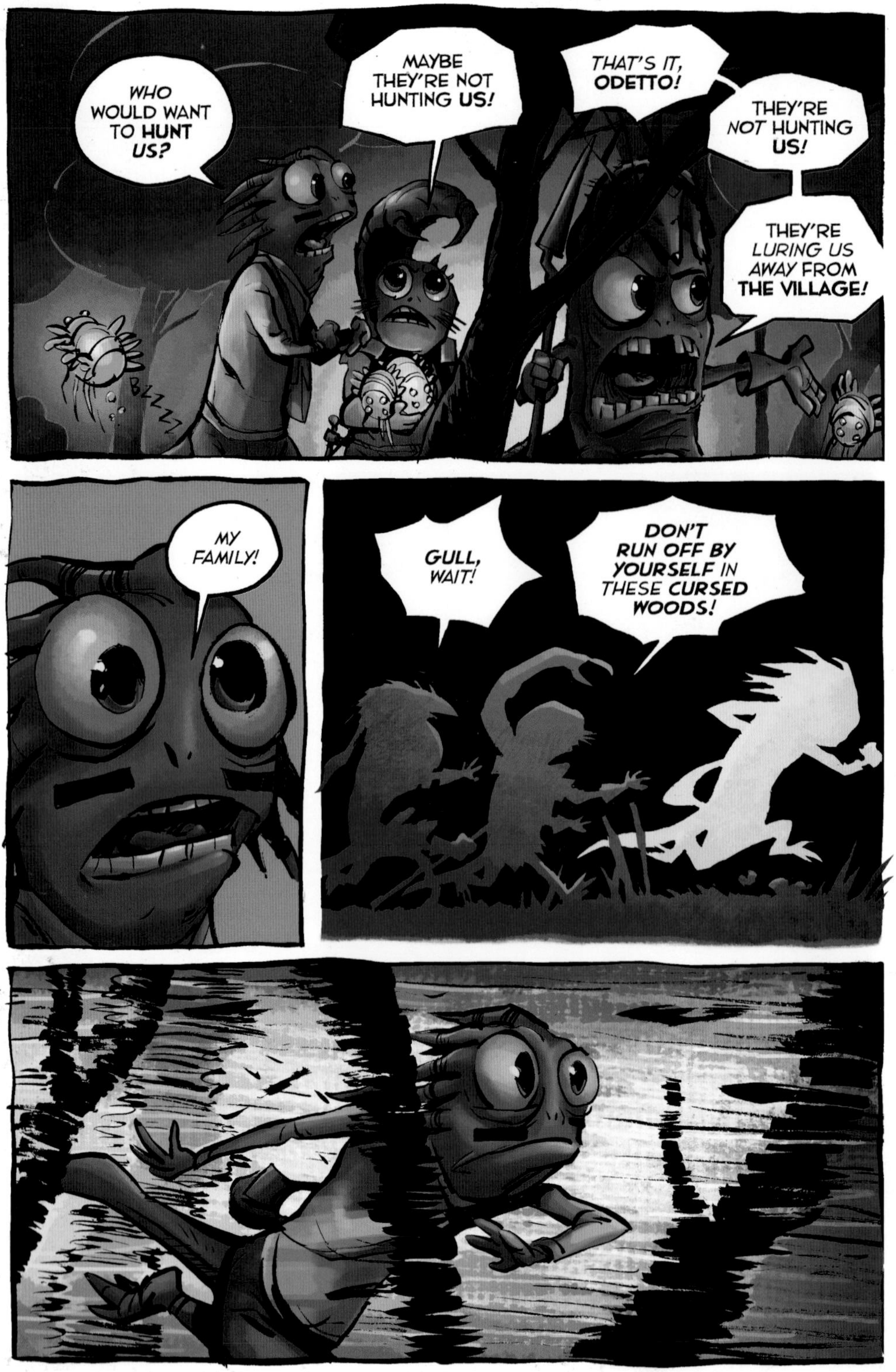
WHO WOULD WANT TO HUNT US?
MAYBE THEY'RE NOT HUNTING US!
THAT'S IT, ODETTO!
THEY'RE NOT HUNTING US!
THEY'RE LURING US AWAY FROM THE VILLAGE!
BZZZZ
MY FAMILY!
GULL, WAIT!
DON'T RUN OFF BY YOURSELF IN THESE CURSED WOODS!

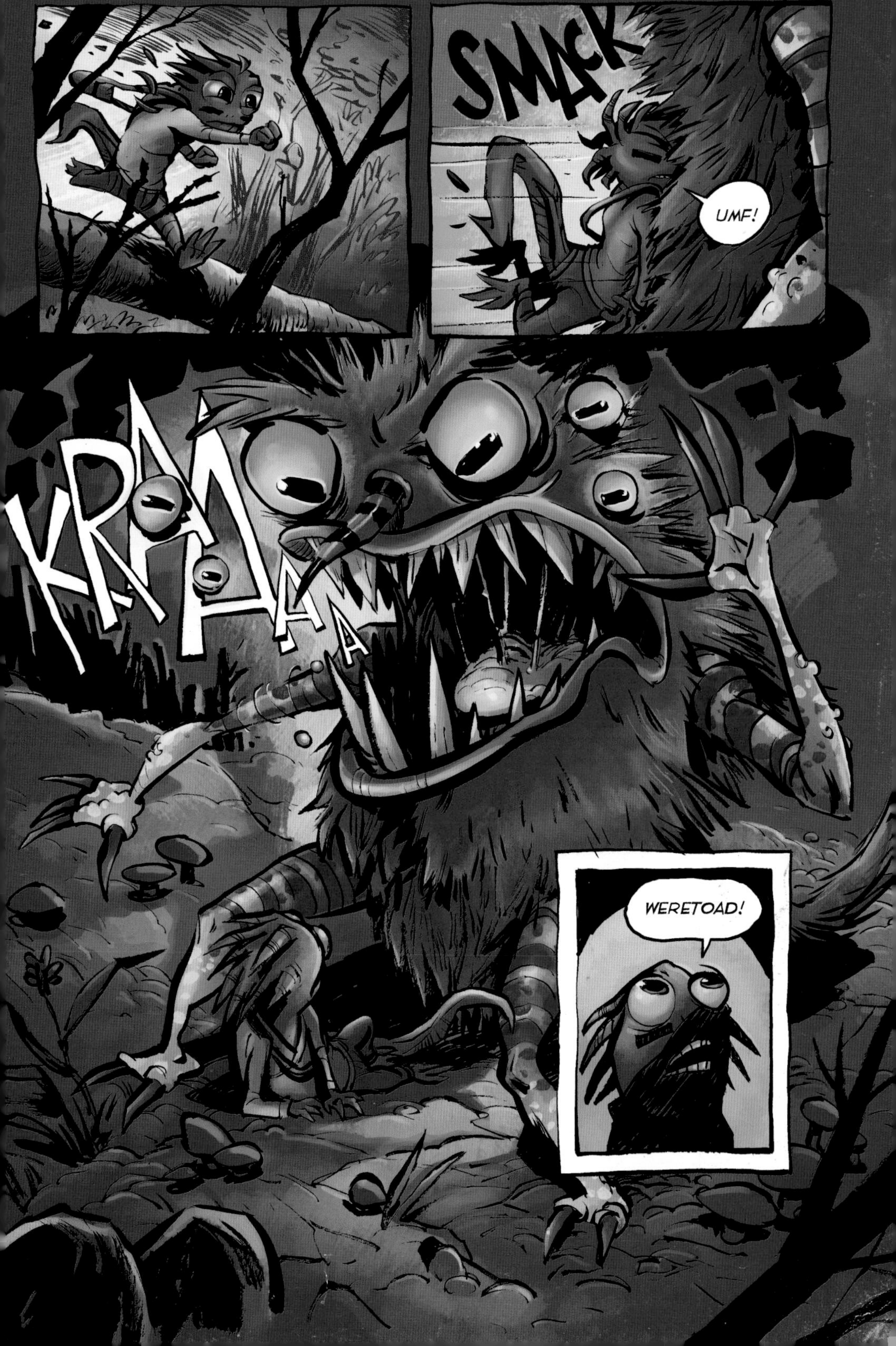
SMACK
UMF!
KRAAAAAA
WERETOAD!

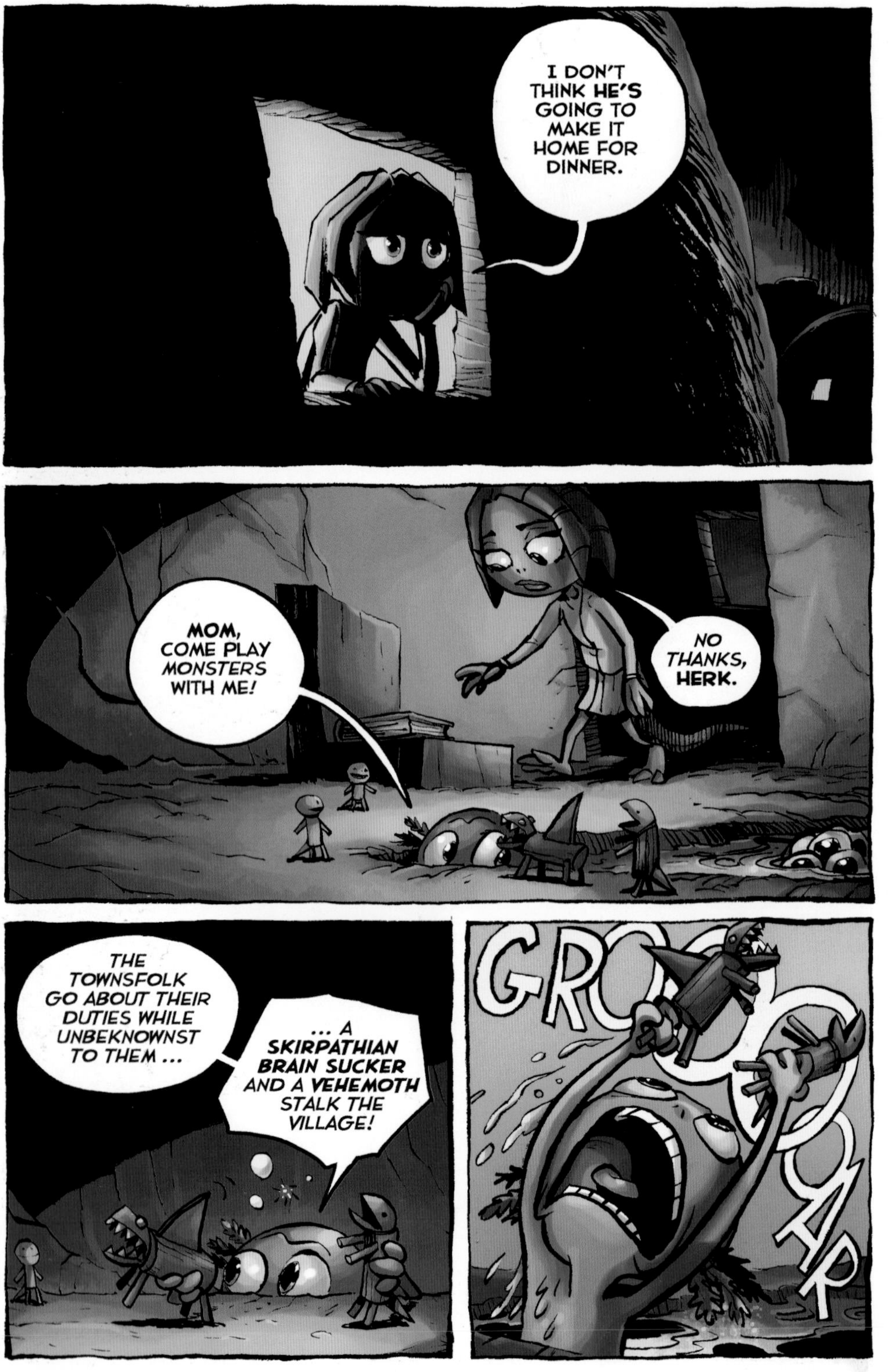
I DON'T THINK HE'S GOING TO MAKE IT HOME FOR DINNER.
MOM, COME PLAY MONSTERS WITH ME!
NO THANKS, HERK.
THE TOWNSFOLK GO ABOUT THEIR DUTIES WHILE UNBEKNOWNST TO THEM ...
... A SKIRPATHIAN BRAIN SUCKER AND A VEHEMOTH STALK THE VILLAGE!
GROOOOOOAR

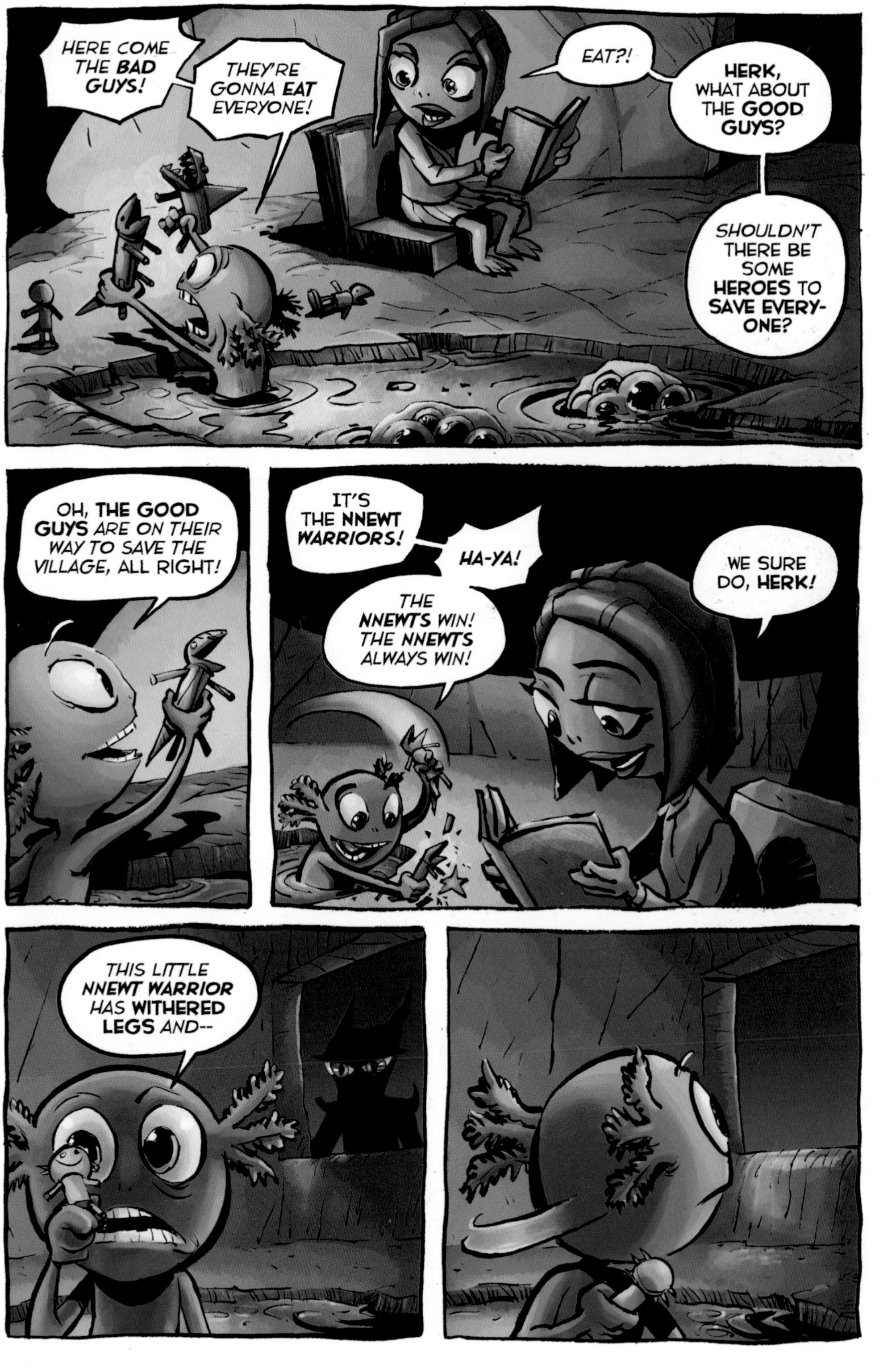
HERE COME THE BAD GUYS!
THEY'RE GONNA EAT EVERYONE!
EAT?!
HERK, WHAT ABOUT THE GOOD GUYS?
SHOULDN'T THERE BE SOME HEROES TO SAVE EVERY-ONE?
OH, THE GOOD GUYS ARE ON THEIR WAY TO SAVE THE VILLAGE, ALL RIGHT!
IT'S THE NNEWT WARRIORS!
HA-YA!
THE NNEWTS WIN! THE NNEWTS ALWAYS WIN!
WE SURE DO, HERK!
THIS LITTLE NNEWT WARRIOR HAS WITHERED LEGS AND--

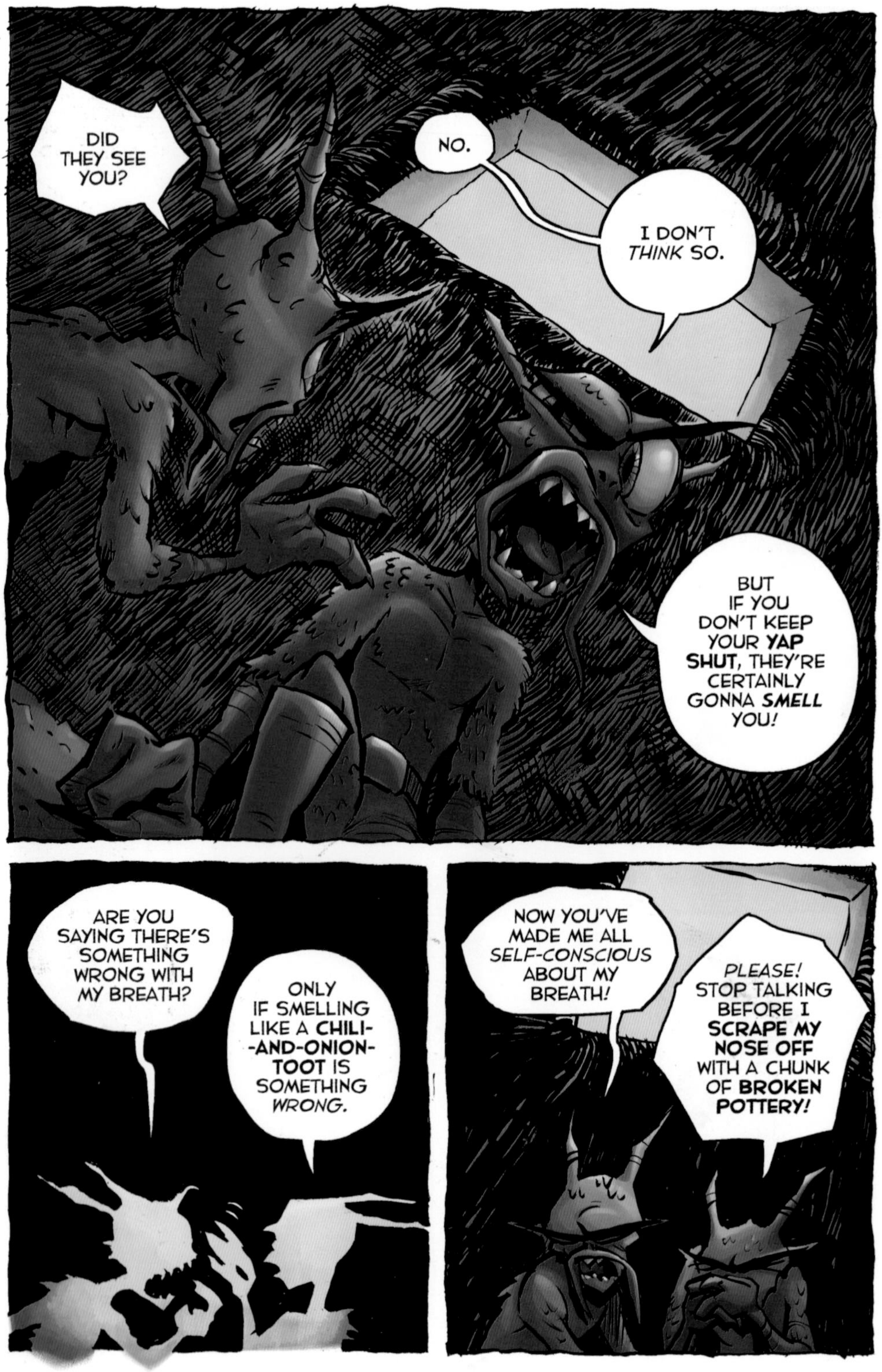
DID THEY SEE YOU?
NO.
I DON'T *THINK* SO.
BUT IF YOU DON'T KEEP YOUR **YAP SHUT**, THEY'RE CERTAINLY GONNA **SMELL** YOU!
ARE YOU SAYING THERE'S SOMETHING WRONG WITH MY BREATH?
ONLY IF SMELLING LIKE A **CHILI-AND-ONION-TOOT** IS SOMETHING *WRONG.*
NOW YOU'VE MADE ME ALL *SELF-CONSCIOUS* ABOUT MY BREATH!
PLEASE! STOP TALKING BEFORE I **SCRAPE MY NOSE OFF** WITH A CHUNK OF **BROKEN POTTERY!**

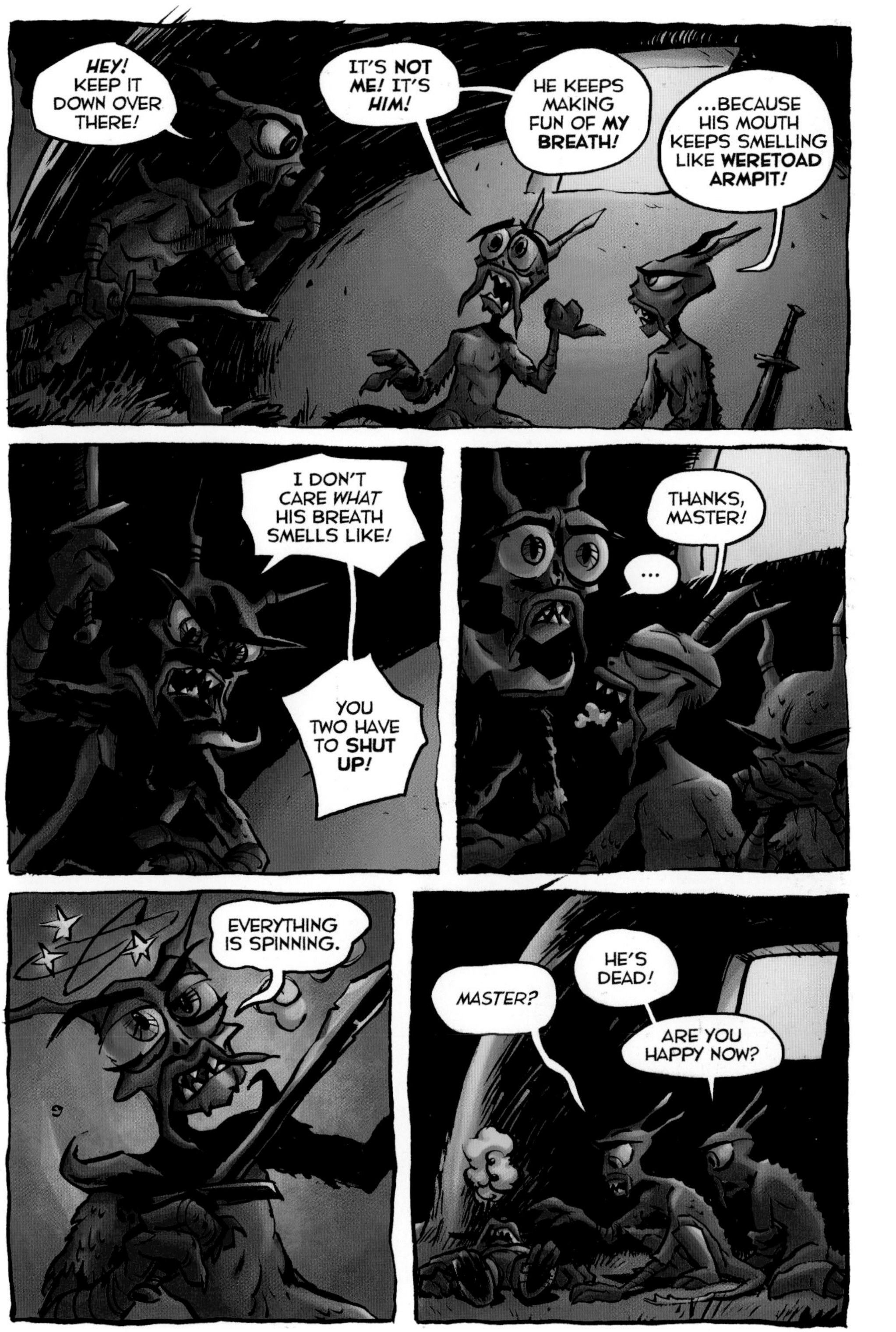
HEY! KEEP IT DOWN OVER THERE!
IT'S NOT ME! IT'S HIM!
HE KEEPS MAKING FUN OF MY BREATH!
...BECAUSE HIS MOUTH KEEPS SMELLING LIKE WERETOAD ARMPIT!
I DON'T CARE WHAT HIS BREATH SMELLS LIKE!
YOU TWO HAVE TO SHUT UP!
THANKS, MASTER!
...
EVERYTHING IS SPINNING.
MASTER?
HE'S DEAD!
ARE YOU HAPPY NOW?

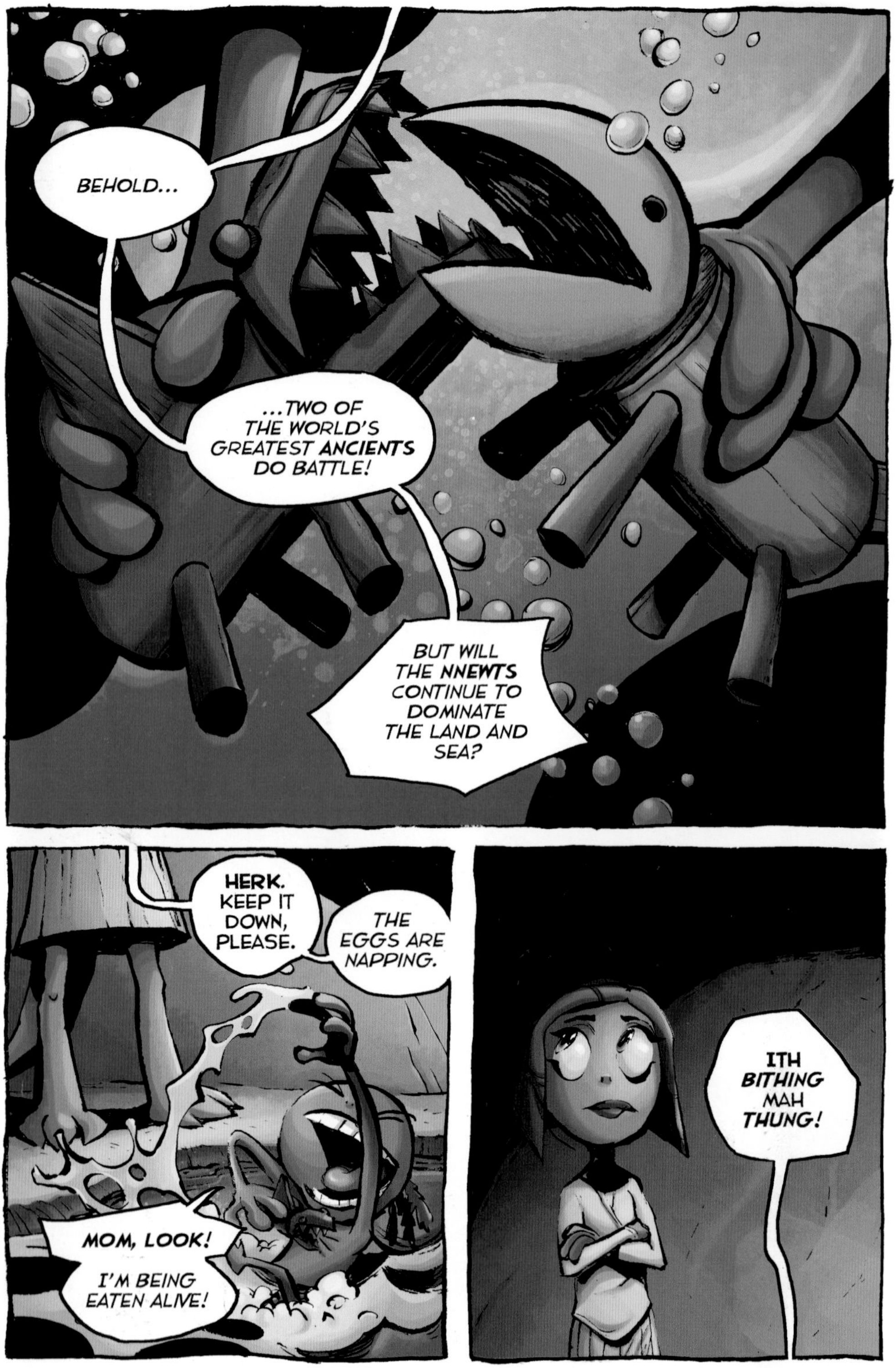
BEHOLD...
...TWO OF THE WORLD'S GREATEST ANCIENTS DO BATTLE!
BUT WILL THE NNEWTS CONTINUE TO DOMINATE THE LAND AND SEA?
HERK. KEEP IT DOWN, PLEASE.
THE EGGS ARE NAPPING.
MOM, LOOK!
I'M BEING EATEN ALIVE!
ITH BITHING MAH THUNG!

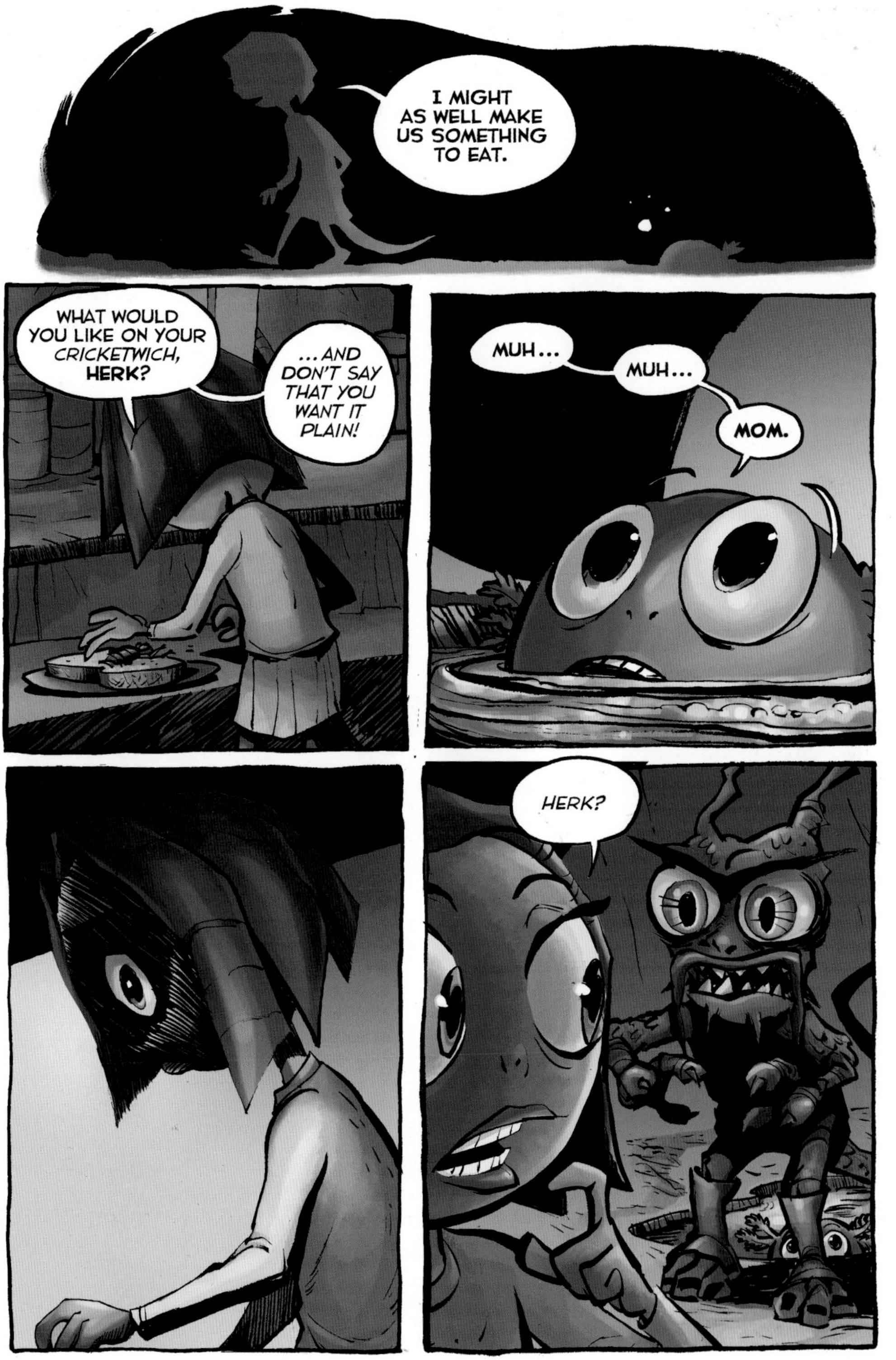
I MIGHT AS WELL MAKE US SOMETHING TO EAT.
WHAT WOULD YOU LIKE ON YOUR CRICKETWICH, HERK?
...AND DON'T SAY THAT YOU WANT IT PLAIN!
MUH...
MUH...
MOM.
HERK?

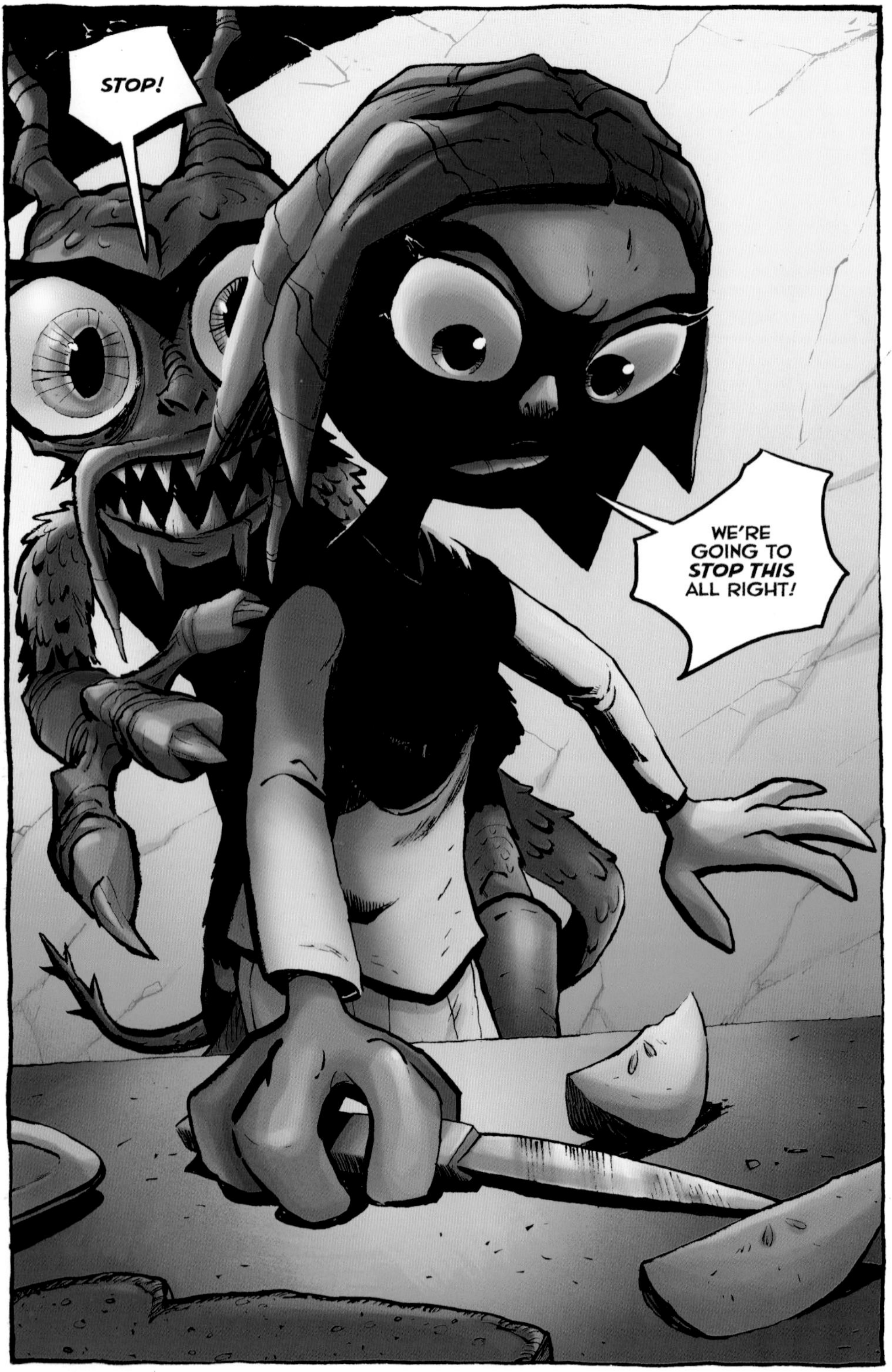
STOP!
WE'RE GOING TO *STOP THIS* ALL RIGHT!

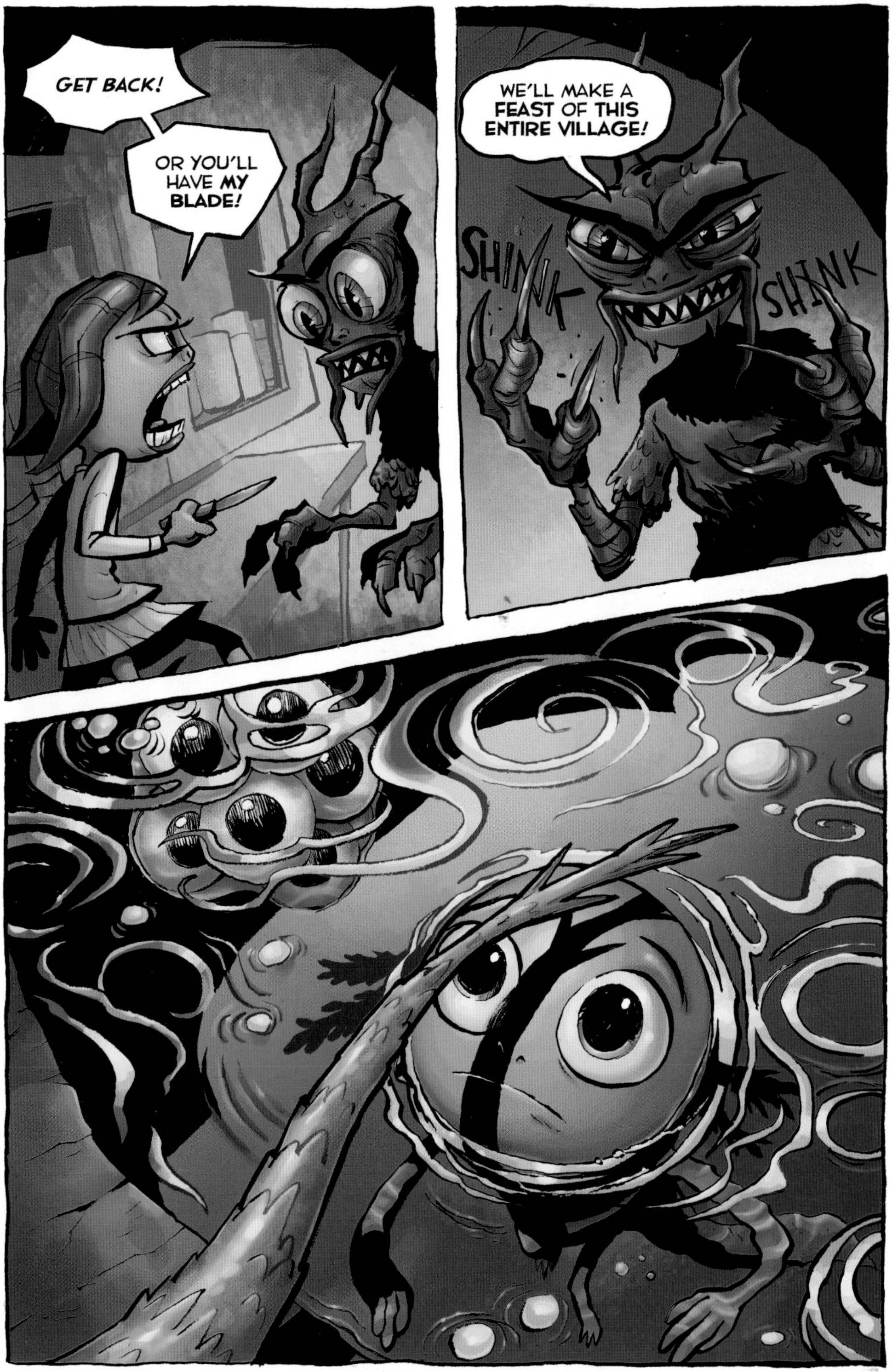
GET BACK!
OR YOU'LL HAVE MY BLADE!
WE'LL MAKE A FEAST OF THIS ENTIRE VILLAGE!
SHINK
SHINK

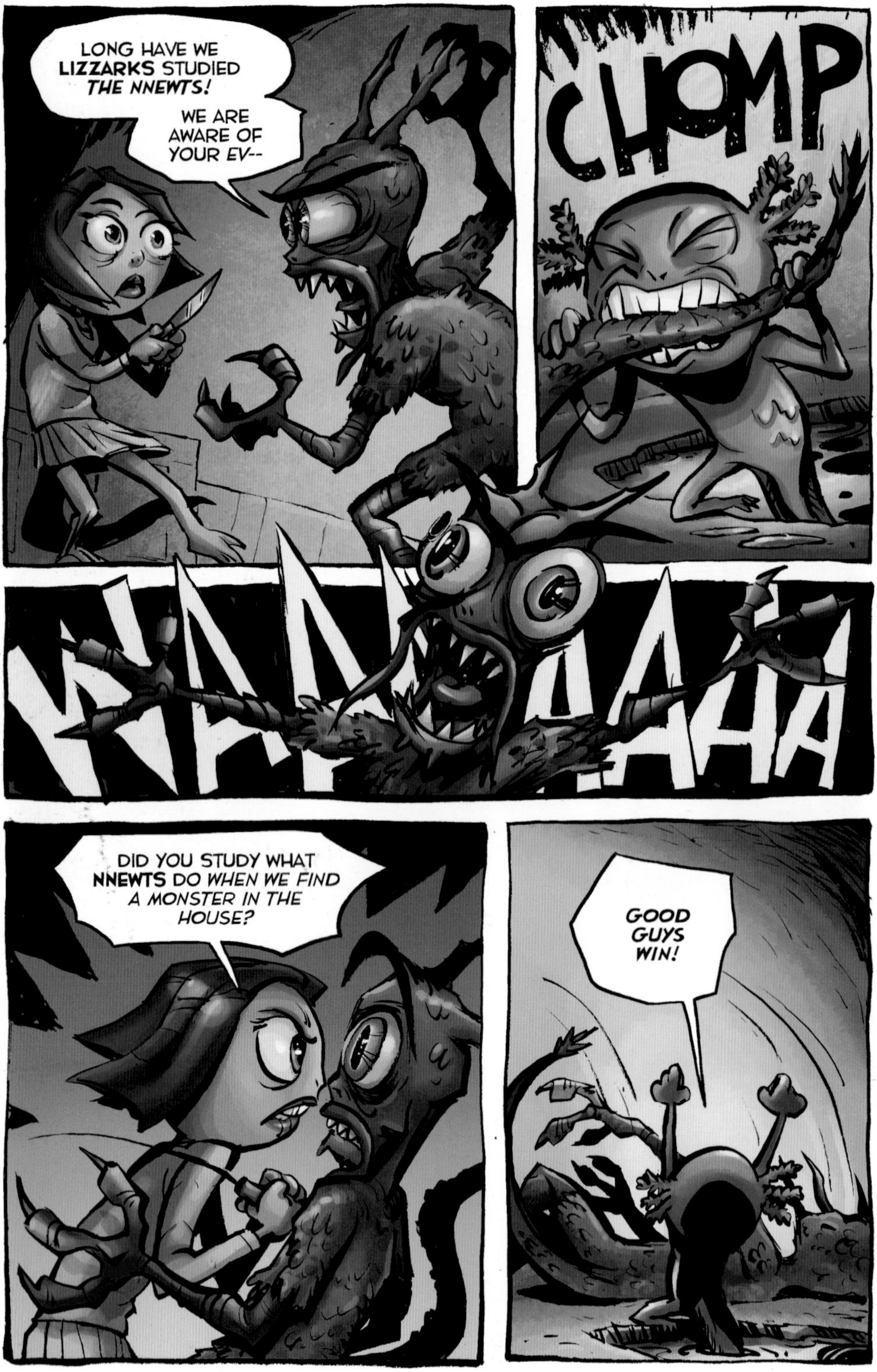
LONG HAVE WE LIZZARKS STUDIED THE NNEWTS!
WE ARE AWARE OF YOUR EV--
CHOMP
DID YOU STUDY WHAT NNEWTS DO WHEN WE FIND A MONSTER IN THE HOUSE?
GOOD GUYS WIN!

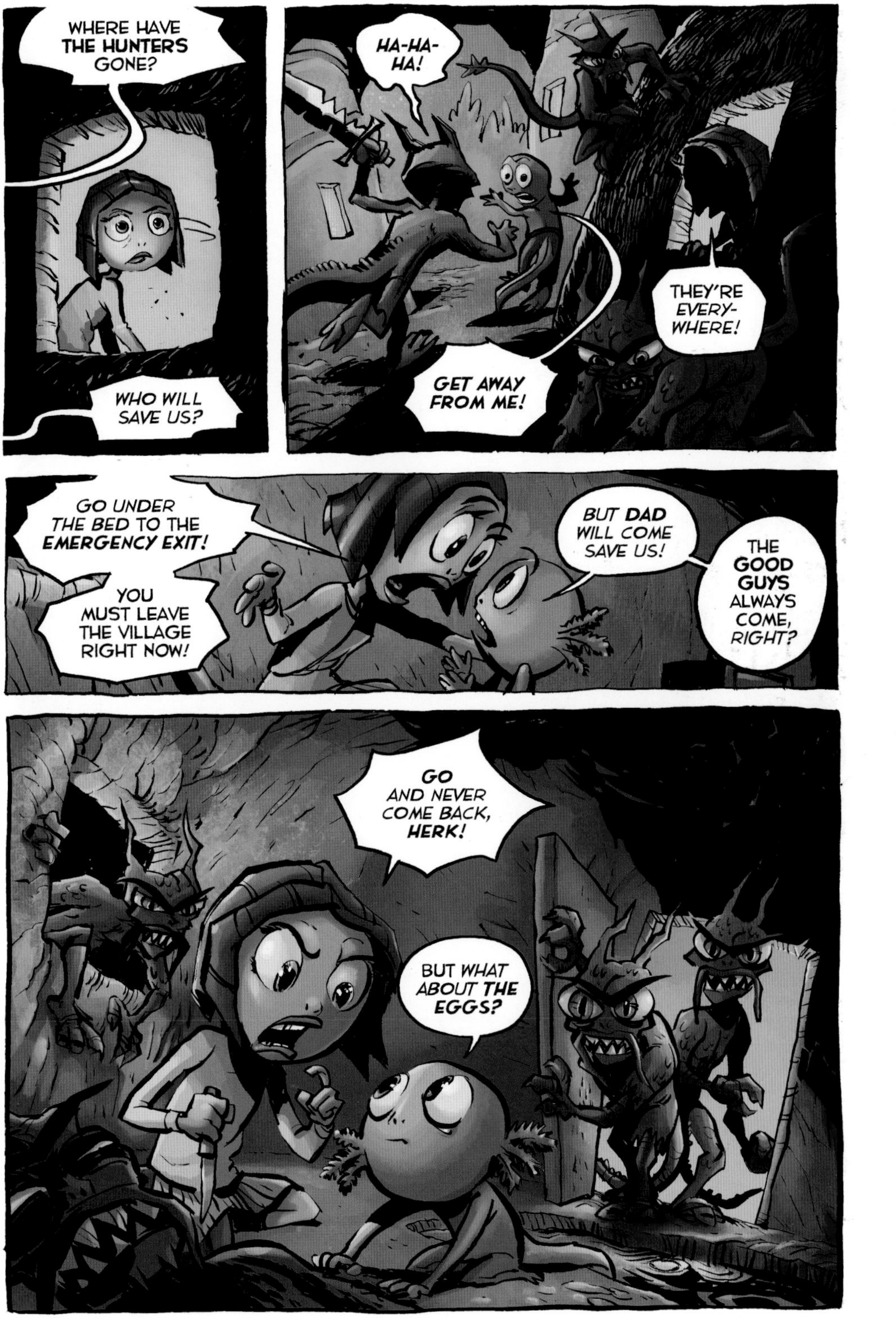

WHERE HAVE THE HUNTERS GONE?
WHO WILL SAVE US?
HA-HA-HA!
GET AWAY FROM ME!
THEY'RE EVERY-WHERE!
GO UNDER THE BED TO THE EMERGENCY EXIT!
YOU MUST LEAVE THE VILLAGE RIGHT NOW!
BUT DAD WILL COME SAVE US!
THE GOOD GUYS ALWAYS COME, RIGHT?
GO AND NEVER COME BACK, HERK!
BUT WHAT ABOUT THE EGGS?

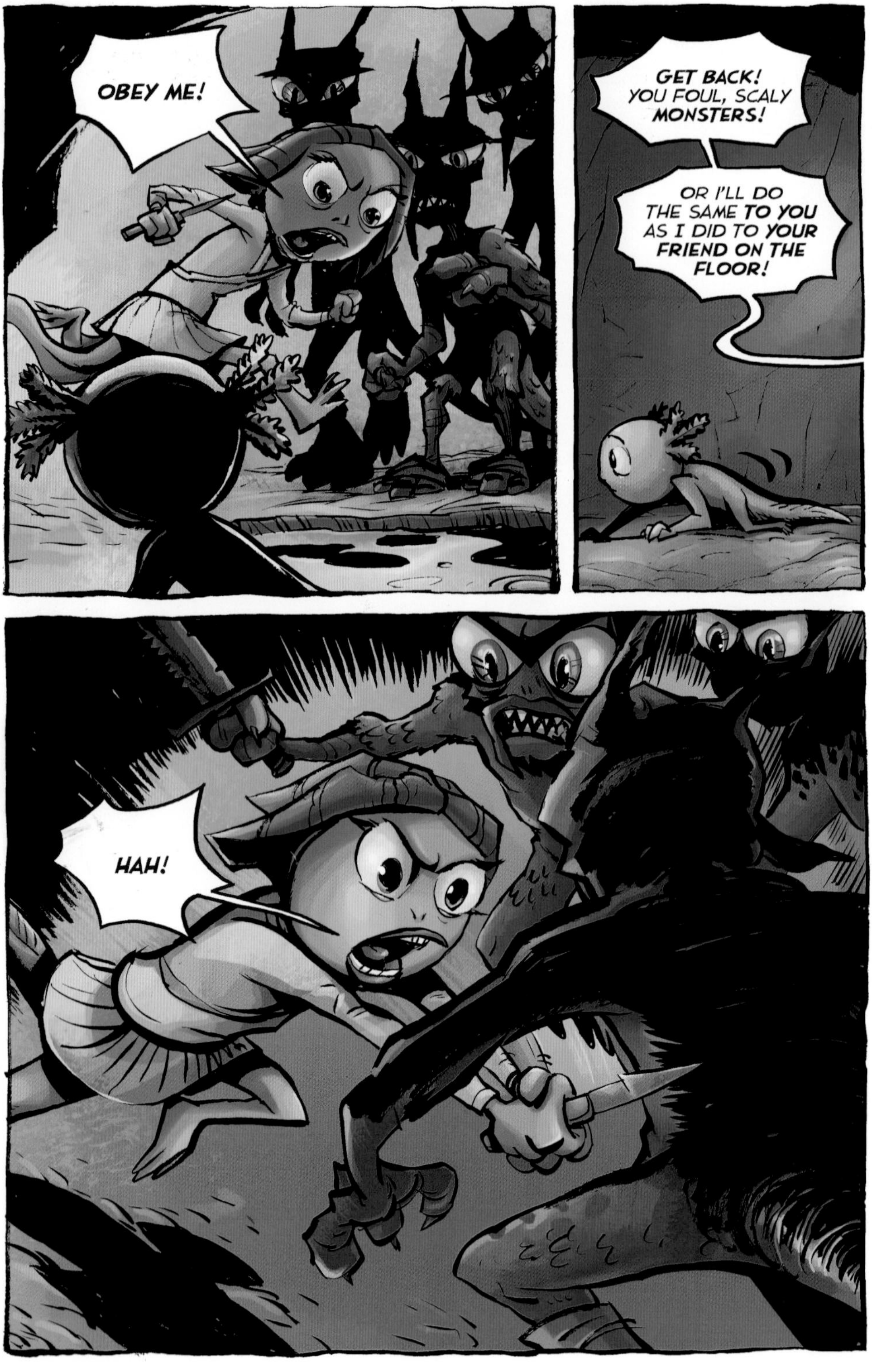

OBEY ME!
GET BACK! YOU FOUL, SCALY MONSTERS!
OR I'LL DO THE SAME TO YOU AS I DID TO YOUR FRIEND ON THE FLOOR!
HAH!

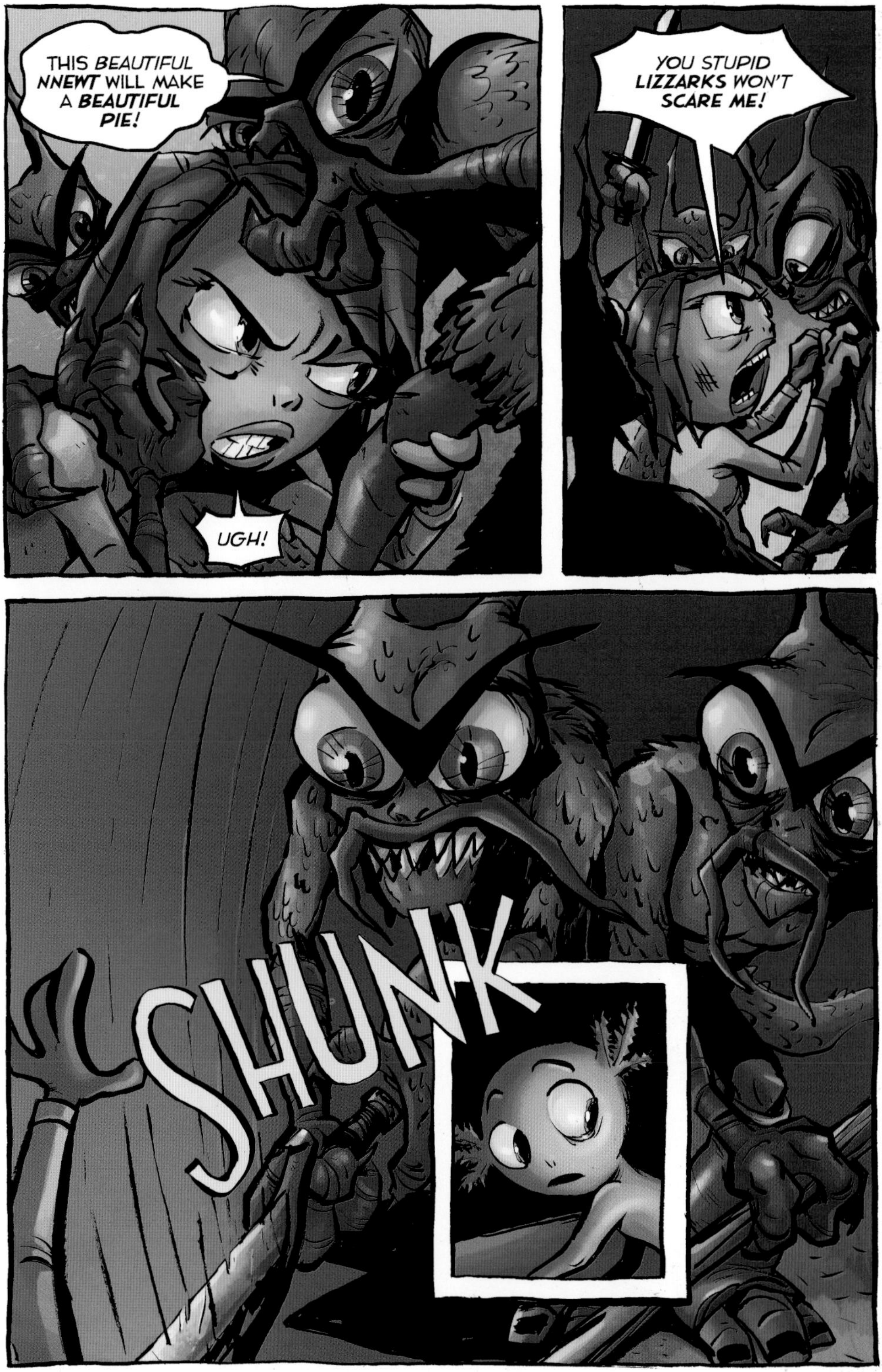
THIS *BEAUTIFUL* **NNEWT** WILL MAKE A **BEAUTIFUL PIE!**
UGH!
YOU STUPID **LIZZARKS** *WON'T* **SCARE ME!**
SHUNK

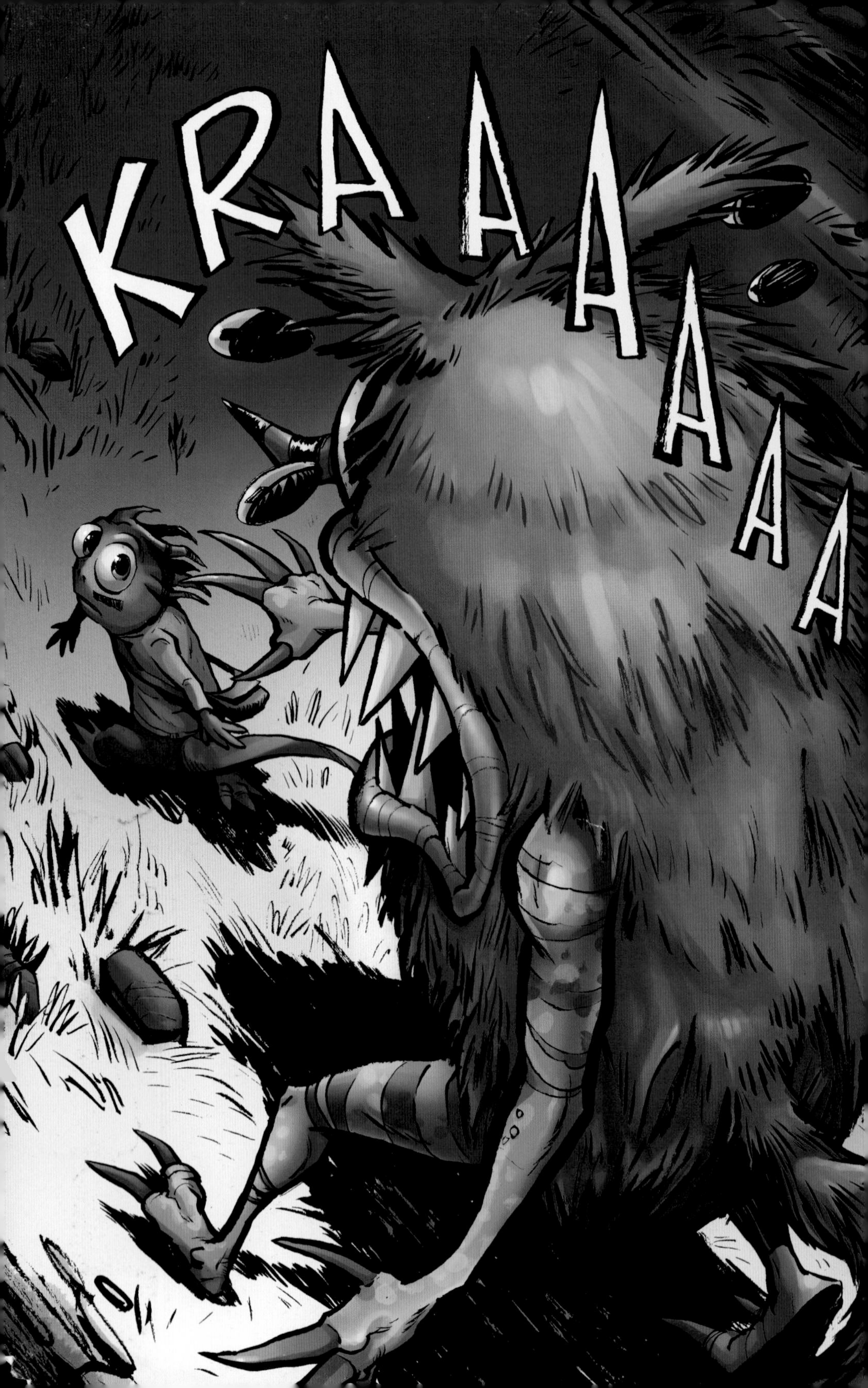
KRAAAAAAAA

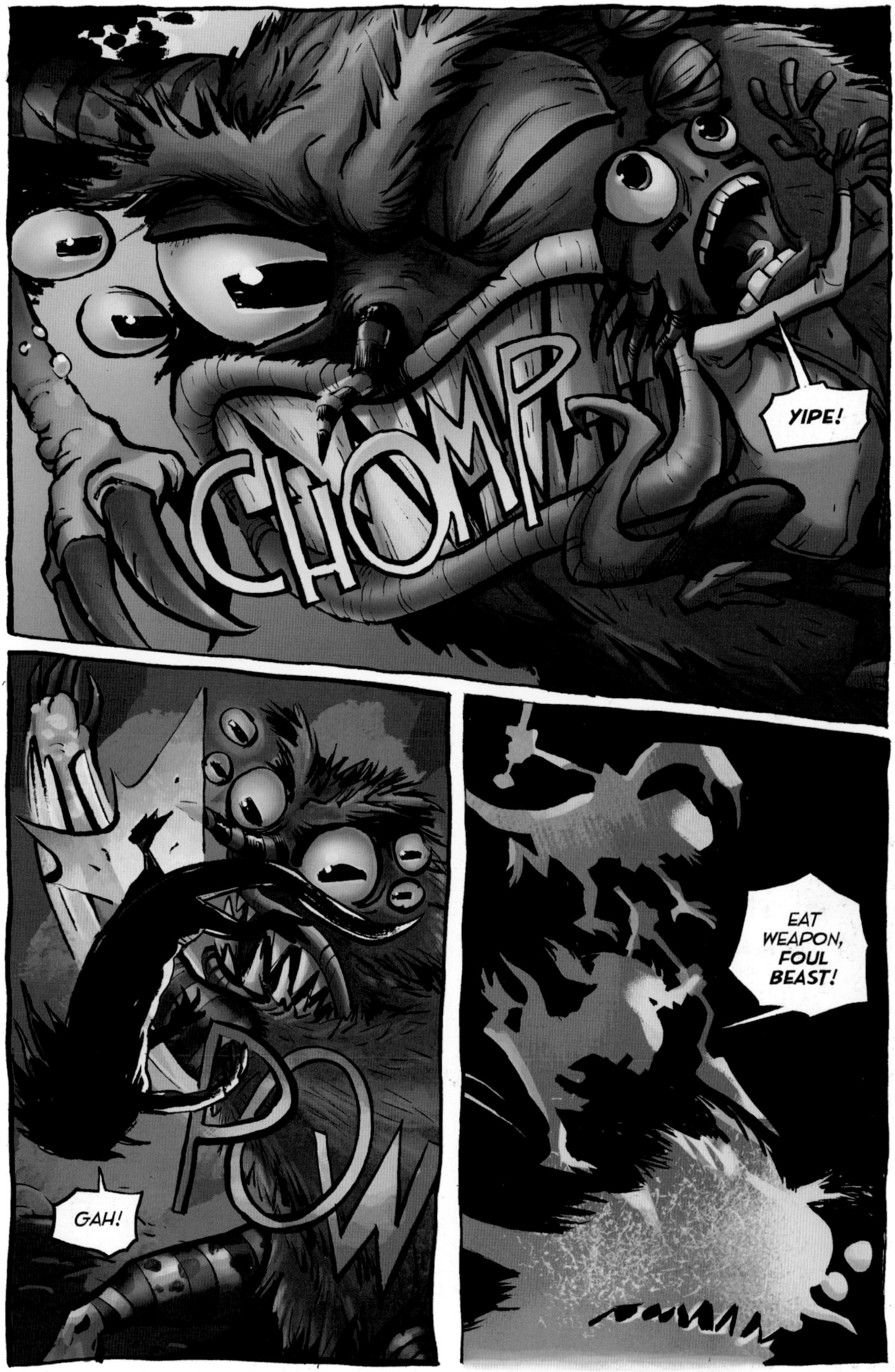
CHOMP!
YIPE!
POW
GAH!
EAT WEAPON, FOUL BEAST!

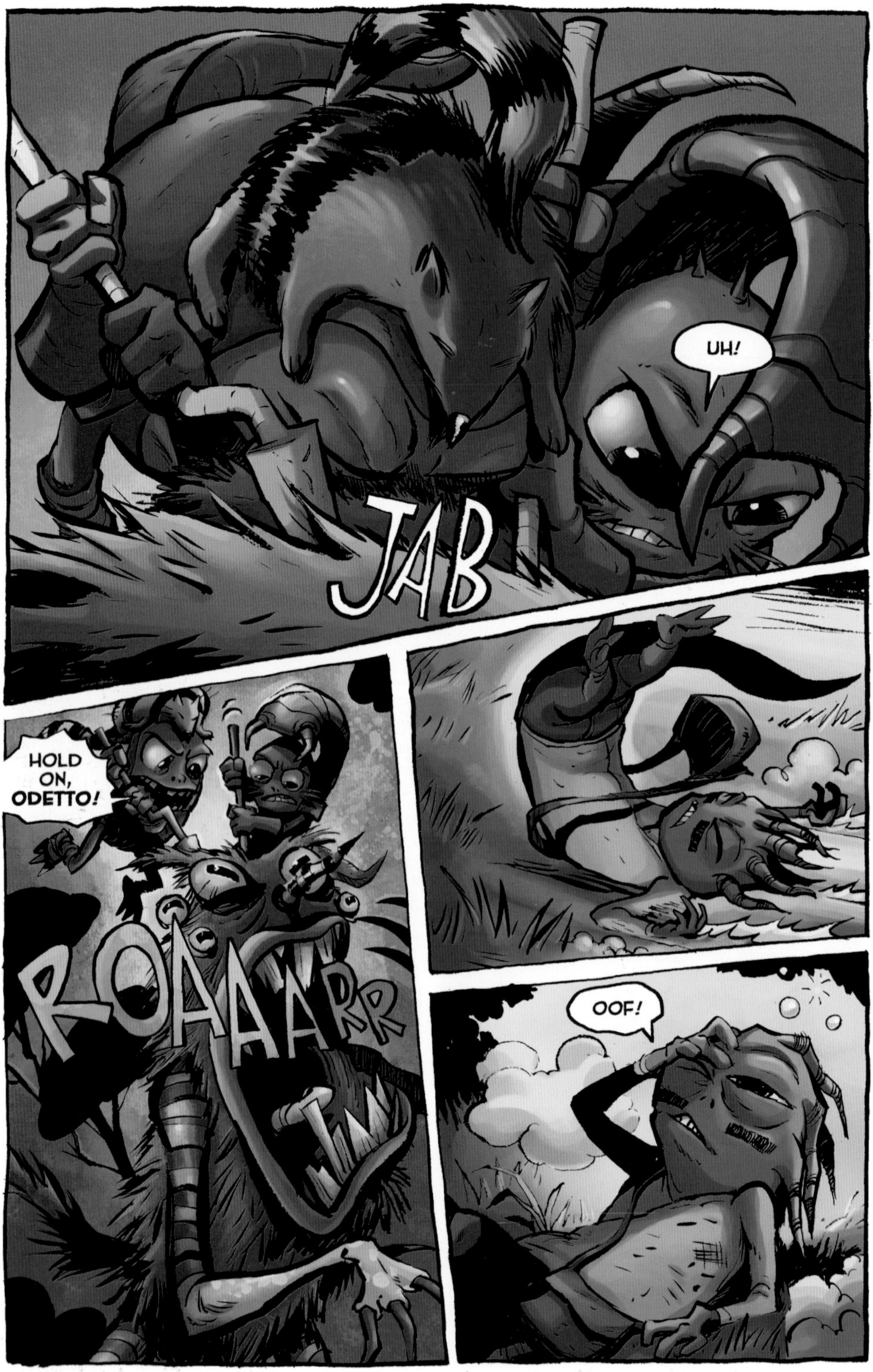
UH!
JAB
HOLD ON, ODETTO!
ROAAAARR
OOF!

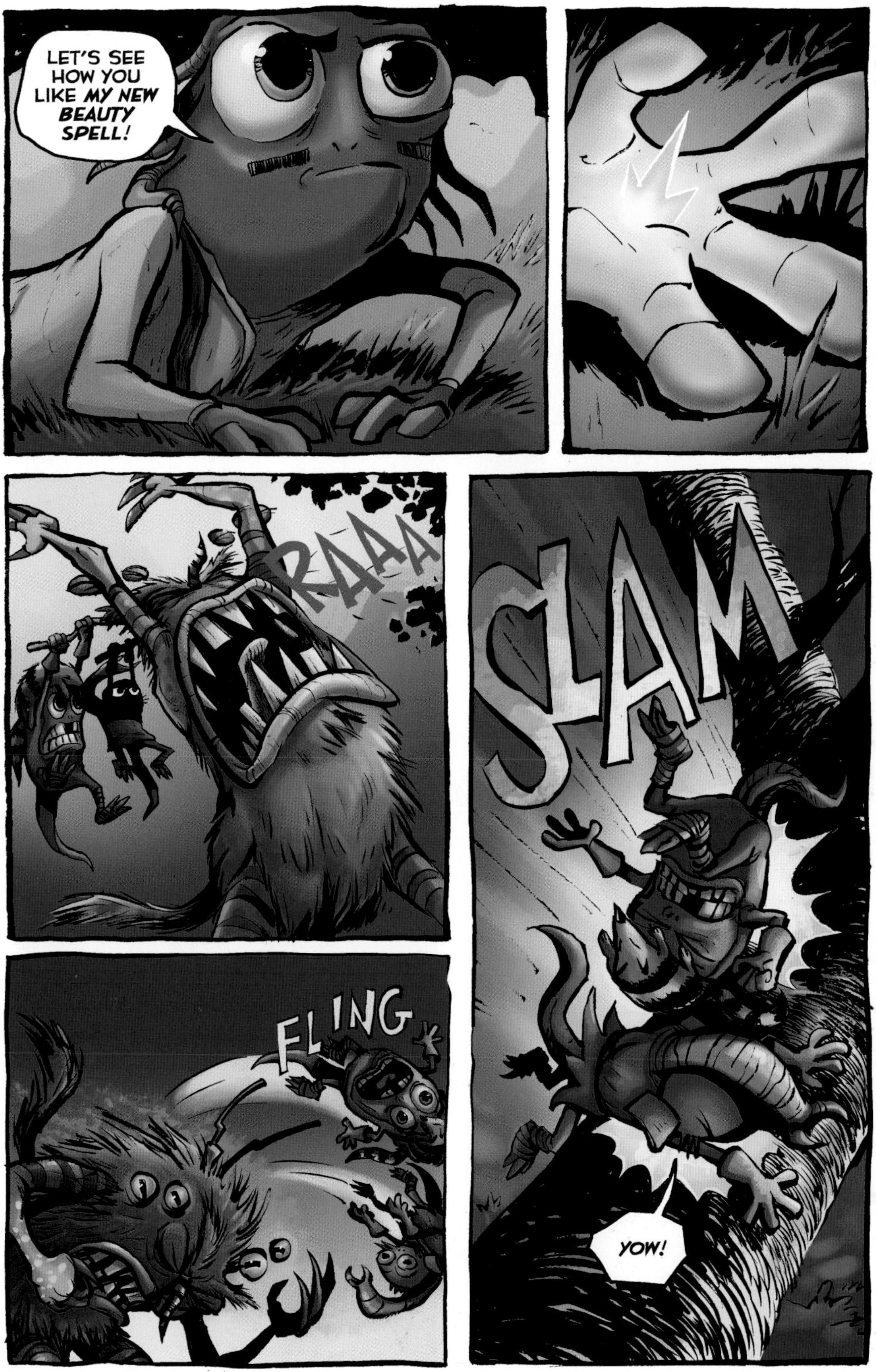
LET'S SEE HOW YOU LIKE *MY NEW BEAUTY SPELL!*
RAAA
SLAM
FLING
YOW!

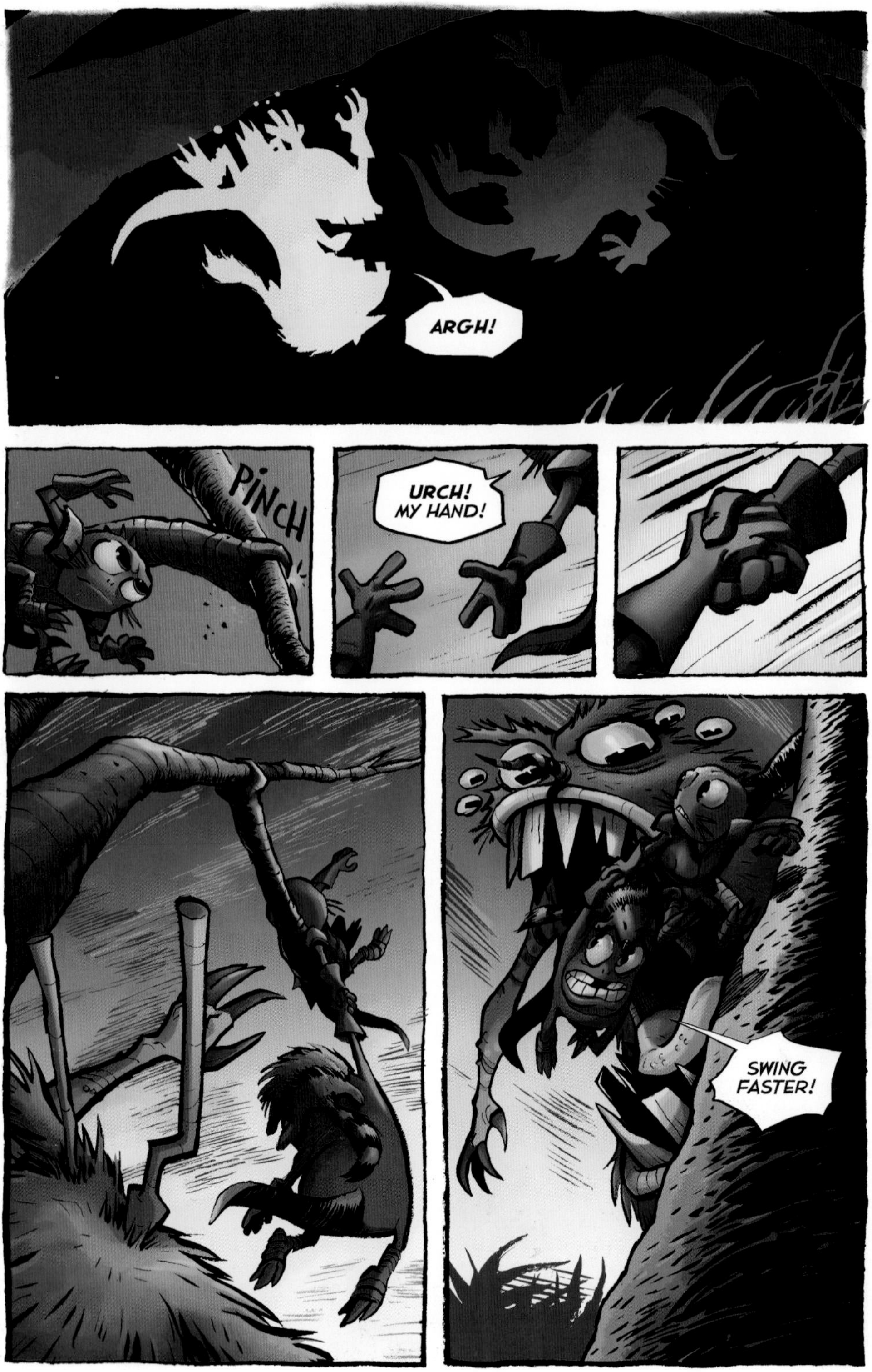
ARGH!
PINCH
URCH! MY HAND!
SWING FASTER!

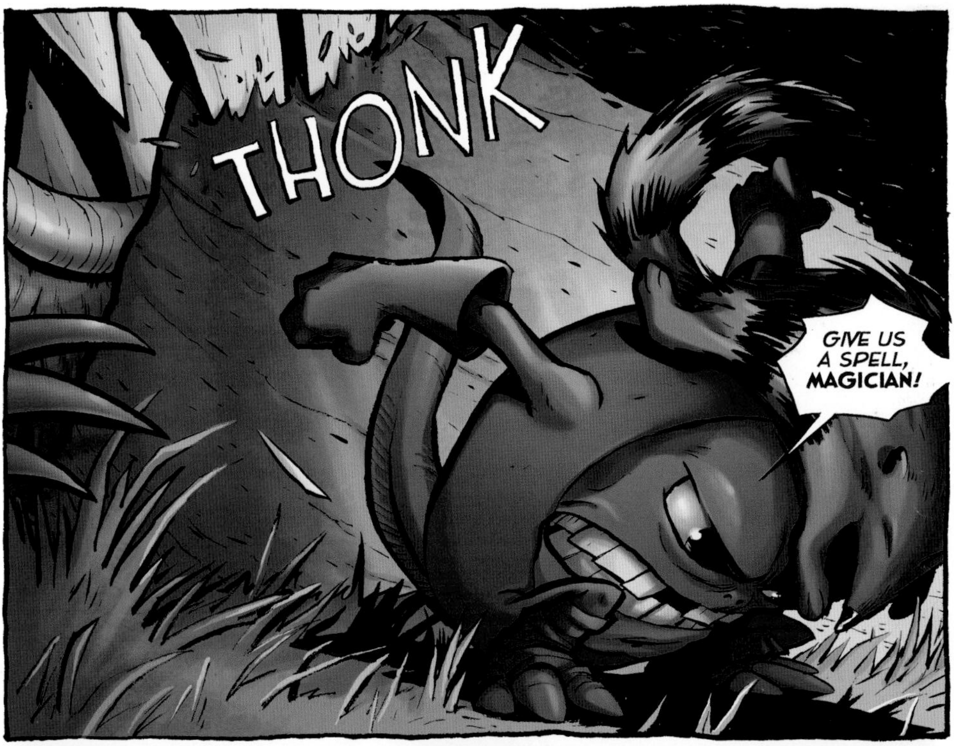
THONK
GIVE US A SPELL, MAGICIAN!

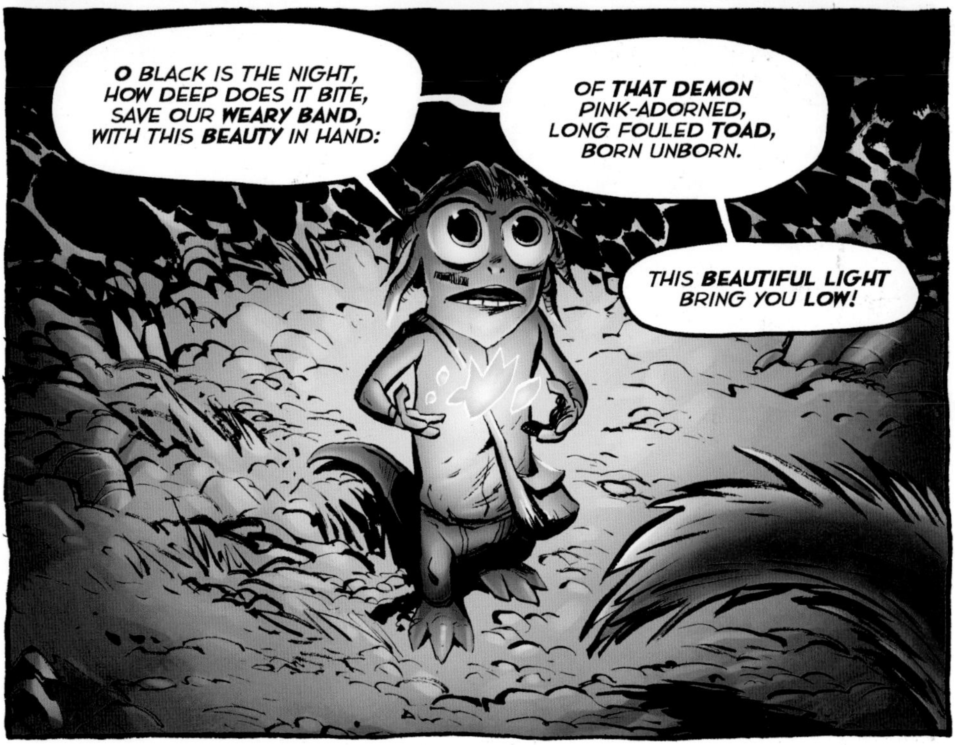
O BLACK IS THE NIGHT, HOW DEEP DOES IT BITE, SAVE OUR WEARY BAND, WITH THIS BEAUTY IN HAND:
OF THAT DEMON PINK-ADORNED, LONG FOULED TOAD, BORN UNBORN.
THIS BEAUTIFUL LIGHT BRING YOU LOW!

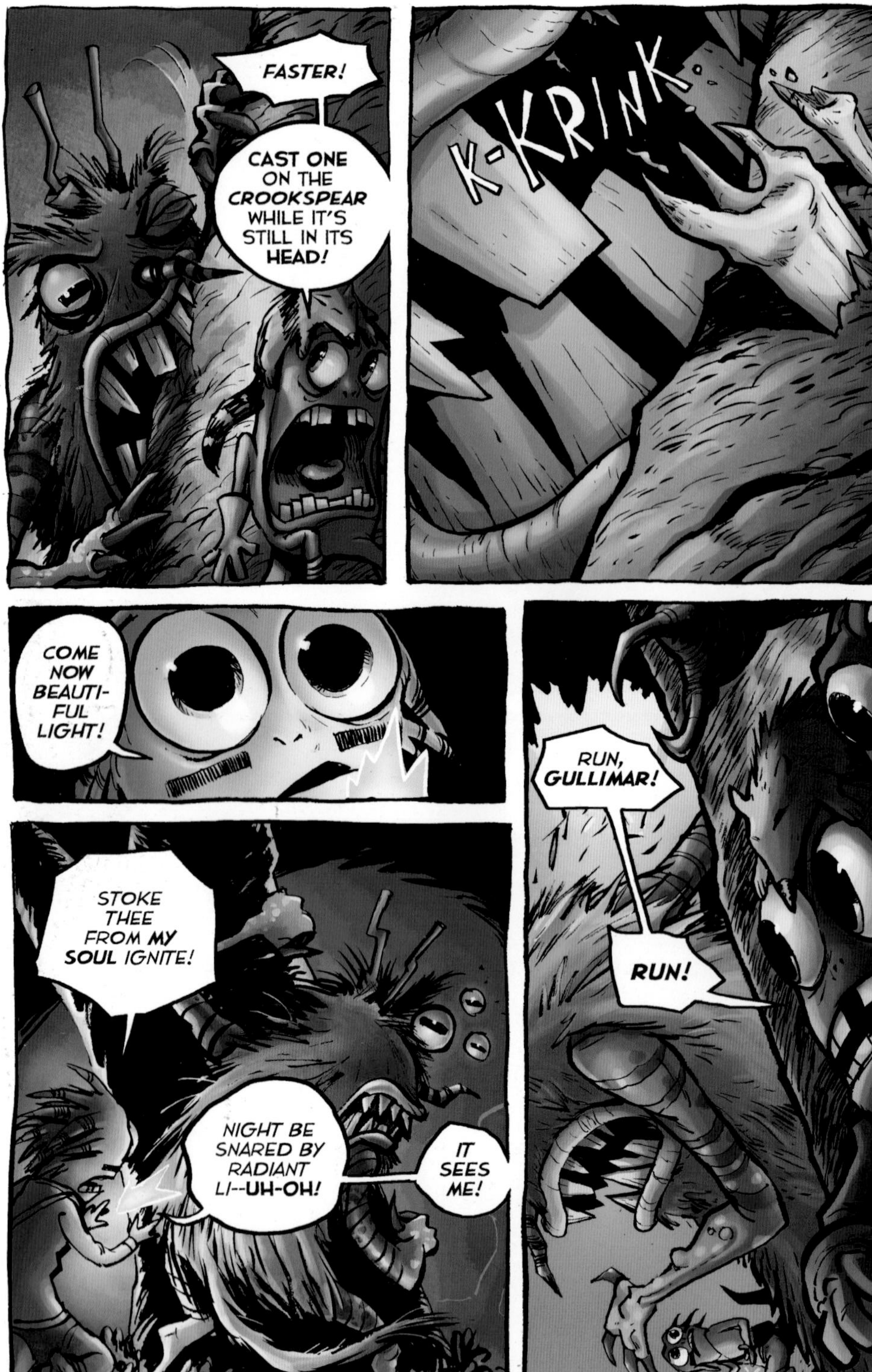
FASTER!
CAST ONE ON THE CROOKSPEAR WHILE IT'S STILL IN ITS HEAD!
K-KRINK
COME NOW BEAUTI-FUL LIGHT!
STOKE THEE FROM MY SOUL IGNITE!
NIGHT BE SNARED BY RADIANT LI--UH-OH!
IT SEES ME!
RUN, GULLIMAR!
RUN!

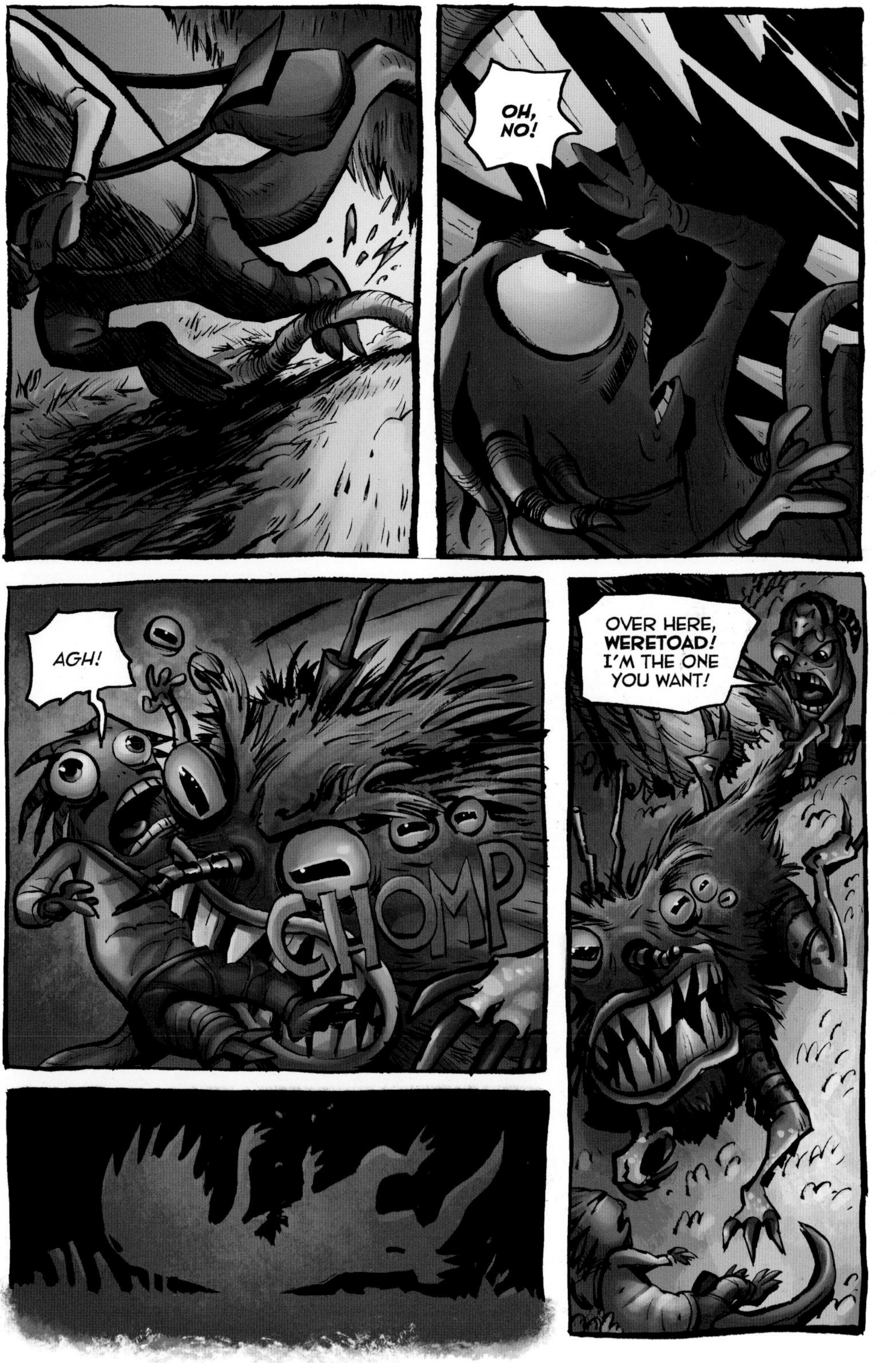
OH, NO!
AGH!
CHOMP
OVER HERE, WERETOAD! I'M THE ONE YOU WANT!

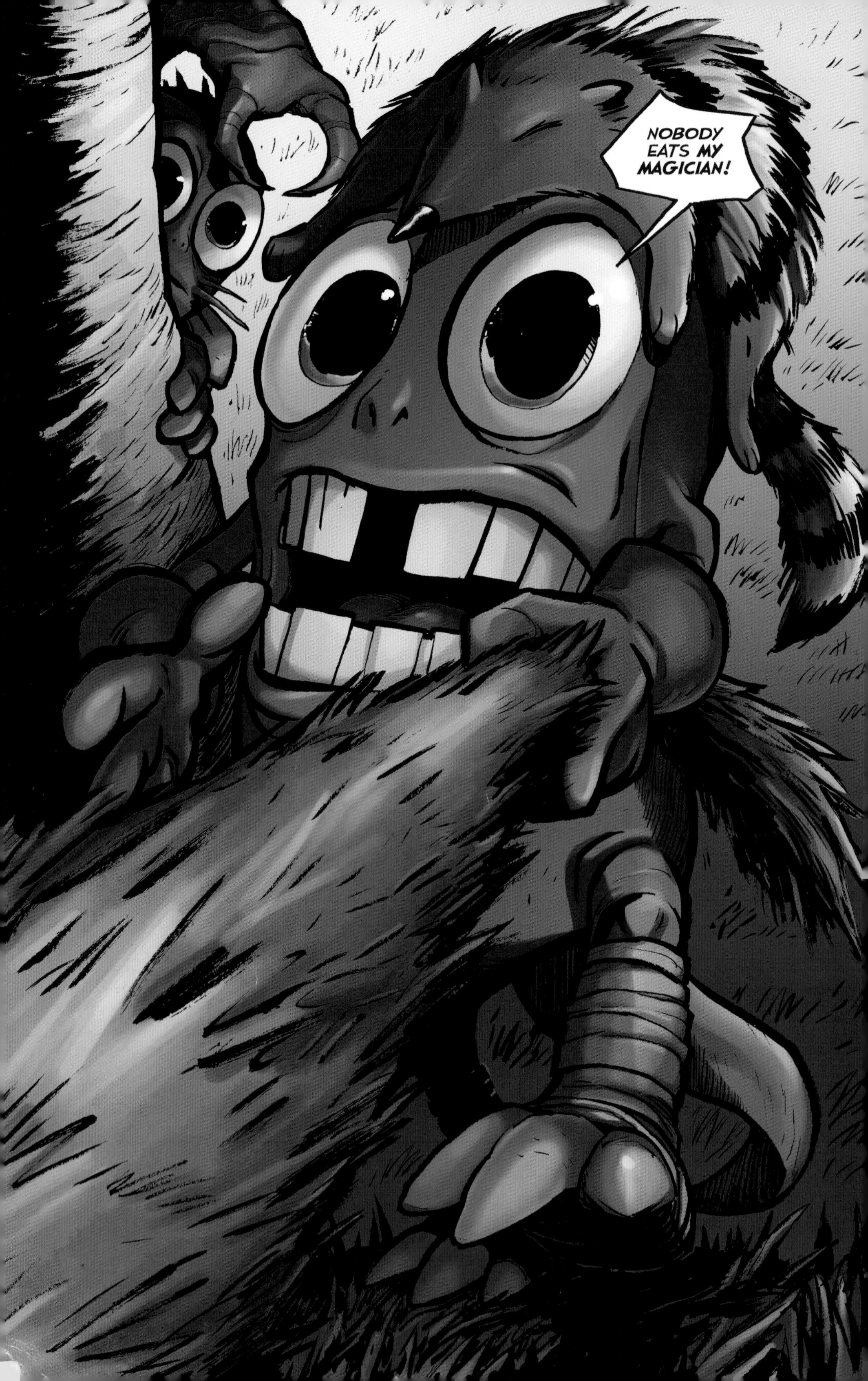
NOBODY EATS MY MAGICIAN!

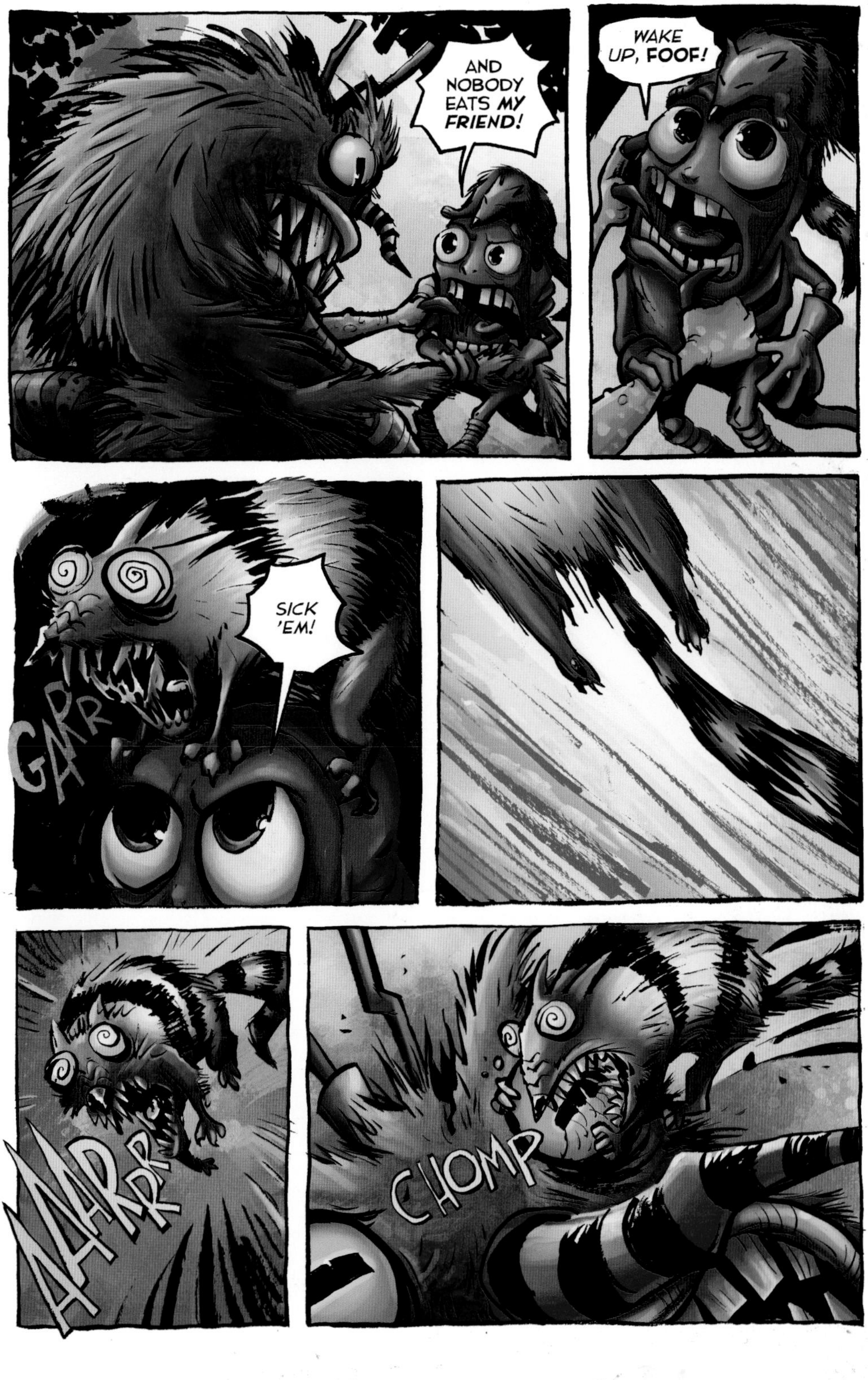
AND NOBODY EATS MY FRIEND!
WAKE UP, FOOF!
SICK 'EM!
GARRR
AAARRR
CHOMP

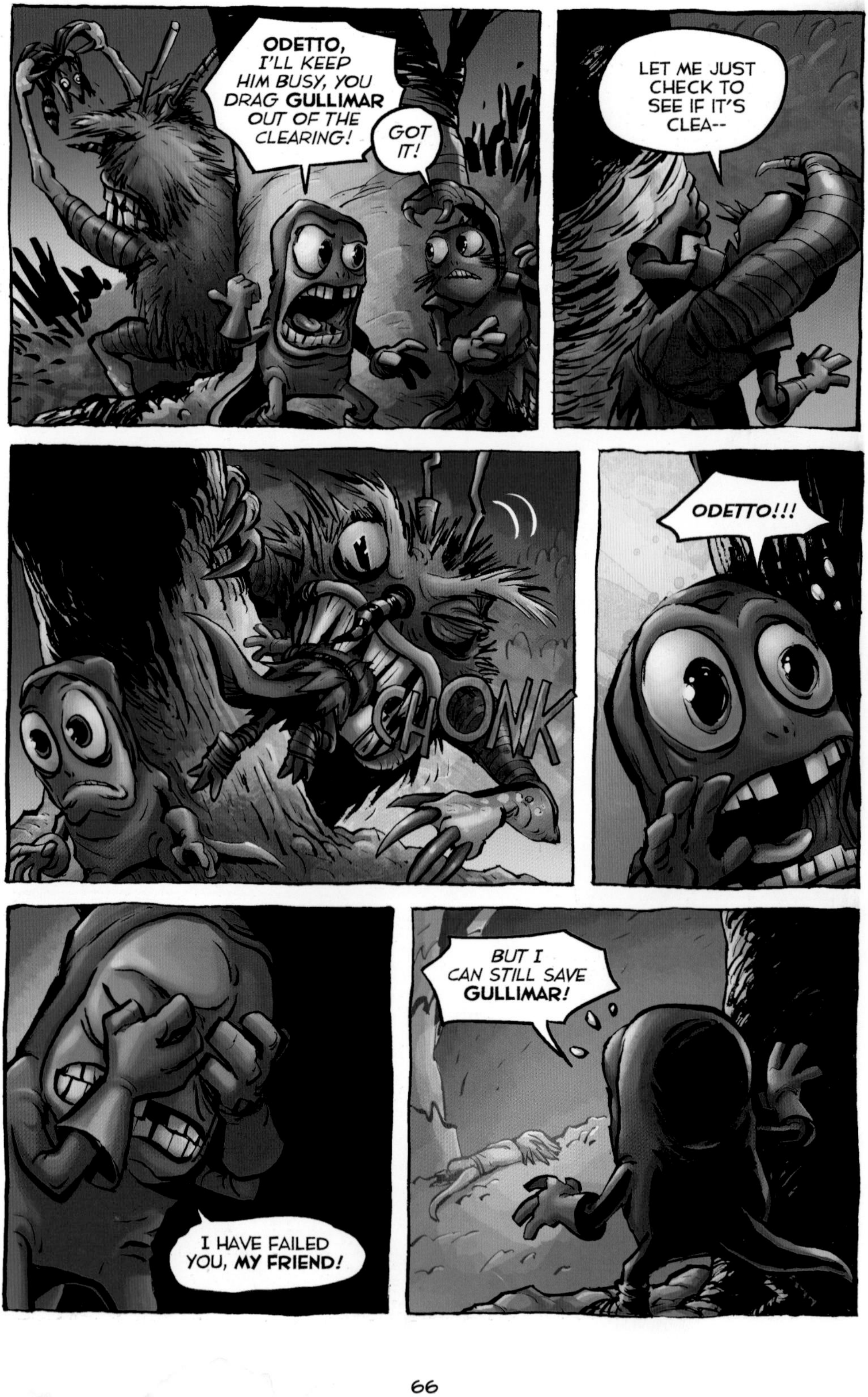
ODETTO, I'LL KEEP HIM BUSY, YOU DRAG GULLIMAR OUT OF THE CLEARING!
GOT IT!
LET ME JUST CHECK TO SEE IF IT'S CLEA--
CHONK
ODETTO!!!
I HAVE FAILED YOU, MY FRIEND!
BUT I CAN STILL SAVE GULLIMAR!

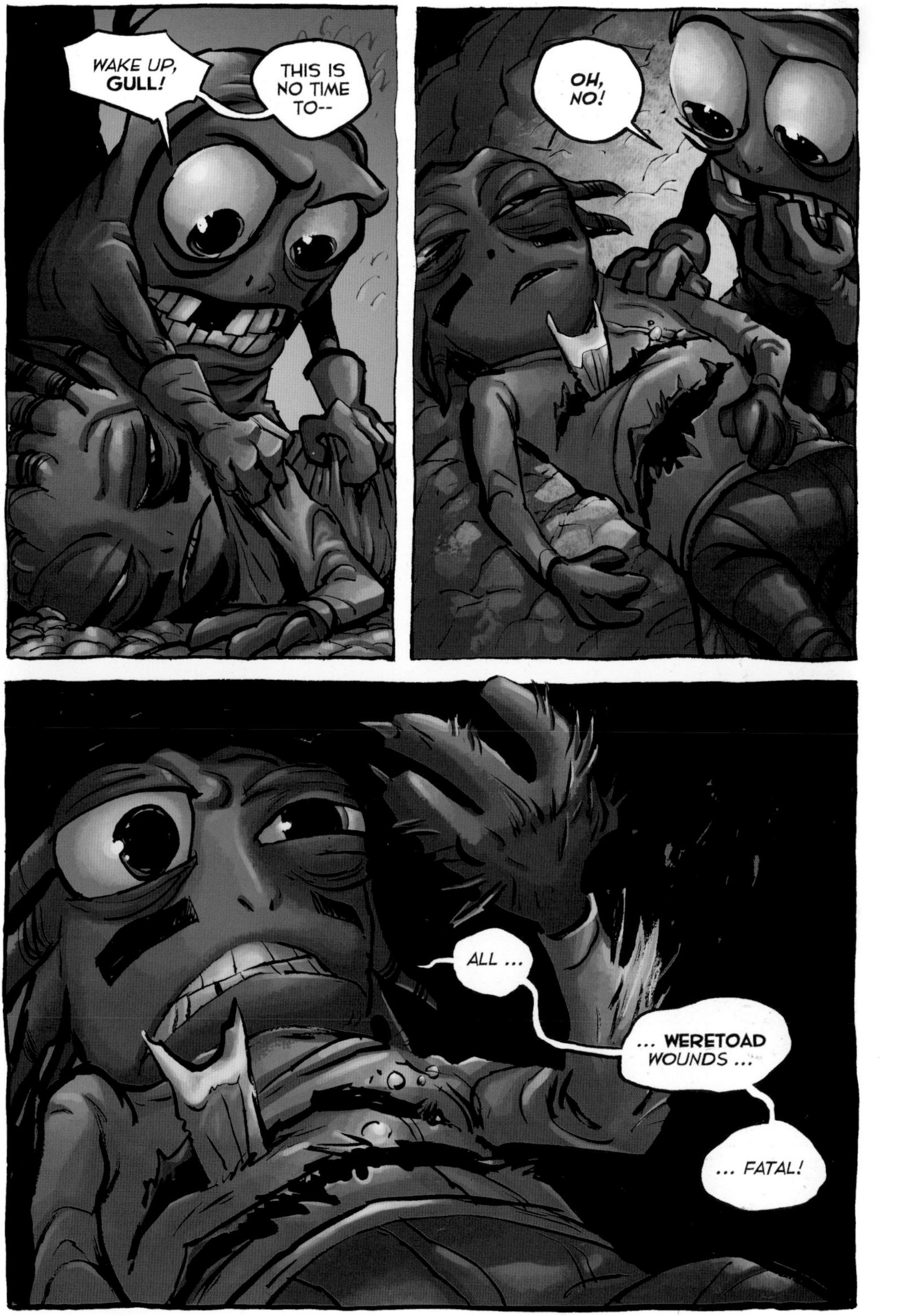
WAKE UP, GULL!
THIS IS NO TIME TO--
OH, NO!
ALL ...
... WERETOAD WOUNDS ...
... FATAL!

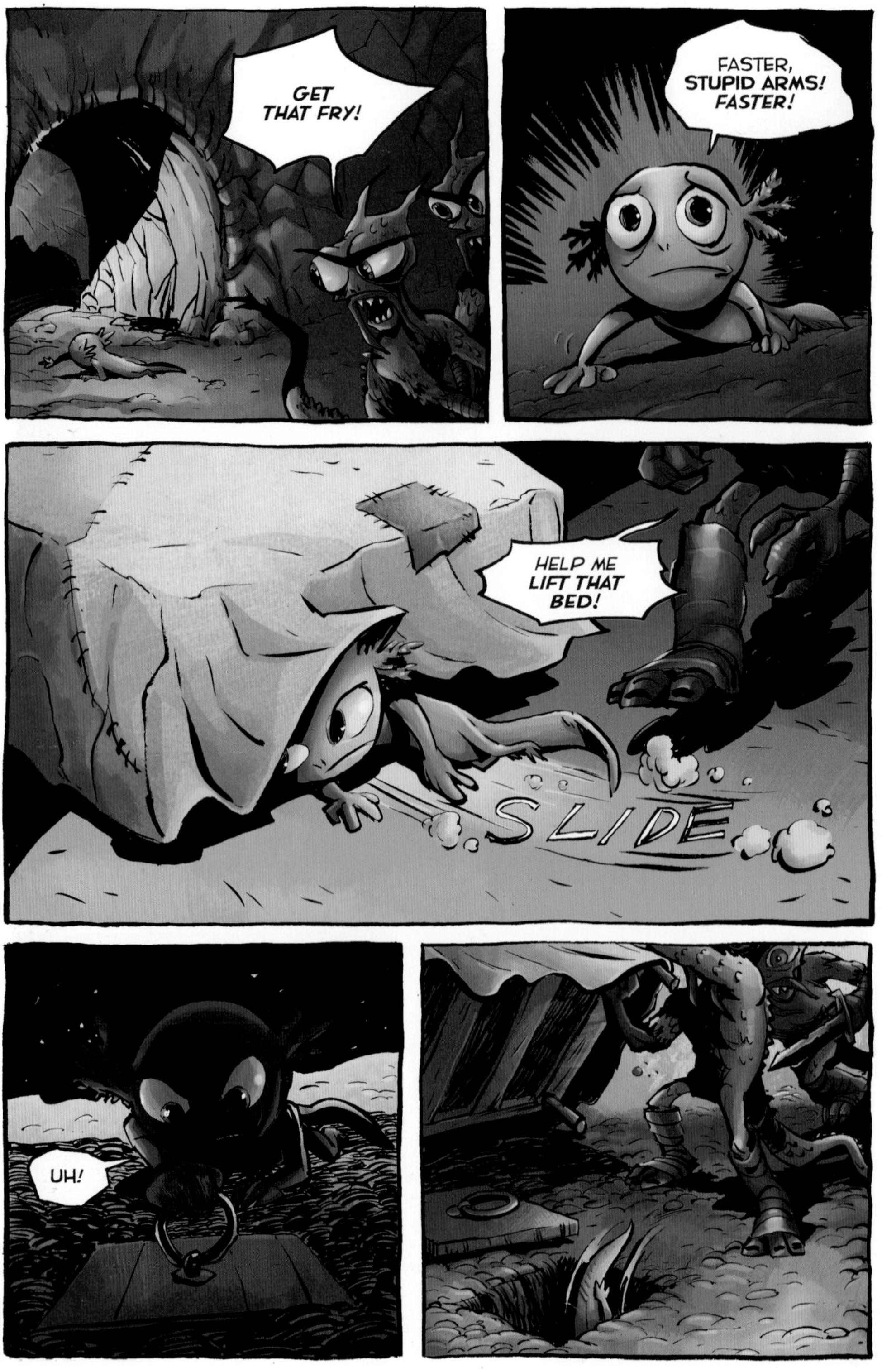
GET THAT FRY!
FASTER, STUPID ARMS! FASTER!
HELP ME LIFT THAT BED!
SLIDE
UH!

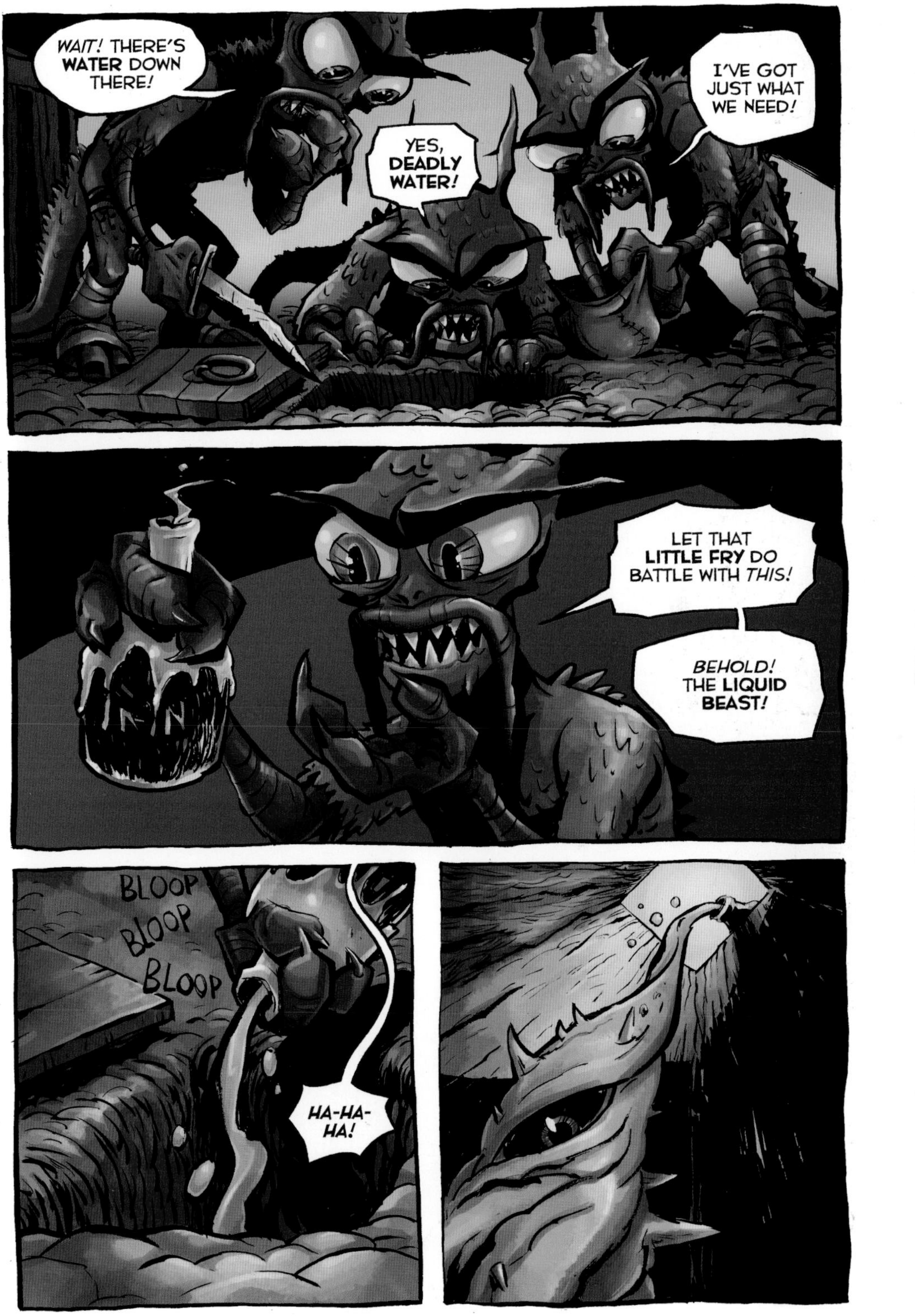
WAIT! THERE'S WATER DOWN THERE!
YES, DEADLY WATER!
I'VE GOT JUST WHAT WE NEED!
LET THAT LITTLE FRY DO BATTLE WITH THIS!
BEHOLD! THE LIQUID BEAST!
BLOOP
BLOOP
BLOOP
HA-HA-HA!

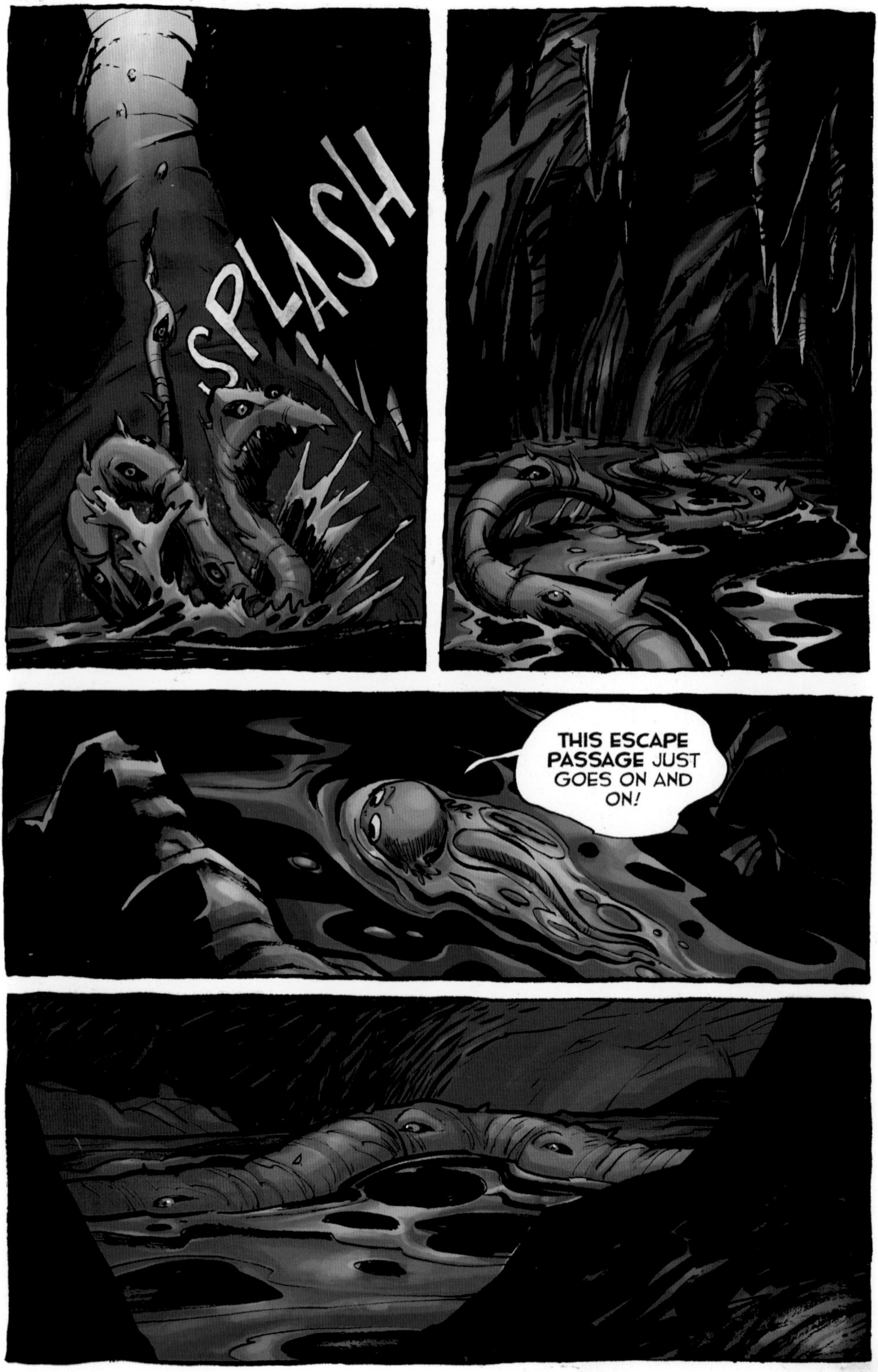
SPLASH
THIS ESCAPE PASSAGE JUST GOES ON AND ON!

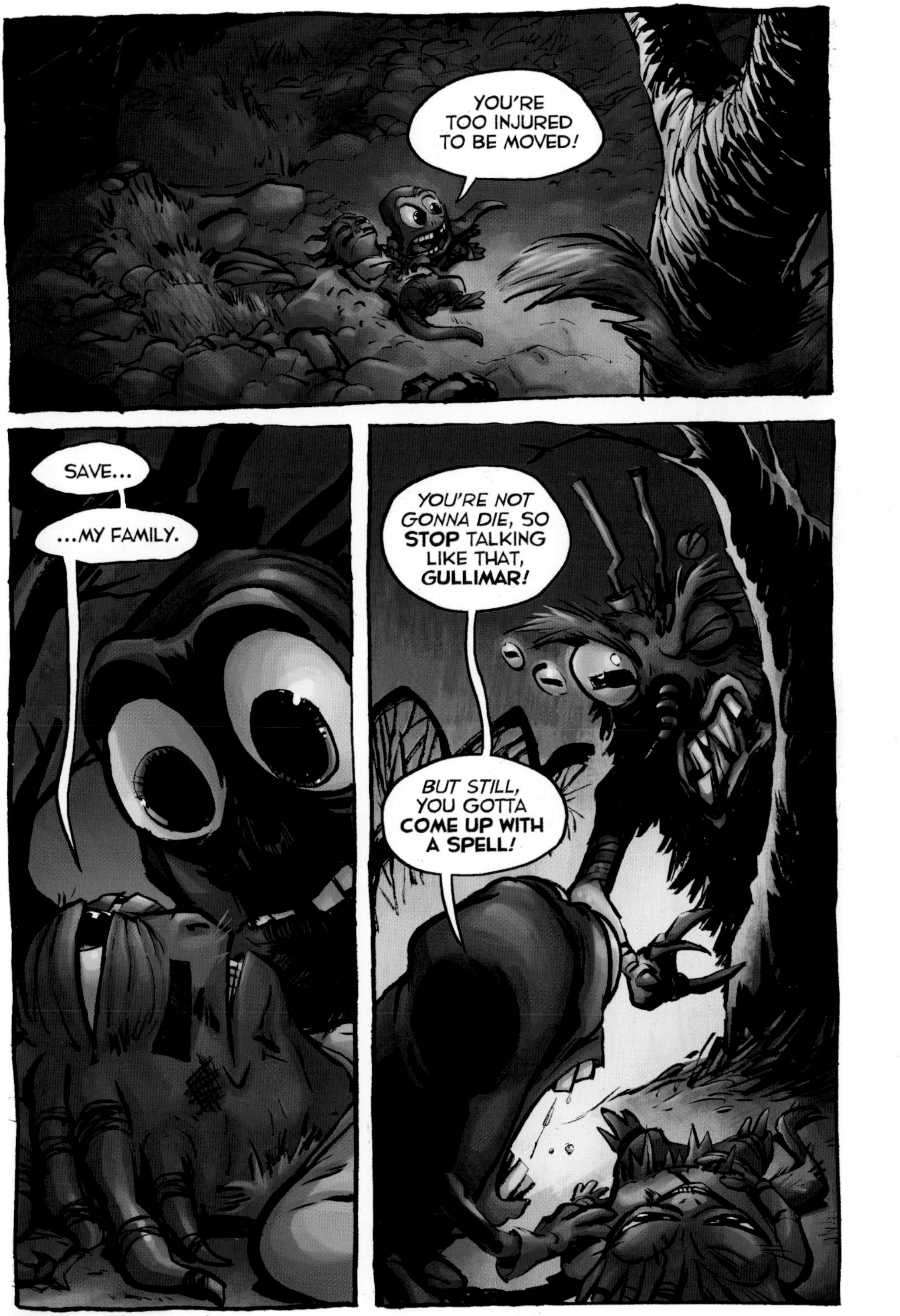
YOU'RE TOO INJURED TO BE MOVED!
SAVE...
...MY FAMILY.
YOU'RE NOT GONNA DIE, SO **STOP** TALKING LIKE THAT, **GULLIMAR!**
BUT STILL, YOU GOTTA **COME UP WITH A SPELL!**

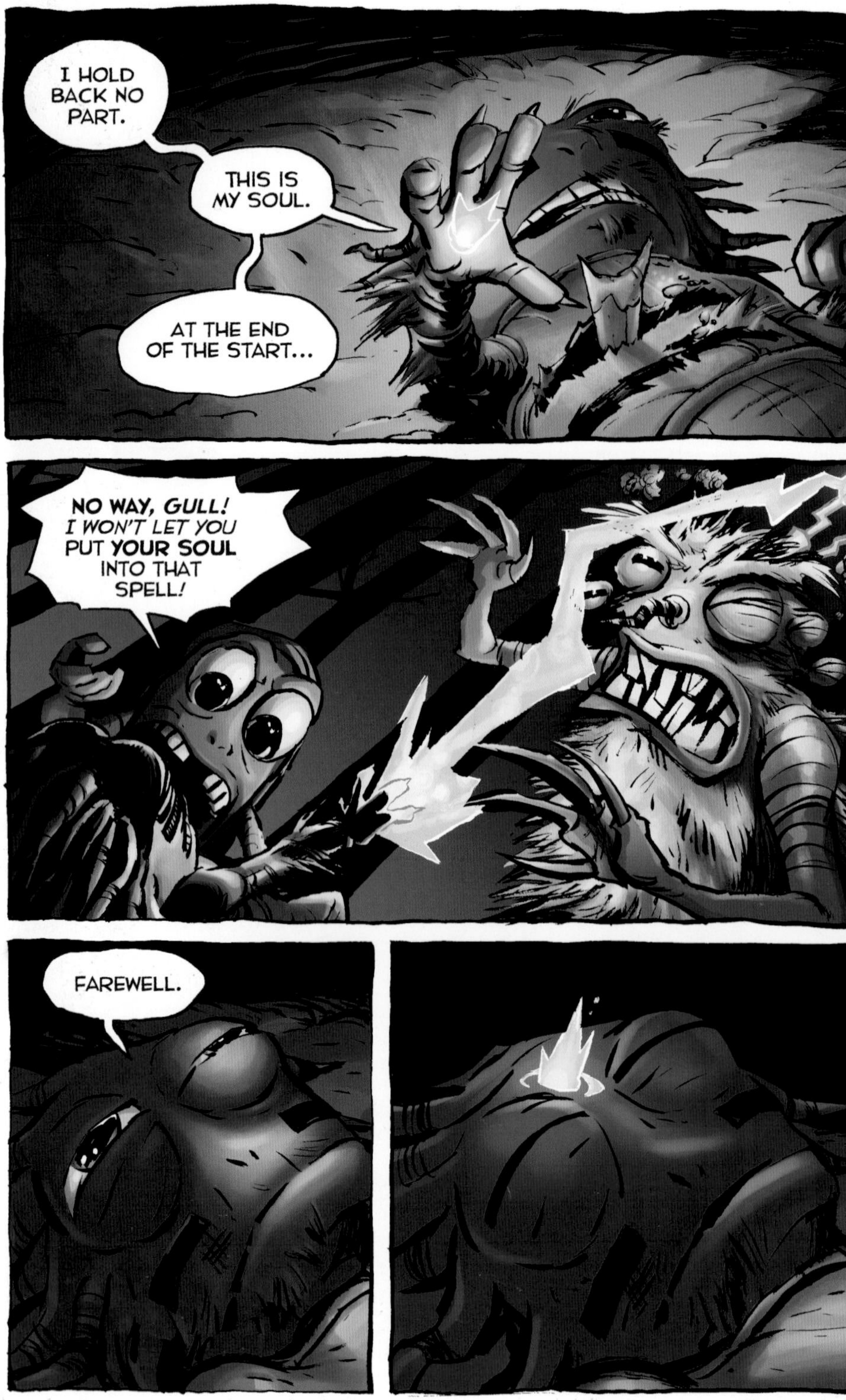
I HOLD BACK NO PART.
THIS IS MY SOUL.
AT THE END OF THE START...
NO WAY, GULL! I WON'T LET YOU PUT YOUR SOUL INTO THAT SPELL!
FAREWELL.

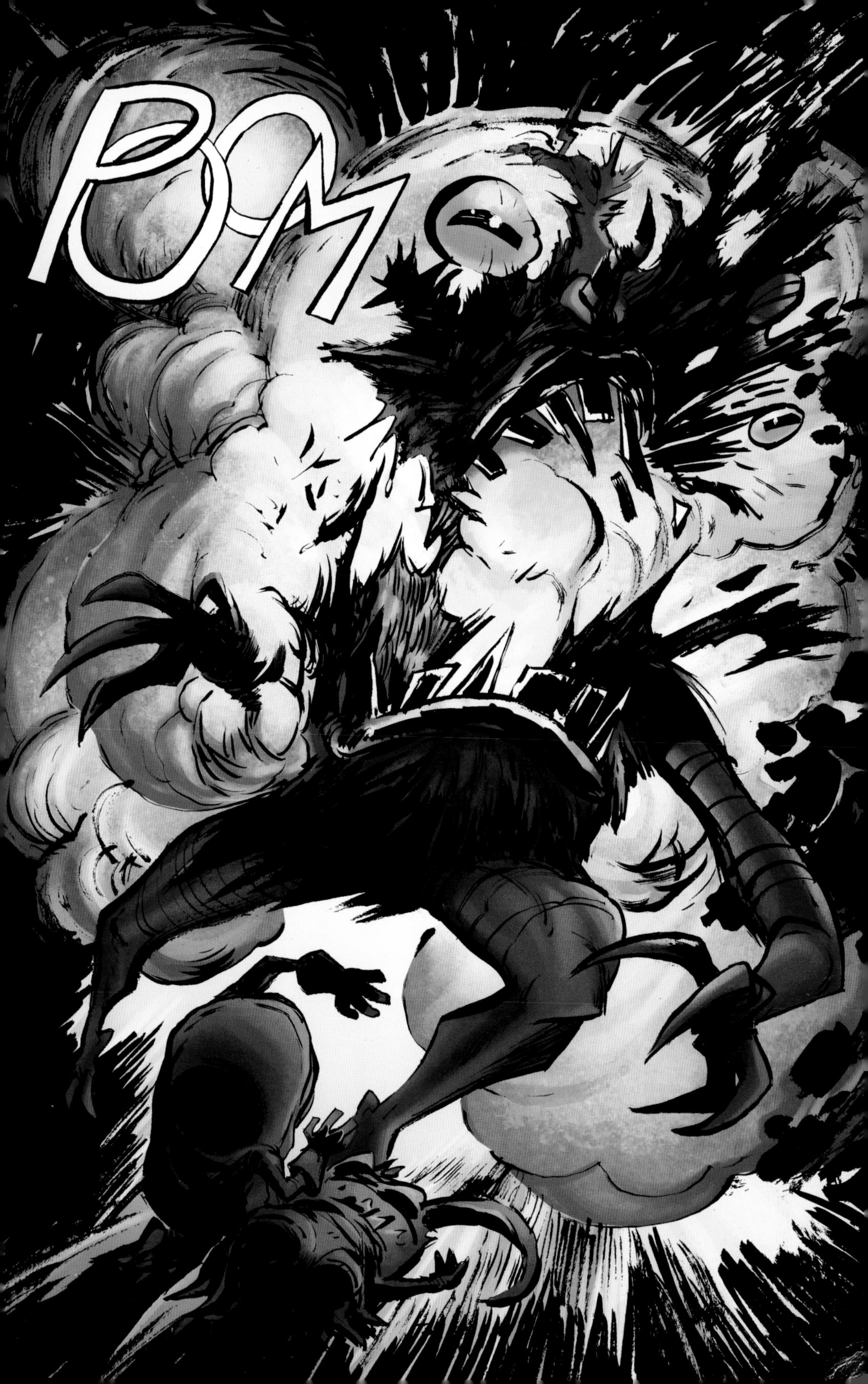
POOM

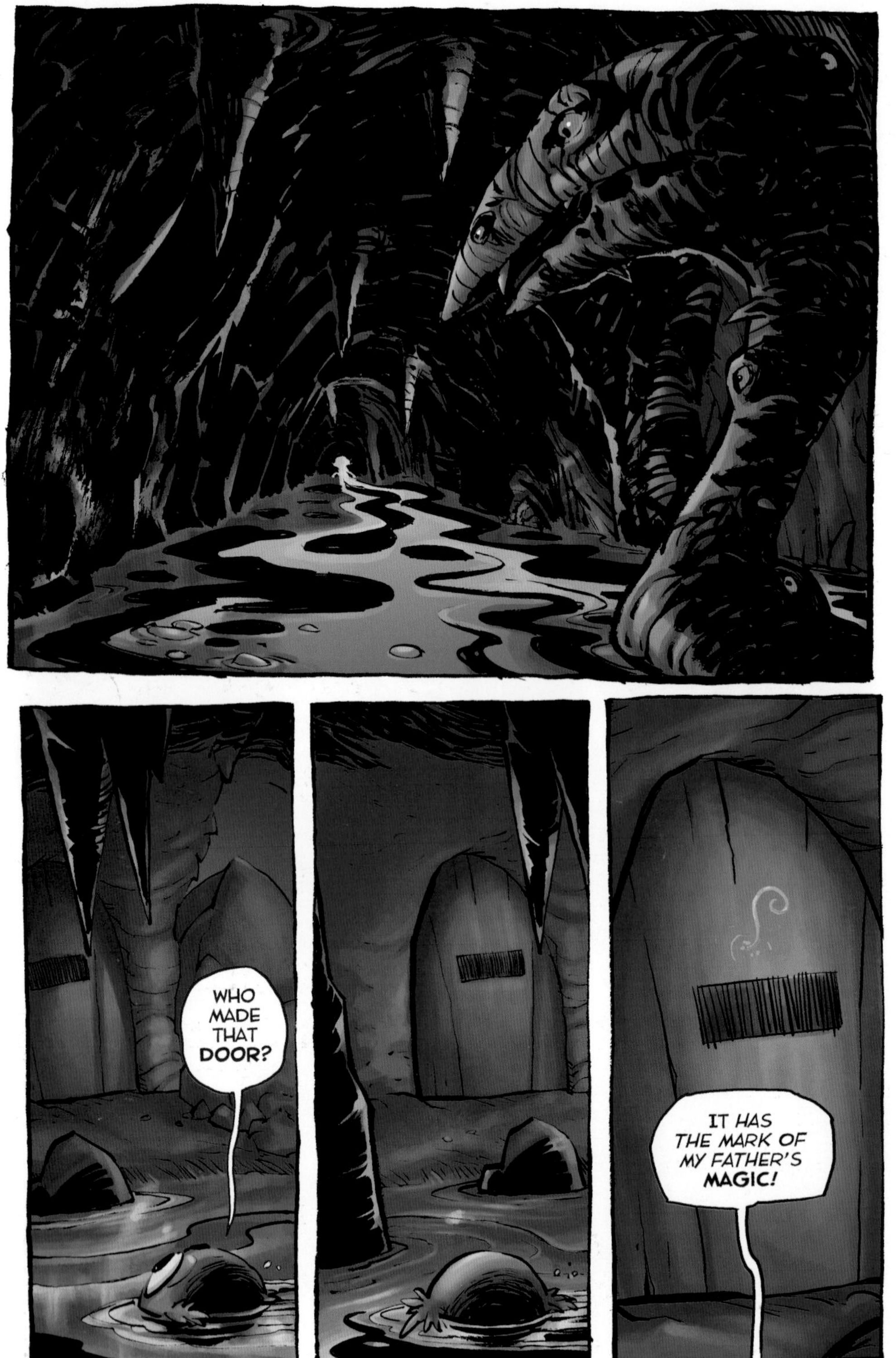
WHO MADE THAT DOOR?
IT HAS THE MARK OF MY FATHER'S MAGIC!

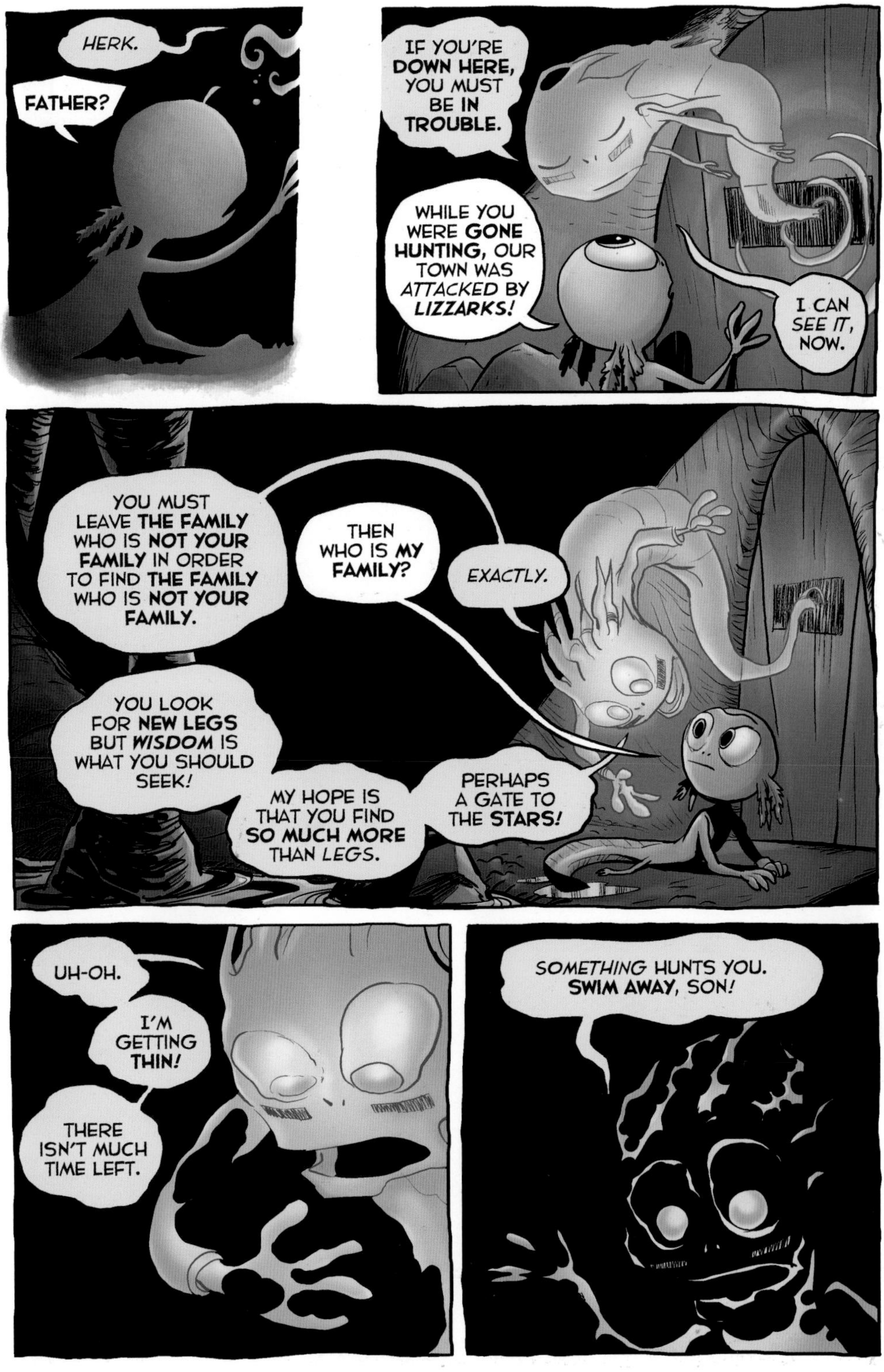
HERK.
FATHER?
IF YOU'RE DOWN HERE, YOU MUST BE IN TROUBLE.
WHILE YOU WERE GONE HUNTING, OUR TOWN WAS ATTACKED BY LIZZARKS!
I CAN SEE IT, NOW.
YOU MUST LEAVE THE FAMILY WHO IS NOT YOUR FAMILY IN ORDER TO FIND THE FAMILY WHO IS NOT YOUR FAMILY.
THEN WHO IS MY FAMILY?
EXACTLY.
YOU LOOK FOR NEW LEGS BUT WISDOM IS WHAT YOU SHOULD SEEK!
MY HOPE IS THAT YOU FIND SO MUCH MORE THAN LEGS.
PERHAPS A GATE TO THE STARS!
UH-OH.
I'M GETTING THIN!
THERE ISN'T MUCH TIME LEFT.
SOMETHING HUNTS YOU. SWIM AWAY, SON!

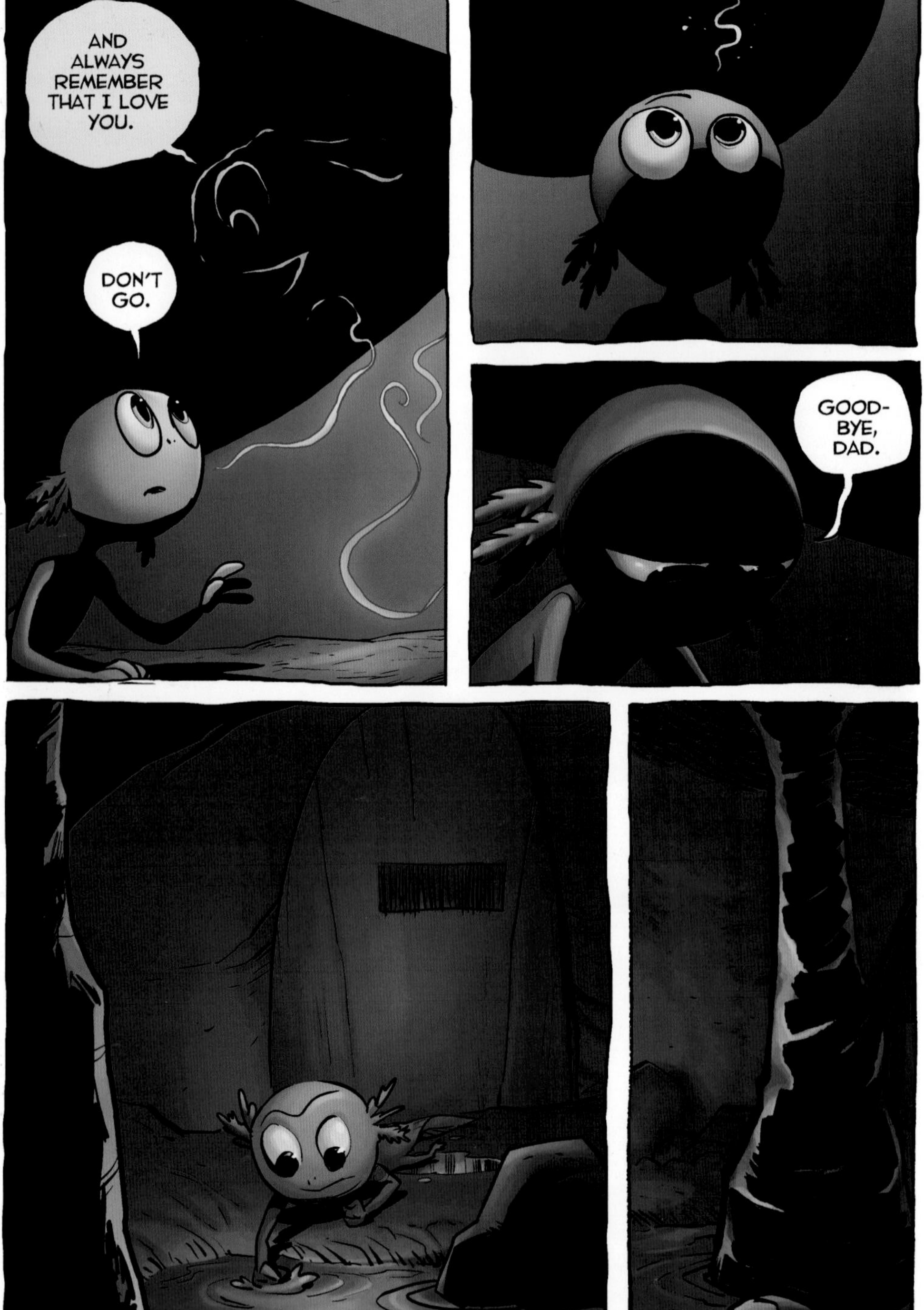
AND ALWAYS REMEMBER THAT I LOVE YOU.
DON'T GO.
GOOD-BYE, DAD.

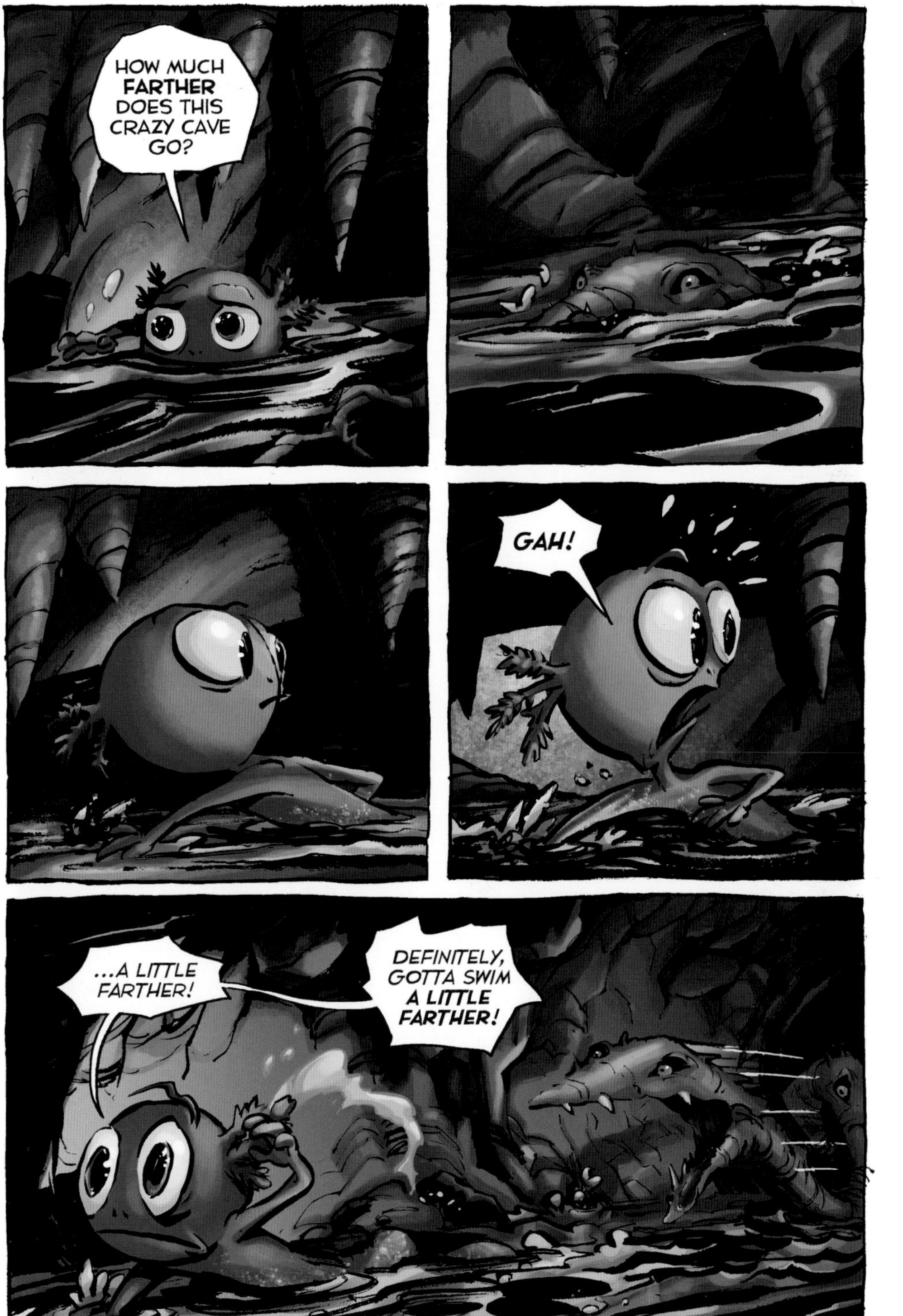
HOW MUCH FARTHER DOES THIS CRAZY CAVE GO?
GAH!
...A LITTLE FARTHER!
DEFINITELY, GOTTA SWIM A LITTLE FARTHER!

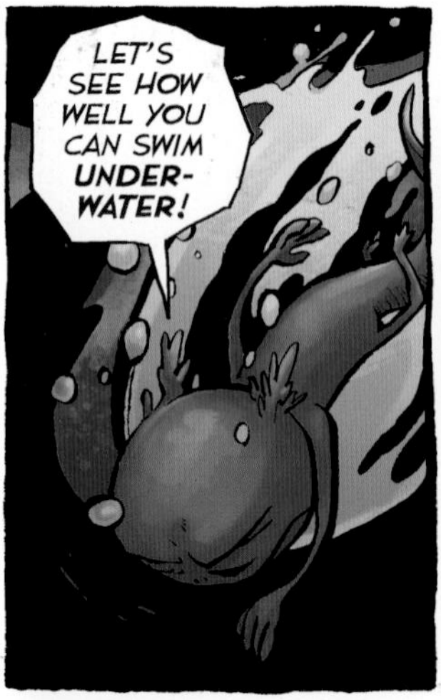
LET'S SEE HOW WELL YOU CAN SWIM UNDER-WATER!

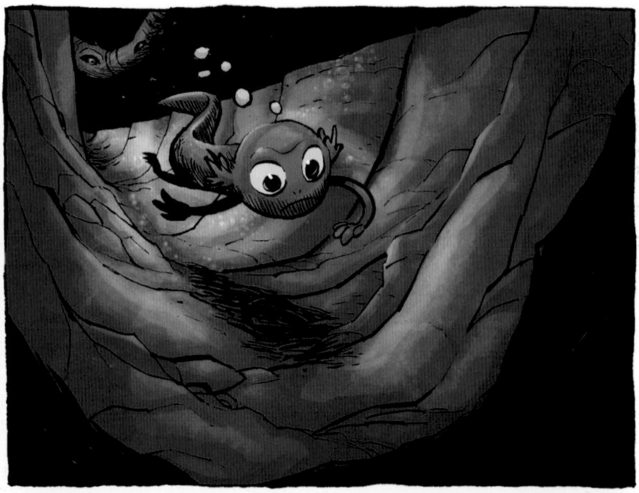

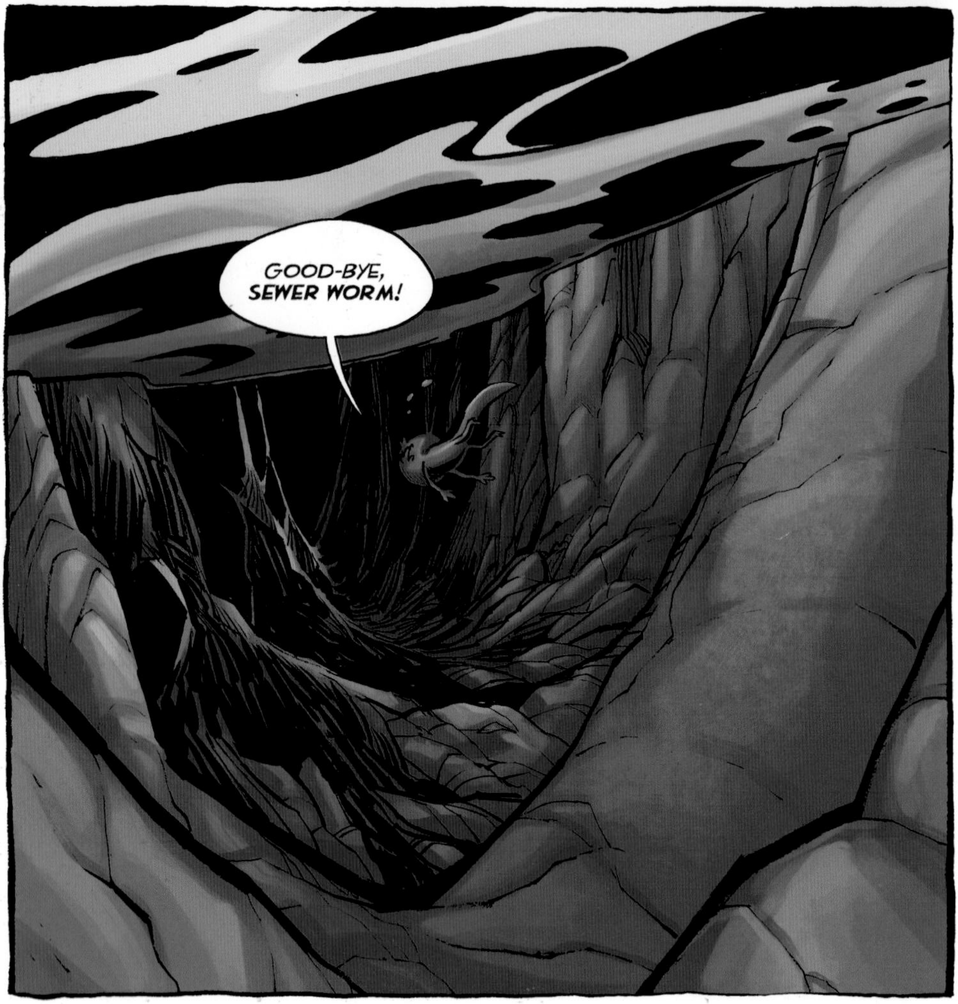
GOOD-BYE, SEWER WORM!

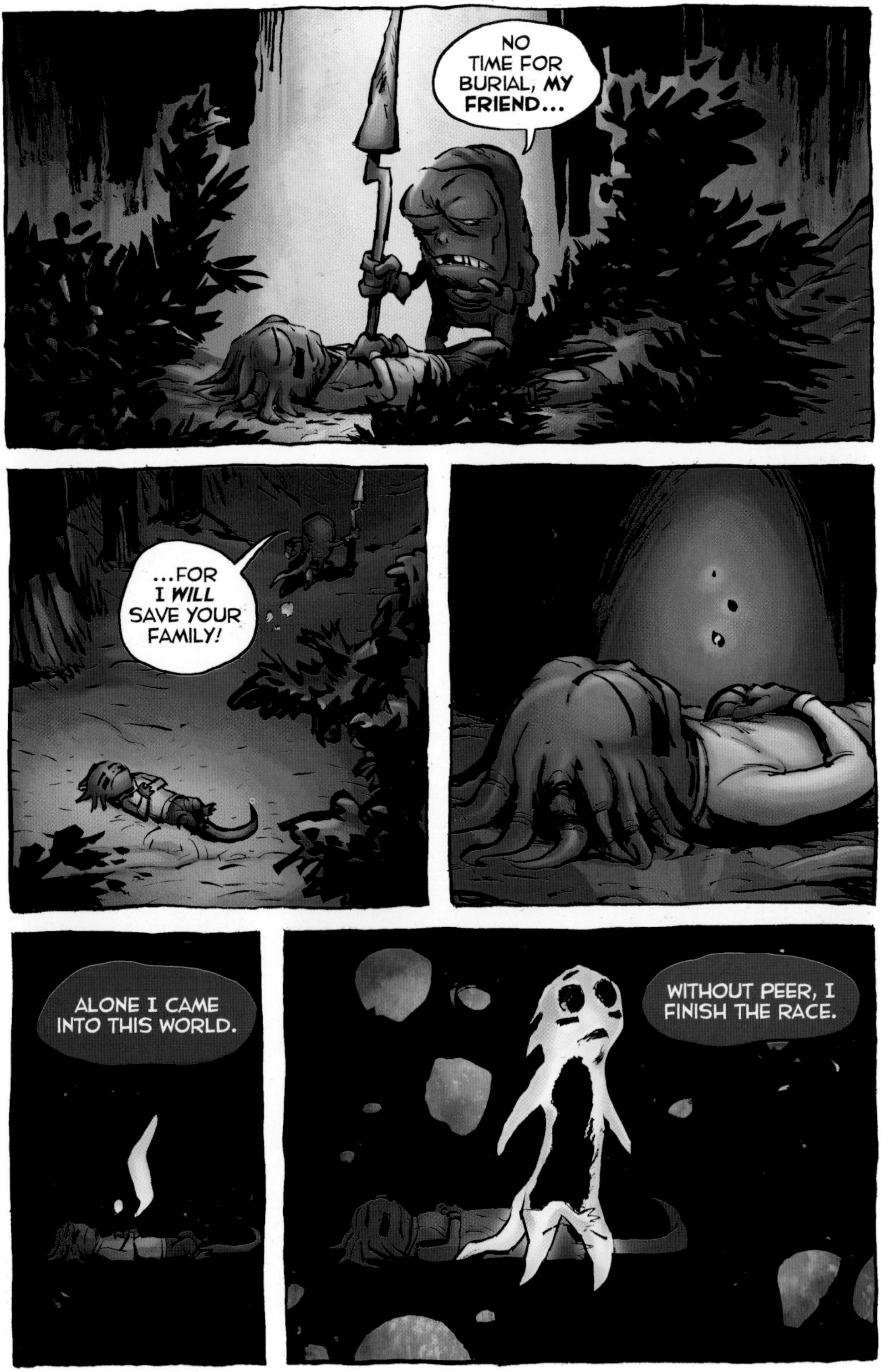
NO TIME FOR BURIAL, **MY FRIEND...**
...FOR I *WILL* SAVE YOUR FAMILY!
ALONE I CAME INTO THIS WORLD.
WITHOUT PEER, I FINISH THE RACE.

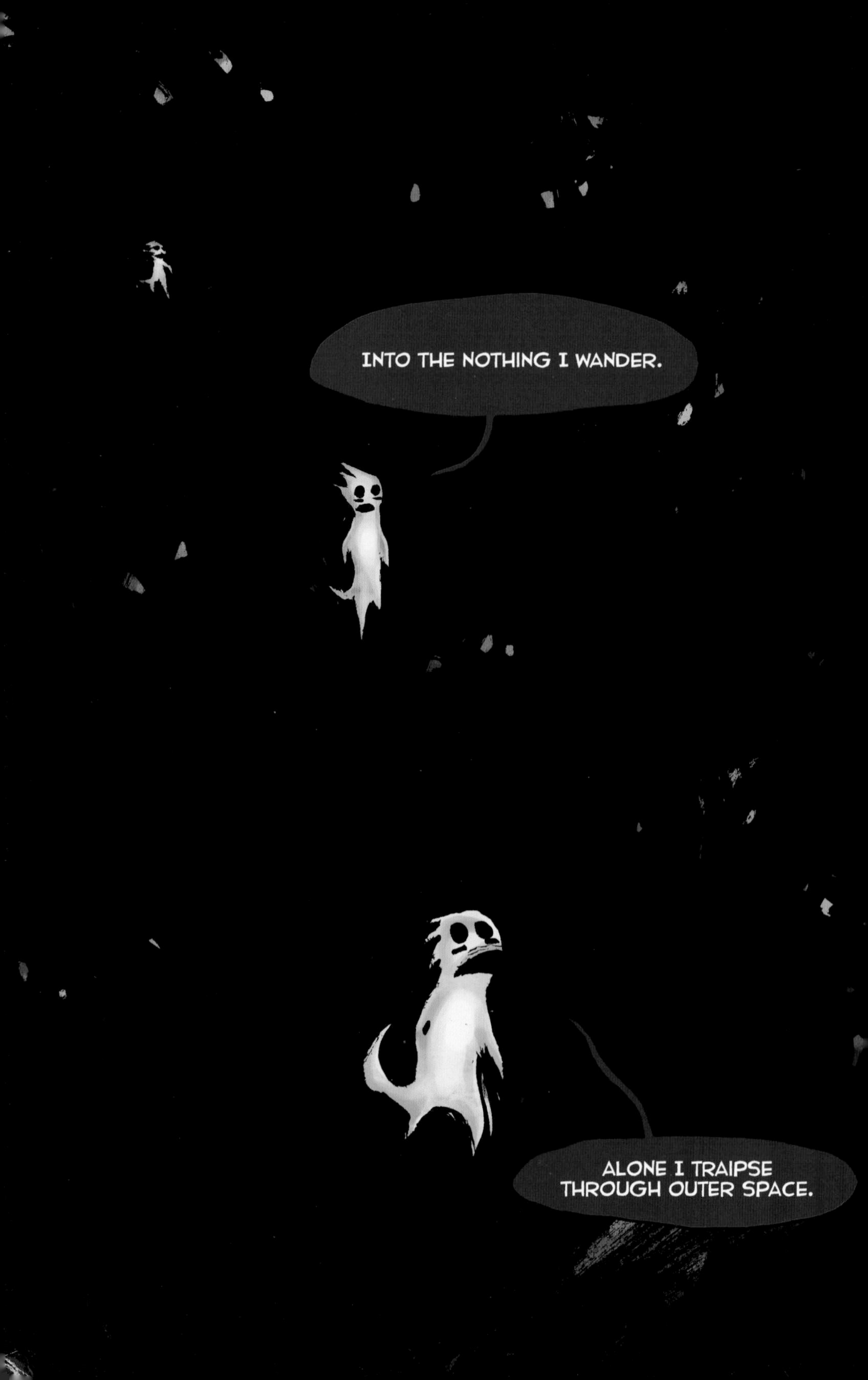
INTO THE NOTHING I WANDER.
ALONE I TRAIPSE THROUGH OUTER SPACE.

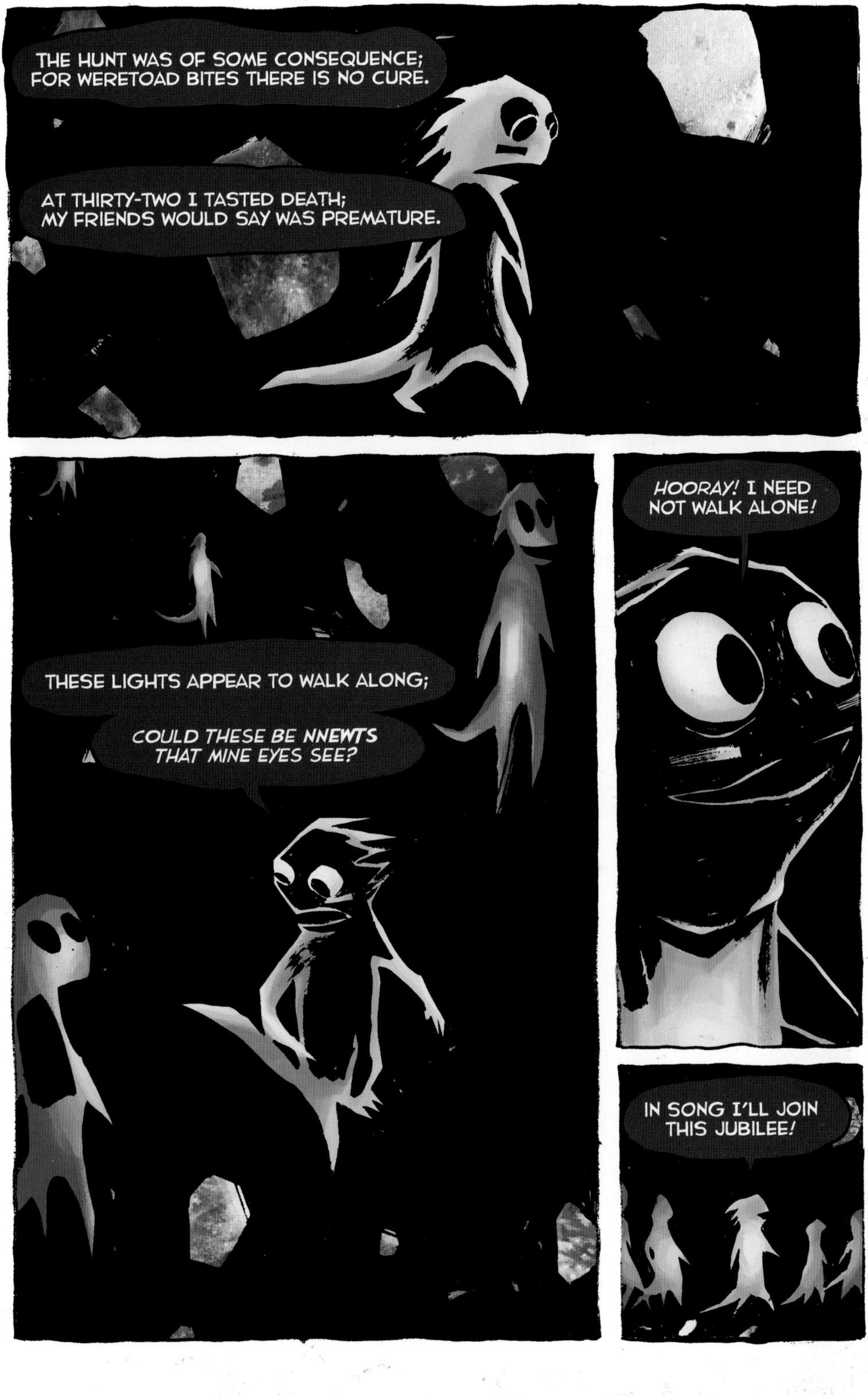
THE HUNT WAS OF SOME CONSEQUENCE;
FOR WERETOAD BITES THERE IS NO CURE.
AT THIRTY-TWO I TASTED DEATH;
MY FRIENDS WOULD SAY WAS PREMATURE.
THESE LIGHTS APPEAR TO WALK ALONG;
COULD THESE BE NNEWTS THAT MINE EYES SEE?
HOORAY! I NEED NOT WALK ALONE!
IN SONG I'LL JOIN THIS JUBILEE!

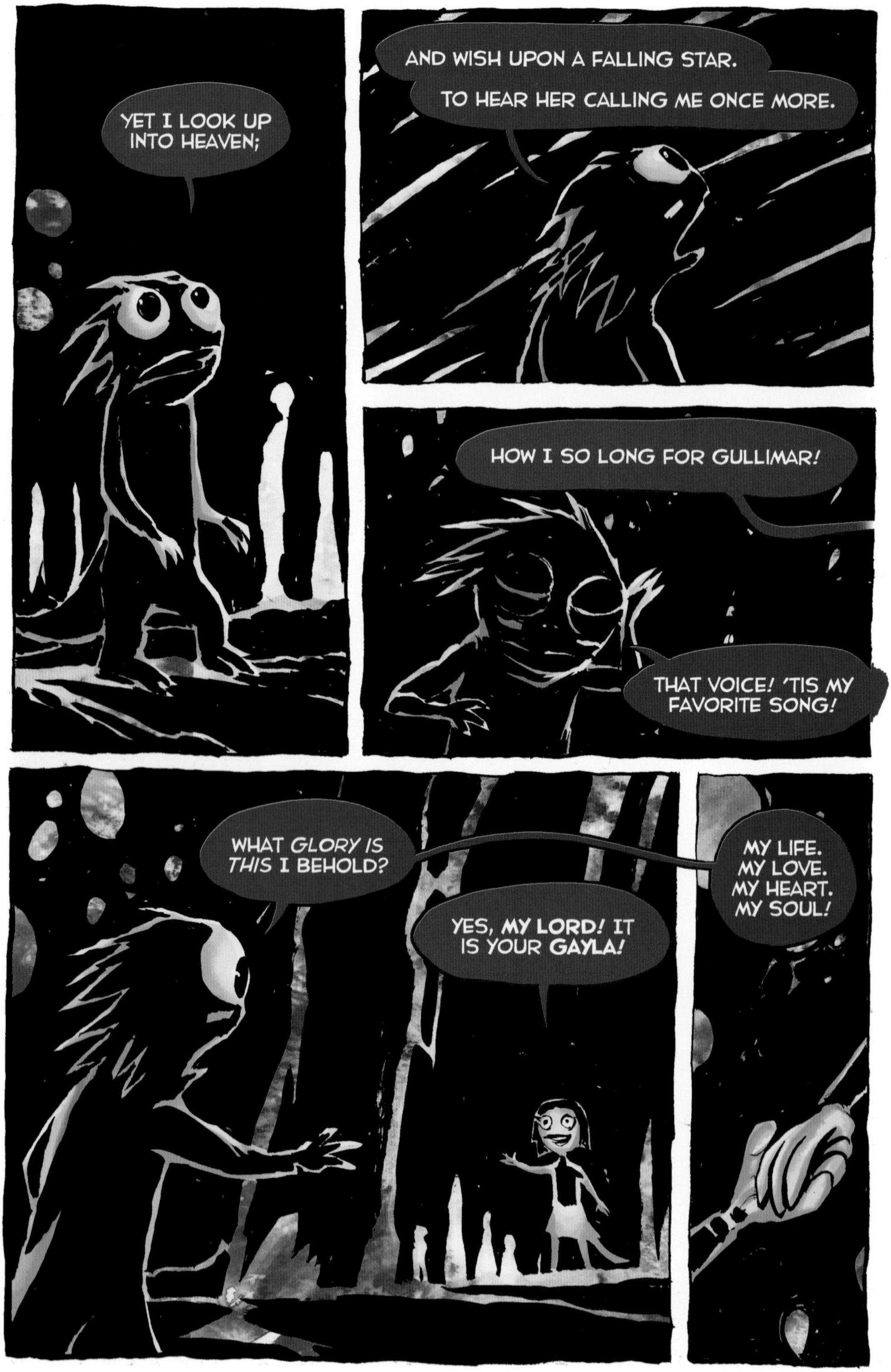
YET I LOOK UP INTO HEAVEN;
AND WISH UPON A FALLING STAR.
TO HEAR HER CALLING ME ONCE MORE.
HOW I SO LONG FOR GULLIMAR!
THAT VOICE! 'TIS MY FAVORITE SONG!
WHAT GLORY IS THIS I BEHOLD?
MY LIFE. MY LOVE. MY HEART. MY SOUL!
YES, MY LORD! IT IS YOUR GAYLA!

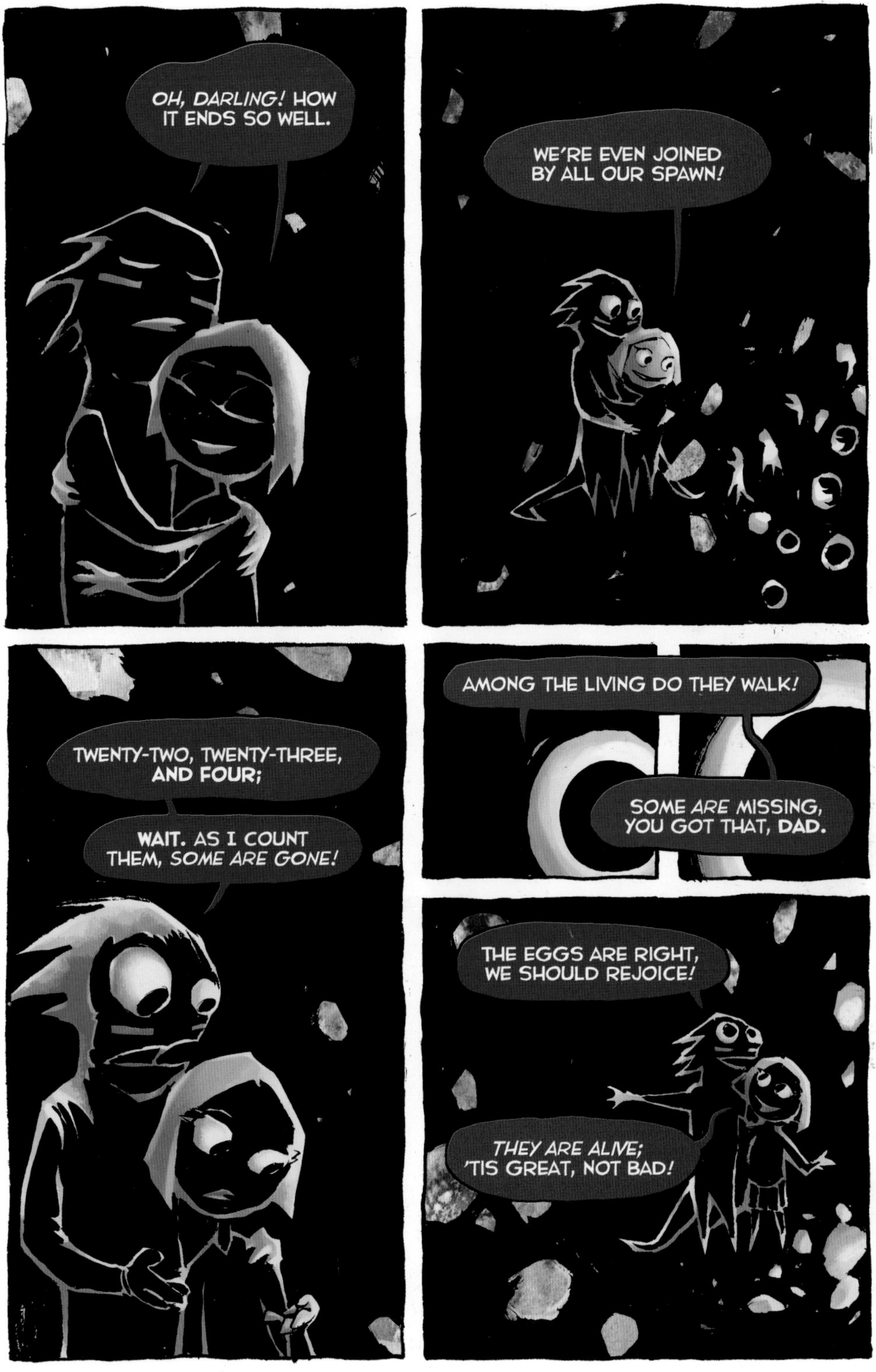
OH, *DARLING!* HOW IT ENDS SO WELL.
WE'RE EVEN JOINED BY ALL OUR SPAWN!
TWENTY-TWO, TWENTY-THREE, **AND FOUR;**
WAIT. AS I COUNT THEM, *SOME ARE GONE!*
AMONG THE LIVING DO THEY WALK!
SOME *ARE* MISSING, YOU GOT THAT, **DAD.**
THE EGGS ARE RIGHT, WE SHOULD REJOICE!
THEY ARE ALIVE; 'TIS GREAT, NOT BAD!

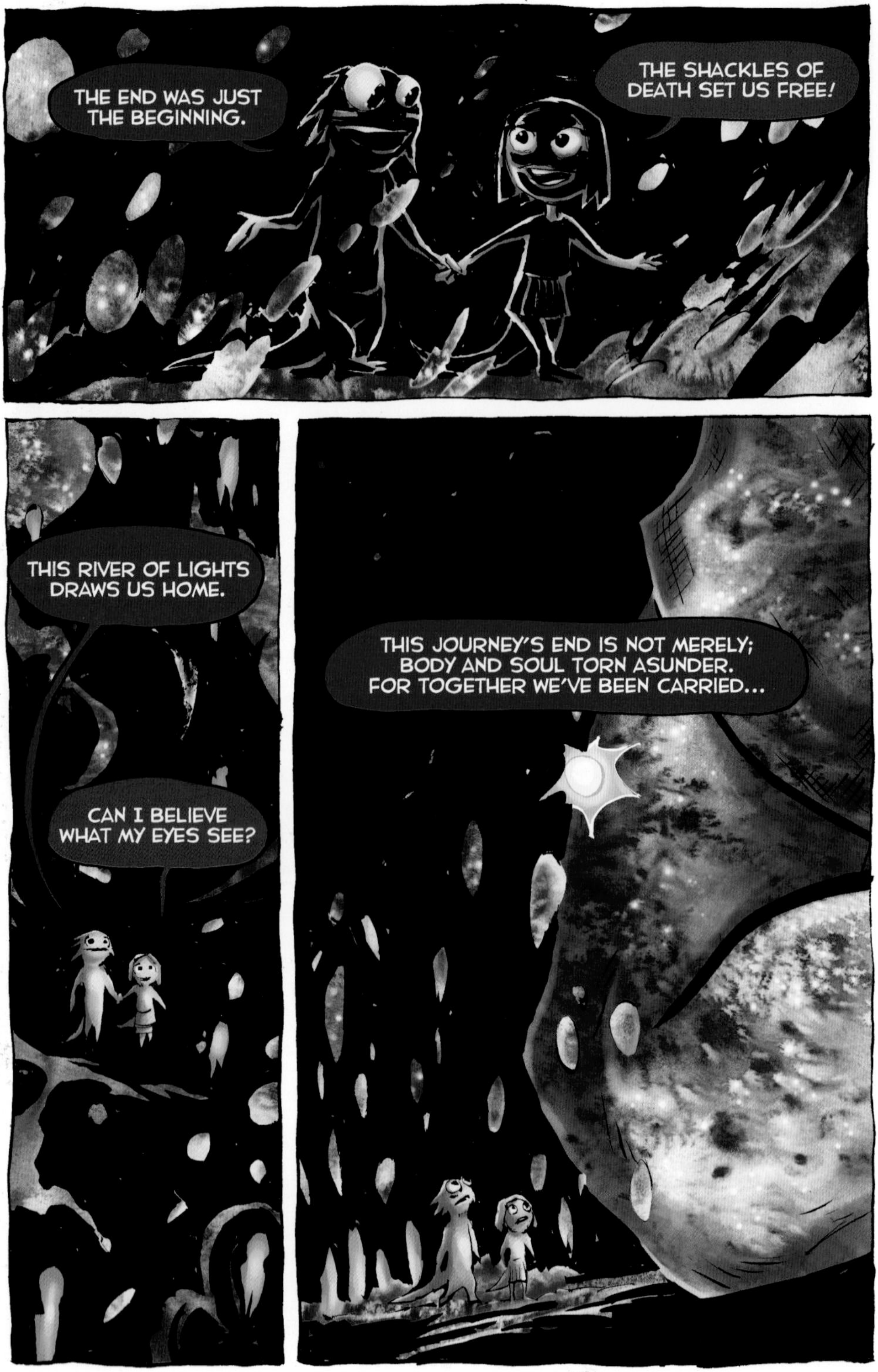
THE END WAS JUST THE BEGINNING.
THE SHACKLES OF DEATH SET US FREE!
THIS RIVER OF LIGHTS DRAWS US HOME.
CAN I BELIEVE WHAT MY EYES SEE?
THIS JOURNEY'S END IS NOT MERELY; BODY AND SOUL TORN ASUNDER. FOR TOGETHER WE'VE BEEN CARRIED...

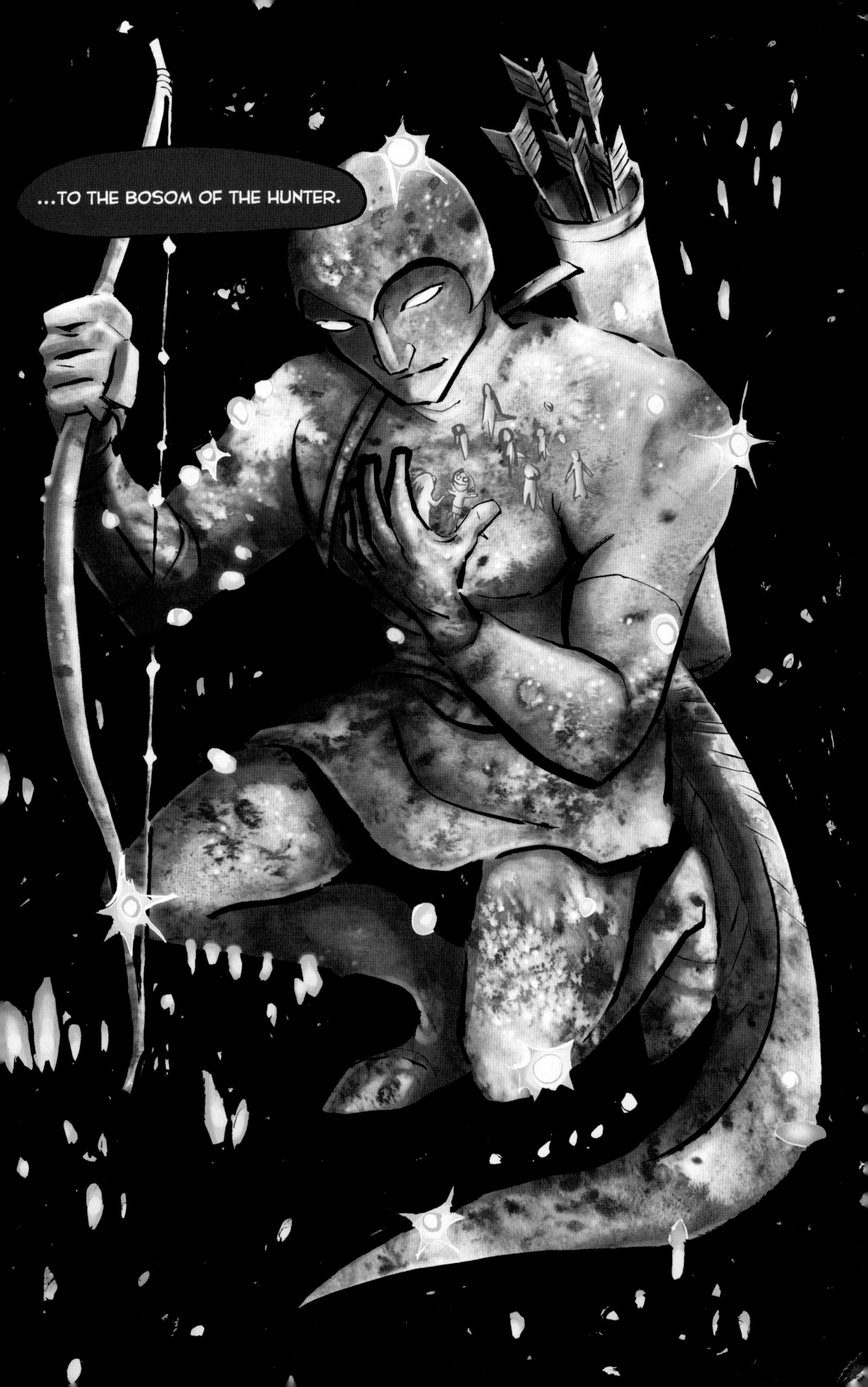
...TO THE BOSOM OF THE HUNTER.

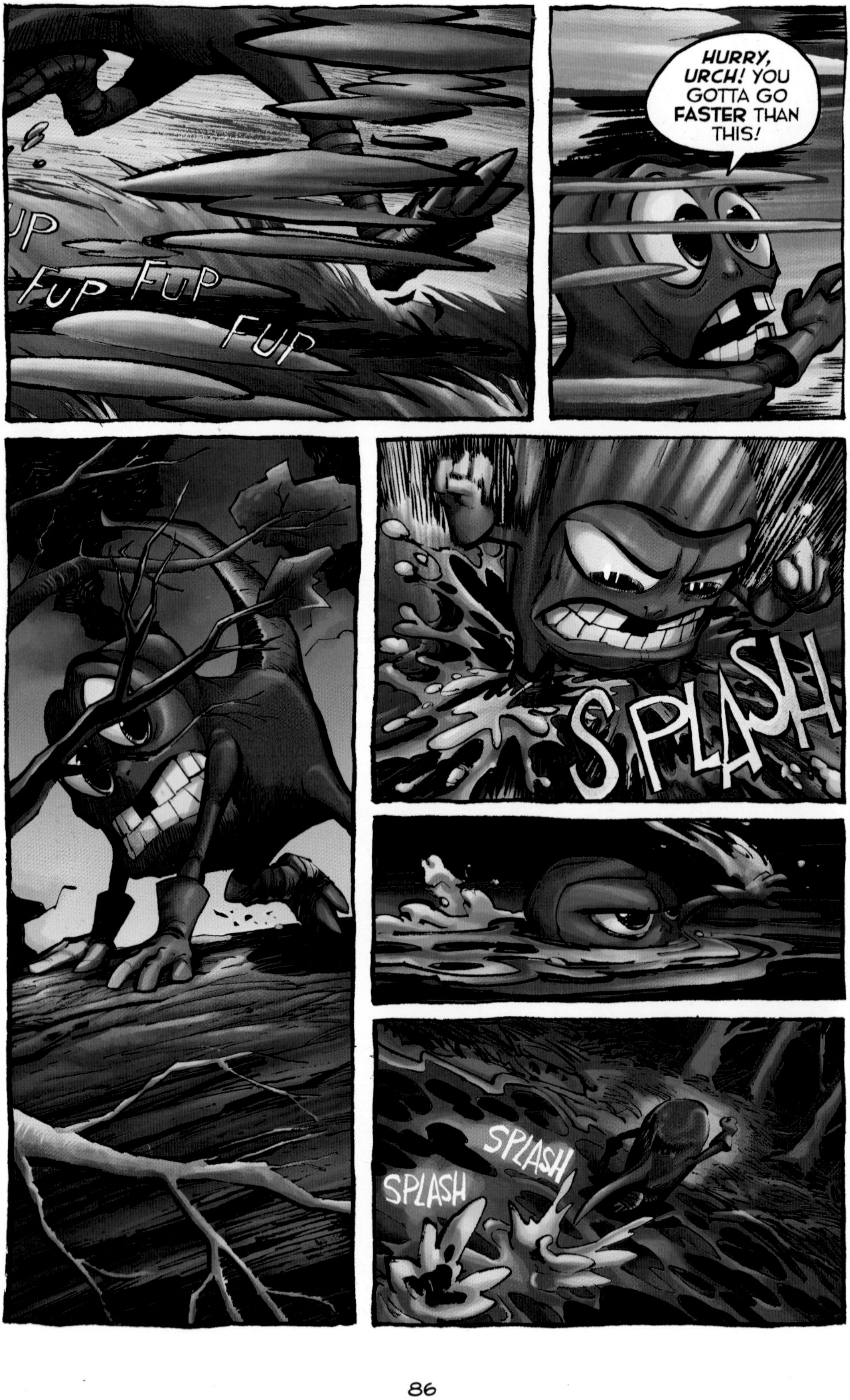
FUP
FUP FUP
FUP
HURRY, URCH! YOU GOTTA GO FASTER THAN THIS!
SPLASH
SPLASH
SPLASH

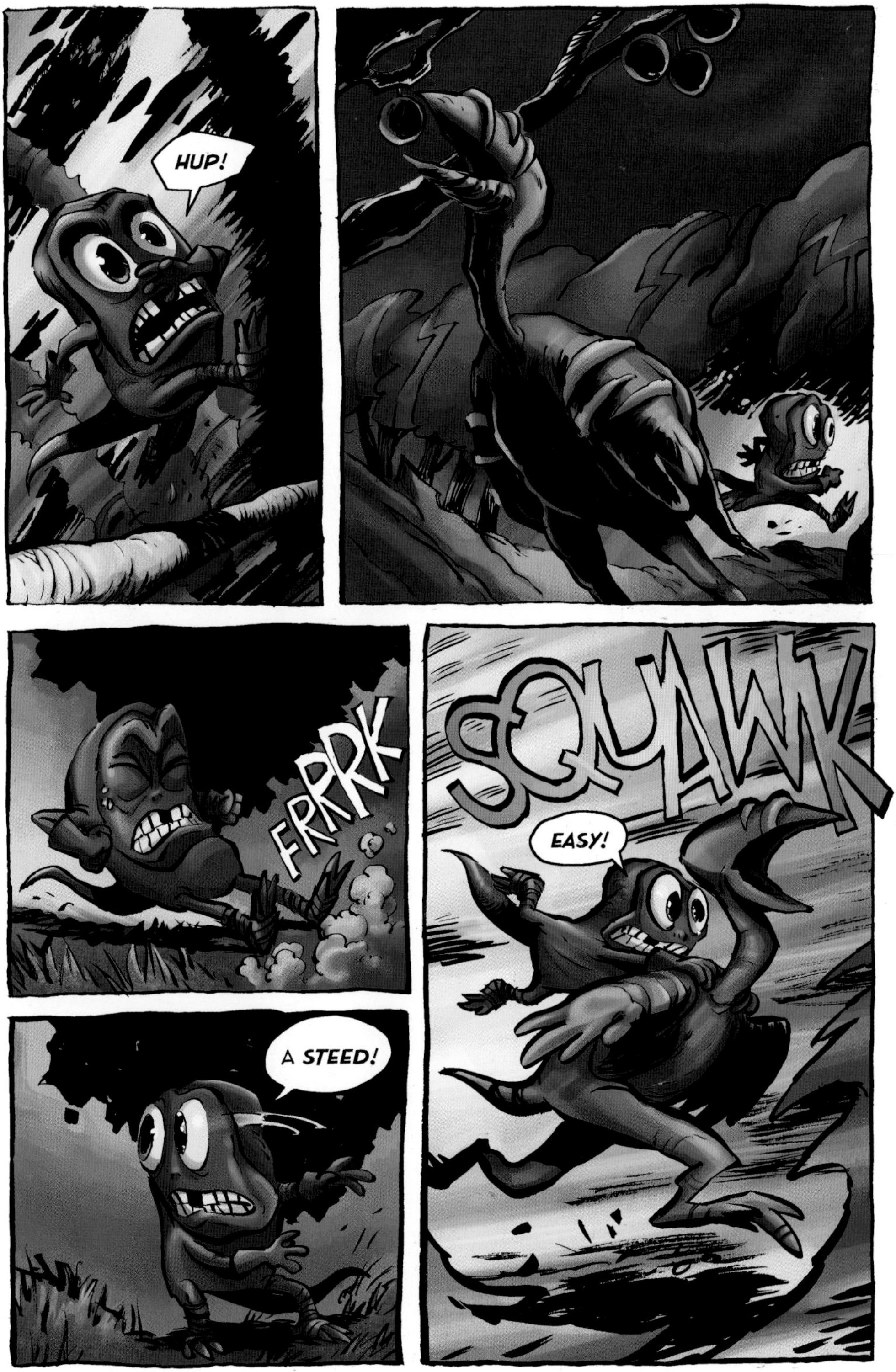
HUP!
FRRRK
A STEED!
SQUAWK
EASY!

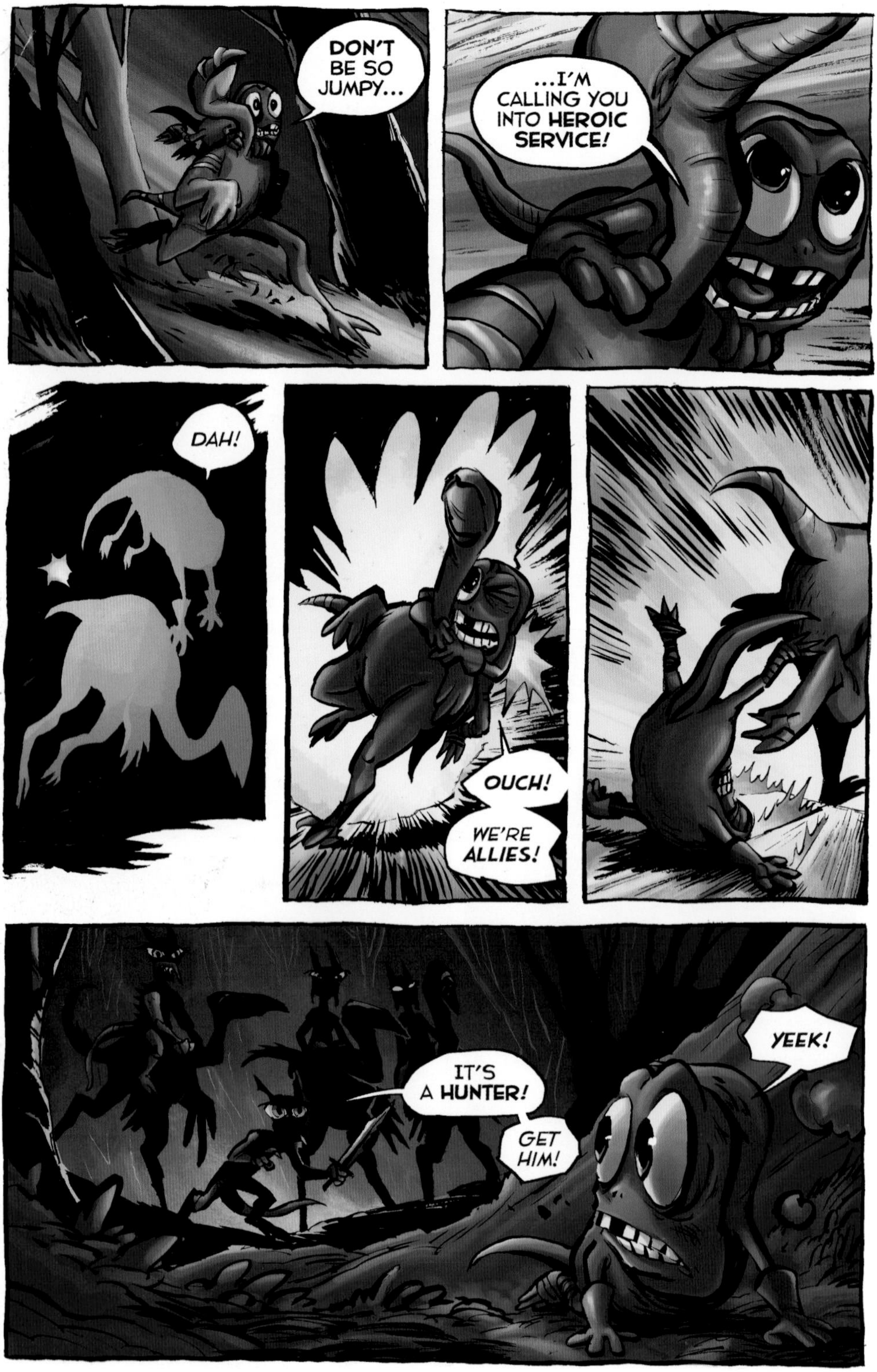
DON'T BE SO JUMPY...
...I'M CALLING YOU INTO HEROIC SERVICE!
DAH!
OUCH!
WE'RE ALLIES!
IT'S A HUNTER!
GET HIM!
YEEK!

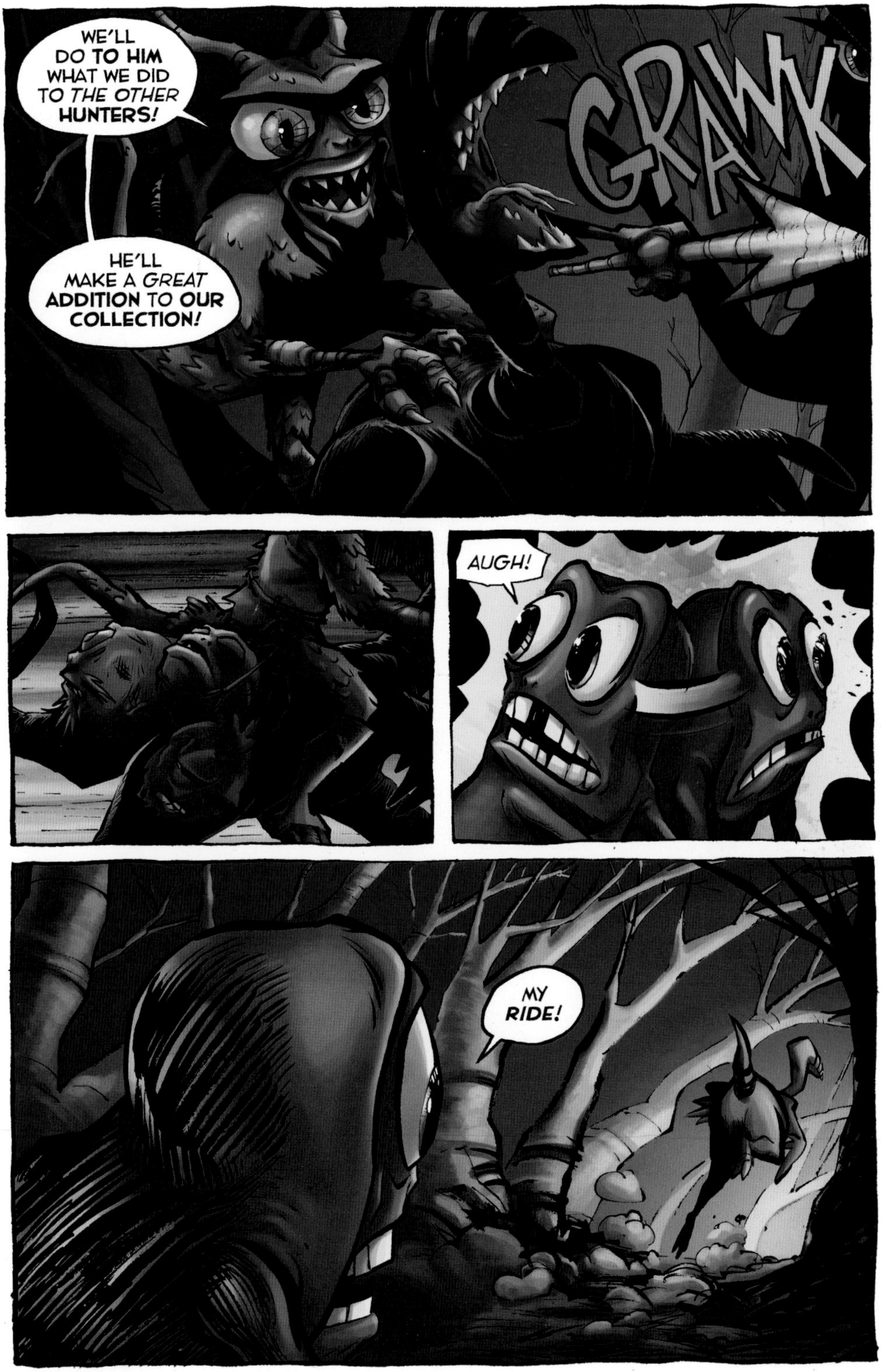
WE'LL DO TO HIM WHAT WE DID TO *THE OTHER* **HUNTERS!**
HE'LL MAKE A *GREAT* **ADDITION** TO **OUR COLLECTION!**
GRAWK
AUGH!
MY **RIDE!**

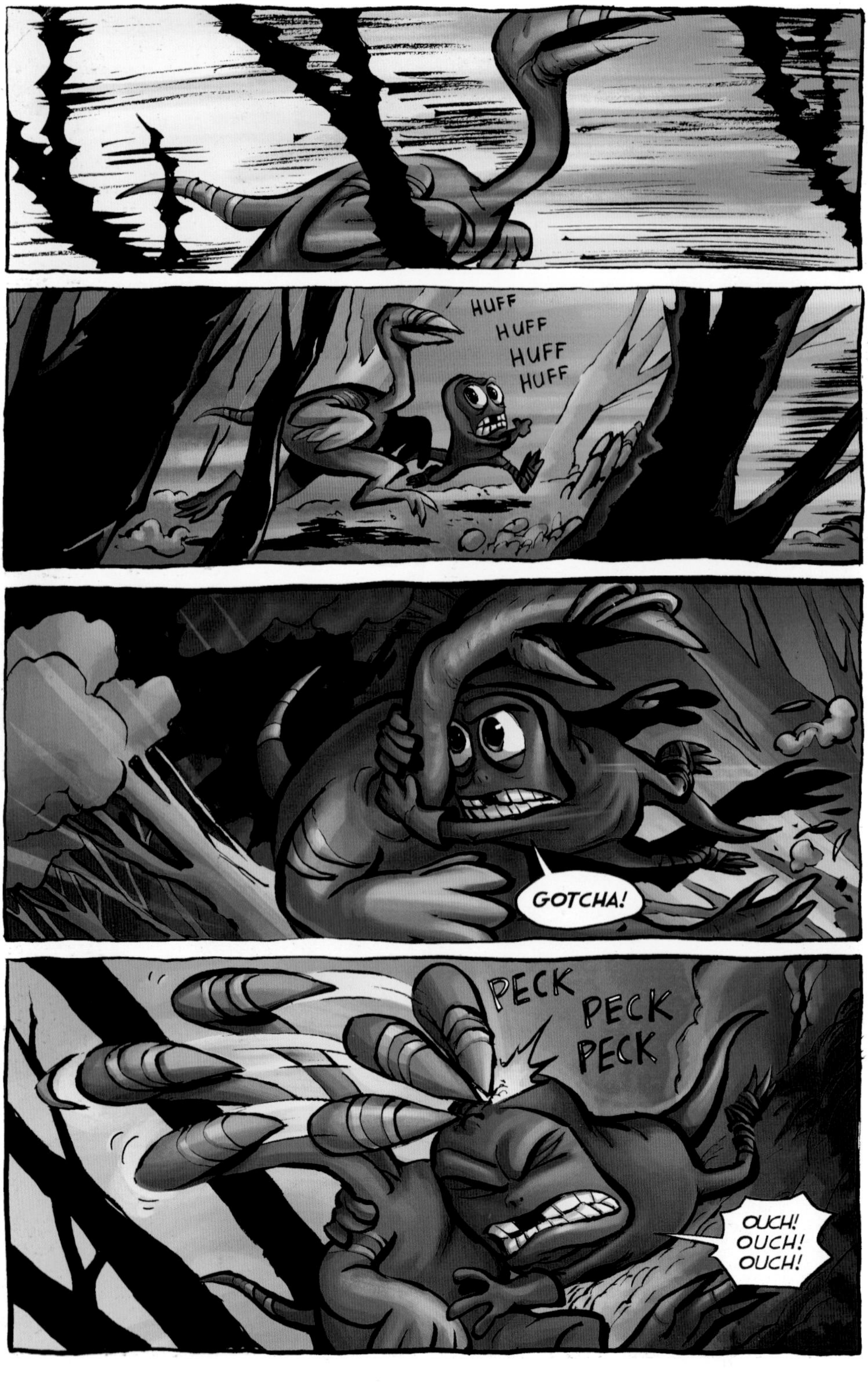
HUFF
HUFF
HUFF
HUFF
GOTCHA!
PECK
PECK
PECK
OUCH!
OUCH!
OUCH!

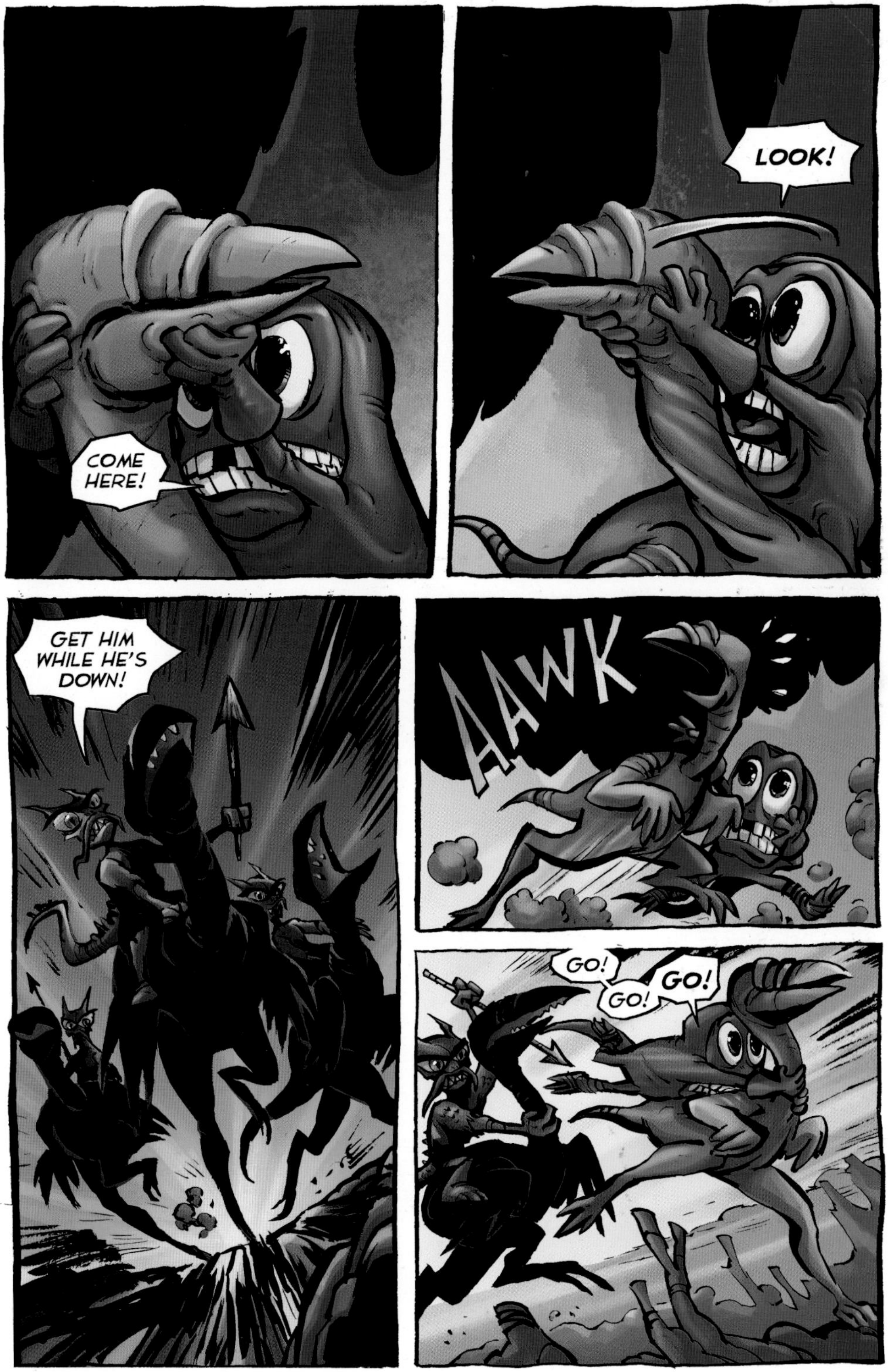
COME HERE!
LOOK!
GET HIM WHILE HE'S DOWN!
AAWK
GO!
GO!
GO!

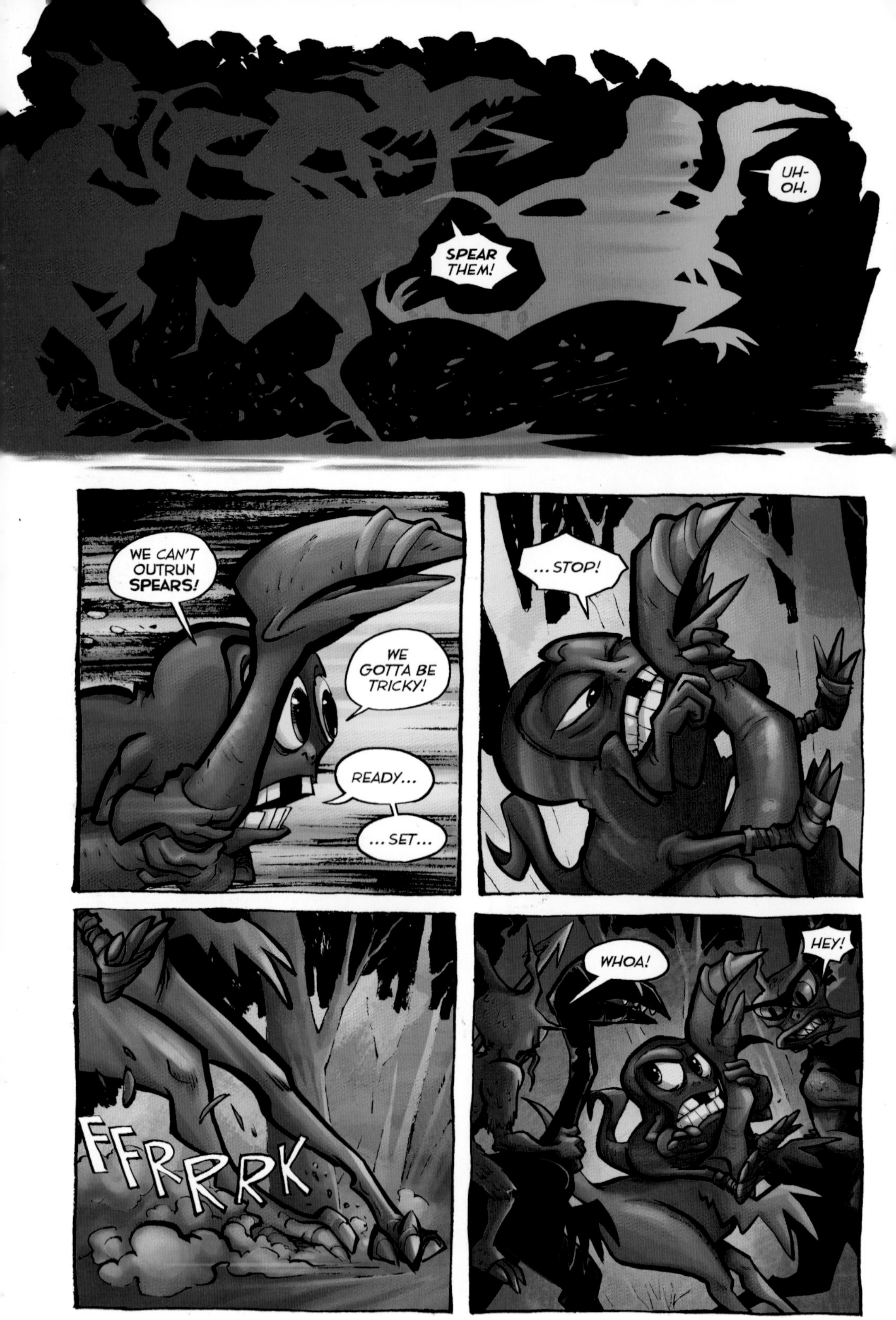
SPEAR THEM!
UH-OH.
WE CAN'T OUTRUN SPEARS!
WE GOTTA BE TRICKY!
READY...
...SET...
...STOP!
FFRRRK
WHOA!
HEY!

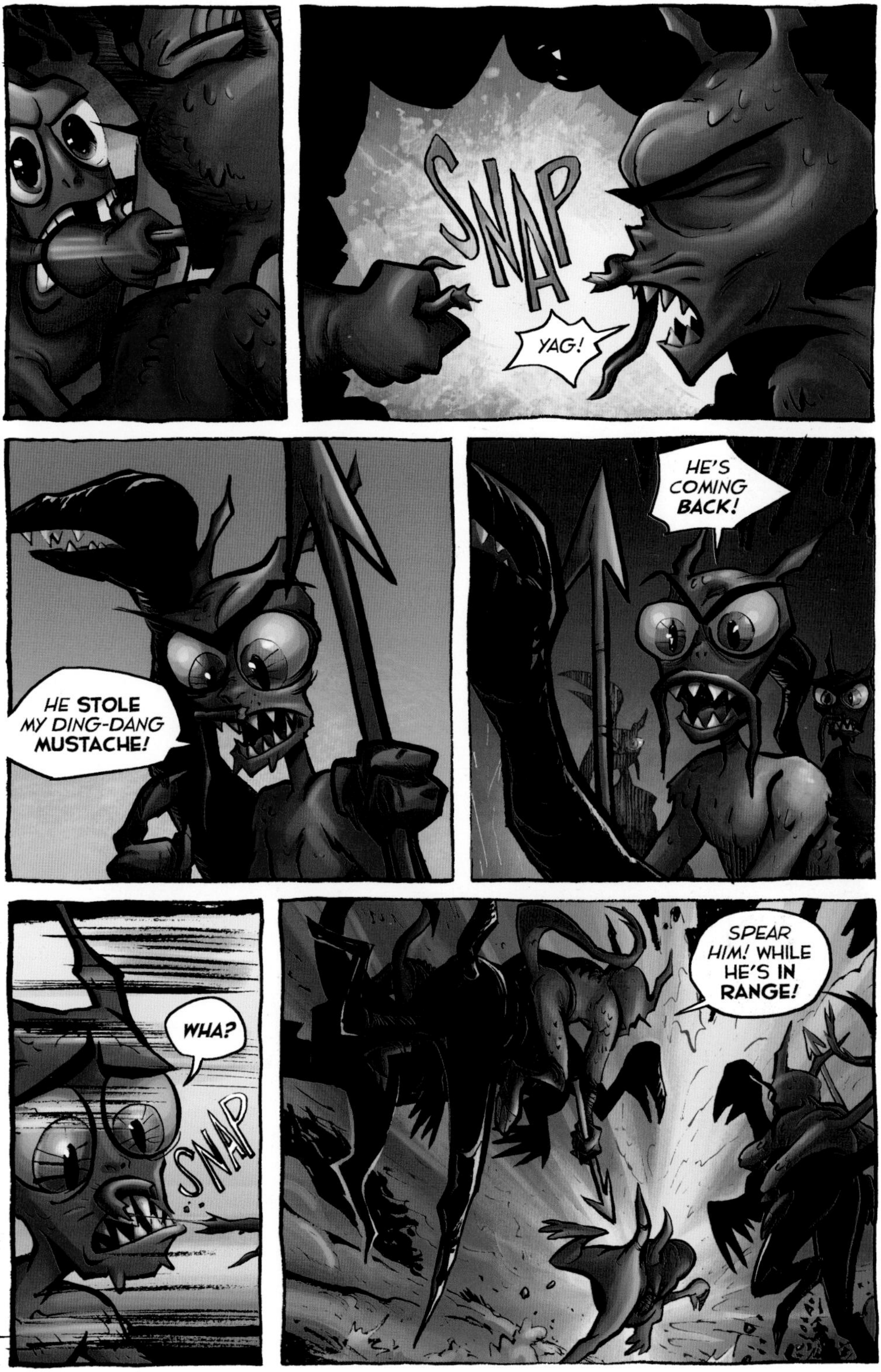
SNAP
YAG!
HE STOLE MY DING-DANG MUSTACHE!
HE'S COMING BACK!
WHA?
SNAP
SPEAR HIM! WHILE HE'S IN RANGE!

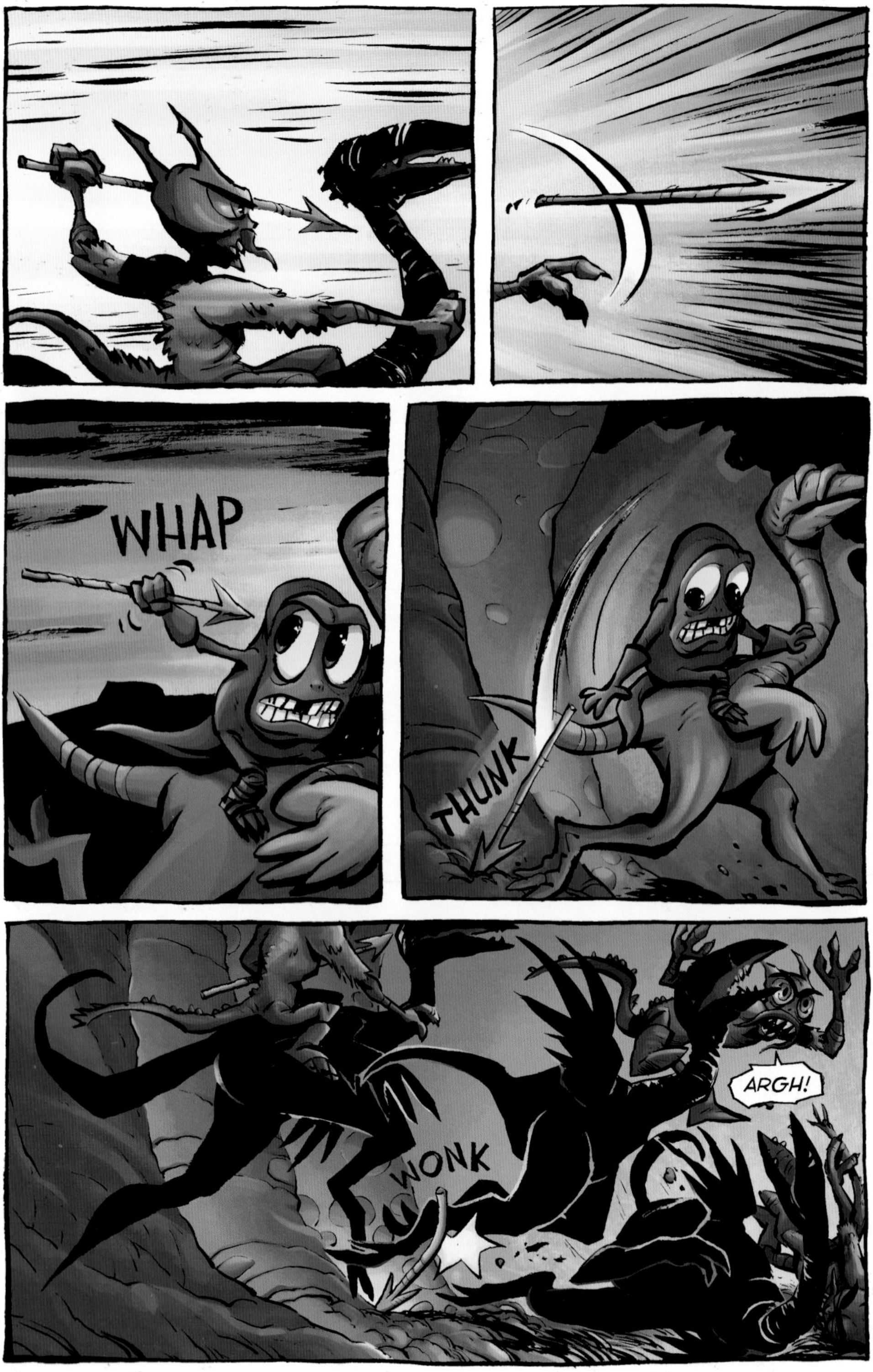
WHAP
THUNK
ARGH!
WONK

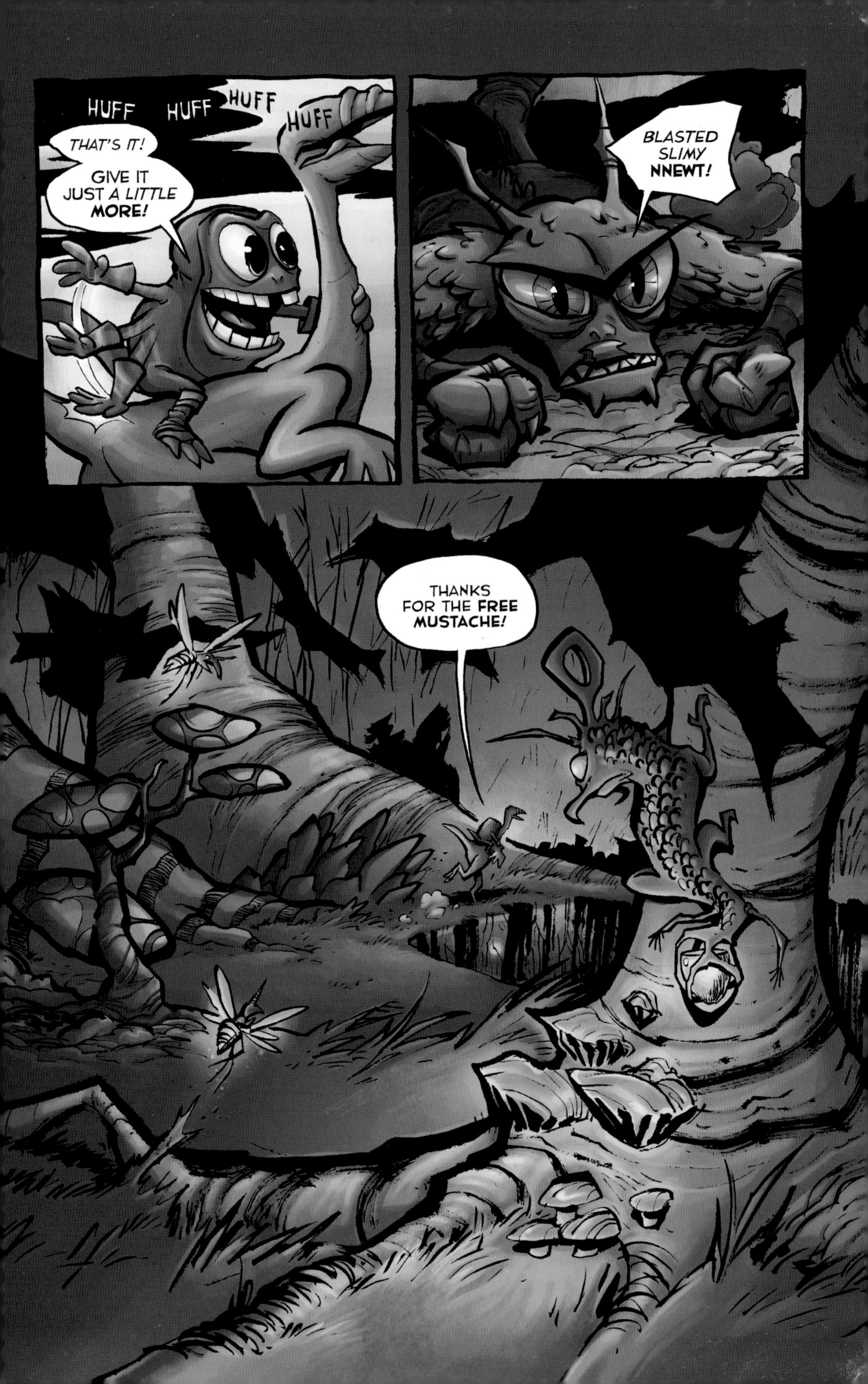
HUFF HUFF HUFF HUFF
THAT'S IT!
GIVE IT JUST A LITTLE MORE!
BLASTED SLIMY NNEWT!
THANKS FOR THE FREE MUSTACHE!

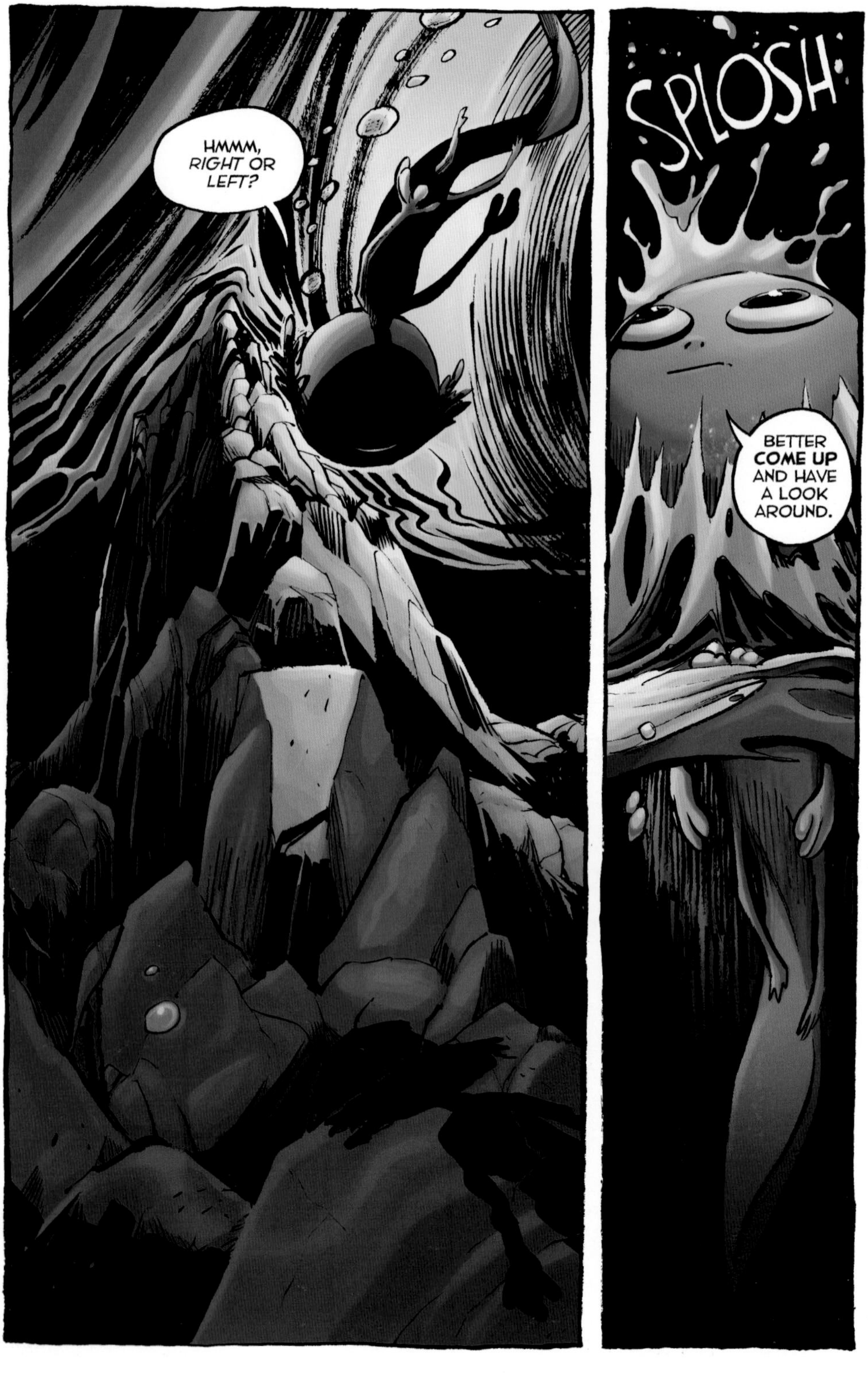
HMMM, RIGHT OR LEFT?
SPLOSH
BETTER **COME UP** AND HAVE A LOOK AROUND.

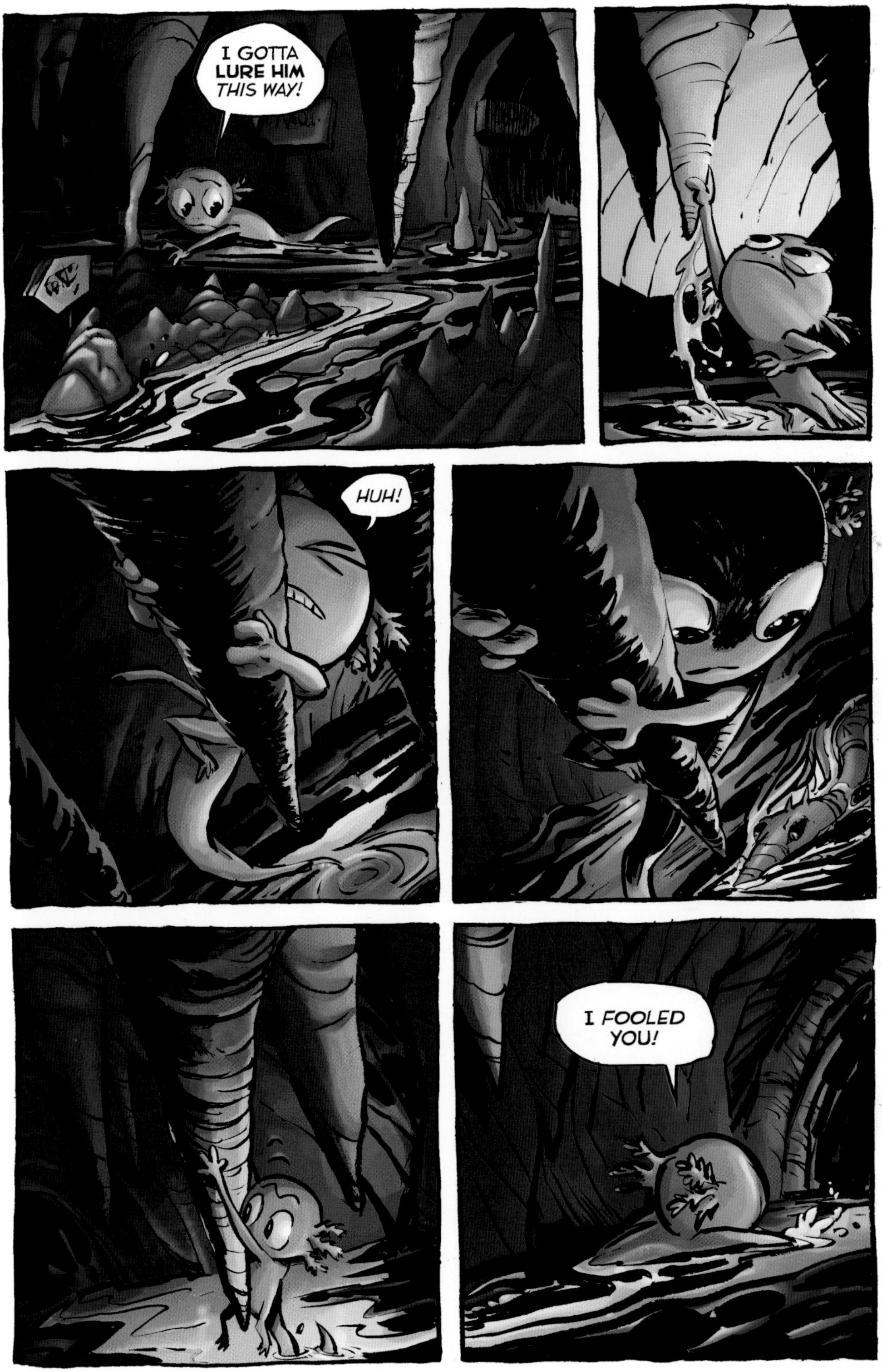
I GOTTA LURE HIM THIS WAY!
HUH!
I FOOLED YOU!

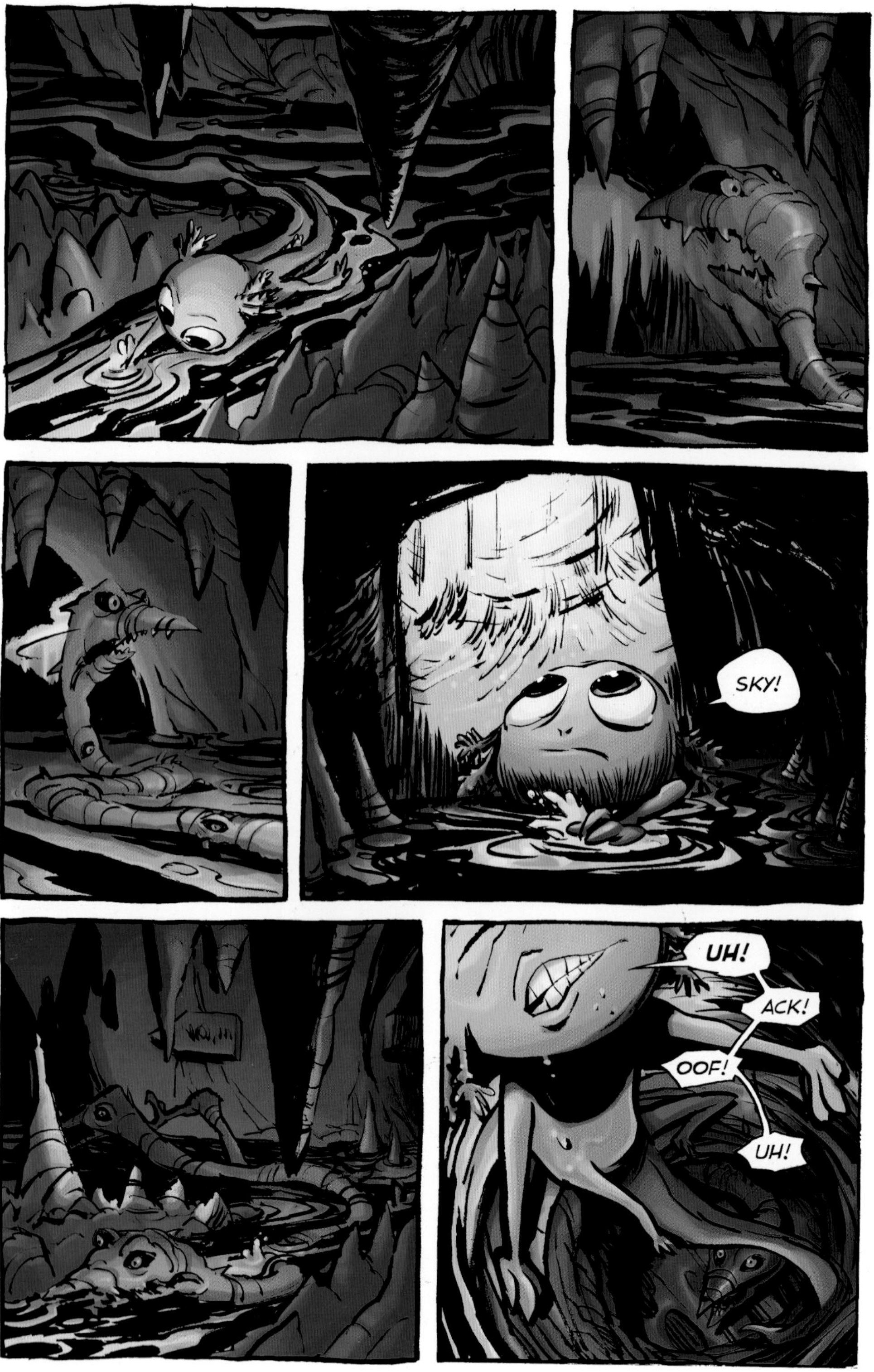
SKY!
UH!
ACK!
OOF!
UH!

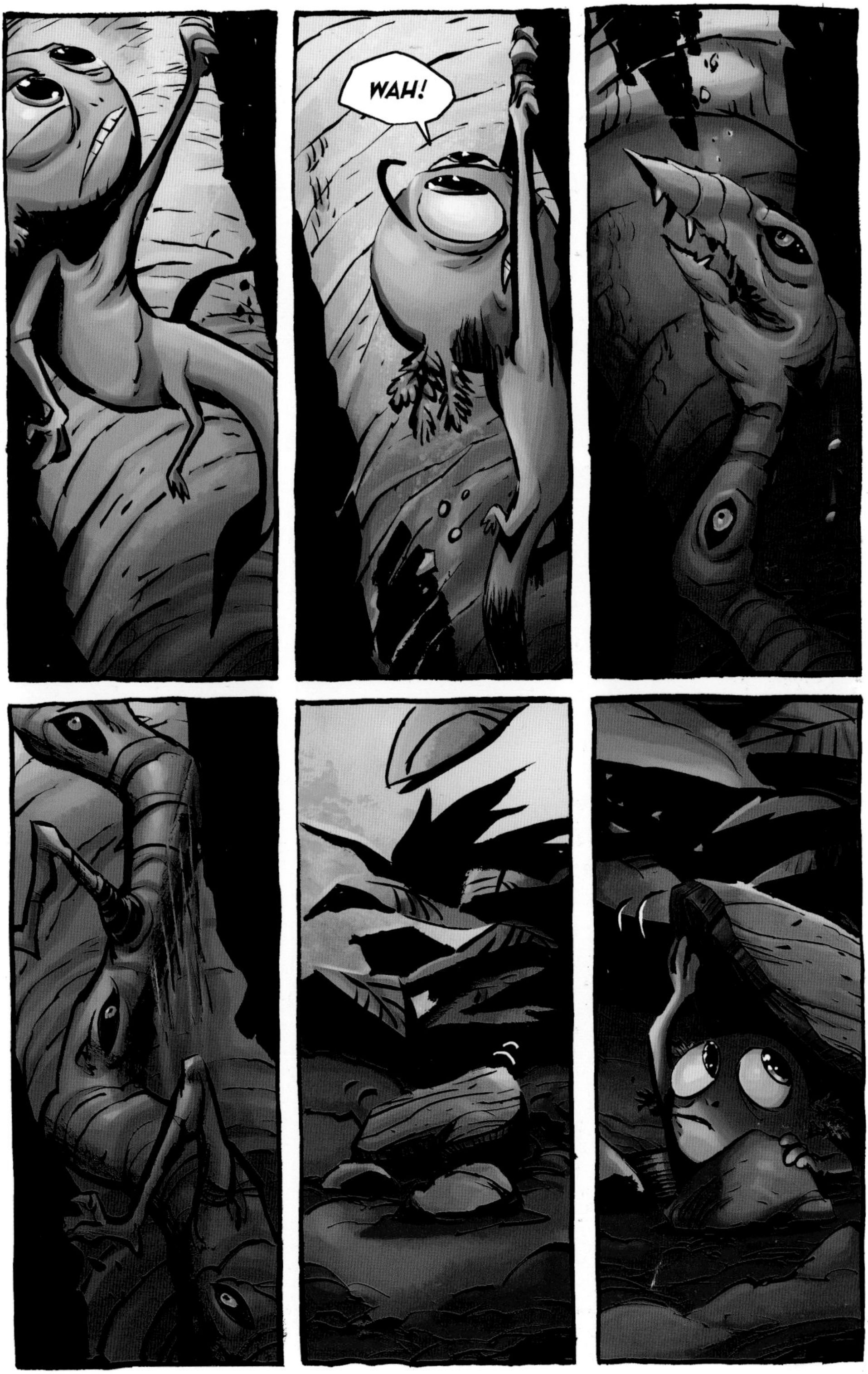
WAH!

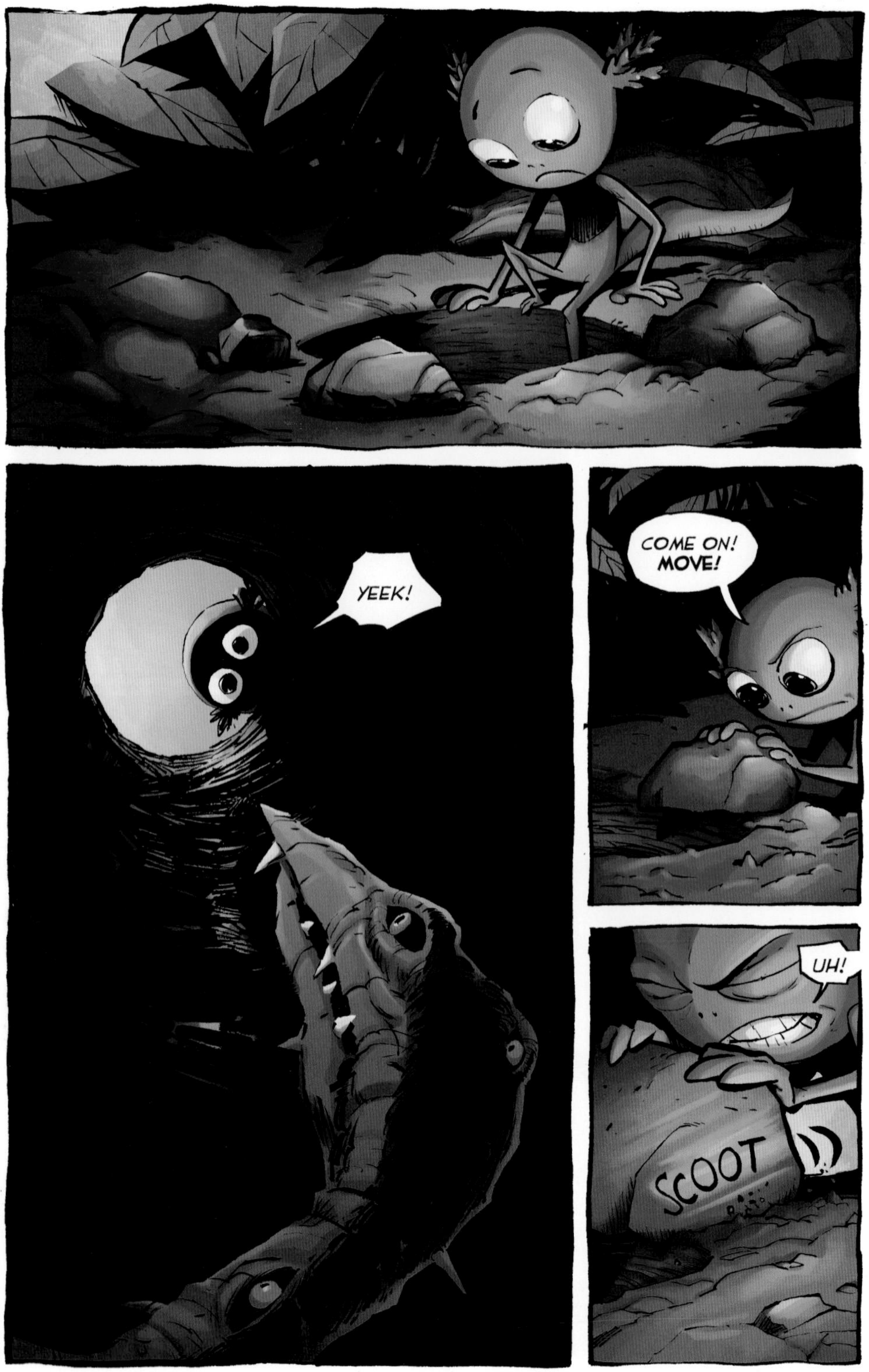
YEEK!
COME ON! MOVE!
UH!
SCOOT

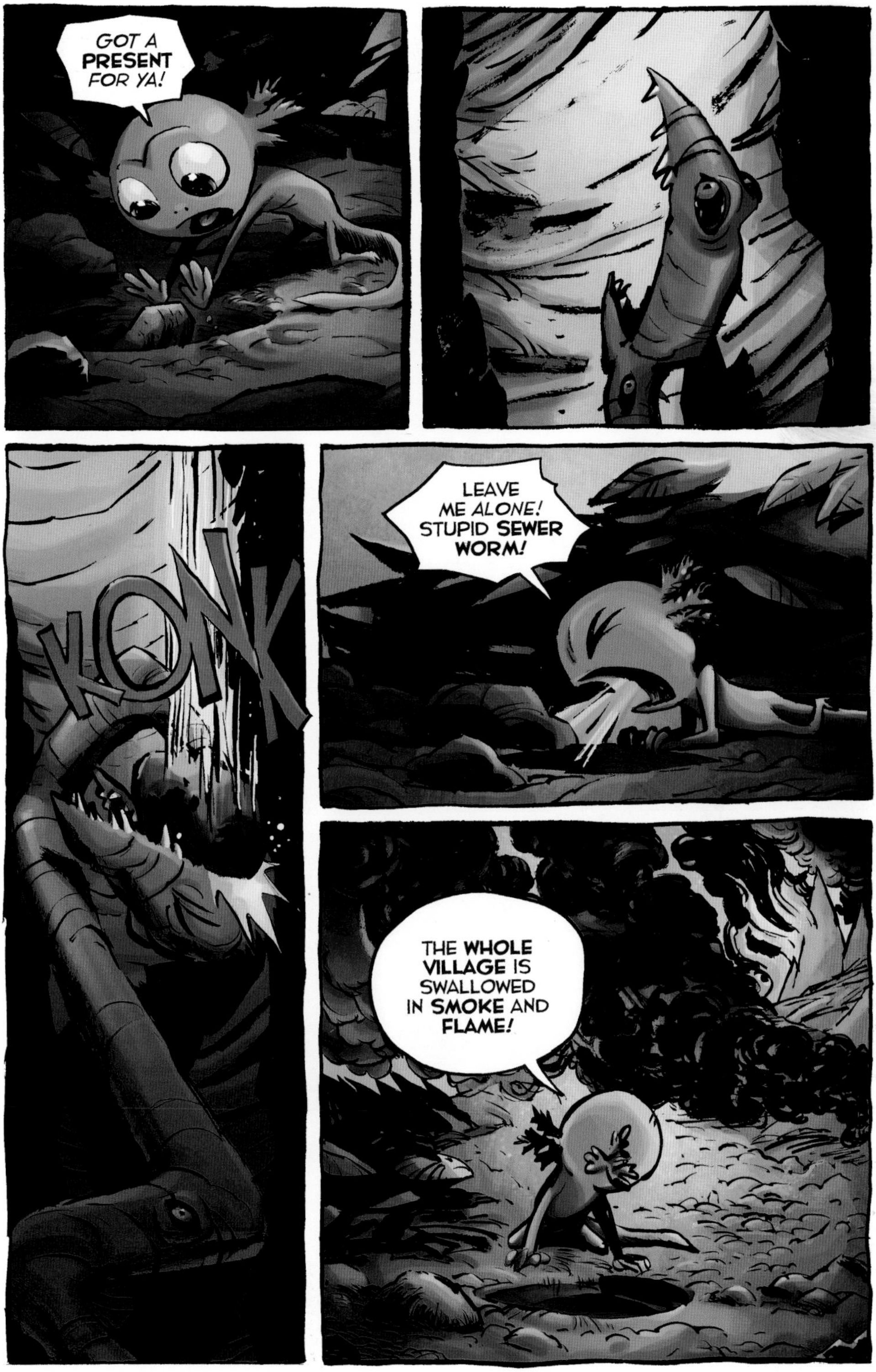
GOT A PRESENT FOR YA!
KONK
LEAVE ME ALONE! STUPID SEWER WORM!
THE WHOLE VILLAGE IS SWALLOWED IN SMOKE AND FLAME!

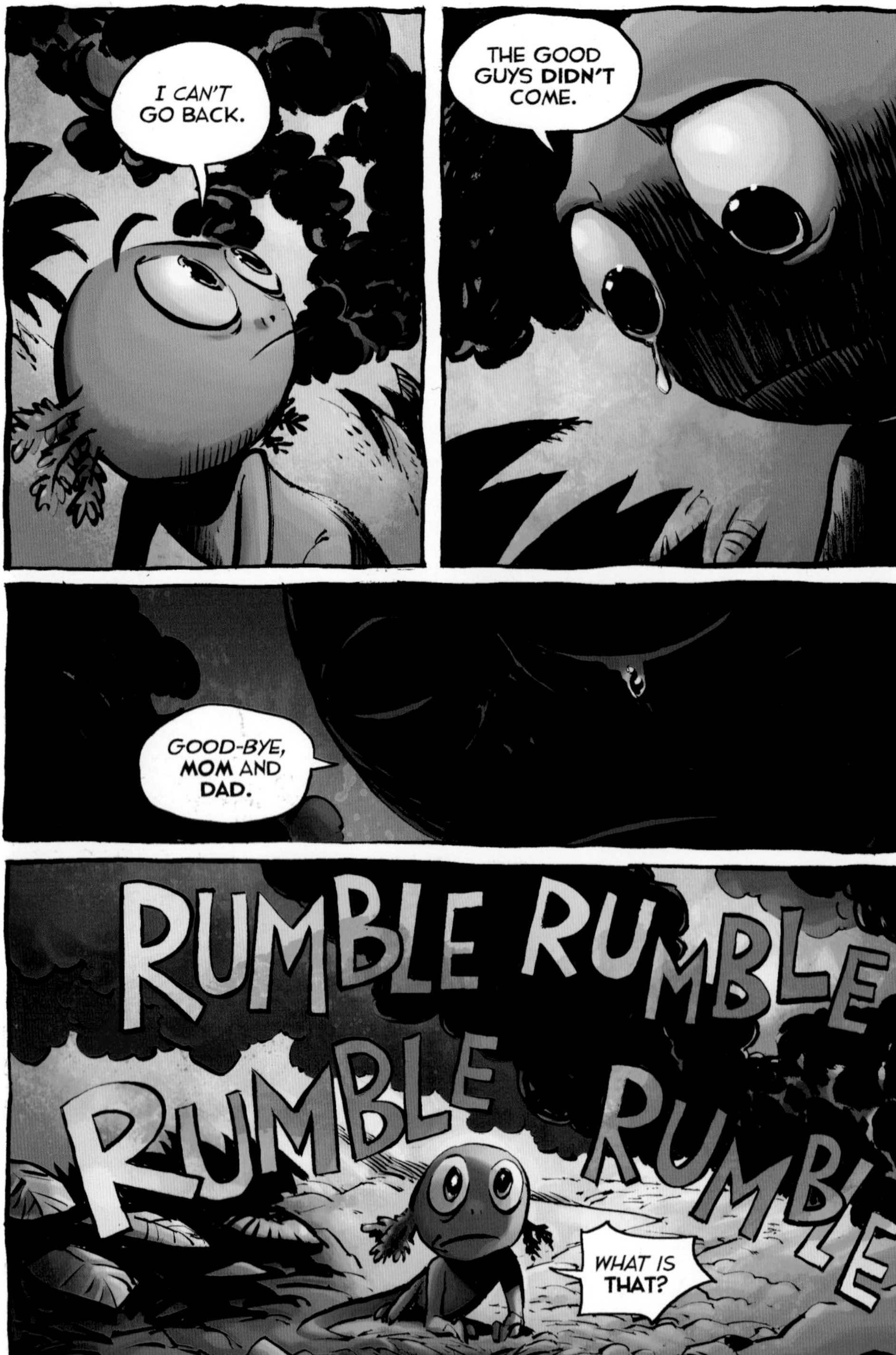
I CAN'T GO BACK.
THE GOOD GUYS DIDN'T COME.
GOOD-BYE, MOM AND DAD.
RUMBLE RUMBLE
RUMBLE RUMBLE
WHAT IS THAT?

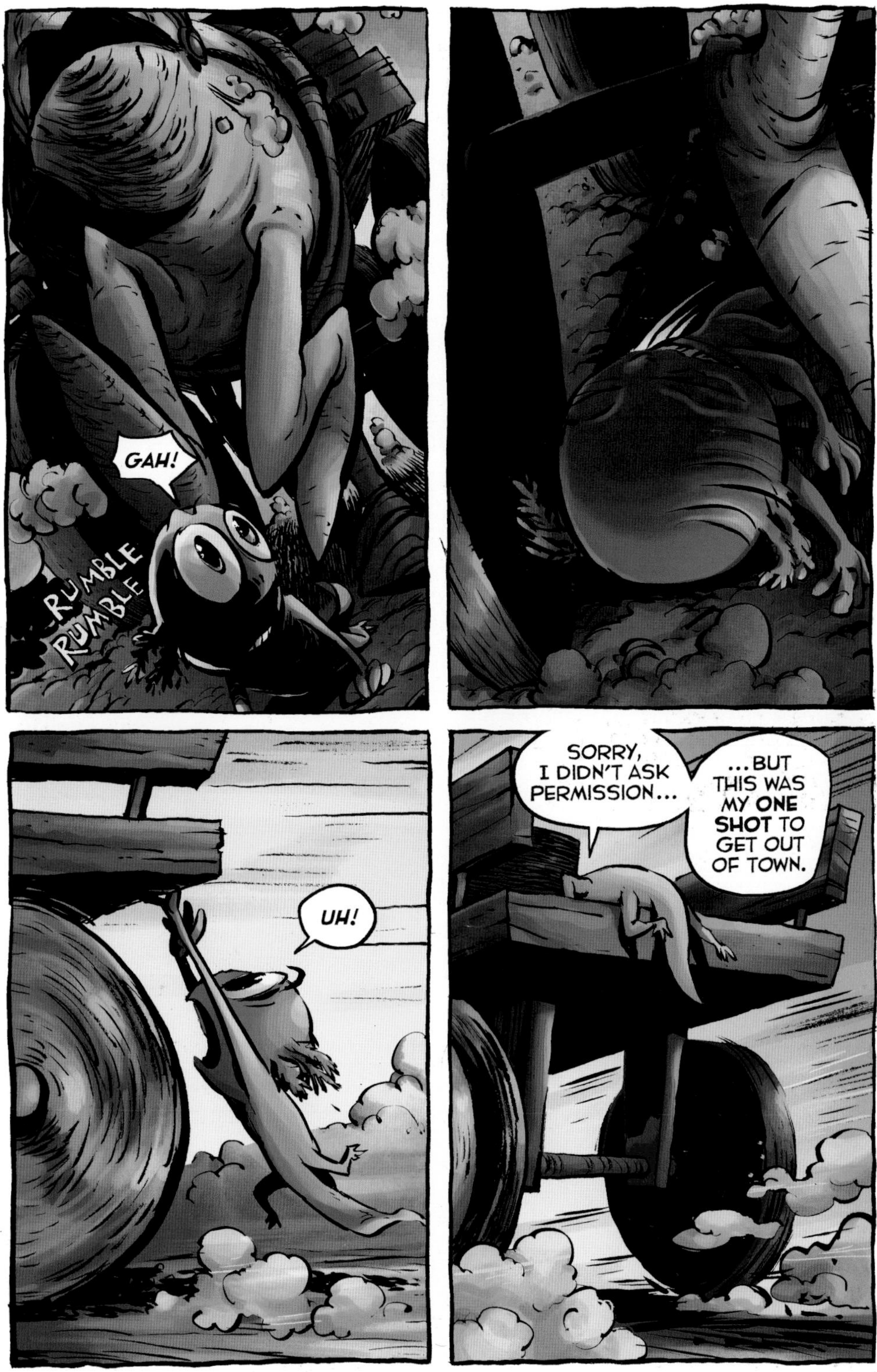
GAH!
RUMBLE RUMBLE
UH!
SORRY, I DIDN'T ASK PERMISSION...
...BUT THIS WAS MY **ONE SHOT** TO GET OUT OF TOWN.

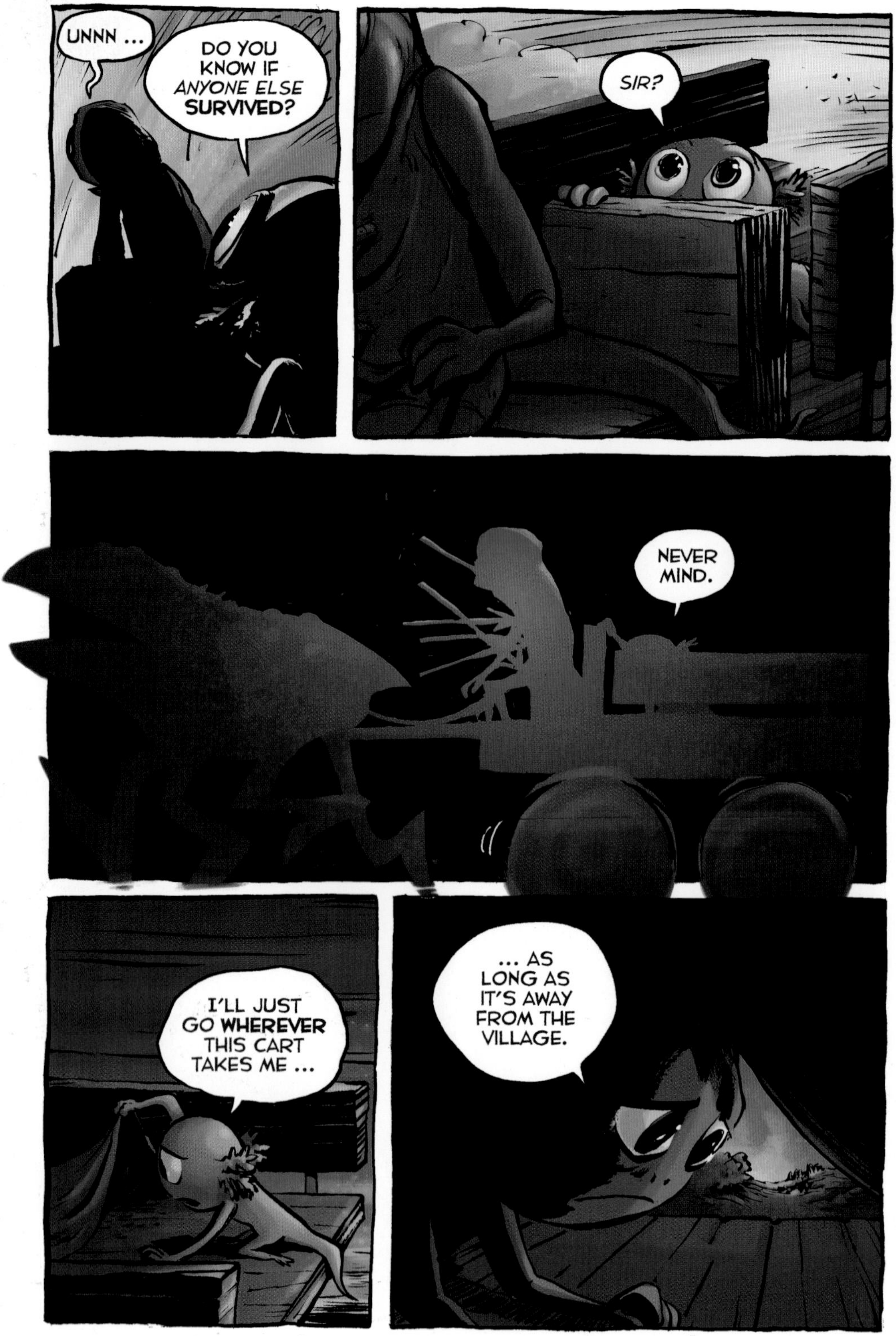
UNNN ...
DO YOU KNOW IF *ANYONE ELSE* **SURVIVED?**
SIR?
NEVER MIND.
I'LL JUST GO **WHEREVER** THIS CART TAKES ME ...
... AS LONG AS IT'S AWAY FROM THE VILLAGE.

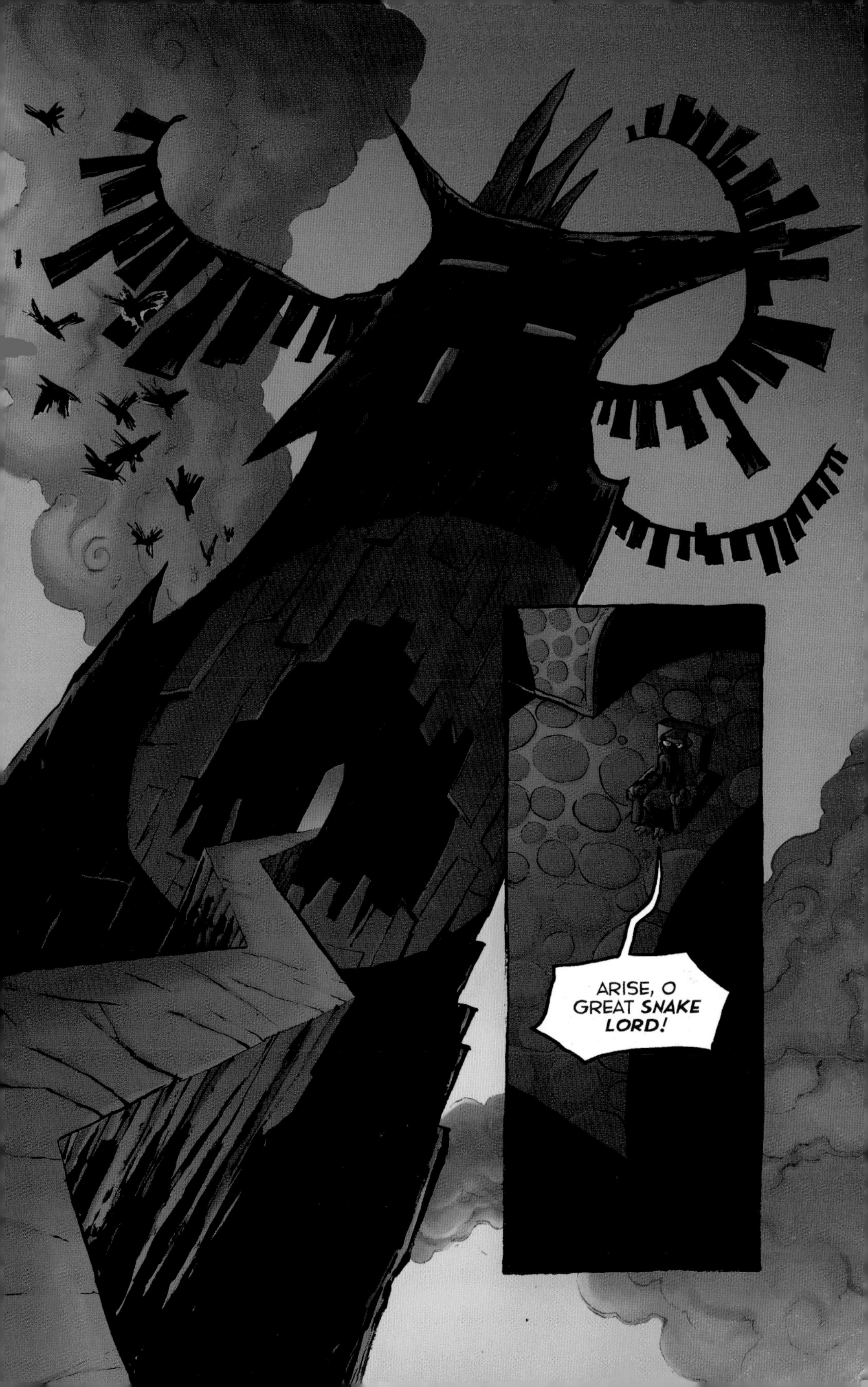
ARISE, O GREAT SNAKE LORD!

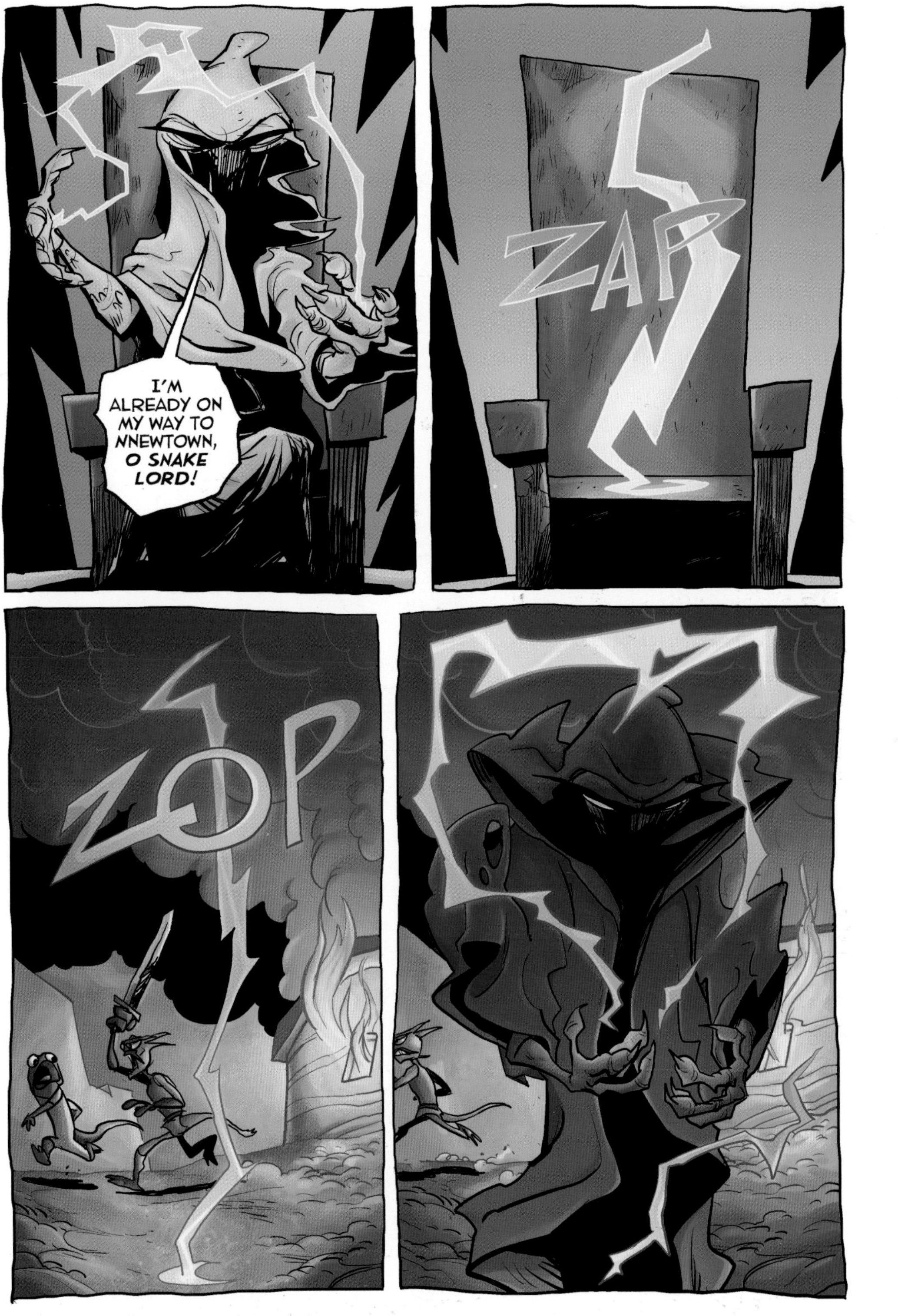
I'M ALREADY ON MY WAY TO NNEWTOWN, O SNAKE LORD!
ZAP
ZOP

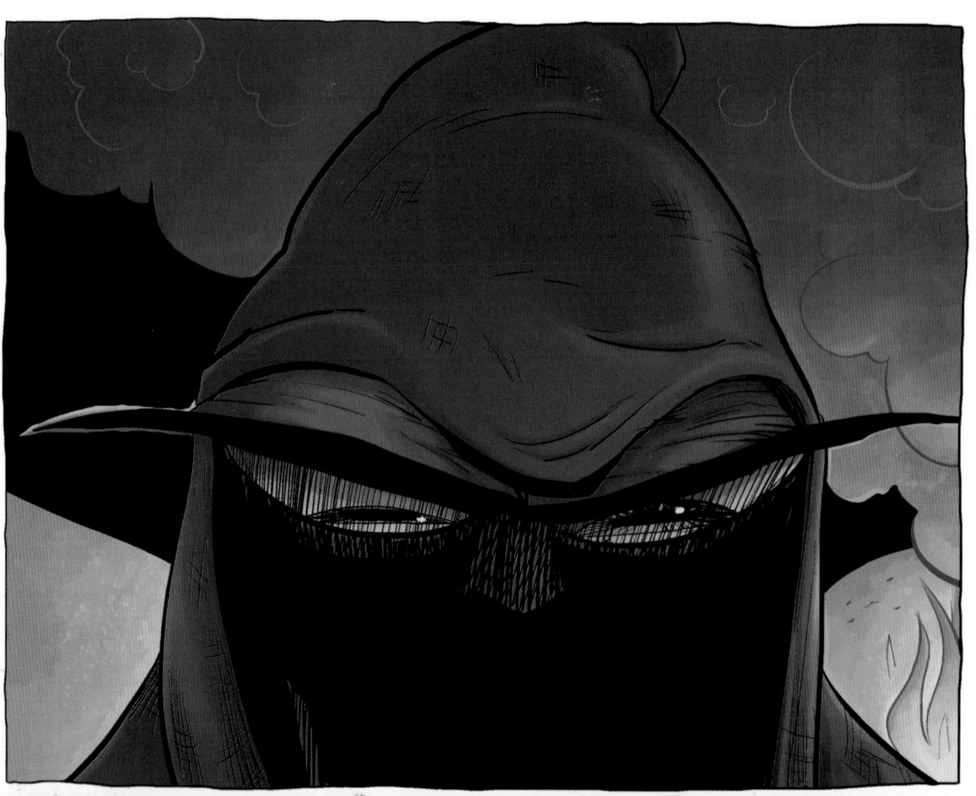

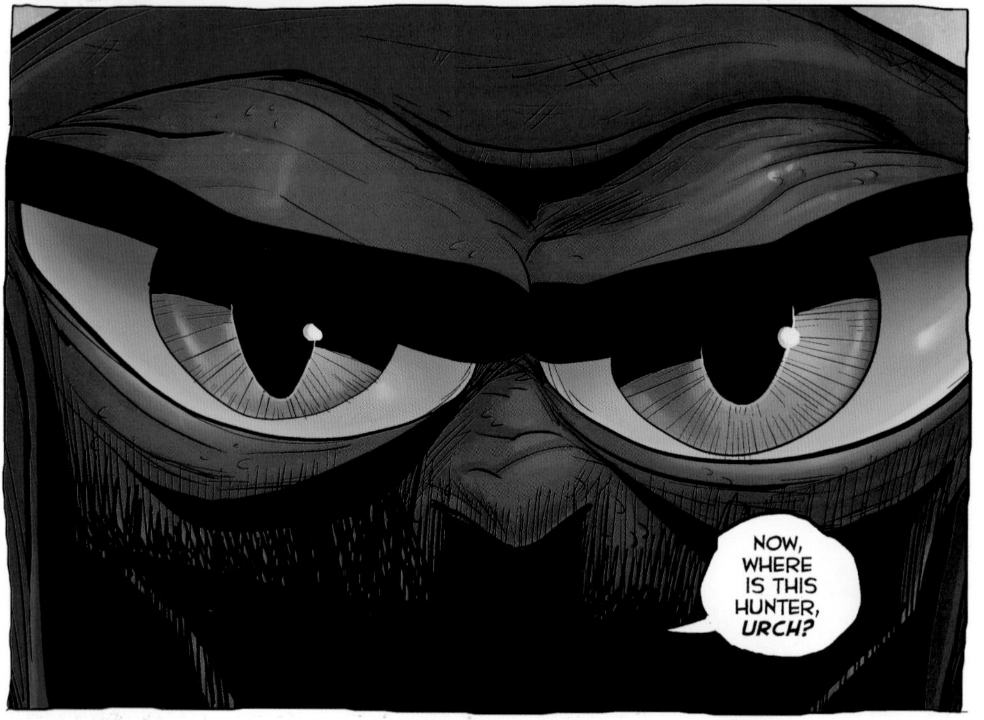
NOW, WHERE IS THIS HUNTER, URCH?

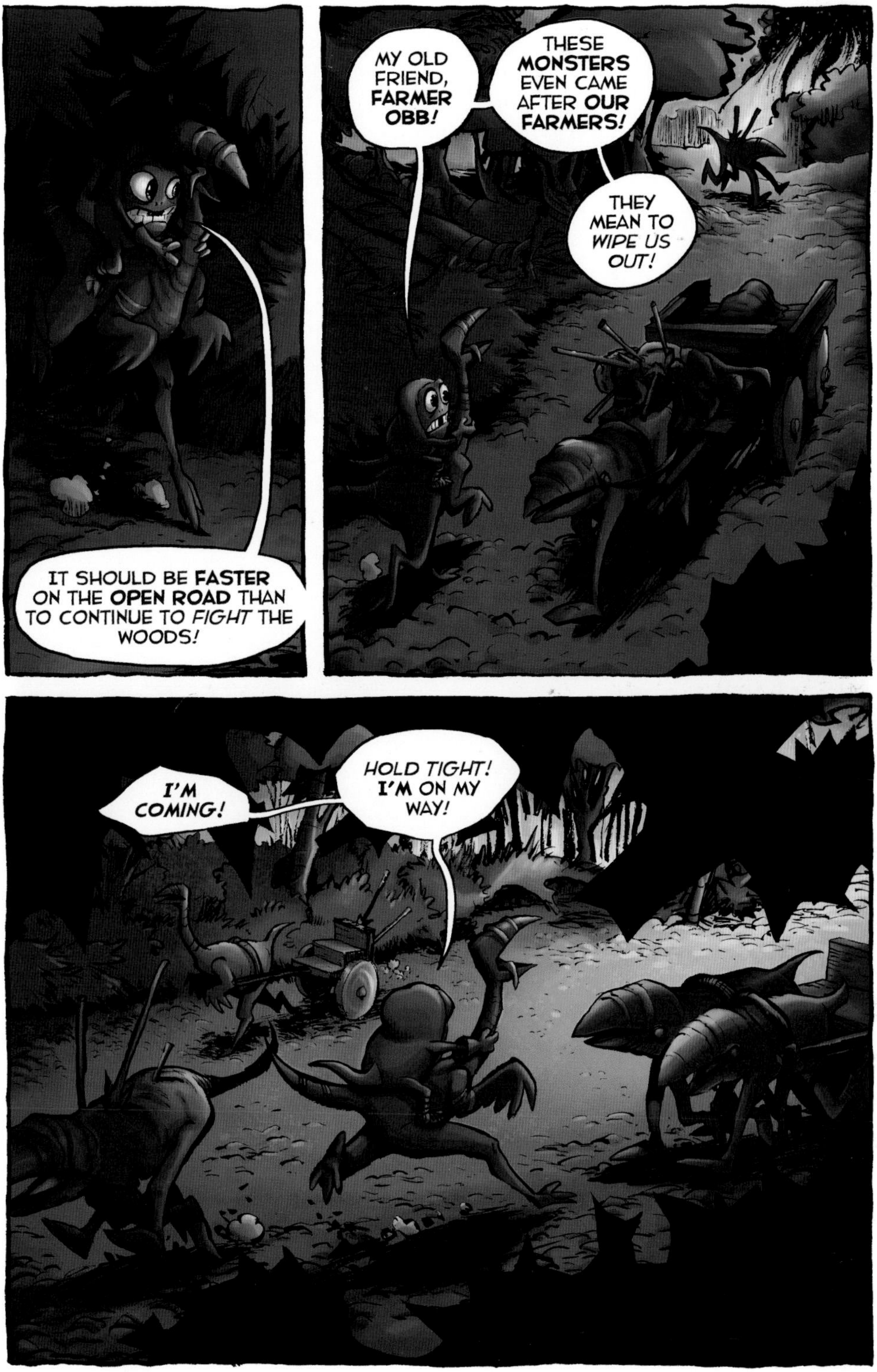
IT SHOULD BE **FASTER** ON THE **OPEN ROAD** THAN TO CONTINUE TO *FIGHT* THE WOODS!
MY OLD FRIEND, **FARMER OBB!**
THESE **MONSTERS** EVEN CAME AFTER **OUR FARMERS!**
THEY MEAN TO *WIPE US OUT!*
I'M COMING!
HOLD TIGHT! ***I'M** ON MY WAY!*

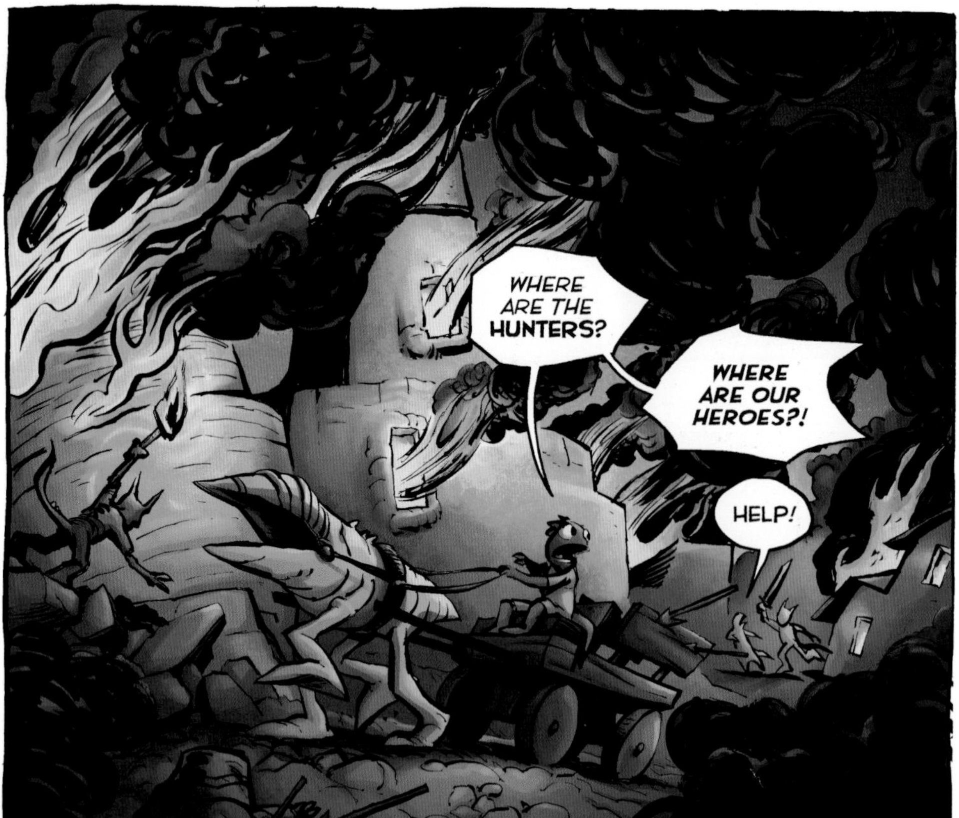
WHERE ARE THE HUNTERS?
WHERE ARE OUR HEROES?!
HELP!

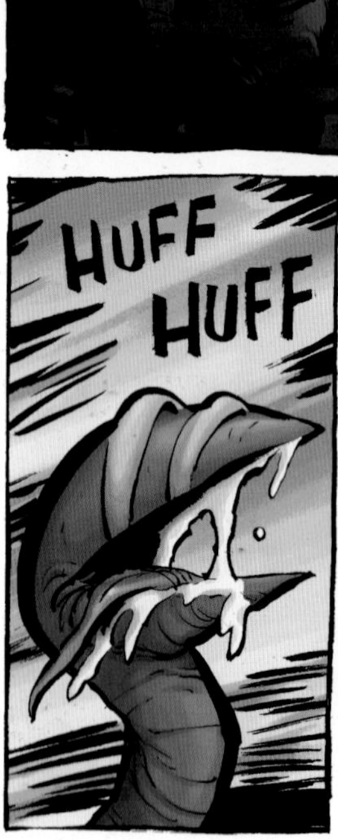
HUFF HUFF

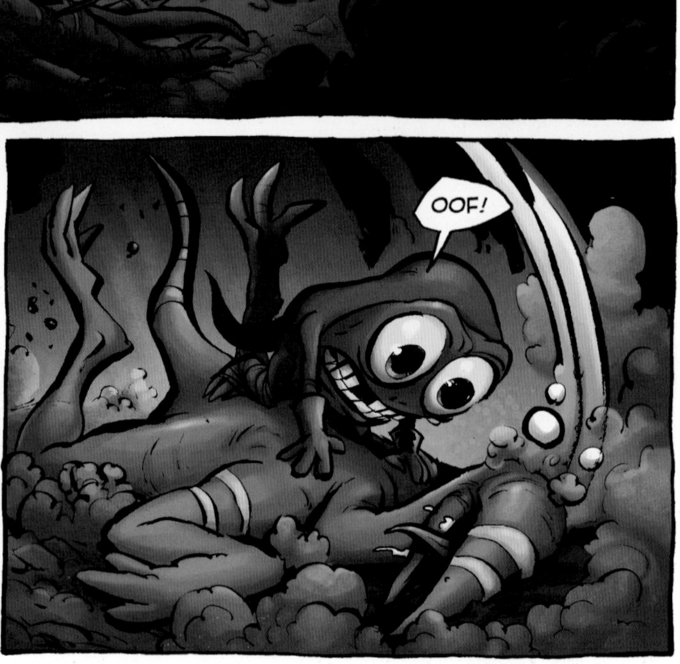
OOF!

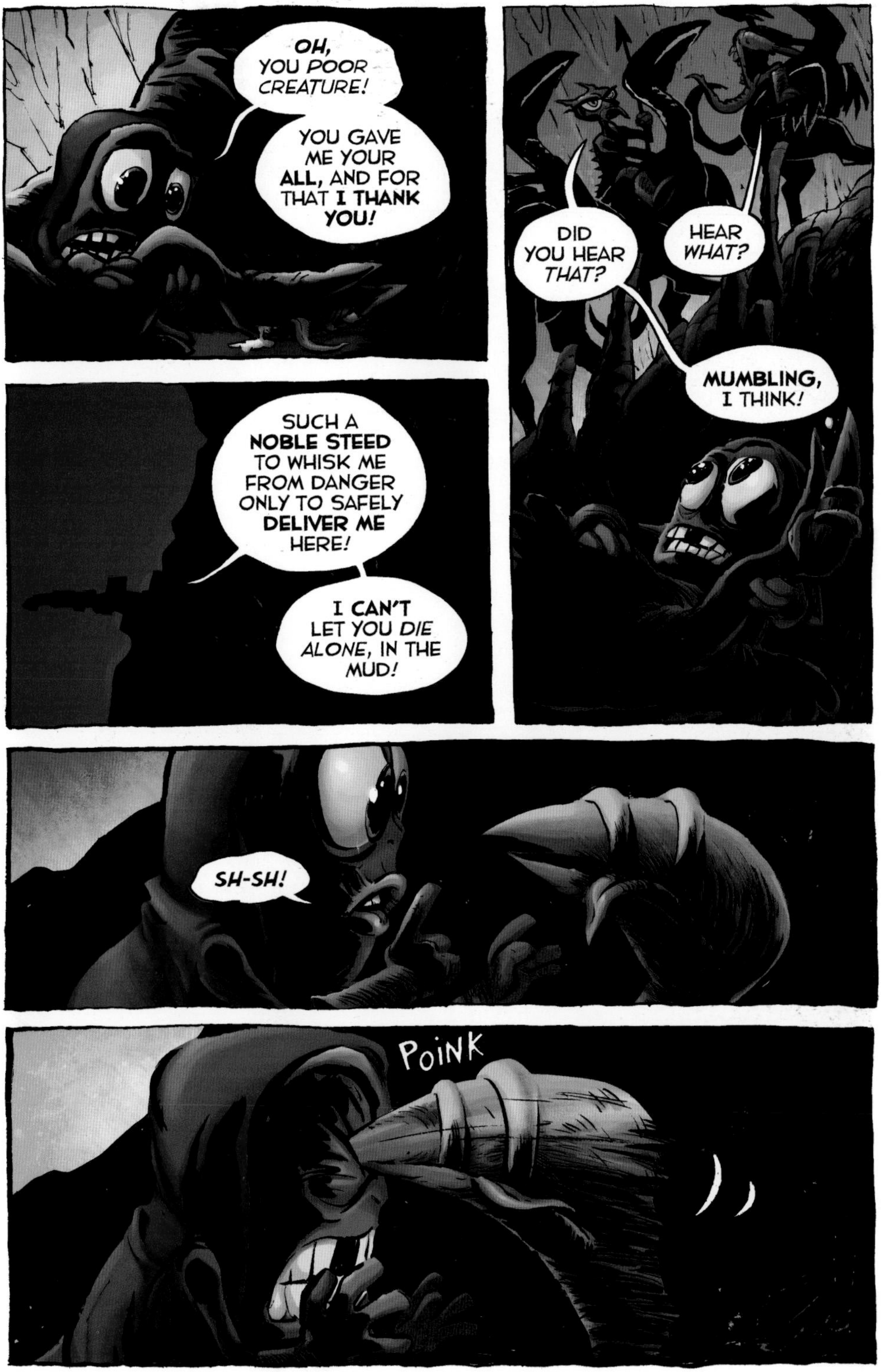
OH, YOU POOR CREATURE!
YOU GAVE ME YOUR ALL, AND FOR THAT I THANK YOU!
DID YOU HEAR THAT?
HEAR WHAT?
MUMBLING, I THINK!
SUCH A NOBLE STEED TO WHISK ME FROM DANGER ONLY TO SAFELY DELIVER ME HERE!
I CAN'T LET YOU DIE ALONE, IN THE MUD!
SH-SH!
POINK

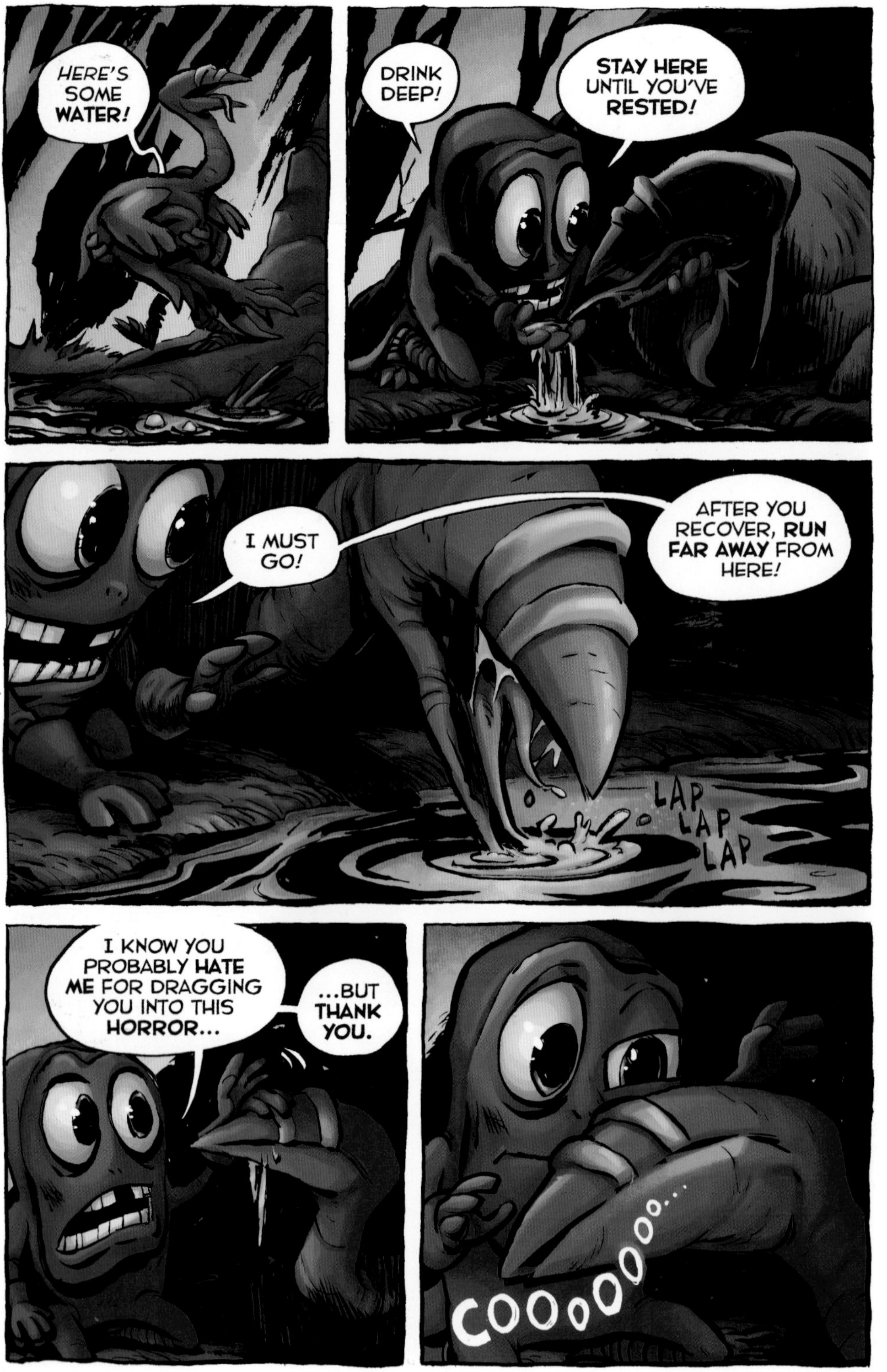
HERE'S SOME WATER!
DRINK DEEP!
STAY HERE UNTIL YOU'VE RESTED!
I MUST GO!
AFTER YOU RECOVER, RUN FAR AWAY FROM HERE!
LAP LAP LAP
I KNOW YOU PROBABLY HATE ME FOR DRAGGING YOU INTO THIS HORROR...
...BUT THANK YOU.
COOOOOOOO...

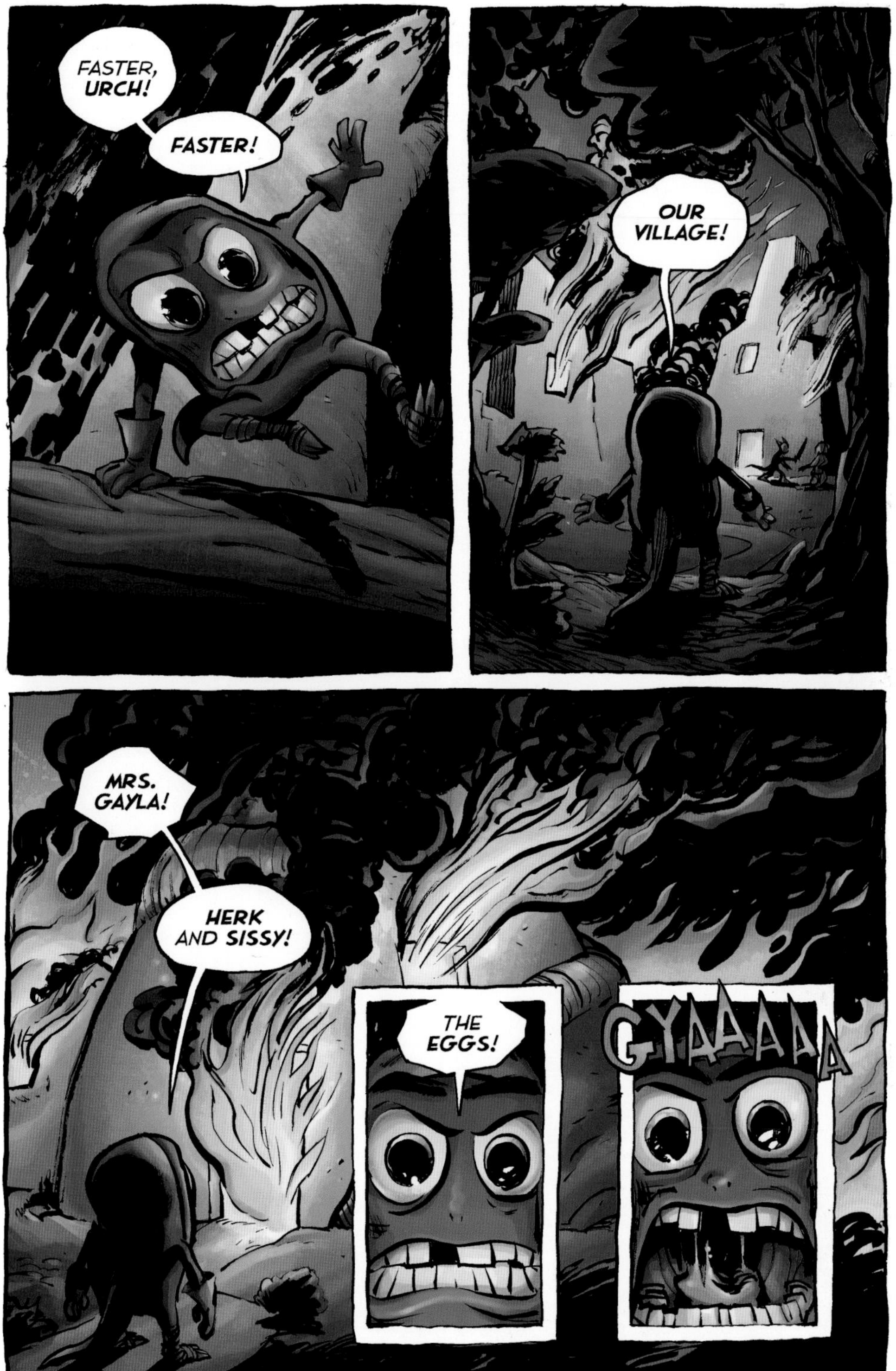
FASTER, URCH!
FASTER!
OUR VILLAGE!
MRS. GAYLA!
HERK AND SISSY!
THE EGGS!
GYAAAAA

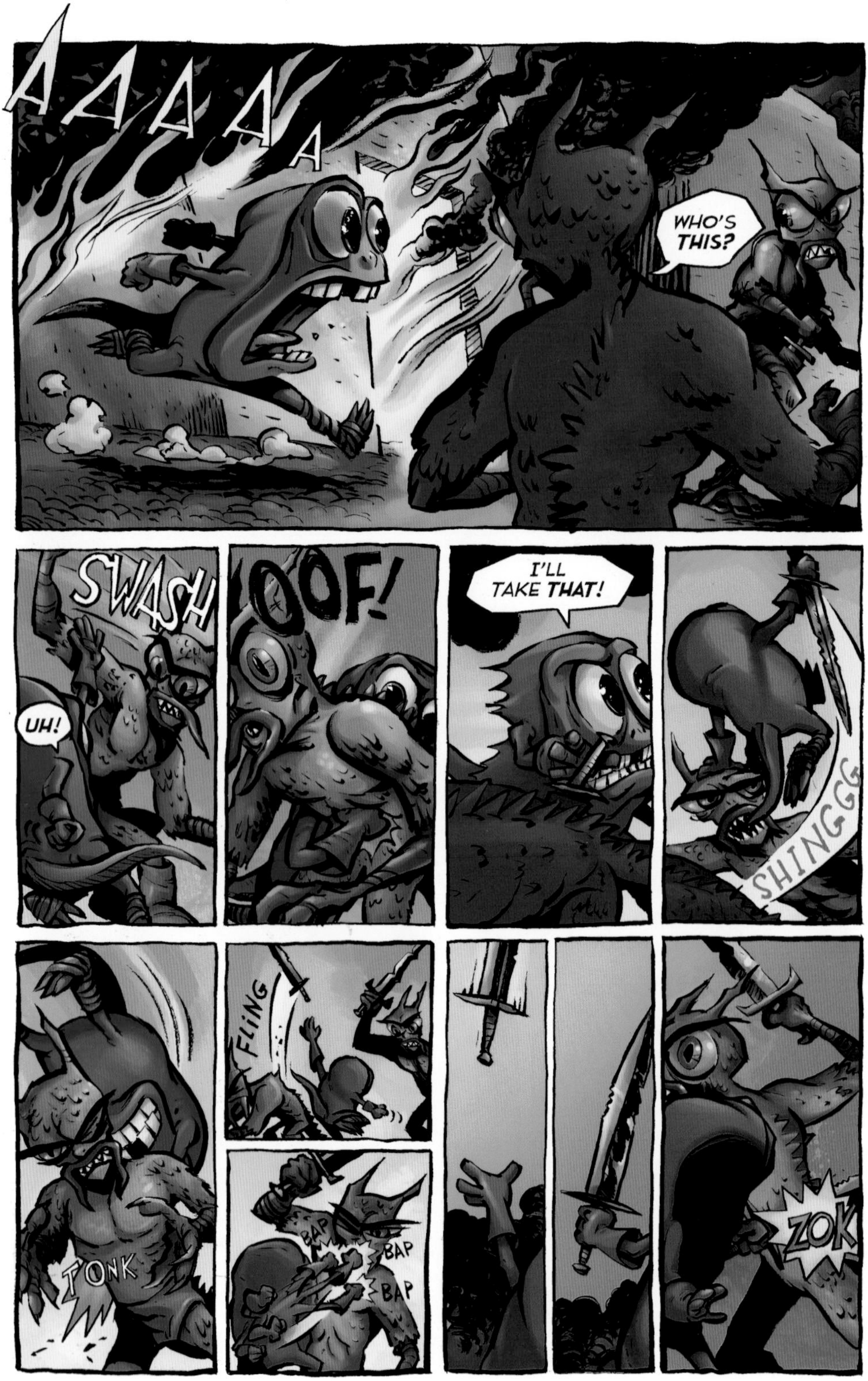
AAAAAA
WHO'S THIS?
SWASH
UH!
OOF!
I'LL TAKE THAT!
SHINGGG
TONK
FLING
BAP
BAP
BAP
ZOK

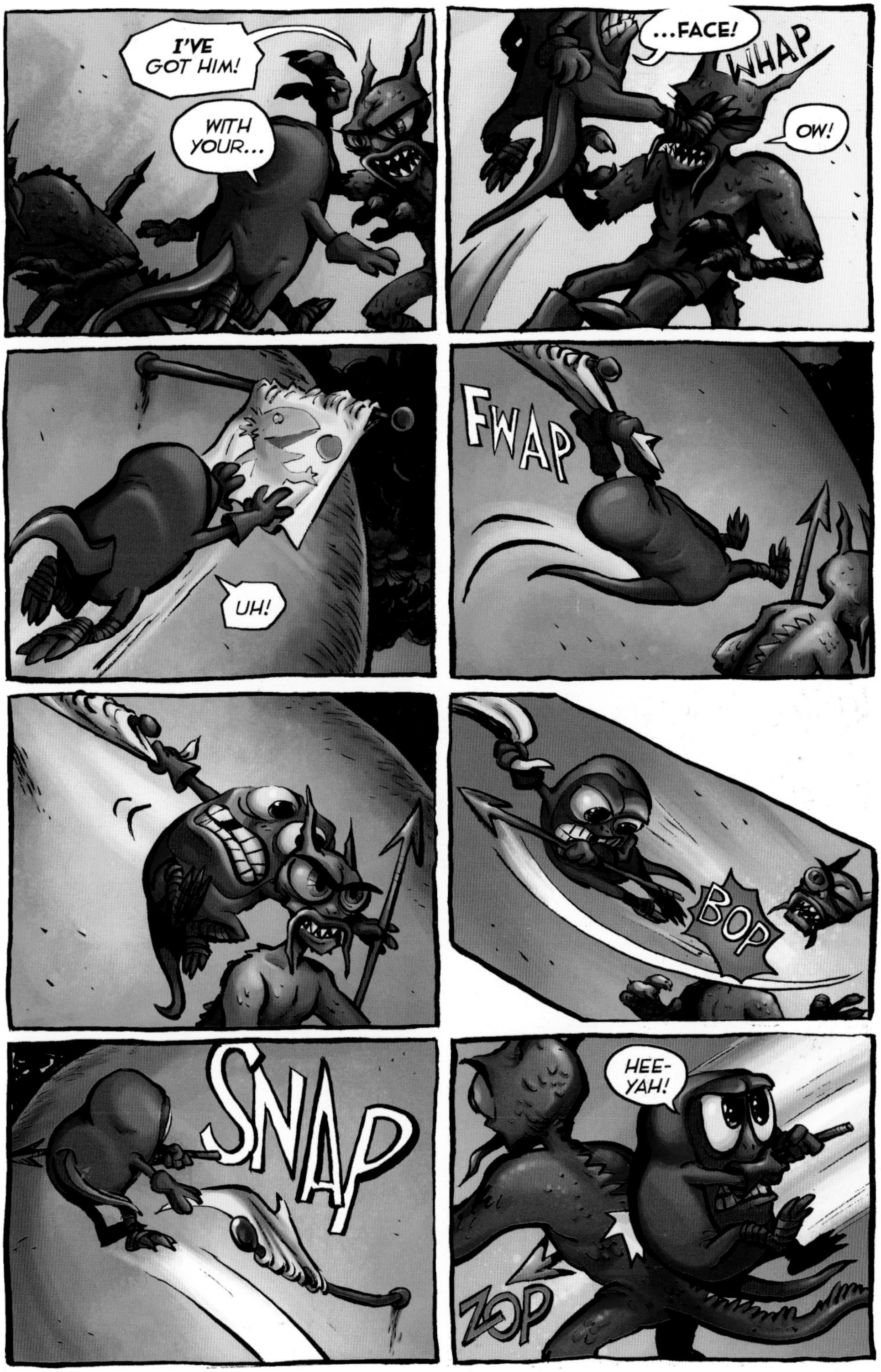
I'VE GOT HIM!
WITH YOUR...
...FACE!
WHAP
OW!
UH!
FWAP
BOP
SNAP
HEE-YAH!
ZOP

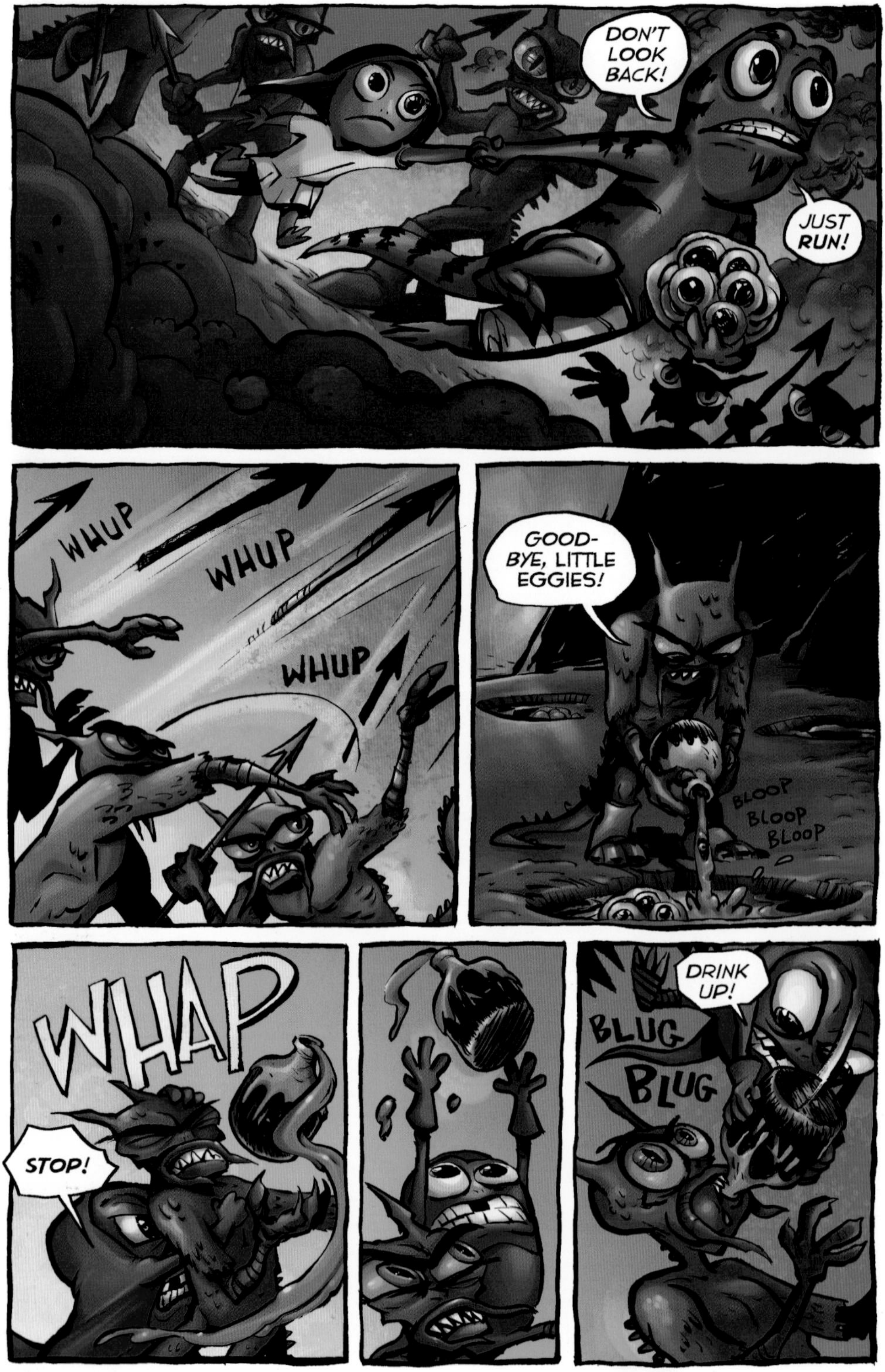
DON'T LOOK BACK!
JUST RUN!
WHUP
WHUP
WHUP
GOOD-BYE, LITTLE EGGIES!
BLOOP
BLOOP
BLOOP
WHAP
STOP!
DRINK UP!
BLUG
BLUG

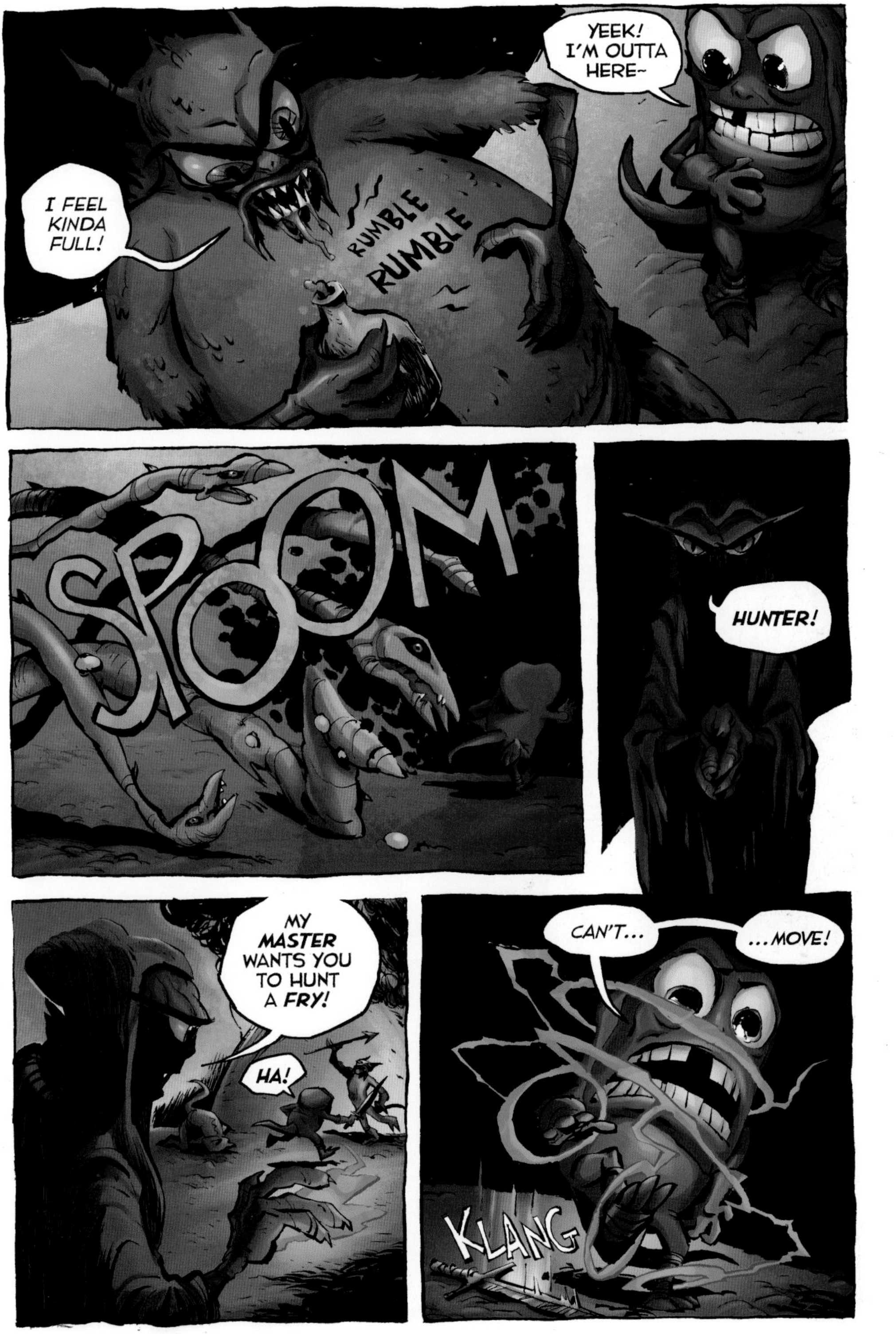
YEEK! I'M OUTTA HERE~
I FEEL KINDA FULL!
RUMBLE RUMBLE
SPOOM
HUNTER!
MY MASTER WANTS YOU TO HUNT A FRY!
HA!
CAN'T...
...MOVE!
KLANG

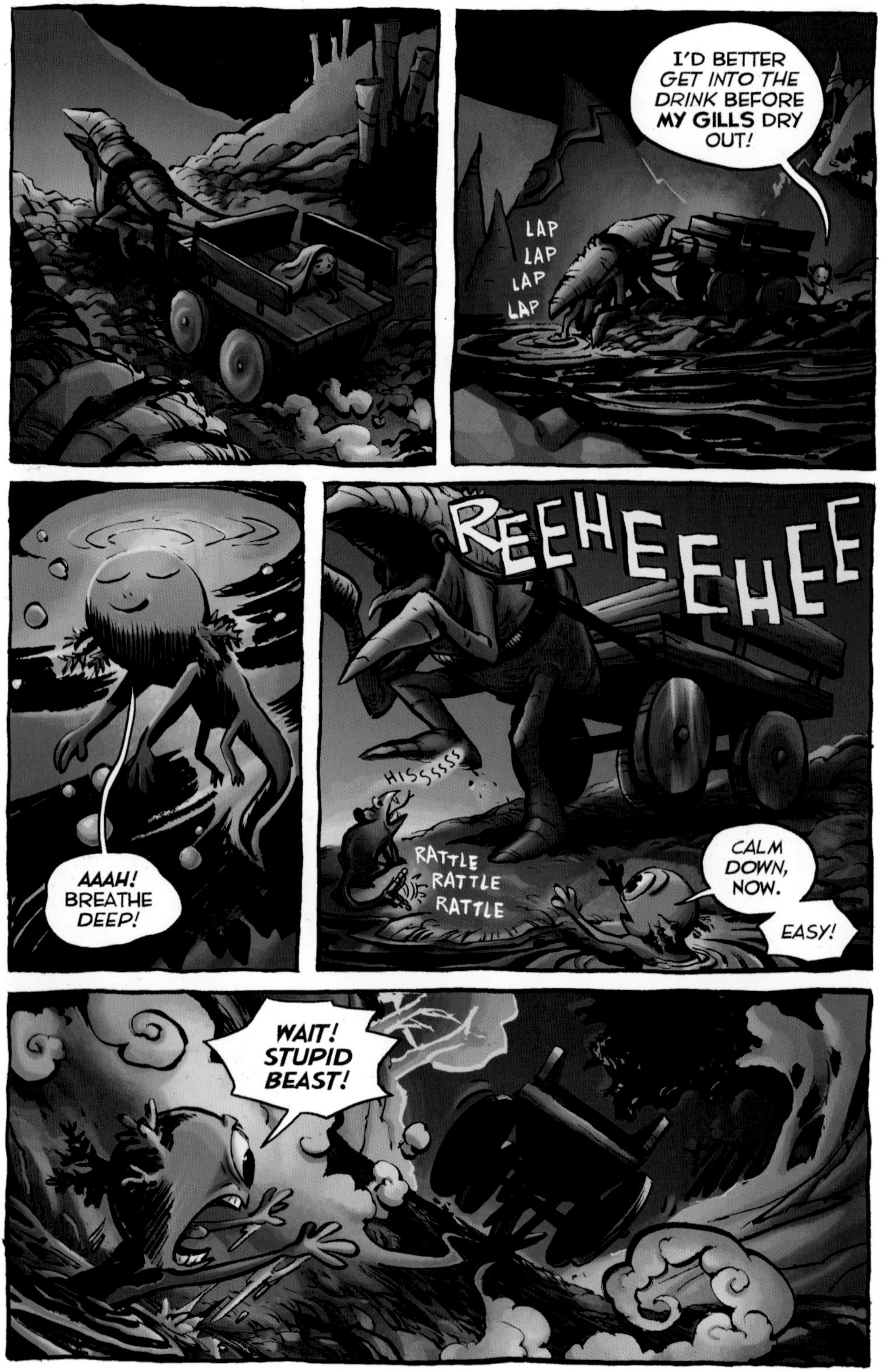
I'D BETTER GET INTO THE DRINK BEFORE MY GILLS DRY OUT!
LAP LAP LAP LAP
AAAH! BREATHE DEEP!
REEHEEEHEE
HISSSSSS
RATTLE RATTLE RATTLE
CALM DOWN, NOW.
EASY!
WAIT! STUPID BEAST!

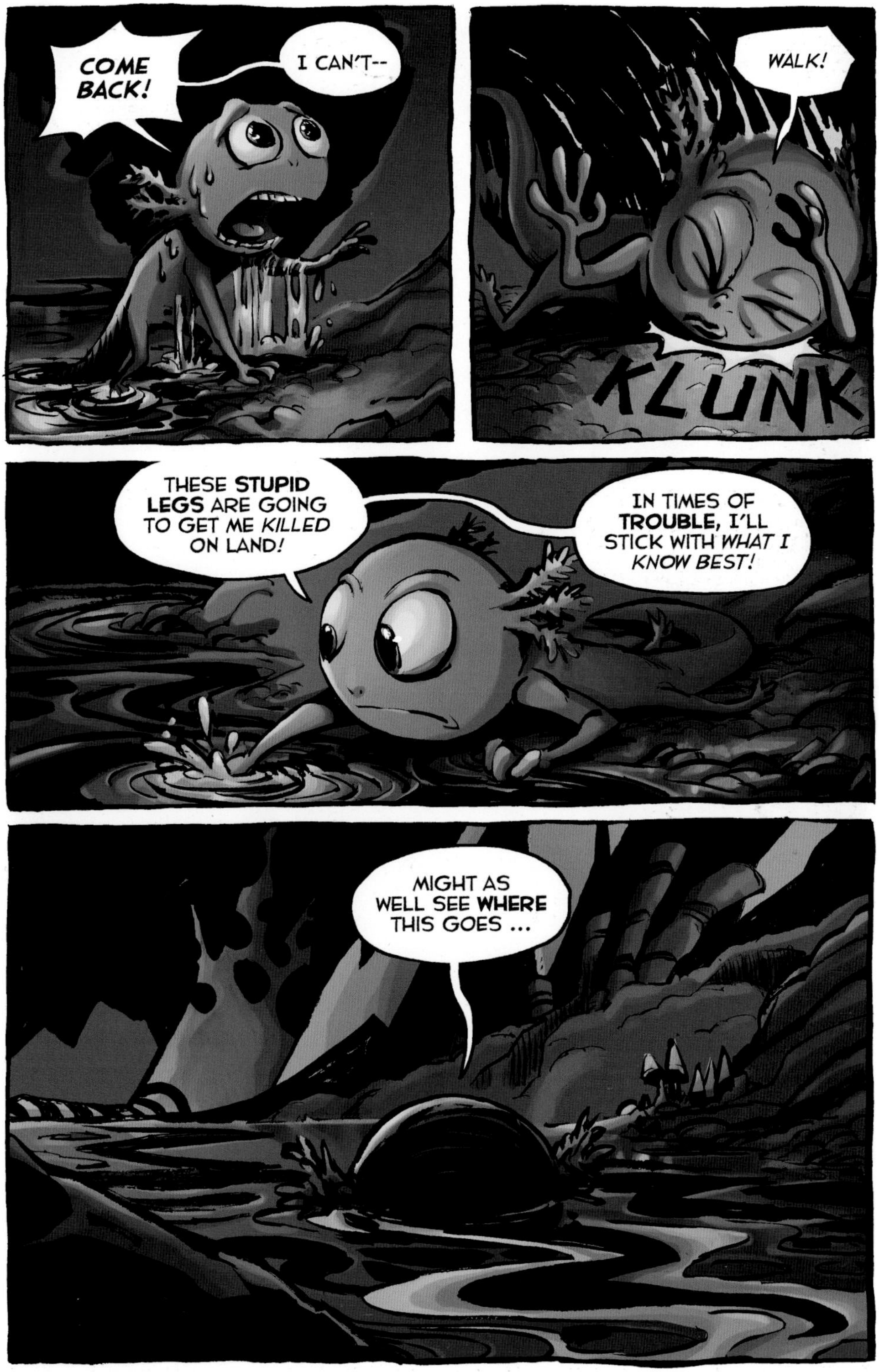
COME BACK!
I CAN'T--
WALK!
KLUNK
THESE STUPID LEGS ARE GOING TO GET ME KILLED ON LAND!
IN TIMES OF TROUBLE, I'LL STICK WITH WHAT I KNOW BEST!
MIGHT AS WELL SEE WHERE THIS GOES ...

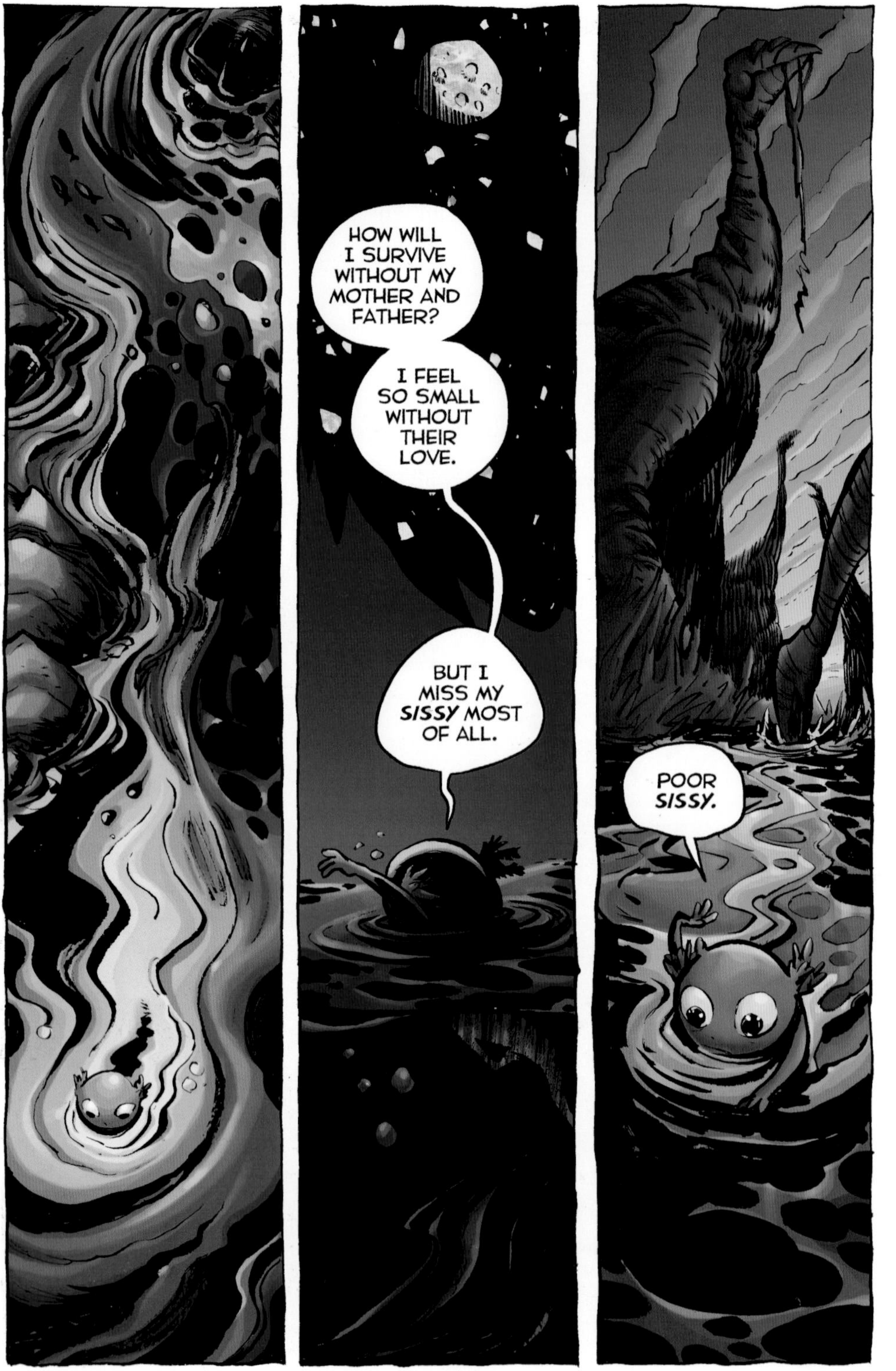
HOW WILL I SURVIVE WITHOUT MY MOTHER AND FATHER?
I FEEL SO SMALL WITHOUT THEIR LOVE.
BUT I MISS MY *SISSY* MOST OF ALL.
POOR *SISSY.*

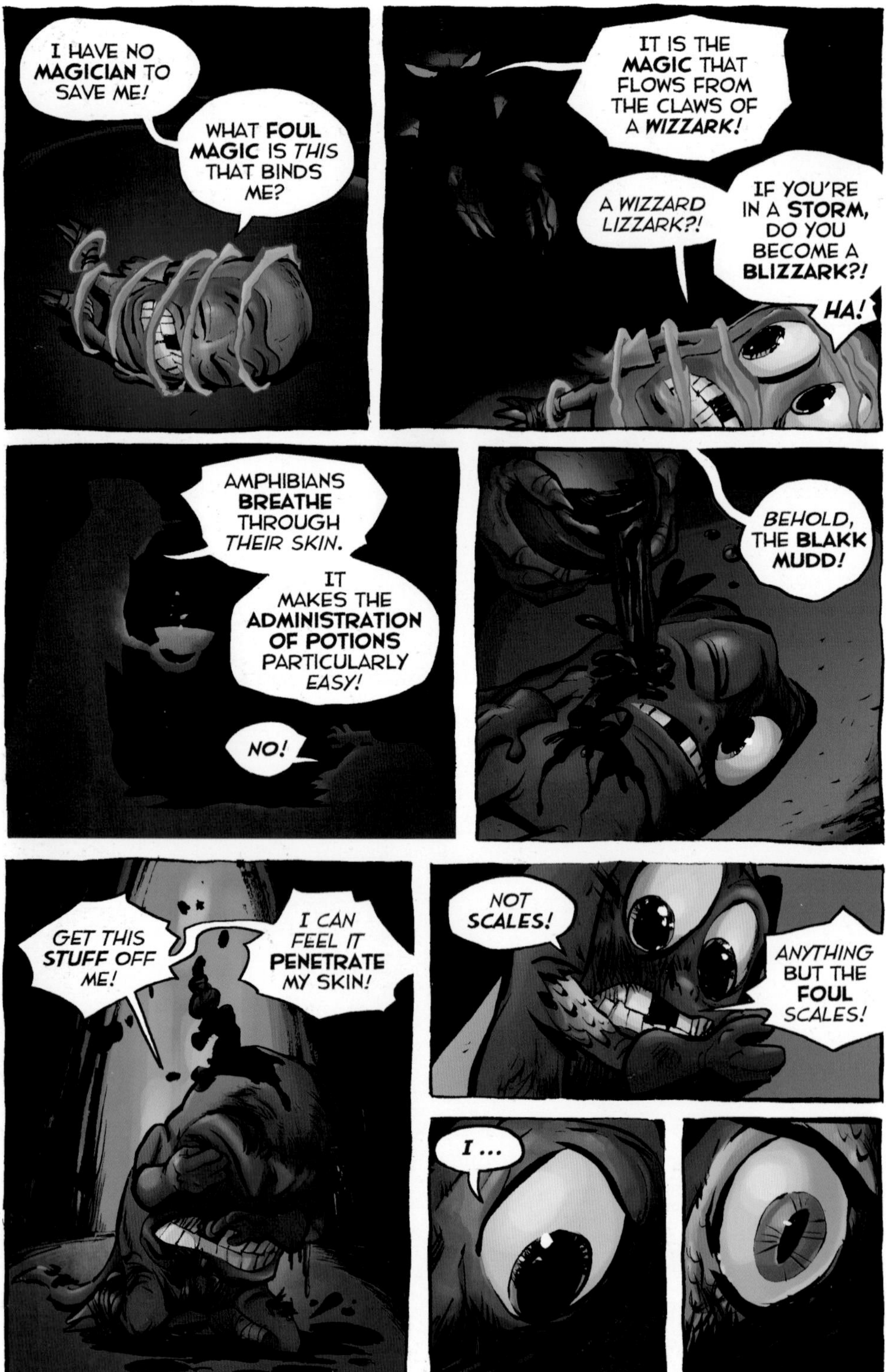
I HAVE NO MAGICIAN TO SAVE ME!
WHAT FOUL MAGIC IS THIS THAT BINDS ME?
IT IS THE MAGIC THAT FLOWS FROM THE CLAWS OF A WIZZARK!
A WIZZARD LIZZARK?!
IF YOU'RE IN A STORM, DO YOU BECOME A BLIZZARK?!
HA!
AMPHIBIANS BREATHE THROUGH THEIR SKIN.
IT MAKES THE ADMINISTRATION OF POTIONS PARTICULARLY EASY!
NO!
BEHOLD, THE BLAKK MUDD!
GET THIS STUFF OFF ME!
I CAN FEEL IT PENETRATE MY SKIN!
NOT SCALES!
ANYTHING BUT THE FOUL SCALES!
I ...

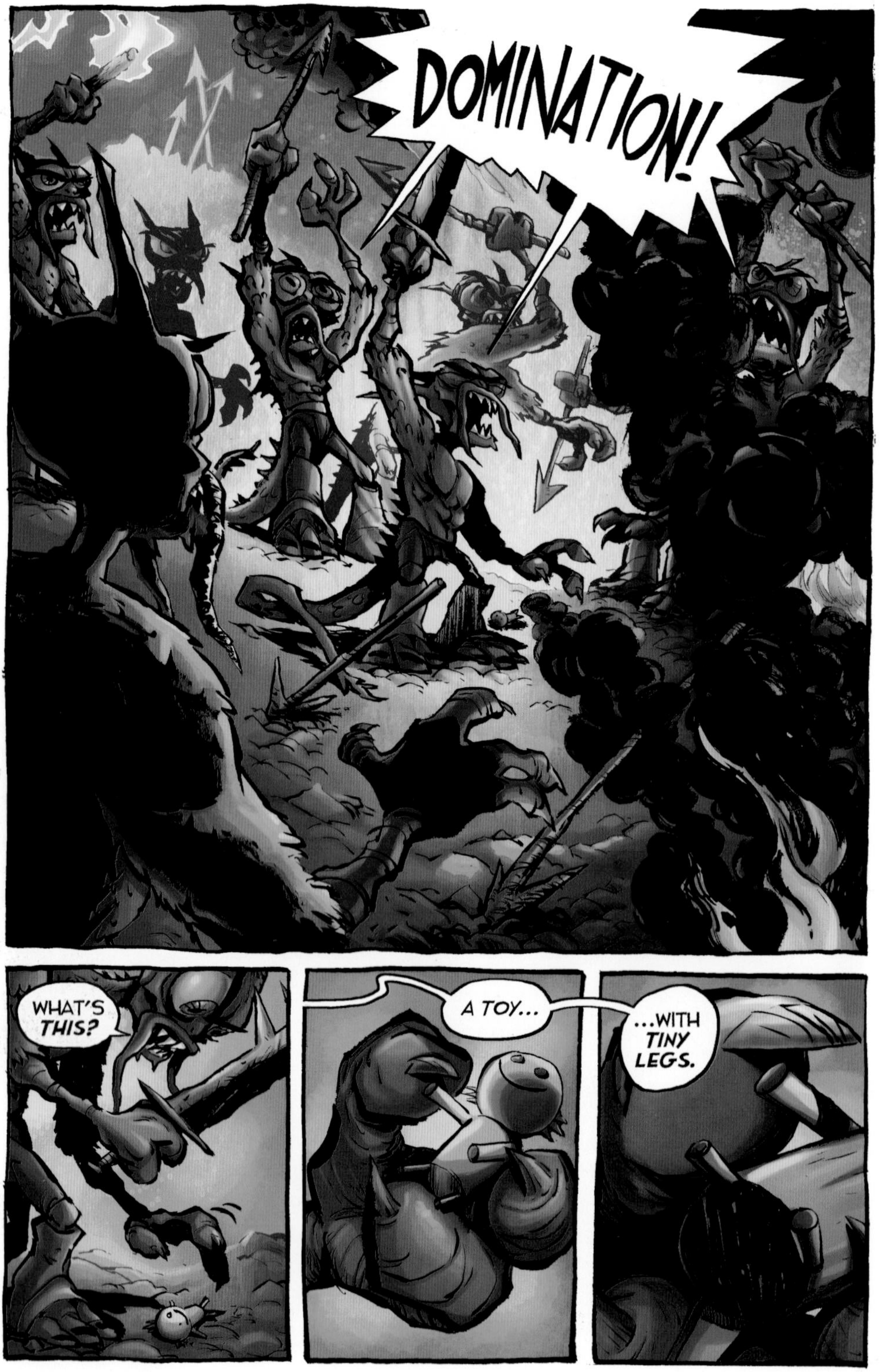
DOMINATION!
WHAT'S THIS?
A TOY...
...WITH TINY LEGS.

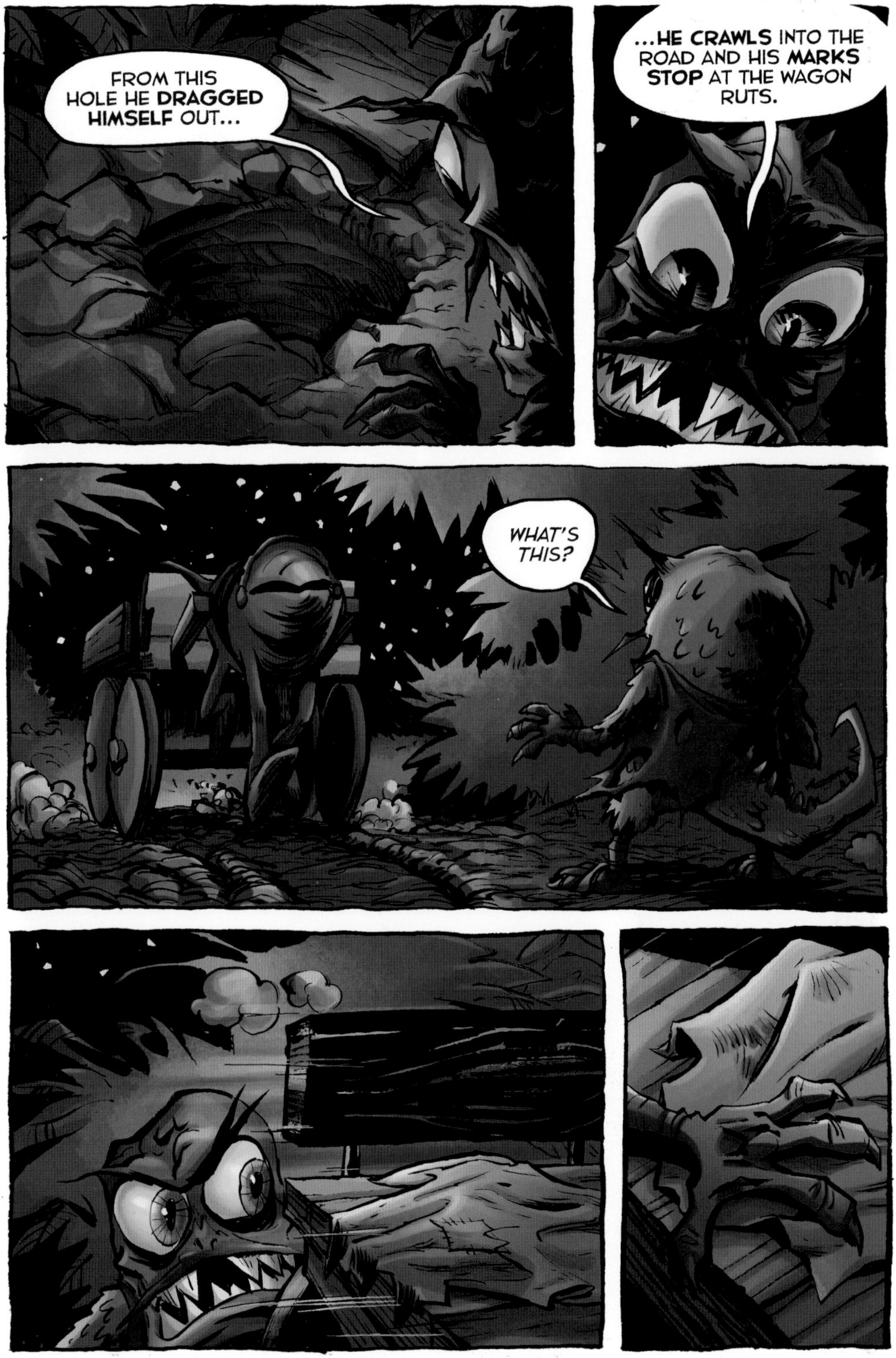
FROM THIS HOLE HE **DRAGGED HIMSELF** OUT...
...**HE CRAWLS** INTO THE ROAD AND HIS **MARKS STOP** AT THE WAGON RUTS.
WHAT'S THIS?

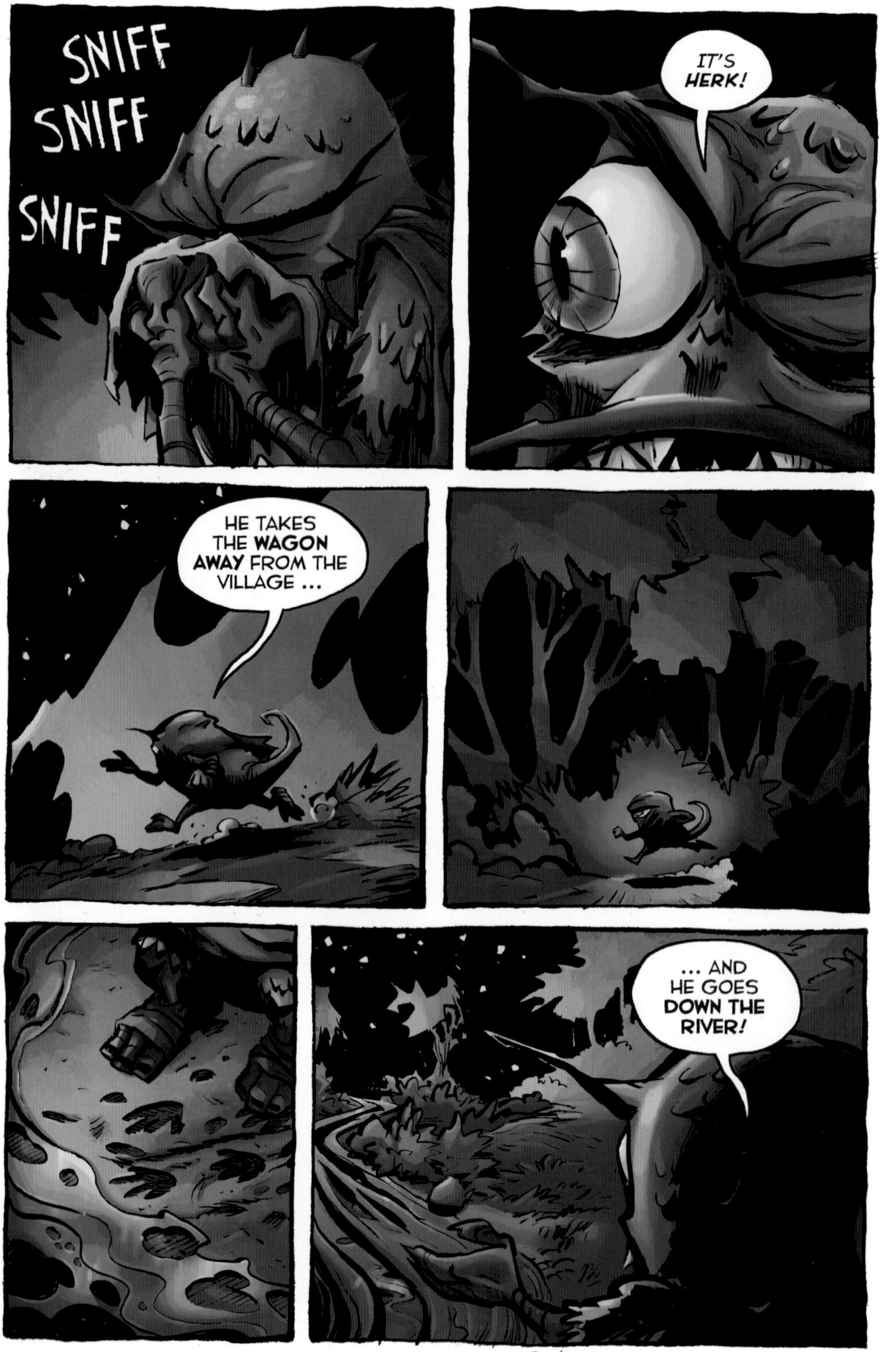
SNIFF
SNIFF
SNIFF
IT'S HERK!
HE TAKES THE WAGON AWAY FROM THE VILLAGE ...
... AND HE GOES DOWN THE RIVER!

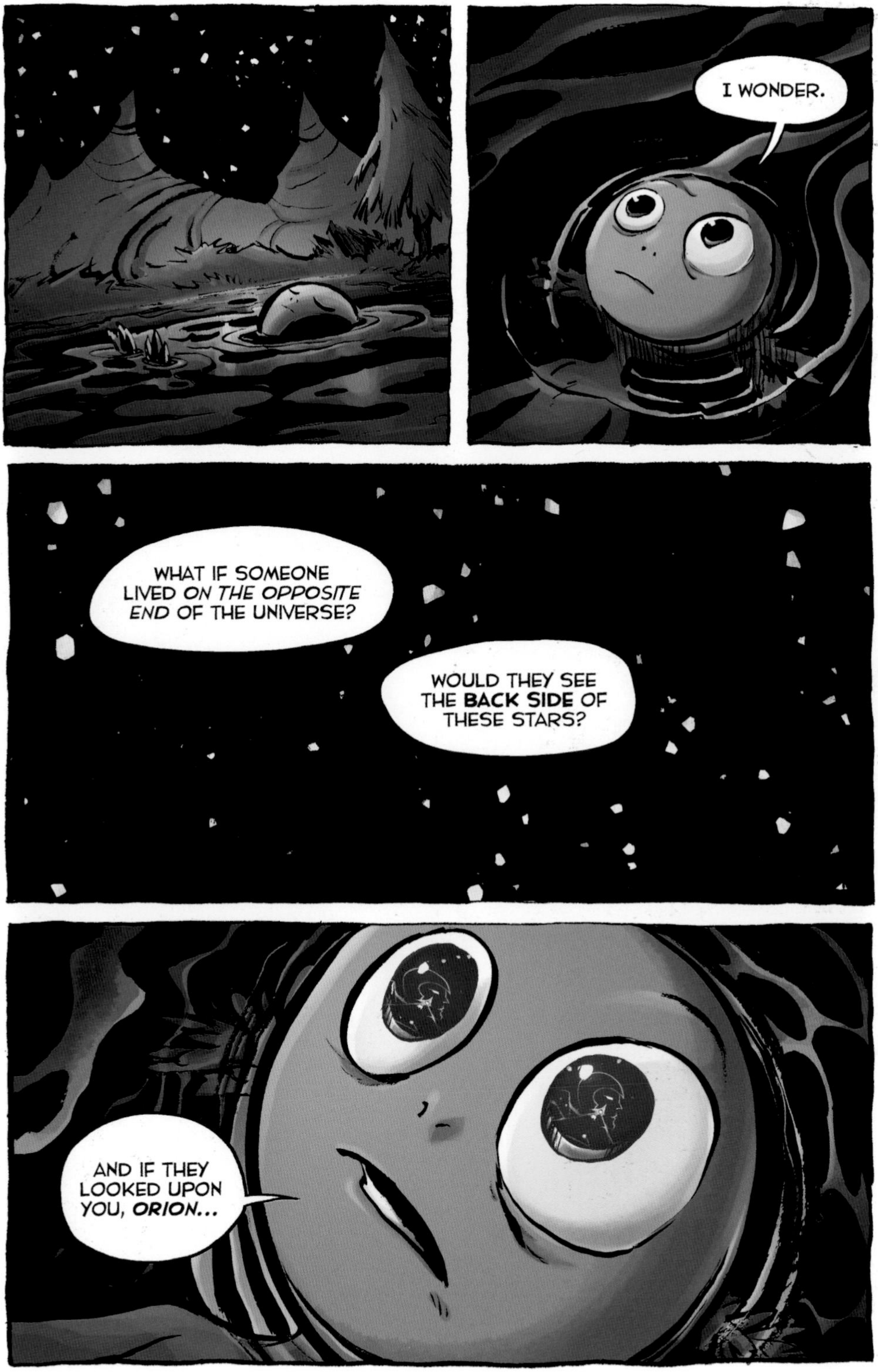
I WONDER.
WHAT IF SOMEONE LIVED *ON THE OPPOSITE END* OF THE UNIVERSE?
WOULD THEY SEE THE **BACK SIDE** OF THESE STARS?
AND IF THEY LOOKED UPON YOU, ***ORION...***

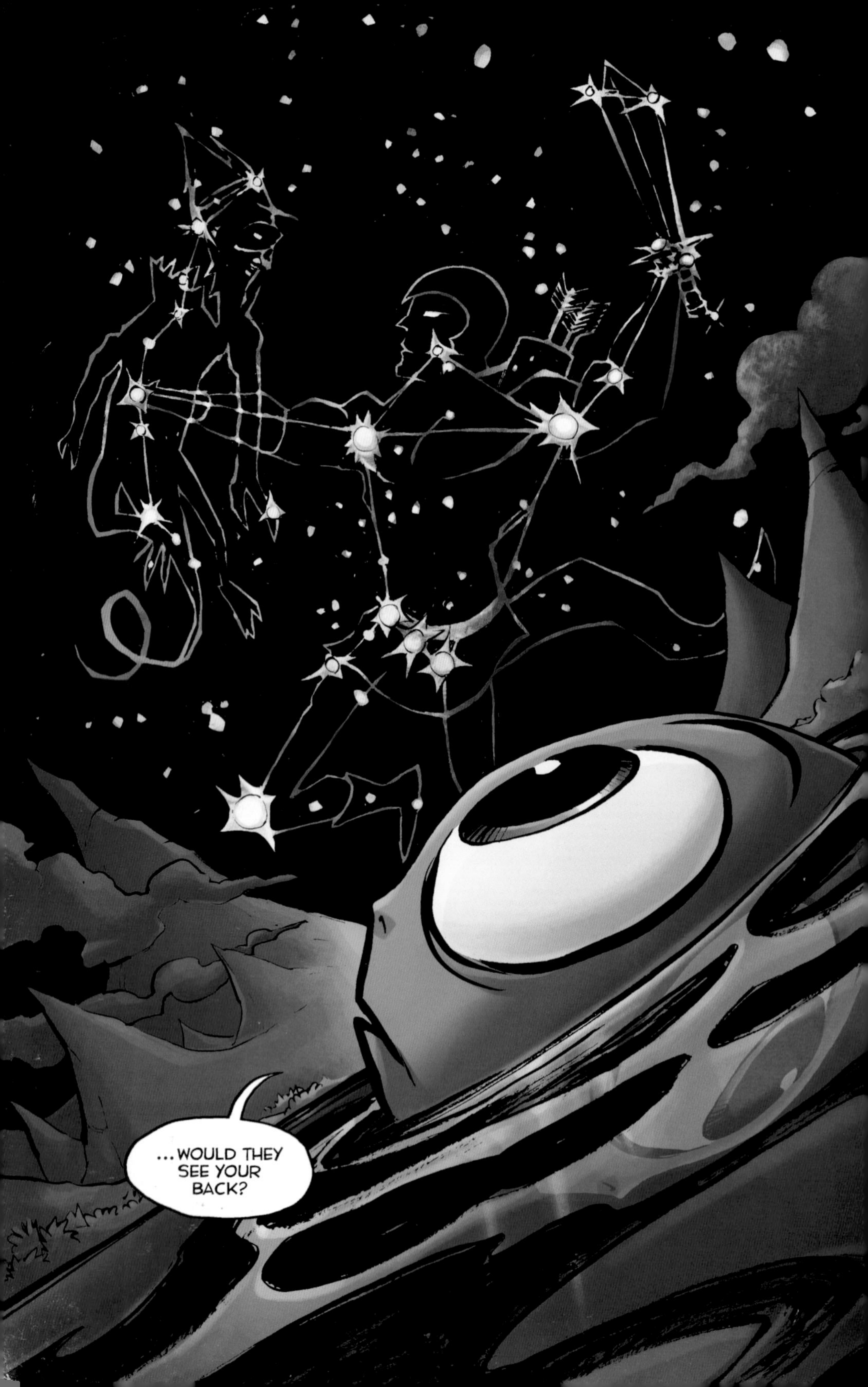
...WOULD THEY SEE YOUR BACK?

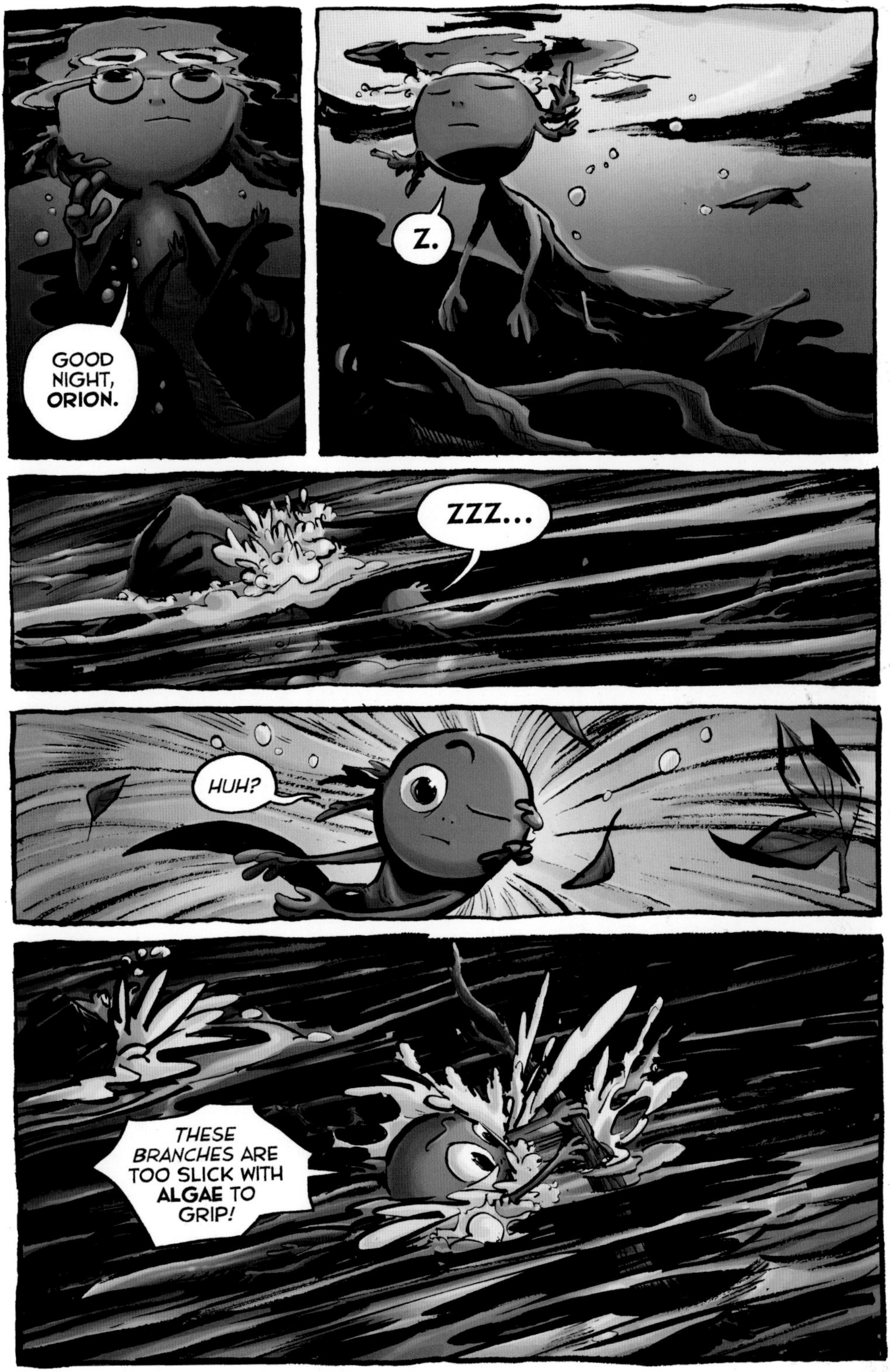
GOOD NIGHT, ORION.
Z.
ZZZ...
HUH?
THESE BRANCHES ARE TOO SLICK WITH ALGAE TO GRIP!

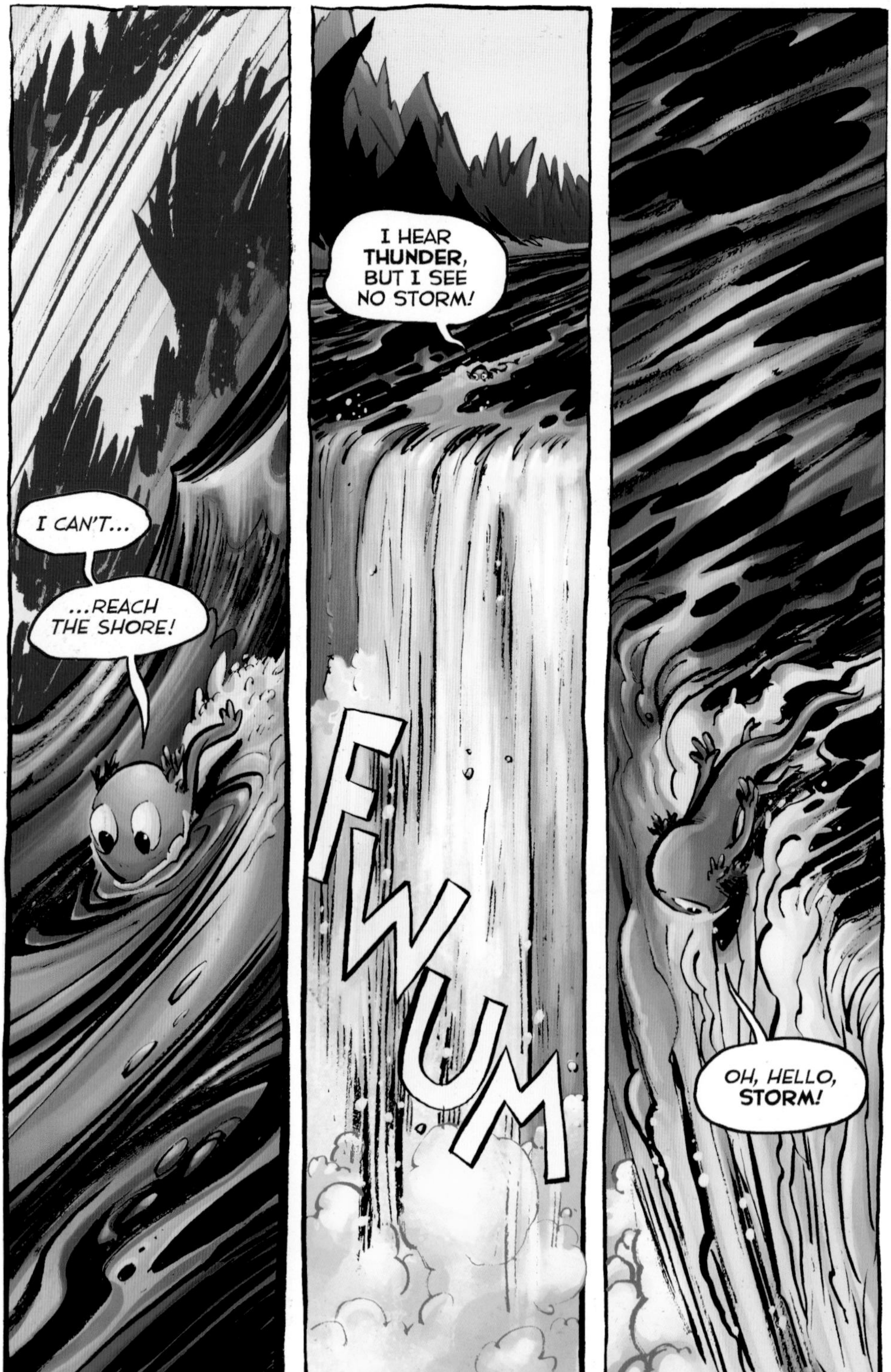
I CAN'T...
...REACH THE SHORE!
I HEAR THUNDER, BUT I SEE NO STORM!
FWUM
OH, HELLO, STORM!

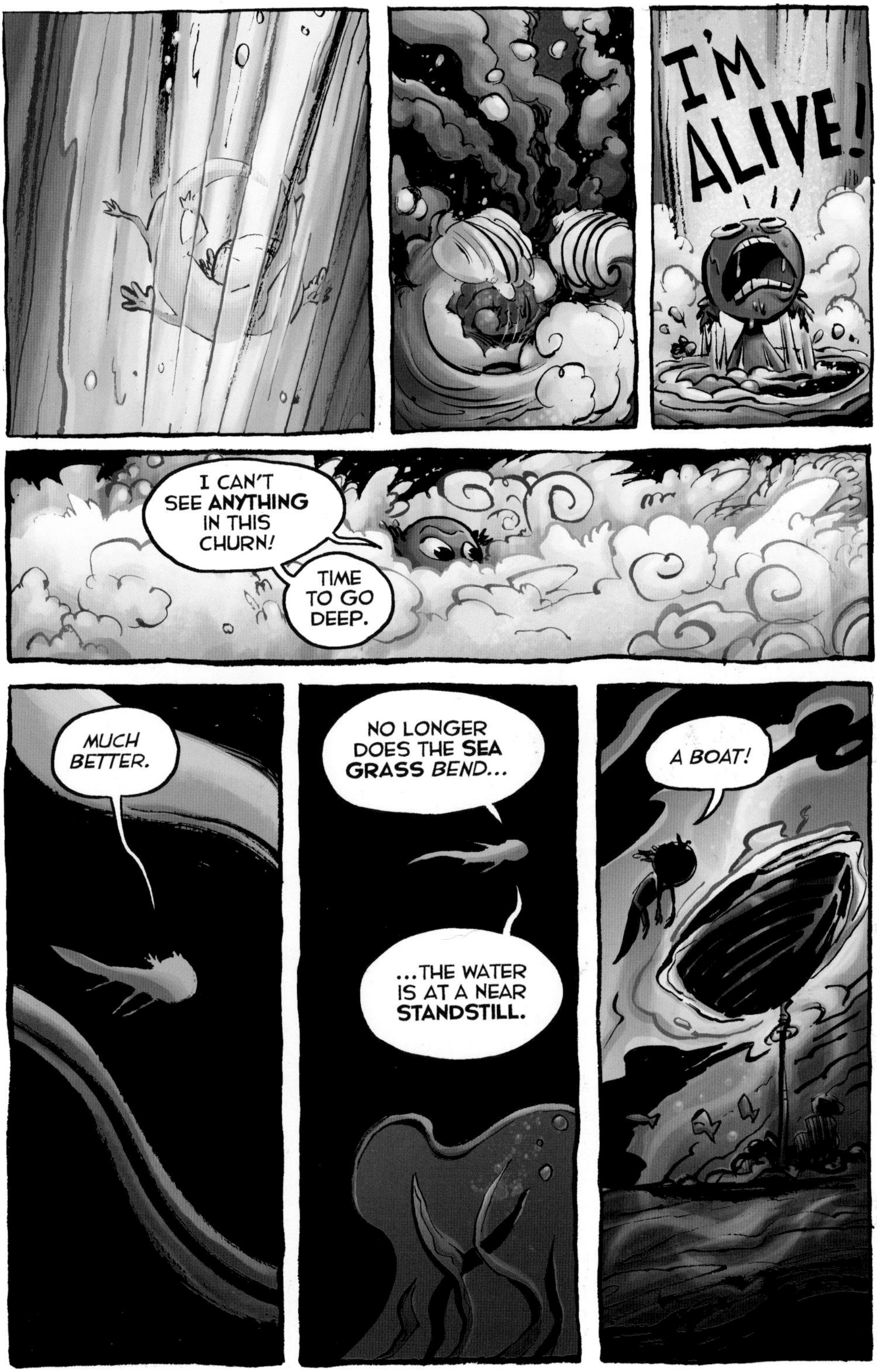
I'M ALIVE!
I CAN'T SEE ANYTHING IN THIS CHURN!
TIME TO GO DEEP.
MUCH BETTER.
NO LONGER DOES THE SEA GRASS BEND...
...THE WATER IS AT A NEAR STANDSTILL.
A BOAT!

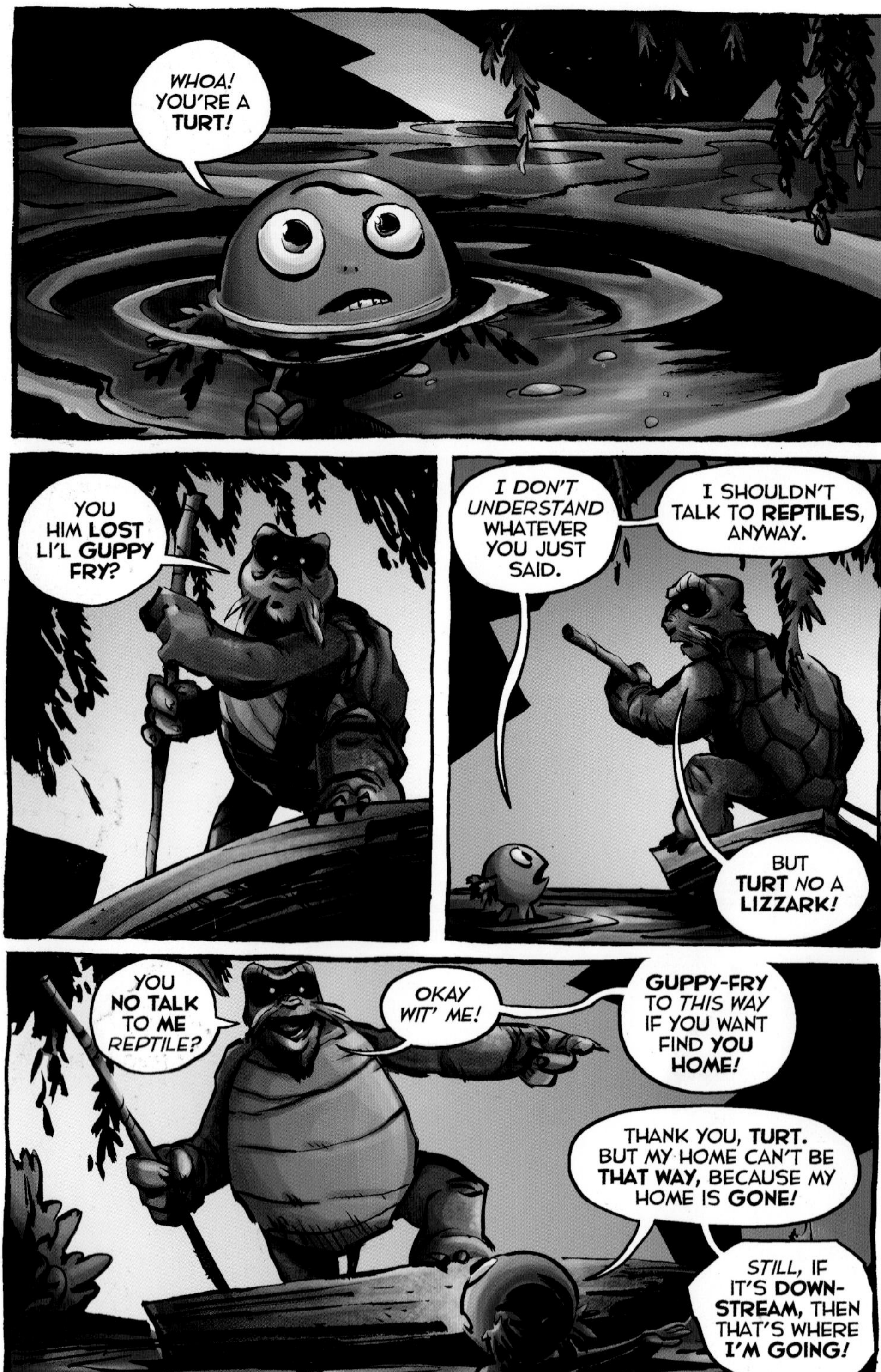

WHOA! YOU'RE A TURT!
YOU HIM LOST LI'L GUPPY FRY?
I DON'T UNDERSTAND WHATEVER YOU JUST SAID.
I SHOULDN'T TALK TO REPTILES, ANYWAY.
BUT TURT NO A LIZZARK!
YOU NO TALK TO ME REPTILE?
OKAY WIT' ME!
GUPPY-FRY TO THIS WAY IF YOU WANT FIND YOU HOME!
THANK YOU, TURT. BUT MY HOME CAN'T BE THAT WAY, BECAUSE MY HOME IS GONE!
STILL, IF IT'S DOWN-STREAM, THEN THAT'S WHERE I'M GOING!

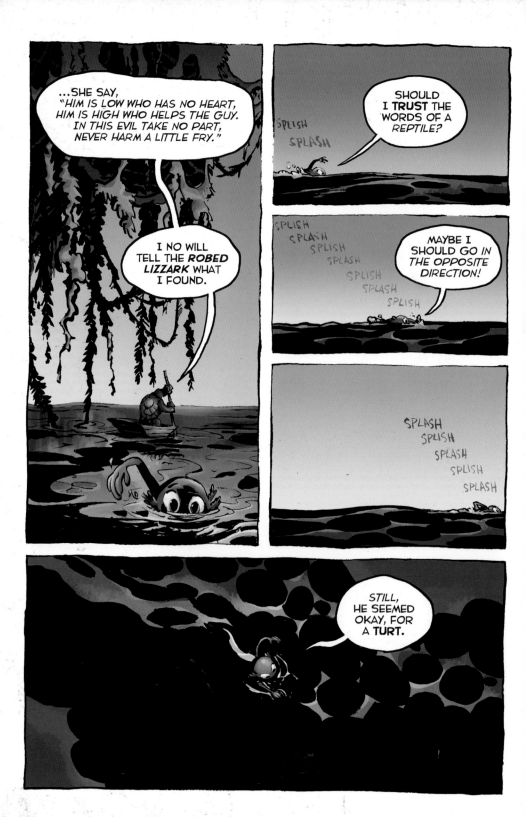

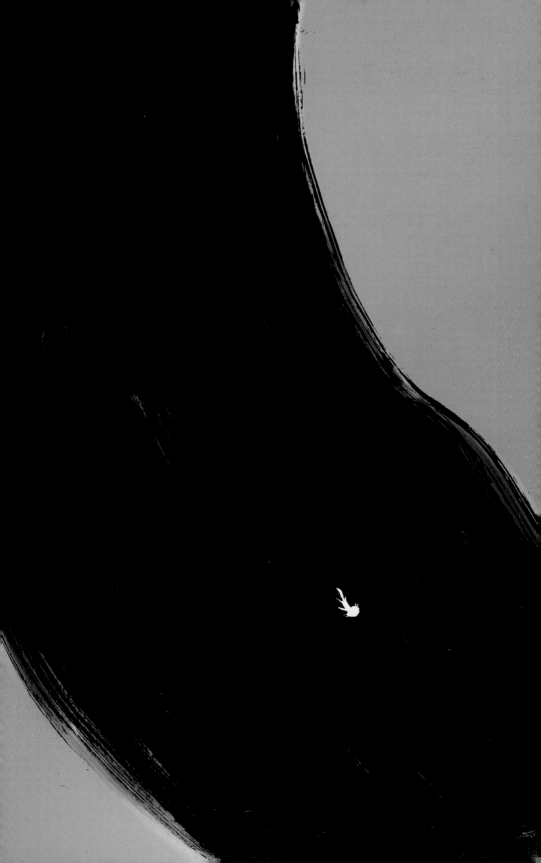

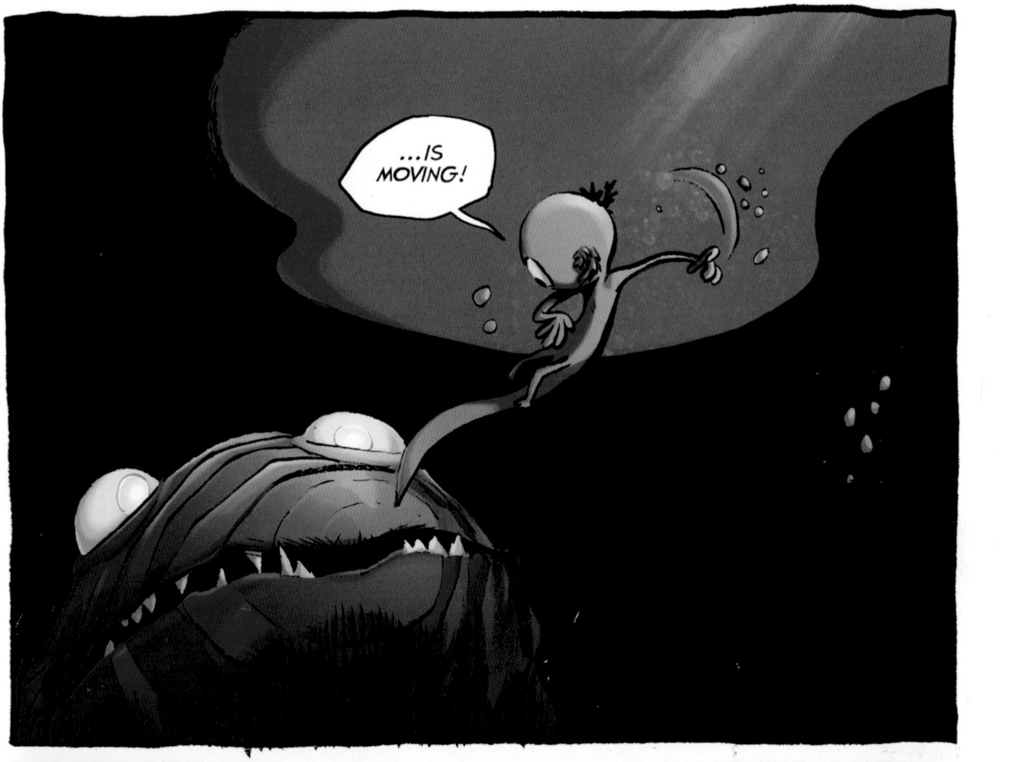
...IS MOVING!

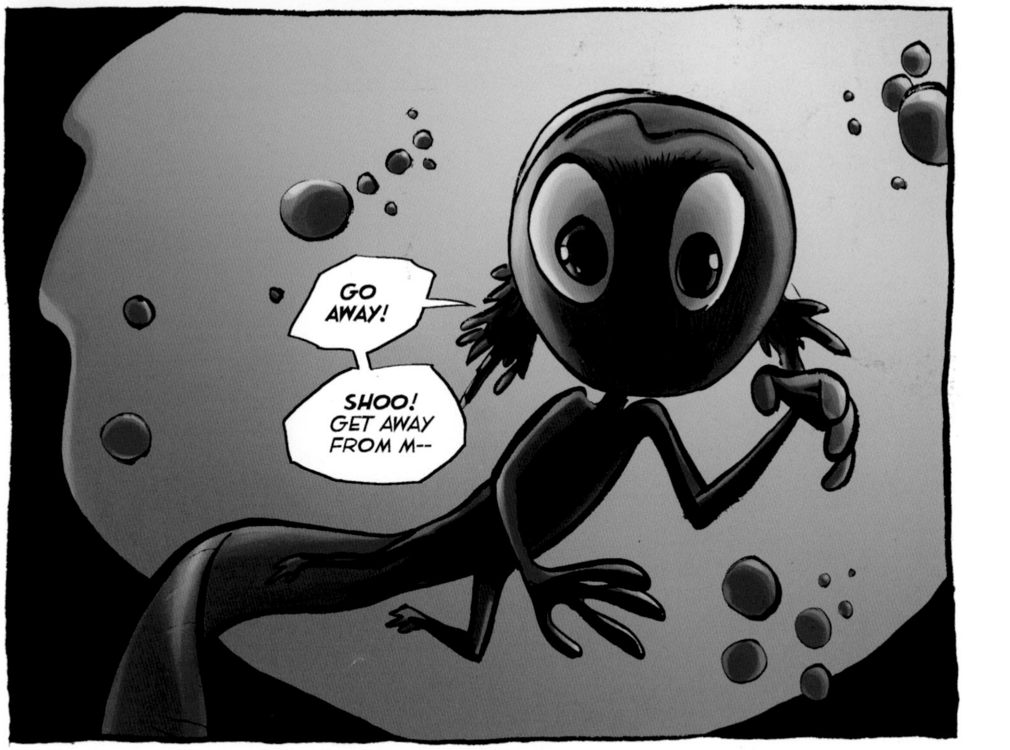
GO AWAY!
SHOO! GET AWAY FROM M--

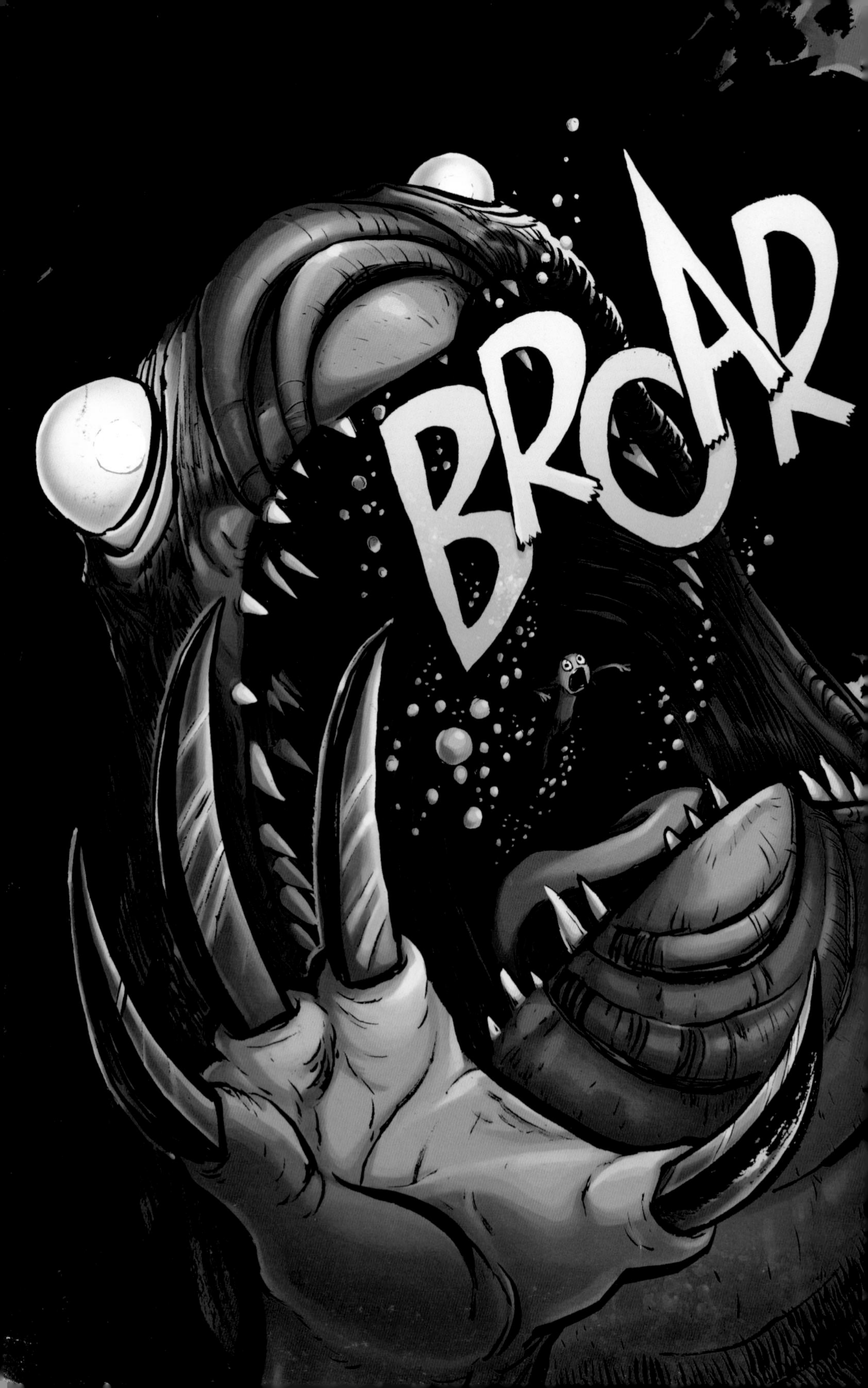
BROAR

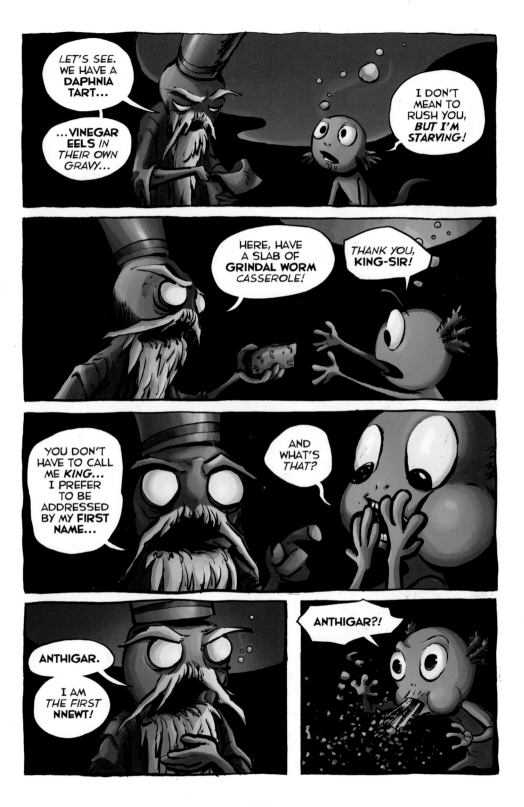

143

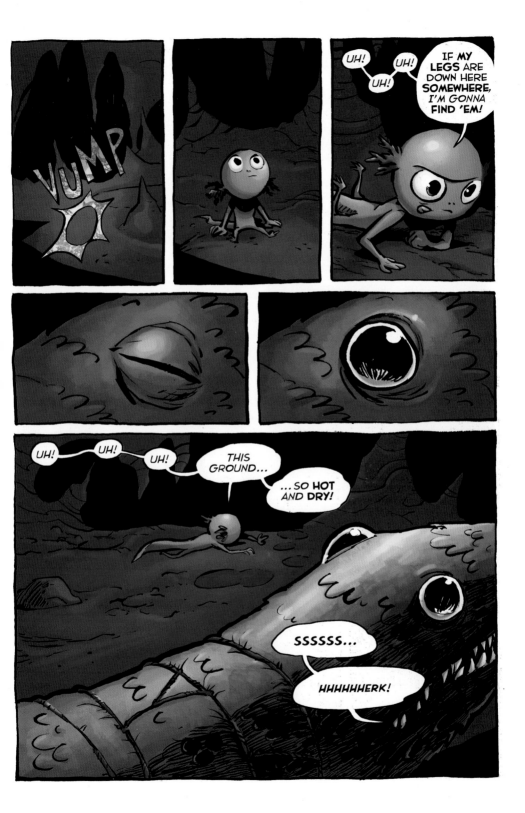

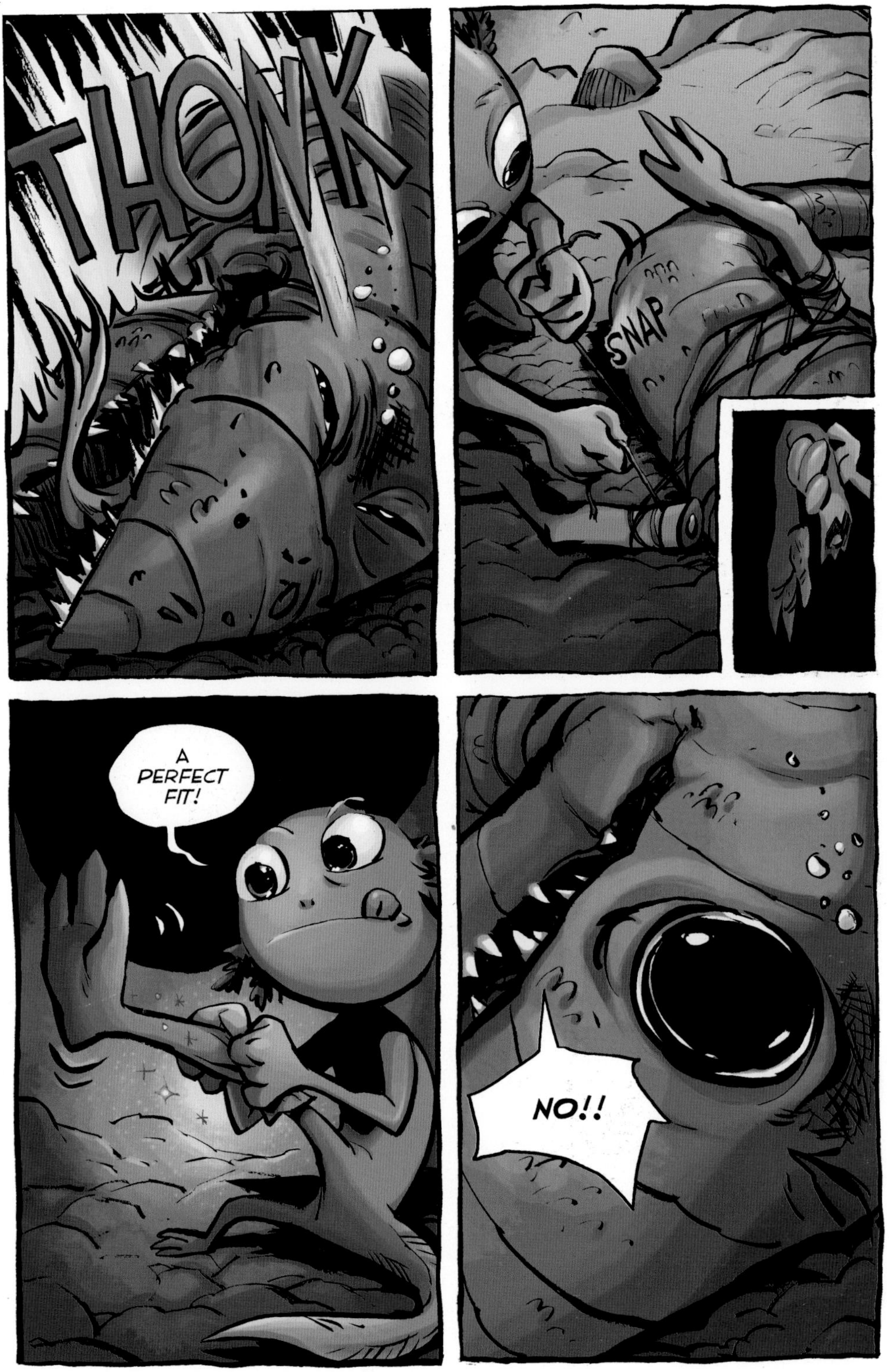
THONK
SNAP
A PERFECT FIT!
NO!!

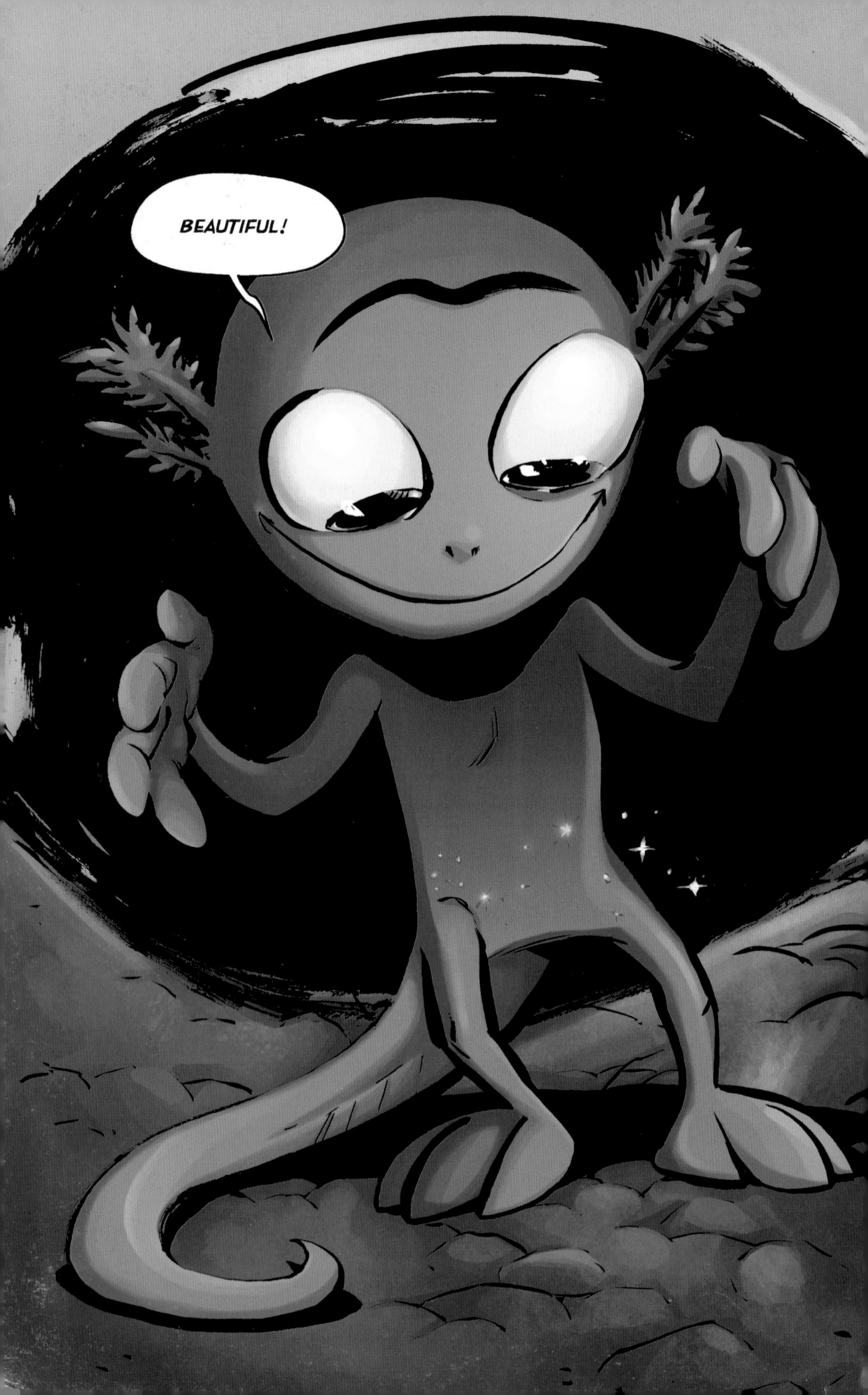
BEAUTIFUL!

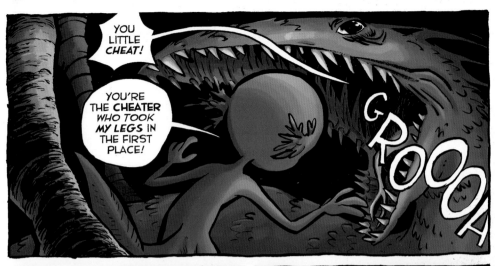

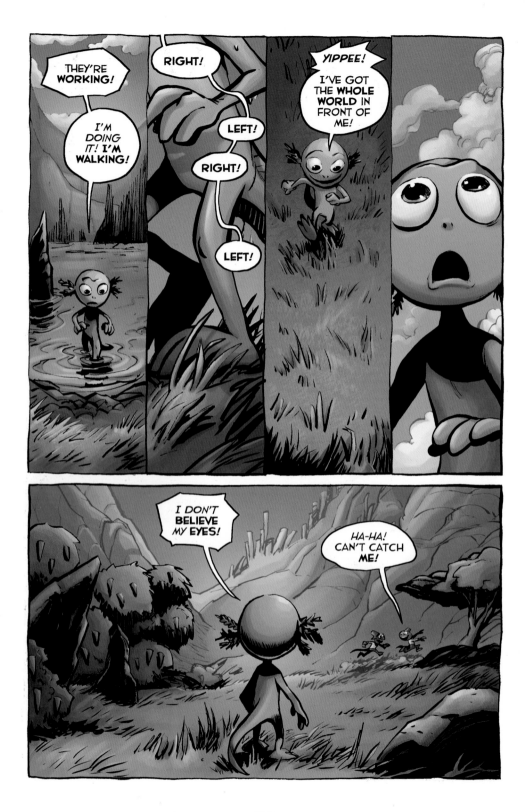

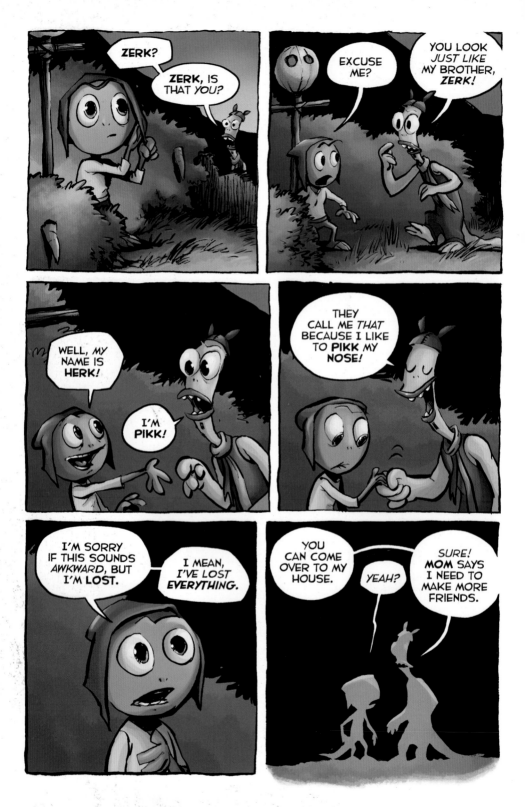

166

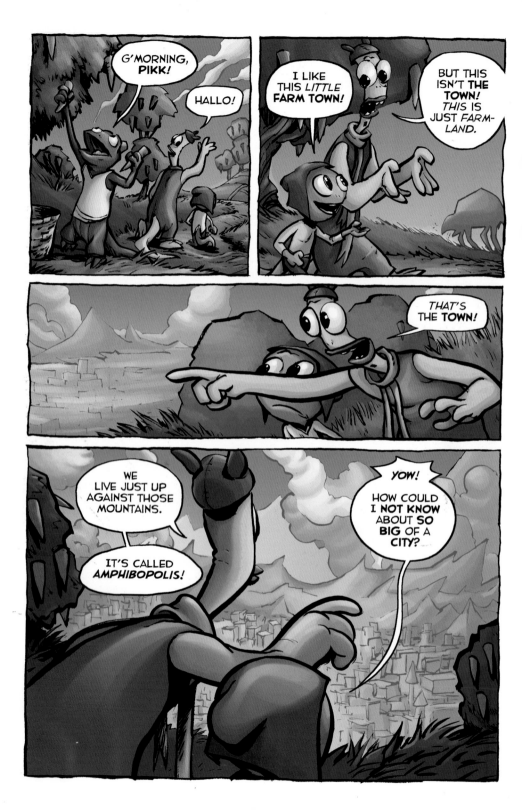

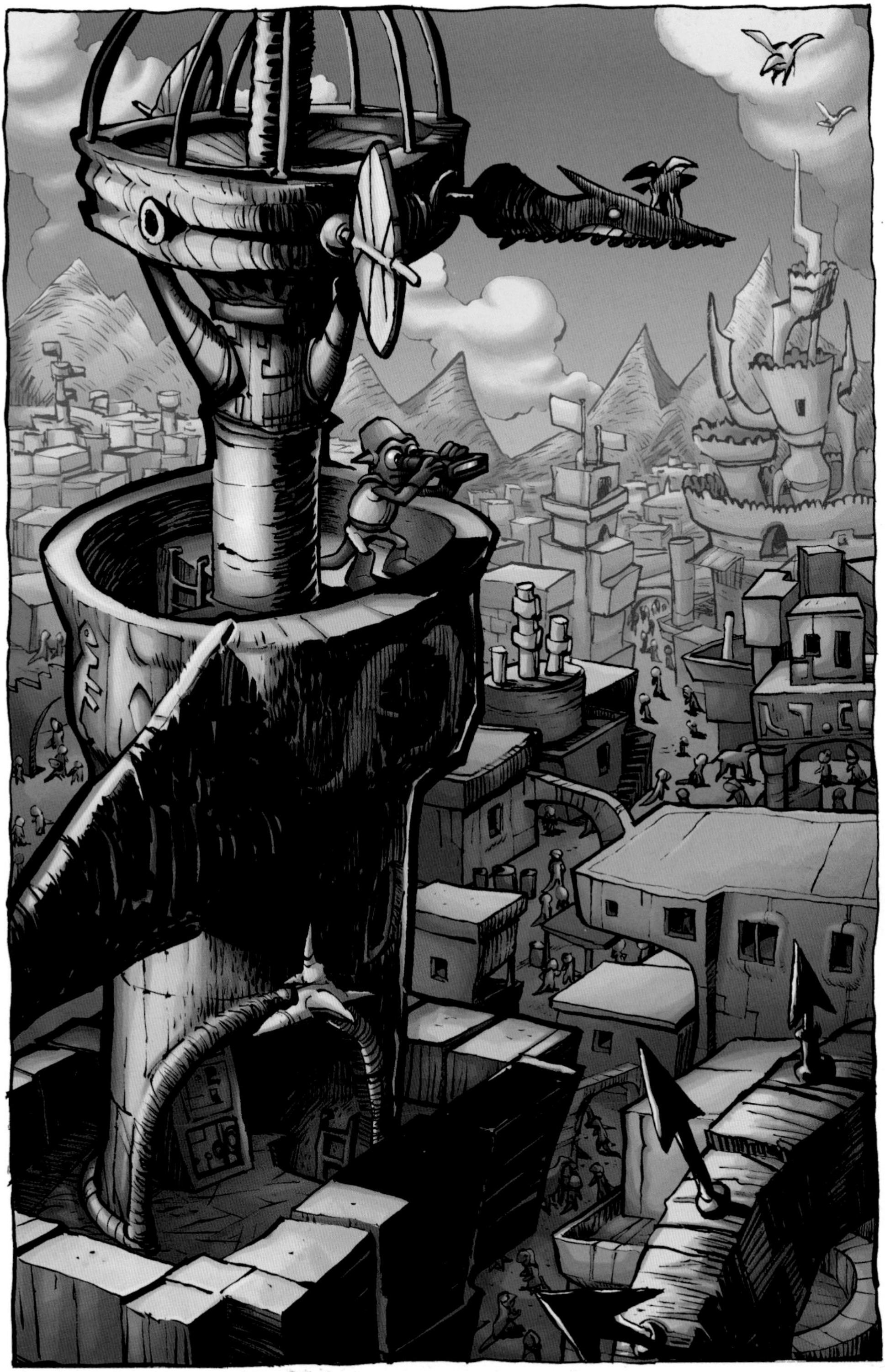

172

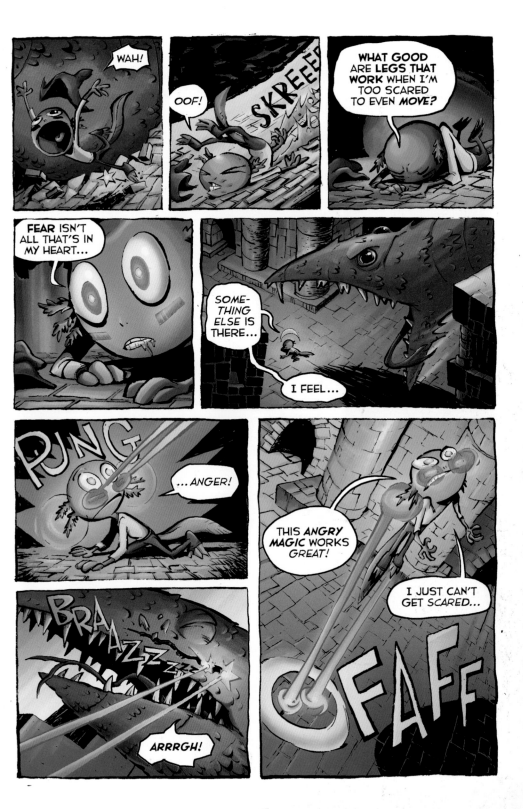

TO BE CONTINUED...

DOUG TENNAPEL is the acclaimed author and illustrator of GHOSTOPOLIS, BAD ISLAND, CARDBOARD, and TOMMYSAURUS REX, all published by Graphix. Among other honors, GHOSTOPOLIS was an ALA 2011 Top Ten Great Graphic Novel for Teens, a 2010 *Kirkus* Best Book of the Year, and a *School Library Journal* Best Comic for Kids published in 2010. BAD ISLAND was a *School Library Journal* Top Ten Graphic Novel for 2011 and a 2012 ALA Great Graphic Novels for Teens selection. CARDBOARD was named to the list of *School Library Journal* Top Ten Graphic Novels of 2012.

Doug is also the creator of the hugely popular character Earthworm Jim. He lives in Franklin, Tennessee, with his wife and their four children.